STORM AND FURY

JENNIFER L. ARMENTROUT

STORM AND FURY

inkyard
PRESS

Recycling programs
for this product may
not exist in your area.

ISBN-13: 978-1-335-01530-3

Storm and Fury

Inkyard Press
22 Adelaide St. West, 41st Floor
Toronto, Ontario M5H 4E3, Canada
www.InkyardPress.com

Printed in U.S.A.

To you, the reader, and to the stars that I can still see

1

"Just a kiss?"

Excitement thrummed through my veins as I tugged my gaze from the TV screen to Clay Armstrong. It took a moment for my wonky vision to focus and piece Clay's face together.

Just a few months older than me, he was beyond cute, with light brown hair that was always flopping over his forehead and just begging for my fingers to run through it.

Then again, I'd never seen an unattractive Warden even though I didn't have it in me to do the mental gymnastics to figure out how they looked like a human and then like a Warden.

Clay sat beside me on the couch in his parents' living room. We were alone, and I wasn't quite sure what life choices I'd made to end up with me sitting here beside him, our thighs touching. Like all Wardens, he was so incredibly bigger than me, even though I was five foot eight and not what one would normally consider a short girl.

Clay had always been friendlier toward me than most of

the Wardens, flirty even, and I liked it—he gave me the kind of attention that I saw between others but never had been on the receiving end of until now. No one in the Warden community besides my friend Jada, and of course Misha, paid much attention to me, and neither of them wanted to kiss me.

But Clay was always nice, complimenting me even when I knew I looked like a hot mess, and for the past couple of weeks, he'd sought me out a lot. I *liked* it.

And there wasn't a damn thing wrong with that.

So, when he'd approached me at the Pit, which was just a really large fire pit where younger Wardens gathered at night to hang out, and asked if I wanted to come back to his place to watch a movie, I didn't have to be asked twice.

Now Clay wanted to kiss me.

And I wanted to be kissed.

"Trinity?" he said, and I flinched when I saw that his fingers were suddenly close to my face. He caught a piece of hair that had fallen against my cheek and tucked it behind my ear. His hand lingered. "You're doing it again."

"Doing what?"

"Disappearing on me," he said. I had, and I did that a lot. "Where'd you go?"

I smiled. "Nowhere. I'm here."

Those Warden eyes, a bright sky blue, peered into mine. "Good."

My smile grew.

"Just a kiss?" he repeated.

The excitement went up a notch and I exhaled slowly. "Just a kiss."

He smiled as he leaned in, tilting his head so our mouths lined up. Mine parted in anticipation. I'd been kissed before. Once. Well, I'd done the kissing. I'd kissed Misha when I was sixteen, and he'd kissed me back, but then it became really weird because he was like a brother to me, and neither of us were about that kind of life.

Plus, things weren't supposed to be like that between Misha and me, because of what he was.

Because of what I was.

Clay's lips touched mine, and they were warm and...dry. Surprise flickered through me. I thought they'd be, I don't know, *wetter*. But it was...nice, especially when the pressure of the kiss increased and his lips parted mine, and then it was *more*. His mouth moved against mine, and I kissed him back.

I didn't want to stop him when the hand along the nape of my neck slid down my back, to my hip. That felt nice, too, and when he eased me down, I went with it, placing my hands on his shoulders as he hovered over me, using his arm to support his weight so he didn't crush me.

Wardens' body temperatures ran high—higher than humans, higher than mine—but he seemed hotter, like he was about to burn up.

And I...I felt sort of...lukewarm.

We kissed and kissed, and those kisses weren't dry anymore, and I liked the way his lower body had settled over mine, how it moved against mine, a mysterious rhythm that felt like it should be, could be, more—if I wanted that.

And that was...*nice*.

Nice like when he'd held my hand on the way to his place. So was the candle he'd lit that smelled like watermelon and lemonade—there was something romantic about that, and about the way his hand opened and closed on my hip. I felt warm and pleasant, not rip my clothes off and let's get it on kind of excited, but this was... It was really nice.

Then his hand was under my shirt and up, over my breast.

Hold up.

I reached down and grabbed his hand as I pulled away, separating his mouth from mine. "Whoa."

"What?" His eyes were still closed, his hand was still on my breast and his hips were *still* moving.

"I said just a kiss," I reminded him, tugging on his hand. "That's more than a kiss."

"You're not having a good time?"

Was I? I had been, key word being *had*. "Not anymore."

I had no idea what it was about *not anymore* that somehow translated into *kiss me again*, but that's what Clay did. He pressed his mouth to mine, and that pressure was no longer nice. It was almost bruising.

Irritation flared to life like a lit match. Tightening my hand on his arm, I pulled it out from under my shirt. I pushed on his chest, breaking the kiss.

I glared up at him. "Get off."

"I was trying to," he grumbled, lifting up, but that was not remotely fast enough for me after that gross comment.

I pushed—pushed *hard*. Clay toppled off me and to the side, into nothing but open space. He landed on the floor, his weight rattling the TV and causing the flames on the candle to flicker.

"What the Hell?" Clay demanded, sitting up. He looked thunderstruck that I was capable of doing what I'd just done.

"I told you I wasn't enjoying this." I swung my legs off the couch and stood. "And you didn't stop."

Clay stared up at me, blinking slowly in shock. It was like he didn't even hear me. "You pushed me off you."

"Yeah, I did, because you're gross." I stepped over his legs and stalked past the window, heading for the door.

He powered to his feet. "You didn't seem to think it was gross when you were begging me to kiss you."

"*What?* Okay. Fake news right there," I snapped. "I didn't

beg you. You asked me if you could kiss me and I said just a kiss. Don't rewrite what just happened."

"Whatever. You know what, I wasn't even into it."

Rolling my eyes, I turned back to the door. "Sure felt like you were."

"Only because you're the only female here that won't expect me to mate with her."

Mating in Warden terms didn't mean hooking up. It meant getting married and having a metric crap ton of little Warden babies, and I was beyond insulted at this point. Not just because that was superwrong of him to say, but it also struck close to home.

There was no one here for me, no relationship that could ever be considered serious. Wardens didn't mix with humans.

They didn't even mix with my kind.

"I'm sure I'm not the only female here that doesn't want to mate with you, you jackass."

Clay moved with the speed of a Warden. One moment he was beside the couch and the next he was in front of me. "You don't need to be a—"

"Choose your words wisely, buddy." Irritation was quickly turning into anger, and I tried to calm down, because…bad things happened when I got angry.

And those bad things usually involved blood.

A muscle thrummed along his jaw and his chest rose with a deep breath before his handsome face smoothed out. "You know, let's start over." His hand moved outside my central vision and landed on my shoulder. I jumped, startled by the unexpected contact.

Wrong move on his part, because I did *not* like to be startled.

I caught his arm. "Can you let me know how much it hurts when you hit the ground?"

"What?" Clay's mouth hung open slightly.

"Because you're about to hit it really hard." I twisted his arm, and there was a brief second when I saw the shock flash across his face. He was a Warden in training, preparing to be the warrior the world knew the Wardens as, and he didn't understand how I'd gained the upper hand so quickly.

And then he wasn't thinking anything.

I spun him around and leaned back on my right leg. I kicked out with my left, not holding a damn thing back as my foot connected perfectly with the center of his back. Incredibly proud of myself, I waited for him to eat the floor.

Except that wasn't what happened.

Clay flew across the room and hit the window. Glass cracked and gave way and then out the window he went, into the yard. I heard him hit the ground. Sounded like a minor earthquake.

"Whoops," I whispered, pressing my hands to my cheeks. I stood there for, like, half a minute and then I sprang forward, hurrying to the front door. "Oh, no, no, no."

Luckily the porch light was on and it was bright enough to see where Clay was.

He'd landed in a rosebush.

"Oh, dear." I went down the steps as Clay rolled out of the bush, onto his side, groaning. He seemed alive. That was a good sign.

"What in the holy Hell?"

I jumped at the sound and looked up, recognizing the voice first. Misha. He came out of the shadows, stopping under the glow from the porch light. Too far away from me to see him clearly, but I didn't need to see his expression to know he had that look on his face, a mixture of disappointment and disbelief.

Misha turned from where Clay lay on the ground, to me, to the window and then back to me. "Do I even want to know?"

There wasn't a single part of me that was surprised to see Misha. I'd known it was only a matter of time before he figured out I'd snuck away from the Pit and ended up here.

We were raised together, receiving the same training as soon as we both could walk upright, and he'd been there for my first scraped knee when I'd tried and failed to keep up with him—which he'd laughed at me for—and he'd been there the first time my life came crashing down around me.

Misha had grown from an adorable, freckle-faced, red-headed dork to quite the cutie. I'd had a crush on him for about two hours when I was sixteen, which was when I'd kissed him.

I'd had a lot of short-lived crushes.

But Misha was more than my sidekick or my best friend in the whole world. He was my *Protector*, bonded to me since I was a little girl, and that bond was intense.

Like, if I died, he died, kind of intense, but if he died first, the bond would be severed and then another Warden would take his place. I'd always thought that was unfair, but the bond wasn't *completely* one-sided. What was in me, what I was, fueled him, and his Warden powers often made up for the human part of me.

In a way, we were two sides of the same coin, and I had violated some kind of heavenly rule when I'd kissed him. According to my father, Protectors and their charges were never supposed to engage in naughty, fun times. Supposedly this had to do with the bond, but I had no idea what that really meant. Like what could it actually do to the bond? I'd asked my father, but he'd looked down his nose at me like I'd asked him to explain how babies were made.

None of that meant I was any less annoyed at the moment.

"I have it under control." I gestured toward Clay, moaning on the ground. I could see tiny dark spots on his face. Thorns? God, I hoped so. "Obviously."

"You did that?" Misha stared at me.

"Yeah?" I crossed my arms as Clay began to pick himself up. "And I don't feel remotely bad about it. He didn't understand what 'just a kiss' meant."

Misha pivoted back to Clay. "Is that so?"

"Totally so," I said.

Growling low under his breath, Misha stalked toward Clay, who had finally risen to his knees. He was about to get some help standing. Gripping him by the back of his shirt, Misha lifted Clay off the ground and turned him around so that he was facing Misha. When he let go, the shorter Warden stumbled back a step.

"Did she tell you no and you didn't listen?" Misha demanded.

Clay lifted his head. "She didn't mean it—"

Moving as quick as lightning, Misha cocked back his arm and planted his fist right in the center of Clay's dumb face. Down the boy went for the second time tonight.

I smirked.

"Just like I didn't mean to do that?" Misha said, crouching down. "When someone says no, they mean it."

"Holy shit," Clay whined, covering half his face with his hand. "I think you broke my nose."

"I don't care."

"Jesus." Clay started to stand but fell back on his ass.

"You need to apologize to Trinity," Misha ordered.

"Whatever, man." Clay struggled to his feet, his voice muffled as he turned to me. "I'm sorry, Trinity."

I lifted my hand and extended a middle finger.

Misha wasn't done with him. "You don't speak to her again.

You don't even look at her or breathe in her general direction. If you do, I'll put you through the window again and do a whole lot worse."

Clay lowered his hand and I could see dark blood running down his face. "You didn't put me through a—"

"You obviously don't get it," Misha growled. "I *did* knock you through a window, and I'll do worse next time. Understand me?"

"Yeah." Clay wiped his hand along his mouth. "I understand."

"Then get the Hell out of my face."

Clay bolted back inside and slammed the door behind him.

"You need to get back to the house." Misha's voice was gruff as he took my hand and led me through the yard, into the shadows.

I let him lead the way, because once we were outside the lights, I couldn't see crap.

"Thierry needs to know about this," I said once we hit the sidewalk that led all the way back to the main house.

"Oh, Hell, yeah, I'm telling Thierry. He needs to know and something more than an epic beatdown needs to be handed to Clay."

"Agreed." A huge part of me wanted to go back and kick Clay through another window, but I'd let Thierry handle it from here even though that was going to lead to a very embarrassing conversation with the man who was like a second father to me.

But Thierry was the one in the position to do more. He was the boss here, and not just a clan leader but a Duke, overseeing all the other clans and the many outposts in the Mid-Atlantic and Ohio Valley. He was ultimately responsible for training all the new warriors and ensuring that the community remained safe and relatively hidden.

He could make sure that Clay learned to never, ever do that again.

Misha stopped once we were far enough from Clay's house. "We need to talk."

I sighed. "I really don't want to be lectured right now. I know you mean well, but—"

"How did you knock him out of a window?" he asked, cutting me off.

A frown pulled at my lips as I stared up at Misha's shadowy face. "I pushed him and then I... Well, I kicked him."

Letting go of my hand, he placed his own on my shoulders. "How did you manage to kick him out the window, Trin?"

"Well, you see, I lifted my leg, like I've been trained—"

"That's not what I meant, you little smart-ass." Misha cut me off. "You're getting stronger. Way stronger."

A shiver curled down my spine and danced over my skin. I *was* getting stronger, but I imagined that with each passing year, that would continue to happen for the both of us until...

Until what?

For some reason I'd always thought that when I turned eighteen, something would change, but my birthday passed over a month ago, and we were still here, secreted away and well hidden, just waiting for the time when I was summoned by my father to fight.

I wasn't living.

Neither was Misha.

The all-too-familiar feeling of discontent started to settle over me like a too-heavy blanket, but I pushed it aside.

Now wasn't the time to think about any of that, because the truth was, I'd been getting stronger for a while now. Faster, too, but I'd been able to hold back when I trained with Misha.

I'd just lost my cool tonight.

Could've been way worse, though.

"I didn't mean to kick him through a window exactly, but I'm glad I did," I said, lowering my gaze to the dark sweater I wore. "He did seem...freaked out by how strong I was."

"Of course he did, Trin, because nearly everyone here thinks you're just a human."

But I wasn't.

I wasn't part-Warden, either, and they were like real-life superheroes, hunting down the bad guys, if superheroes were, well, gargoyles.

Until a little over ten years ago, the beastly looking statues perched on churches and buildings throughout the world were seen only as architectural wonders, but then they went public, exposing to the world that many of those statues were actually living, breathing creatures.

After an initial period of shock, people realized Wardens were just another species, and they accepted them. Well, most humans did. There were fanatics like the Church of God's Children who believed Wardens were a sign of the end times or something lame, but most people were okay with Wardens, and while the Wardens did sometimes help law enforcement if they happened upon a human committing crimes, Wardens were mostly gunning for bigger baddies.

Demons.

The general public had no idea demons were real or what they looked like or how many different species there actually were. Hell, they had no idea that many demons blended in among them so well that some of them had even been voted into government positions of great power and influence.

The majority of people believed demons were creatures of biblical myth, because some kind of heavenly rule demanded that mankind was to stay in the dark when it came to demons, centering around the incontrovertible idea of blind faith.

Man must believe in God and Heaven and their faith must

come from a pure place and not from fear of celestial consequence. If man was ever to find out Hell *truly* existed, things would go south fast for everyone, including the Wardens.

It was up to the Wardens to dispatch the demons and keep mankind in the dark so that people could live and thrive with their free will and all that jazz.

At least, that was what we've been told, what we believed.

When I was younger, I didn't understand it. Like, if mankind knew that demons were real, they could protect themselves. If they knew that, say, killing one another actually did mean they'd get a one-way ticket with no refunds to Hell, they might *act* right, but those actions might not be of their own free will. Thierry had explained it to me once.

Humankind must always be in the position of exercising free will without fear of consequence.

But the Wardens of the Potomac Highlands, the ancestral seat of power for the Mid-Atlantic and Ohio Valley clans, where the warriors were trained to protect the human cities and fight the ever-increasing population of demons, had a purpose that extended beyond training the warriors.

They were hiding *me*.

Most who lived in the community didn't know that, including Clay and his stupid, floppy hair. He didn't even know I could see ghosts and spirits, and yes, there was a world of difference between the two. I could count on one hand how many knew the truth. Misha. Thierry and his husband, Matthew. Jada. That was all.

And that would never change.

Most Wardens believed I was just an orphaned human that Thierry and Matthew had felt sorry for, but I was far from being just a human.

The part of me that was human came from my mother. Every time I looked in the mirror, I saw her staring back at me. I got my dark hair and brown eyes from her, as well as the olive skin tone courteous of her Sicilian roots. I also had her face. Big eyes. Maybe a little too big, because I could make myself look bugged out without much effort. I had her high cheekbones and small nose that curved slightly to one side at the end. I also had her wide, often expressive mouth.

That wasn't the only thing that came from my mother's side. I also had her crap family genetics.

My nonhuman side… Well, I didn't *look* like my father.

At all.

"A human can't punch or kick a Warden around, not even an inch," Misha said, pointing out the obvious. "I'm not saying you shouldn't have done what you did, but you need to be careful, Trin."

"I know."

"Do you?" he asked quietly.

My breath caught as I closed my eyes. I did know. God, did I ever. Clay had deserved what I did and more, but I needed to be careful.

And while Thierry needed to know what had gone down with Clay, because if he behaved that way with me, it was unlikely I would be the only one, Thierry already had a lot on his plate.

Ever since the leader of the Warden clan in DC died back in January, things had been tense here. There'd been a lot of closed-door meetings, more so than normal, and I had overheard—well, eavesdropped on—Thierry talking about escalating attacks and not just on outposts but on communities nearly as large as ours, which was rare.

Just a couple of weeks ago, demons had come close to our walls. That night…

That night had been bad.

"Do you think Clay will say anything?" I asked.

"If he has two working brain cells to rub together, he won't." Misha curled an arm around my shoulders and tugged me forward. I face-planted against his chest. "He's probably too scared to say anything."

"Of me," I said, and grinned.

Misha didn't laugh like I thought he would. Instead, I felt his chin rest atop my head. A long moment passed. "Most of the Wardens here have no idea what they're hiding. They cannot know what you are." He said what I knew, what I've always known. "They can never know."

Jerking awake with a gasp, I sat straight up in bed. There were demons outside the compound walls.

There were no sirens warning the residents to seek shelter, which was what happened when demons neared the wall. The estate was as silent as a tomb, but I knew there were demons nearby. Some kind of internal demon radar system was telling me this.

The soft, luminous glow of the stars plastered to my ceiling faded as I turned the bedside lamp on and rose swiftly from the bed.

I quickly pulled on a pair of black sweats and a tank top, because going out and investigating while in undies that had the words *Hump Day* plastered across the ass wasn't exactly the best of ideas.

Going out there at all would probably be considered a bad idea, but I wasn't giving myself time to think about that.

I toed on my running sneakers as I snatched the iron daggers from my dresser, an eighteenth birthday present from Jada, and quietly stepped out into the brightly lit hallway. All the lights in the house were left on for me, just in case I got the munchies in the middle of the night. No one wanted me to trip due to lack of depth perception, breaking my neck falling down the steps, so the mansion was like a freaking lighthouse.

I couldn't even begin to fathom what the electricity bill was like.

The cool metal of the daggers warmed against my palm as I deftly made my way from the third to the main floor, hurrying before anyone, namely my ever-present shadow, discovered I was up and about.

Misha would flip if he caught me, especially after everything that had just gone down with Clay the night before.

So would Thierry.

But this was the second time in a month that demons had gotten close to the walls, and last time I'd done what was expected of me. I'd stayed safely ensconced in the fortress-like walls of Thierry's home, guarded not only by Misha but by an entire clan of Wardens who were willing to lay down their lives for me even if they didn't know that was what they were doing.

Two had died that night, disemboweled by the razor-sharp claws of an Upper Level demon. Ripped apart in such a terrible way there was barely anything left of them to bury, let alone to show their loved ones.

That wasn't going to happen again.

Doing what I was told, doing what was expected of me, almost always ended up in someone else paying the price for my inaction.

For my safety.

Even my mother.

I slipped out the back door and into the cool mountain air of early June, then took off in a jog toward the left branch of the wall, the section I knew wouldn't be monitored as heavily as the front. The faint glow of city lamps and solar lights faded, pitching the cleared grounds into utter darkness. My eyes didn't adjust. They never would at night, but I knew this path like the back of my hand, having explored nearly every inch of the several mile long and wide community over the years. I didn't need my crap eyes to guide me through the thick cropping of trees as I picked up my pace. The wind lifted strands of long dark hair from my face. As I cleared the last of the ancient elms, I knew exactly how many feet existed between me and the wall even though I couldn't see it in the darkness.

Fifty.

The wall itself stood at a tremendous size, the height equivalent to a six-story building. The first time I'd tried to jump it, I ended up smacking into the side of it like a bug into a windshield.

That had hurt.

Actually, it had taken a couple dozen tries before I cleared the wall, and at least double that before I could do it successfully multiple times.

I dug in as a burst of power and strength exploded through me. Arms pumping, I shifted the daggers into one hand as I reached twenty feet out from the wall and then I *jumped*.

It was like flying.

The rush of air, the weightlessness and nothing but darkness and faint twinkling lights in the sky. For a few precious seconds, I was free.

And then I slammed into the wall, near the top. Smacking my hand down on the smooth cement of the top, I caught myself with my free hand before I fell. Muscles in my arm screamed as I hung there for a precarious few seconds and then I curled, swinging myself up onto the top.

Breathing heavy, I shook out the burning in my left arm and then palmed the daggers in both hands as I strained to hear anything in the darkness, a sign of where the action was going down.

There.

My head cocked to the right. I heard the sound of low male voices near the entrance. Wardens. Even though their heightened senses would alert them to the presence of demons, they were unaware. My senses were just more keen, and I knew it would be only a matter of minutes before the Wardens became aware of the demons.

I had a choice.

Sound the alarm and send the Wardens into the hilly forest surrounding the community. There was a good chance some would get hurt, maybe even die, but that was what Thierry would demand of me, what Misha was destined to ensure.

That was what I'd done, time and time before, in different situations, and all of them had ended the same way.

Me without a scratch and someone else dead.

Or I could change that outcome, take care of the demons before the demons even knew what they were dealing with.

My mind had already been made up when I'd left the house.

Jumping from the wall to the ground would result in a broken bone or two for me, and since prior experience had proved that, I carefully worked my way along the narrow ledge to the place where I knew a nearby tree stretched toward the wall even though I couldn't see it. I stopped twenty feet to my left, took a deep breath, said a little prayer and then crouched. Leg muscles tensed. My hands gripped the daggers.

One. Two. Three.

I jumped into the void, lifting the daggers high as I brought my knees up to my stomach. I felt the first whisper-soft brush of leaves, kicked my legs out and then I slammed the daggers down. The wickedly sharp ends dug into the bark, clawing deep as I slid down the tree, stopping when my feet touched a thick branch.

Exhaling heavily, I pulled the daggers free and then knelt,

using my hands to guide my way. I closed my eyes and let instinct take over. Slipping from the branch, I landed in a crouch, silent as I remained there for a heartbeat before rising. I took off toward my left, heading deeper into the forest, letting the increasing pressure along the back of my neck guide my way. About a hundred feet later, I stopped in a clearing cut by a narrow creek and dimly lit by silvery moonlight. The scent of rich soil filled me as I looked around. My heart rate kicked up as the feeling of heavy oppressiveness settled on my shoulders.

Fingers relaxing and tightening around the handle of the daggers, I scanned the shadows crowding the trees. They seemed to pulse as I squinted, and impulse demanded that I charge forward, but I knew not to trust what my eyes were telling me. I stood perfectly still, waiting—

Crack.

A twig snapped behind me. Spinning around, I swung the dagger in a high, sweeping arc.

"Jesus," a voice grunted, and then a hard, warm hand circled my wrist. "You nearly took my head off, Trin."

Misha.

I squinted, unable to make out his face in the darkness. "What are you doing out here?"

"Did you seriously just ask that question?" He held on to my arm as the air stirred around us. Misha leaned down, and all I could make out was the vibrant, bright blue eyes of a Warden. "What are you doing outside the walls in the middle of the night with your daggers?"

No point in lying now. "There are demons here."

"What? I don't sense any demons."

"That doesn't mean they're not here. I can feel them," I told him, tugging on my arm. He let go. "They're close even if you can't feel them yet."

Misha was quiet for a moment. "That's even more reason

why you should be anywhere but out here." Anger threaded his voice. "You know better than this, Trinity."

Irritation prickled over my skin as I turned away from Misha to stare rather pointlessly into the shadows as if I could magically get my eyes to work better for me. "I'm tired of knowing better, Misha. Knowing better gets people killed."

"Knowing better keeps *you* alive, and that is all that matters."

"That's so wrong. That can't be the only thing that matters." I almost stomped my foot, but somehow managed to stand still. "And you know that I can fight. I can fight better than any of you."

"Try not to be too overconfident, Trin," he replied, tone as dry as the desert.

I ignored that. "Something is going on, Misha. This is the second time in a month that demons have gotten close to the wall. In the last six months, how many communities have been attacked? I stopped counting when it hit double digits, but it doesn't take a genius to figure out that each community that's been attacked has been closer and closer to this one, and each time they'd managed to breach the walls in the other communities, it's clear they're looking for something. They're doing sweeps."

"How do you know that? Have you've been eavesdropping on Thierry again?"

I flashed a quick grin. "It doesn't matter how I know. Something is going down, Misha. You know that. Demons may go after the smaller compounds in the cities, but they aren't stupid enough to try to raid a place like this—like they did to some of the other communities."

He was quiet for a moment. "You think...they know about you? That they're looking for you?" he asked, and a fine shiver curled its way down my spine. "That's impossible. There's no way they know you exist."

Unease festered in the pit of my stomach. "Nothing is impossible," I reminded him. "I'm living proof of that."

"And yet again, if what you suspect is true, the last place you should be is out here."

I rolled my eyes.

"I saw that," he snapped.

"That's impossible." I looked over my shoulder, in the general vicinity of where he was standing. "You're standing behind me."

"Thought you just said nothing is impossible?"

"Whatever," I muttered.

Misha's sigh could've rattled the trees around us. "If your father knew you were out here…"

I snorted, like a little piglet. "As if he's remotely paying attention to me."

"You don't know that he isn't," Misha replied. "He could be watching us right now. Hell, he could've been watching you with Clay last night—"

"Ew, come on. Don't say that."

"I'm just…" He trailed off.

Misha felt it then.

I knew this because he cursed under his breath and the pressure on the nape of my neck gave way to a series of sharp tingles that spread to the space between my shoulder blades.

The demons were here.

"If I tell you to get back to the wall, will you listen?" Misha asked as he stepped into the moonlight. The silvery glow glanced off slate-gray skin and large wings. Two horns curled back from his skull, parting auburn curls.

I snickered. "What do you think?"

Misha sighed. "Don't get yourself killed, because I'd like to keep living."

"More like don't get *yourself* killed," I snapped back, scanning the ever-increasing shadows. "Because I really don't want to end up bonded to some stranger."

"Yeah, that would totally suck for you," he muttered, his shoulders straightening as his stance widened. "Meanwhile, I'll just be dead."

"Well, if you're dead, it's not like you'd care about anything anymore," I reasoned. "Because, you know, you'd be *dead*—"

Misha held up one large, clawed hand, silencing me. "Do you hear that?"

At first, I didn't hear anything other than the distant call of a bird or possibly a chupacabra. We were in the mountains of West Virginia; anything was possible. But then I heard it—a rustling of bushes and broken branches, a series of clicking and chattering. Goose bumps rose all over my arms.

I didn't think a chupacabra was making that sound.

Floodlights positioned high on the wall flicked on, filling the forest with intense blue-white light, signaling that the Wardens on the walls now sensed the demons.

And I was most likely going to be caught out here and be in big, big trouble.

Too late now.

The rustling grew louder and the shadows between the trees seemed to warp and spread. Every muscle in my body tensed, and then they came, bursting from the shrubs and scurrying across the clearing. Dozens of them.

Raver demons.

2

I'd never seen a Raver demon before; I'd only read about them in class and heard some of the other Wardens talk about them. Nothing they'd ever described did these creatures justice.

They were like rats—giant hairless rats that ran on two legs, had teeth that a great white shark would envy and claws that could cut through even the Warden's stone-like skin.

"Well, that's a bucket full of nightmares," I murmured.

Misha huffed out a laugh.

Ravers were bottom feeders, scavenger demons that prayed on weak humans and corpses of animals and, well, anything dead. They didn't attack Warden compounds.

"Something's not right here," whispered Misha, obviously following the same train of thought as me. "But that doesn't matter right now."

No.

It didn't.

At least six of them went straight for Misha, seeing and sensing that he was a Warden. Me? They pretty much ignored, probably because I smelled like a good ol' human.

That was their first and last mistake.

Hand-to-hand combat wasn't exactly easy for me, not when my vision was constricted to a narrow tunnel, so I had to be careful. I had to be smart and keep my distance.

Misha shot forward, spinning in a wide circle. One of his wings caught the closest Raver, knocking the creature back several feet as he jabbed his clawed hand into the center of another Raver's chest.

The crunchy wet sound turned my stomach.

Another Raver launched into the air, using its powerful legs. It was heading straight for Misha's back.

I let honed instinct take over. I cocked back my arm, then let the dagger fly.

It struck true, embedding deep in the Raver's chest. The thing shrieked as it plummeted from the air and landed on its side, already dead.

Misha spun toward me, his mouth slightly agape. "How do you do that?"

"I'm special." I switched the other dagger to my right hand. "And you have another one right behind you."

He turned, catching that one and pile-driving the sucker into the hard ground.

My knife throwing had caught the attention of several more Ravers. One broke off, charging me as its chattering sound grew louder. It swiped at me, and I dipped down, feeling the wind of its swing stir my hair. I popped up behind the creature and kicked out, catching it in its back. The Raver hit the ground and rolled, but I didn't give it time to recover. I brought the iron dagger down, cutting off its squeal of rage.

I spun but didn't see the tail on the other Raver until it

smacked into my leg. I squealed and jumped back, totally feeling its thick, rubbery texture through my sweats.

"Oh God, you have a tail," I groaned, shuddering. "You all have tails. I'm going to vomit."

"Can you hold off on that?" Misha asked from somewhere behind me.

"No promises." Shuddering again, I leaped to the side and spun to shove the dagger into the chest of another Raver. A hot spray of gunky demon blood splattered my chest. "Oh, man, now I'm going to have to shower."

"God, you're whiny."

Grinning, I darted to the right and found the rapidly decomposing body of the Raver that I had taken down with the first blade. Heart thumping, I pulled the blade out of its chest and then scanned the clearing. Six were left. I took a step forward.

"Beside you!" Misha shouted.

A bolt of panic lit up my chest as I twisted at the waist. Leaping back, I narrowly avoided being swiped by those claws. That would have been bad—*very* bad.

If my blood spilled, the moment it hit the air, they'd sense what I was.

They'd go into a frenzy—a feeding frenzy.

The thing charged me, mouth opening wide. A gust of rancid breath slammed into me as I slammed the dagger into its chest. "What in the Hell have you've been eating?"

"You probably don't want the answer to that," Misha grunted.

That was true.

I turned, finding another Raver coming for me. One side of my lips kicked up as a surge of adrenaline lit up my veins. That feeling was so much better than kissing. I flipped the daggers in my hands, completely showing off as I took a step forward—

A huge mass landed in front of me, shaking the ground and the elms.

That's what it looked like to me at first, just a solid mass of pissed-off fury that was so powerful it was a tangible entity in the woods. Six-foot wings spread out, blocking my view of just about everything.

And then my eyes focused. I saw shoulder-length red hair, and my heart sunk. Matthew.

Not only was he Thierry's husband, he was the second in command here at the ancestral seat, answering only to Thierry.

He looked over his shoulder at me. His features were a blur, but there was no mistaking the anger in his tone. "Please tell me I'm hallucinating and you're not really standing out here."

I looked around. "Well..."

"Get her back to the house," Matthew thundered as several more Wardens landed, causing what felt like a mini earthquake. "If you think you can actually handle that, Misha."

Oh dear.

Misha dropped a Raver and then seemed to disappear from where he'd been standing.

I opened my mouth to defend Misha and to also point out that I didn't need to be carted off, but for once in my life, I wisely snapped my mouth shut.

But then Matthew, who was like a third father to me, spoke once again. "You know better than this, Trinity."

And then I unwisely opened my mouth. "I had it handled. Obviously."

Matthew spun toward me, and I saw those blue eyes then, burning with barely restrained fury. "You're so lucky it is me here and not Thierry."

That was probably true.

Misha was suddenly beside me, and I wasn't given much of an option. He folded an arm around my waist and then crouched. Whatever else I was about to say was lost in a rush of cool air and night sky.

I was in so, so much trouble.

Misha wasn't speaking to me.

He was sitting in the living room, long legs kicked up on the couch, arms folded across his chest. His entire body took up all three cushions. He was watching an info commercial on some kind of magic frying pan like it was the most interesting thing ever committed to screen.

I was pacing behind the couch, nerves stretched thin. I could've hidden away in my bedroom, pretended that I was asleep, but that would've made me a coward. And there was no point in delaying the massive lecture that was coming my way.

A blur of movement shot in front of the TV. Misha didn't react to it, so my eyes narrowed. Was it Peanut, my sort of, not exactly alive, friend? I hadn't seen that punk all day or night. God only knew what he was up to.

A door opened somewhere in the massive house, slamming shut a few seconds later. I stopped pacing. Only then did Misha look at me. He raised his brows.

Heavy footsteps echoed down the hall outside the living room, and I turned to the arched opening. Thierry entered, tugging a fresh shirt on over his bald head. He was still too far away for me to gain much from the expression on his dark brown face. Matthew was right behind him, only slightly shorter and less broad. I clasped my hands together.

"I have several things I need to say, but I want to know something first," Thierry's deep voice boomed. "What in the Hell was she doing outside those walls?"

My mouth opened.

"I have no idea." Misha pulled his legs off the couch and sat up, twisting at the waist so he could see Thierry. "I was happily asleep when she snuck off."

I snapped my jaw shut, wondering exactly how in the world Misha knew I was outside the walls if he'd been asleep. The bond wouldn't have alerted him to that. It didn't work that way.

"It is your responsibility to know where she is at all times," Thierry responded. "Even if you're asleep."

"Okay, that seems a bit implausible," I said, jumping into the conversation. "And I'm the one who went over the wall, so I don't know why you're asking him why I did it."

Thierry slowly turned to me, and now that he was closer, I could see the hard lines of his jaw and his narrowed eyes. Eek! Probably should've kept my mouth shut.

"He is your Protector. He should know where you are."

Without even looking at Misha, I could feel him glaring daggers into me. "He can't be responsible for me while—"

"I'm not sure if you fully understand his role, but yes, he is *always* responsible for you. Asleep or awake, it doesn't matter," Thierry interrupted while Matthew leaned against the back of the couch. "Why were you outside those walls, Trinity?"

For what felt like the thousandth time tonight, I explained myself. "I woke up and I knew there were demons nearby. I sensed them—"

"While you were asleep?" Matthew asked, reddish brows snapping together. I nodded, and he glanced at Thierry. "That's new."

"Not exactly," I said. "The last time they came, I sensed them in the middle of the night. It woke me up."

"And that night you did what you knew you should have," Thierry responded. "You stayed inside, where—"

"Where it's safe. I know that." Frustration rose. "And that night two Wardens died."

"It doesn't matter how many die." Thierry took a step toward me. "Your safety is the number one priority."

I inhaled sharply. "I can fight. I can fight better than most Wardens! It's what I've been trained for since I could walk, but I'm expected to sit around twiddling my thumbs while people die? And don't say their lives don't matter. I'm tired of hearing that." My hands curled into fists. "Misha's life matters. Matthew's life matters. Your life matters! Everyone here matters." Except for Clay, but that was splitting hairs. "I'm tired of sitting around and doing nothing when people are dying. Knowing better gets people killed. It killed my mother—" I cut myself off with a sharp inhale.

It was so silent you could hear a cricket sneeze.

The vibe of the entire room shifted. Misha rose as if he was going to come to where I was standing, but I took a step back. I didn't want him to touch me. I didn't want his sympathy or empathy.

I didn't want anything other than to do what I was put on this Earth to do. Fight.

Everything about Thierry softened, even his voice. "You didn't get your mother killed."

Yeah, that was his opinion and not a fact.

"I know you want to get out there and help," he continued, "and I know you're trained and you're good, but, Trinity… you need to be careful with your vision, especially at night."

Steel shot down my spine. "I know what my vision is like at night, but it didn't stop me from kicking some demon ass. It never will."

All of us in the room knew that was a lie, because eventually my vision would stop me.

It would stop me from doing a lot of things, which kind of canceled out the whole being superspecial thing I had going on.

But that wasn't going to be today or even tomorrow.

I lifted up my chin as Matthew and Thierry exchanged helpless looks. "At some point, my father is going to summon me, and I doubt that whatever fight he wants me involved in will happen only during the daytime, and even then, my vision still sucks. That's not going to change. That's why I train eight hours a day and practice all the time. I should be out there, getting real experience, before I'm summoned."

Thierry turned away, running his hand over his smooth head. Misha finally decided to speak up. "She didn't have any problems," he said, and that was about ninety-nine percent true. I hadn't seen that one Raver until it was too late. "She did really well."

I smiled at him, big and bright.

He shot me a look. "And we should probably be getting real-life experience."

Matthew was watching his husband closely. He sighed as he folded his arms. "It's a little too late at night to have that discussion."

While I wanted to have that discussion, I also wanted to have what felt like a way more important one. "Isn't it super-weird that Ravers were out here? That was the first time I'd ever seen one, and wow, they're really creepy, but I thought they were scavenger demons. Way lower level."

"They are," Thierry answered as he looked at Matthew. "They're not supposed to be topside. They don't remotely blend in."

Due to the same cosmic rule that made it impossible to tell humans that demons were real, only demons who could blend in with humans were allowed topside. There were quite a few that, at first glance, looked perfectly human. Giant walking rats totally weren't one of them.

"And not only that, Ravers are usually a sign of a much bigger problem," Matthew added. "Where you see Ravers, you almost always find Upper Level demons."

My heart nearly stopped in my chest. That little tidbit was probably taught in class, but I'd forgotten. I glanced over at Misha, and he looked just as uneasy as I felt.

Upper Level demons were the Big Bads.

Their abilities ran the gamut. Some could sway human minds to do bad, bad things. Others could summon fire and rain down brimstone, change their appearance at the drop of a hat, becoming human one moment and an animal the next. Many of them were biblically old. All of them could take out a Warden.

And if the Ravers being here meant that there was an Upper Level demon nearby, that was a big deal.

I crossed my arms, almost not wanting to ask what I already suspected. "Do you think it's possible that an Upper Level demon knows about me?"

Thierry hesitated. "Every last one of your kind has been slaughtered, Trinity. If an Upper Level demon knew you were here, those walls would already be breached. Nothing would stop it from getting to you."

There was a ghost in the driveway.

Again.

Could be worse, I supposed. But the Raver attack was two days ago, and our walls hadn't been breached by an Upper Level demon hell-bent on devouring me.

Literally.

Even with my crap eyes, I knew the figure pacing in front of the hedges lining the wide driveway was superdead. I knew this mainly because his body kept flickering in and out like poor reception on an old television.

He definitely wasn't a spirit, and I'd seen enough of the two in my eighteen years to know the difference. The man below in his gold-colored shirt hadn't crossed over yet.

Spirits were the deceased who had seen the light—and there was almost always a light—had gone to it and then had come back for some reason or another. Usually they had a message or just wanted to check in on their loved ones.

Kneeling on the ledge of the Great Hall, I grasped the rough edge of the roof with one hand and placed my other on the curved shoulder of the stone gargoyle beside me. Heat radiated from the shell, warming my palm. I squinted behind my sunglasses and leaned as far as I could without falling face-first off the roof. The Great Hall was almost as tall as the wall and at least two stories higher than Thierry's house.

Watching the ghost pace back and forth, obviously confused, I wondered where in the world he'd come from. The community wasn't exactly easily reachable, nestled in the hills of the mountain and accessed only by back roads—winding, curvy back roads.

Probably a car accident.

Many a tired, unsuspecting traveler had fallen victim to those treacherous roads, with their sharp curves and steep, sudden embankments.

The poor dude had probably lost control and woken up dead before wandering here, like a lot of ghosts did. Last week it was a hiker who'd gotten lost on the mountain and fallen to her death. Two weeks ago it was an overdose—an older man who'd died on one of those back roads, too out of it to realize he was dying and too far away from help even if he had. Last month there'd been a girl, and hers had been the worst death I'd seen in a long time. She'd wandered away from her family during a camping trip and crossed paths with a kind of evil that was all too human.

The weight of that memory, of the girl's screams for her mother, settled heavily in my chest. Moving her on hadn't been easy, and there wasn't a day that went by that I didn't remember her cries.

Shaking off those memories, I focused on the newest ghostie down below. Car accidents were unexpected and often traumatic, but nothing like murder victims or those who died angry deaths. He wouldn't be hard to move on.

I hadn't seen any spirits lately, because I hadn't been outside the community in over a year. The few times I had managed to sneak off, I hadn't made it far enough to run across one.

Restlessness crawled over my skin and dug deep. The feeling of being trapped bit and chewed its way to the surface. How long did they plan to keep me here? Forever? Desperation sprang to life and guilt quickly followed.

Thierry and Matthew were still upset with me, and I hated that they were angry, that they didn't understand why I couldn't just sit back any longer.

My stomach churned as I turned my gaze to the statue beside me. I was close enough to make out all the details. The smooth layer of stone and the two fierce, thick horns that could puncture the toughest metal. The deadly claws that could tear through cement were currently relaxed. The face, even as frightening as it could be with its flat nose and wide mouth parted by vicious fangs, was at peace. Resting. Asleep.

Misha hadn't let me out of his sight since the night of the Ravers. I was surprised he hadn't tried to camp out on my bedroom floor the last two nights.

I'm not trapped.

This was my home and not my prison. Everything that I needed could be found here. I knew exactly how many homes lined the idyllic streets and parks. Besides Thierry's house, there were one hundred and thirty-six single-family homes and several dozen duplexes and townhomes for those unmated. The walled community was a small city, complete with its own hospital, shopping center, theater, gym and various restaurants and clubs designed to serve every whim or need. Those who were not trained as warriors worked within the community. Everyone had a purpose here.

Except for me.

Mostly everyone here had accepted my mother and me into their clan when we arrived. Thierry protected us—well, protected *me*. Not my mother. He'd cared for her. He'd welcomed her and treated her like a queen and me like her princess, but he hadn't been able to protect her.

Protecting her was never a part of the equation.

However, at the end of the day, I wasn't a Warden, and I…I was running out of time to get out there, to really *see* the world beyond the mountains of West Virginia and Maryland.

I was eighteen, and no Warden law surpassed the legality that I was, in fact, an adult and could do as I pleased, but leaving wasn't simple.

Sighing, I pulled my gaze from the resting gargoyle and focused on the road as cool June air lifted the few loose strands of my dark hair, tossing them around my head.

I must look like Medusa.

Squinting didn't help me see any better, even with the fading sunlight dipping behind Green Mountain, but I saw the ghost stop and turn toward the road. A second later, he fragmented like smoke in the wind, and he didn't piece back together.

He'd be back, though, that I knew in my bones. They always came back.

My gaze lifted to the road beyond and the thick crush of

tall, ancient elms that crowded the paved road. All of it was a blur of colors—greens, whites and blues. Down below, I heard the doors open, and a heartbeat later, I saw the top of Thierry's dark head as he stepped out onto the driveway.

I really hoped Thierry didn't look up.

Granted, I wasn't grounded or anything. Hell, Thierry had never grounded me. Mom, on the other hand, had been a different story. She'd grounded me about every other five seconds.

Nibbling on my thumbnail, I watched Thierry stare at the empty hedge-lined road. Even from where I was perched, I could sense the tension rolling off him, filling the cool mountain air, flowing with the wind.

A moment later, Matthew joined him. He came to stand beside Thierry, placing his hand on the man's lower back.

"It's going to be okay," Matthew said, and I tensed.

Thierry shook his head. "I don't like it."

"We don't have to, but…they requested our help." Matthew pressed his lips to Thierry's temple. "It'll be okay."

Thierry didn't respond. They stood in silence then, as if they were waiting for something or someone.

Minutes passed, and I heard them before I saw them. The crunching of tires on gravel warred with the distant call of birds. I knelt and peered around the slumbering Misha as a large, black SUV came down the road and rolled to a stop below.

Curiosity bubbled to life as my eyes widened. The sound of car doors slamming shut was too hard to ignore. Rising just the slightest bit, I looked over the ledge and saw Matthew and Thierry walking forward to greet…

Holy crap on a cracker the size of Texas, we had *visitors*, and I was completely unaware that we were going to have visitors. If our clan needed to meet with another, one of the Wardens left to carry out said meeting elsewhere. Rarely, if ever, was a meeting held here at the seat. Young Wardens from the Mid-Atlantic region were brought here only once a year, in September, to be trained by the elder Wardens until they reached maturity, and since it was only June, our visitors couldn't be here with a young Warden.

I squinted, but all I could make out was that there were three male Wardens in addition to Matthew and Thierry. One had longish brown hair, another had shorter brown hair cropped close to the skull and the other was a blond. No females were with them. That wasn't at all surprising. Female Wardens rarely traveled outside of their home communities or the outposts, because they were often targeted by demons, just as the children were.

Demons were astonishingly clever and logical. They knew that, if they took out those who could produce the next generation of Wardens, they could level a blow near impossible to recover from.

And it was one of the reasons that, collectively, all the classes of demons outnumbered the Wardens by the *millions*.

I was kind of like a female Warden, caged here for my safety, but for very, very different reasons.

Thierry greeted each of the visitors, shaking their hands, and I wished I could see their faces. The group turned to walk into the Great Hall.

What in the world was going on?

Reaching over, I rapped my knuckles of the stone shell and was immediately rewarded with a low, rumbling growl of annoyance. I giggled. Misha loved his late-afternoon naps in the fading sun. It's where he always went after training and classes.

"Go to your room," came the gruff reply from Misha. "Read a book. Watch a movie. Find a hobby."

I ignored what Misha said, taking a perverse amount of joy in annoying the utter living crap out of him whenever I could.

"There are Wardens here," I said, the words coming out in an excited rush.

"There are always Wardens here, Trinity."

I stared at him, brow wrinkled. "These Wardens don't live here."

The statue shifted, the stone becoming slightly less hard and turning from dark gray to a quicksilver as the wings unfurled behind me. Reddish-brown hair appeared around the horns, the curls blowing in the wind.

Vibrant blue eyes with thin, vertical pupils met mine. Irritation shone in those eyes. Wardens had weird sleeping patterns. Some stayed up all night and slept in the mornings and late afternoons. Misha's schedule was based on whatever I was doing. "Trinity…"

Dipping under a wing, I took off as Misha rose from his perch, spinning around. "Dammit!" he shouted.

I knew the roof like the back of my hand, not even needing to really see where I was going. I was already on the other side, hopping up on the ledge, when Misha took flight behind me.

"Don't let them see you!" he yelled as I jumped. "I swear to God, Trinity, I will lock you in your room!"

No, he wouldn't.

Hitting the small alcove below, I skidded down the rounded roof. The moment my feet hit nothing but air, I twisted onto my stomach. Gripping the edge of the roof, I swung my body inward, through the window I left open when I first joined Misha on the roof.

I landed in the empty, dimly lit hallway and spun around to close the window behind me and then I locked it just in case Misha tried to follow me through. After shoving my sunglasses into the back pocket of my jeans, I took off down the hall, passing several closed doors to guest rooms and apartments that were almost never in use before throwing open the door to the musty-smelling stairwell. I took the steps three and four at a time and reached the first level in ten seconds.

From there, I slowed my steps and kept close to the wall, slipping past a kitchen that was used only when there were banquets and ceremonies. Activity was bustling for the upcoming Accolade, a massive ceremony held to celebrate Wardens becoming full warriors. It involved a lot of eating, a lot of drinking and whole lot of secret squirrel stuff that went down with the newly ordained Wardens.

Beyond the kitchen, I found the room I was looking for, which was a staging area of sorts and filled to the brim with folding tables and stacked chairs. I was careful not to knock into any of them, which required me to walk extraordinarily slowly.

And that took a lot of effort.

I didn't do slow.

Voices grew louder as I neared the deep maroon curtains that separated the staging area from the Great Hall.

Stopping in front of the curtains, I carefully curled my fingers around the edge of one and tugged it a few inches aside, revealing the wide, cylinder-shaped hall in all its glory as dust spit into the air.

Good Lord, when was the last time anyone touched this curtain?

My gaze immediately lifted to the ceiling even though I couldn't see the paintings anymore, no matter how brightly lit the hall was. Angels adorned the ceiling, many of which were battle angels—the Alphas. Those were the angels that oversaw the Wardens and often communicated with them, sometimes even in person, though I'd never seen one in real life. Painted in their armor and wielding righteous swords, they were a fearsome sight to look upon.

"How was the trip here?" Thierry was asking as he walked into my line of sight, and I refocused. The visitors stood on the raised dais, waiting. "I hope uneventful?"

Matthew followed Thierry to the center, toward a seat that wasn't supposed to be called a throne, according to Thierry, but that, with its oversize seat and a back carved out of granite and shaped into a shield, sure looked like a throne to me.

But what did I know?

"Yes," answered the one standing the closest to the dais. I couldn't see him quite clearly, but he was the one with the longish brown hair. "The drive was long but it was a beautiful one."

"It's been many years since I've been to the nation's capital," Matthew said, hands clasped behind his back. "I imagine our community is vastly different than what you're used to."

Wow.

They were from Washington, DC? The DC clan was a large outpost and their clan leader had died recently, which was right around the time Thierry had begun to act more stressed than normal.

My gaze shifted to the one who'd been speaking. He looked like he was in his late twenties and seemed too young to be a clan leader, but he was the one doing all the talking.

"It is very different," the male Warden answered with a chuckle. "I don't think I've seen this much open space in years."

Thierry sat. "Well, we're glad that you were able to make it here, Nicolai."

I mouthed his name, sort of liking it.

"Thank you for receiving us," Nicolai responded. "We were surprised that our request was accepted."

So was I.

"We don't approve many requests," Thierry replied. "But we thought it would be best to meet in person with you and your clan."

So he *was* the new clan leader. My gaze shifted to the other Wardens. The one with the shorter dark hair was standing near the blond, who was the closest to me, standing maybe a foot or two from where I stood behind the curtain. I couldn't see the blond's face yet, but goodness, he was tall, around six and a half feet, and the black thermal he wore stretched across broad shoulders. His shoulder-length hair was pulled back and secured at the nape of his neck.

"As I'm sure you're aware, the demon activity around several of the cities has been steadily decreasing over the last three months," Nicolai said, drawing my attention back to the clan leader. "Before, we spotted maybe two or three Upper Level demons a week. We haven't seen one in *months*."

That sounded like good news to me, especially since one might be sniffing around here.

"Well, that doesn't sound like a problem," Thierry commented.

"It doesn't on the surface, but there's also been an increase in Fiends and, even more disturbingly, lower level demons that couldn't blend in with the populace if they tried," Nicolai continued. "Zayne has come across four hordes of Raver demons this month alone. It's odd to see so much activity from lower level demons without an Upper Level being behind it."

My gaze shifted to the blond. Zayne. That must be his name. He turned slightly, and every thought I had scattered like ashes in the wind as I got my first look at him. A tiny, still-functioning part of my brain knew how bad being that distracted by appearance was, but I was... I was *stunned*.

Stunned straight into stupidity.

I liked to think that I wasn't someone who could be easily distracted by a gorgeous face, but he was... He was *beautiful*. And that was saying something, because I was constantly surrounded by gorgeous Wardens who rocked some great DNA when they appeared human.

His skin was golden, like he spent a decent amount of time in the sun. He had a strong jaw that looked as if it were carved from stone, and those lips... How could they look so soft and so hard at the same time? And wasn't that a weird thing to notice, but I *so* noticed, which probably meant I was veering into creepy territory. High, angular cheekbones matched a straight, proud nose. I was too far away to see his eyes, but I assumed they were like all the other Wardens. The deepest, brightest blue possible.

From where I was standing, this Warden looked like he was only a few years older than me, and he reminded me of the many painted angels that covered the ceiling of the Great Hall—paintings I could no longer see in detail.

"Whoa," I whispered, my eyes going so wide that I probably looked like a squeezed bug.

He stiffened, and I held my breath, fearing he'd heard me. When he didn't look to his left, to where I stood, my shoulders relaxed a little.

"Something has the Upper Level demons afraid enough that they've all gone into hiding." Nicolai was speaking again. "And that something is killing us—killing Wardens."

3

I sucked in a sharp breath. Something was killing *Wardens*? With the exception of Upper Level demons and, well, me, Wardens were practically indestructible, bred to withstand the fiercest of battles.

They weren't easy to kill.

"At first, we thought it was a demon—an Upper Level, taking out some of its own." Zayne spoke up. "But while they do fight among themselves, they don't kill like this, as if they have no fear of exposure. Then Wardens started turning up dead in the same way. What's happening now is happening to demons *and* Wardens."

The Warden with shorter hair moved forward. "If I may speak?"

"Dez, you know I don't stand on formality," Thierry replied.

A faint smile appeared on Dez's face. "I know that Zayne and I don't have the decades of experience that you and Matthew have, but what we're seeing is something altogether new.

Some of our best warriors have died, Wardens who would not be easy to gain the upper hand on."

"Why is it impossible that this is the work of a highly skilled Upper Level demon?" Matthew asked. "Why do you all think this is something else?"

"Maybe we're wrong. Maybe a demon is orchestrating all of this," added Nicolai, and I noticed that Zayne's jaw clenched, as if he were forcing himself not to speak. "We don't know yet, but this week we lost another Warden. We need reinforcements. That's why we're here."

Thierry leaned back, his shoulders tensed. "Well, you've come at the perfect time. The Accolade is about to begin. We will have new recruits."

Nicolai exchanged a look with Zayne and Dez but said nothing.

"We have your rooms readied, and food is being prepared. I'm sure many of you would like to rest," Thierry was saying. "You will be staying for the Accolade."

Nicolai appeared to take a moment before answering. "We are honored to stay, but it is imperative that we return to the city—"

"Do you think that spending a week here will somehow tip the balance? I don't think so," Thierry said, and I recognized the tone that brokered no room for argument. I'd heard it enough myself, but if Wardens were dying, they needed to get back with help. "We have plenty of time to discuss your needs." There was a pause. "And ours."

The corners of my lips turned down. My fingers tightened on the curtain as Zayne inexplicably took a step back, turned his head and…

And looked directly at where I was standing.

Something… Something happened.

A shock of awareness shot through me, followed by a feeling of déjà vu, as if I'd been here before, but that made no sense. This was the first time I'd seen Zayne. I would've remembered if I had seen him before.

I didn't move as he stared at me. I couldn't. I was rooted to the spot, and I was close enough to see his mouth, to read his lips when they began to move.

I see you.

Oh my God.

Jerking back, I let go of the curtain, letting it slide into place. I slowly backed up.

Holy crap, he'd seen me—well, seen part of me at least, but probably enough to recognize me later. Besides the fact we weren't that far apart, Wardens had amazing eyesight, especially at night—

My hip knocked into the edge of a stacked table, sending a sharp flare of pain down my hip. Cursing under my breath, I whirled around and steadied the table before the whole thing could come crashing down. Once I was sure that wouldn't happen, I hightailed my butt out of the Great Hall and into the cool evening mountain air.

The sun had set, but the path was well lit as I walked around the vast gardens behind the hall. My thoughts went back to what I'd overheard. Something that might not be a demon was killing Wardens *and* demons?

What could that be?

Crossing the field toward the main house, I slowed my pace as I neared the thick cropping of trees. From this point on there was only the silvery glow of the moonlight to lead the way, which meant I could barely see crap, but I'd walked this path so many times that my steps were sure, if still a little cautious—unlike the night of the Ravers. Then I had been so full of adrenaline that all my steps had been confident. It wasn't always like that.

My thoughts shifted from what I'd overheard to my reaction to Zayne, that weird feeling. It was so bizarre, but probably had to do with my overactive imagination—

A twig snapped directly behind me. Too close. Stomping down the unexpected bite of surprise, I reacted first, as I'd been trained.

Reaching up, I gripped an arm. There was a jolt. A shock of static charge that registered as I whirled around, twisting the arm as I anchored my weight on my right leg. I caught the vague shape of someone much larger as I swung my fist.

With a startling quickness, my hand was caught and I was spun around to face the other direction, hauled backward against a hard chest and stomach that was most definitely male. In a matter of seconds, he had my arms pinned and the scent of…winter mint surrounded me.

"Is that how you normally greet people?" a vaguely familiar, deceptively soft voice whispered in my ear.

I bent forward, intent on getting enough space between us to deliver a vicious back kick.

"That would be very unwise."

My breath came out harsh and ragged as I straightened, straining against his hold. "Grabbing people from behind in the dark isn't wise."

"I didn't grab you," he responded, tightening his hold on me once I managed to get a few inches between us again. "I called out to you and you didn't answer."

"I didn't hear you." I turned my head to the side. "But is that what you normally do when someone doesn't respond to you? Grab them from—"

"I didn't grab you."

"You were *right* behind me," I said, beyond irritated that he'd incapacitated me so quickly. "Can you let me go?"

"I don't know." There was a pause. "Are you going try to hit me again? Kick me?"

"Not if you don't try to grab me again," I shot back.

A stuttered heartbeat passed and then the arms around me dropped. I launched forward like there were springs attached to my feet, putting several feet between us before I whirled around. There was just enough light from the moon to see him.

"Holy crapsicles," I whispered, taking another step back.

It was *him*.

The utterly beautiful blond Warden.

Zayne.

He tilted his head. "You're...human."

Yeah. Sort of. "Were you expecting something else?"

"Ye-ess." He drew the word out, and he took a moment before he continued, as if he were choosing his words wisely. "Especially considering where we are."

It *was* fairly uncommon for humans to live in Warden communities, so I wasn't surprised that he was surprised.

"Unless," he said, taking a measured step toward me, "you're not supposed to be here."

I tensed. "I'm supposed to be here."

"Just like you were supposed to be behind the curtain in the Great Hall, eavesdropping?"

Well, dammit.

"I live here," I said, instead of answering his question. Thank God most of his features were shadowed and I could actually speak to him and not stand there drooling like I'd never seen an attractive guy before. "And why are you out here? Aren't you supposed to be going to your room, then having dinner provided for you?"

"I got kind of curious when I saw you behind the curtain. Thought I should investigate."

"I don't think you're supposed to be out here following me."

"Didn't realize that as a Warden I couldn't come and go as I pleased."

I kept my arms loose at my sides. "Have you visited here before?" I asked, even though I knew the answer.

"No."

"Then maybe you shouldn't assume what you can and can't do."

Zayne was quiet, and then he let out a deep, rough chuckle. I frowned.

"You have a point," he admitted, and there was another beat of silence. "I am made of questions."

Unsure if that was a good or bad thing, I looked around but was unable to see beyond the dark trees and the faint glow of solar lights. "Are you?"

"Yes. How in the Hell did you end up here? A human living in the regional community—a human who appears to know that demons are real? And obviously you know this, because you didn't run screaming or laughing from the hall when we talked about the demonic activity."

Now I wished I could see his expression as I rubbed my hands along my hips. "I'm not the first or the last ordinary person to know about demons."

That was true. There were humans who did know—most of them worked for police departments or held positions within the government and worked closely with the Wardens. But they were few and far between.

He moved closer, and more of his face came into view, but he was still mostly a blur. "I'm willing to wager that there isn't one thing ordinary about you."

I wasn't sure if he meant that as a compliment or not. "Why would you think that?"

"You live here, at the seat of power for dozens of clans, and you almost punched me in the face in under five seconds flat," he explained. "And you were also hiding behind a curtain, being a little snoop."

I folded my arms. "I'm not a snoop."

"You're not?"

"Just because I happened to be there—"

"Behind a curtain."

I ignored that. "Just because I happened to be behind a curtain—"

"*Hiding* behind a curtain," he amended.

"Just because I was *partially obscured* by a curtain doesn't mean I was snooping around."

Zayne was only about a foot from me now, and I caught the scent of winter mint again. "Do you often find yourself partially obscured by curtains?"

I snapped my mouth shut and then took a deep, long breath. "Why are we talking about this?"

He lifted a shoulder and dropped it. "Because you're claiming you're not a snoop. I mean, maybe you spend your free time standing behind curtains all the time. What do I know?"

My eyes narrowed. "Oh, yeah, I actually do like hanging out behind curtains. I like how dusty they are."

"Since I detect sarcasm, you're basically admitting you were snooping."

"I admitted no such thing."

He dipped his chin. "Why not just admit it?"

I started to tell him there was nothing to admit, but I *had* been snooping. Obviously. I sighed. "We don't get a lot of… visitors, so when I saw you guys arrive I was curious. I had no idea you would be talking about anything important."

"Now, was that so hard to admit?"

"Yes," I replied dryly. "It hurt me. Deep inside. I may never recover."

"How did you end up living here?" he asked, directing the subject back to his original question.

"It's a long story I have no intention of telling you."

A moment passed, and even without seeing his eyes, I could feel his heavy gaze on me. "You're...frustrating."

My brows shot up. Wow. "Well, you're judgmental. Guess which is worse?"

Zayne laughed, and it wasn't like that deep chuckle from before. It was dry as sand. "I'm probably the least judgmental person you'll ever meet."

"You know, I'm going to have to say that's probably not the case."

"You don't know me."

"You don't know me, and you just said I was frustrating," I pointed out.

"I'm making that educated observation after speaking to you for a few minutes."

My hands curled into fists as the urge to punch him filled me, which would be wrong, but also satisfying, but still wrong. I needed to get out of here. "You know, I'm not going to even lie and say it was nice chatting with you. I'm just going to leave now." I started to turn.

"What's your name?"

I stopped and faced him again. "Seriously?"

"What is your name?" he repeated—no, he *demanded.*

My hackles raised. "It's Mindya Business."

"That's exceedingly...lame," he retorted.

I snorted. Like a little piglet. "I thought it was pretty clever."

"We obviously have two very different ideas of what makes something clever," he said, and my eyes narrowed. "You do realize I'm going to find out sooner or later?"

He would, but I'd be damned if I told him what it was.

"Well, I guess you're just going to have to wait for later. Peace out."

I flipped him the middle finger, sure he could see it with his Warden eyes, and then I spun around, prepared to flounce from his sight—

"Trinity Lynn Marrow!" Misha called out. "I swear to Jesus, girl, when I get my hands on you…"

Drawing up short, I closed my eyes.

"I'll admit I didn't expect to find out *that* soon." Wry humor dripped from Zayne tone.

"I don't know you," I said, turning back around. "But I do not like you."

"That's not very nice," Zayne demurred.

Before I could inform him that I didn't even remotely care, Misha stormed into the small clearing. In a heartbeat, he was in front of me, standing between Zayne and me as if he thought Zayne was some wild animal about to attack.

"Back off," growled Misha, lifting a hand of warning in Zayne's direction as I peered around him.

Zayne didn't back off.

He came forward, stopping a mere inch from Misha's hand as he leaned to the side, looking to where I was standing. "You guys really aren't friendly here, are you?"

My lips twitched into a reluctant grin. "Like I said, we don't get a lot of visitors."

"I can tell," Zayne replied dryly.

Misha shifted so that Zayne was once again blocked, causing me to roll my eyes. "Who the Hell are you and what are you doing here?"

"His name is Zayne," I answered for him. "And he's from the DC clan. They were *invited* here."

"No one is randomly invited here," Misha clipped out.

"Well, I guess there's a first for everything." The coolness of Zayne's tone could've frozen the leaves on the trees around us.

I used to think that Misha was one of the tallest and scariest Wardens I'd ever seen in human form, but right now, I was thinking Zayne was going to take that number one spot.

"I don't care if you're invited or not," Misha responded as heat rolled off him, and with that, he jumped ahead of Zayne in the unofficial scary Warden contest. "You shouldn't be out here lurking around and talking to her."

"First off, I wasn't lurking around," Zayne said. "And second, why can't I talk to her? Is it because she's human, or because she swings first, then speaks?"

Oh my God! I sidestepped Misha and glared at the blond Warden. "I swung on you because—"

"I walked up behind you? I'm sorry. I'll try not to do that again," he replied, and even though I couldn't see his face, I heard the smile in his voice.

"What are you doing out here?" Misha demanded, and for once, it wasn't directed toward me.

Zayne paused before saying, "Just needed fresh air. It was a long drive."

I arched a brow, surprised he hadn't tossed me under the bus and backed up over me.

"Well, now that you got your fresh air, I suggest you head back to the Great Hall."

Part of me expected Zayne to refuse. He seemed like the combative sort.

But he surprised me by stepping back. "Yeah, I do think it's time I head back."

"Perfect," Misha snarled.

Zayne inclined his head in my direction. "Nice to meet you…Trinity *Lynn* Marrow."

I started to go off like a firework, the kind that screeches, but Misha took hold of my arm, and I ended up swallowing a mouth full of curses as I yelled, "I'm going to take the high road and ignore that."

"But going low sounds a lot more fun," Zayne echoed back.

I spun back toward where Zayne had been, but Misha didn't let go and all but dragged me away before I could come up with a worthy retort.

"Dammit, Trin."

"What?" I had to take extra big steps to keep up with his freakishly long legs. "I didn't do anything."

"You never do anything."

I frowned. "What's that supposed to me?"

"Oh, I don't know. How about when you got mad and hid in the Great Hall for an entire day, causing everyone to believe you were missing? And then when you were found, you were, like, 'I didn't do anything wrong.'"

"What?" I threw one arm up dismissively. "I was, like, eight years old at the time, and you were being really mean to me."

"How about when you whined until I took you to the movies outside the community and then you ditched me to meet up with some kids you met online?"

"I was working."

"No, you were playing *Ghost Whisperer*," he corrected.

"That's not playing! There was a spirit who needed an extremely important message relayed."

"And what about the time you fell off the roof and then I got blamed for it? That was, like, a month ago."

I pursed my lips.

"And how about the night you went beyond the walls and started fighting Ravers, Trin?"

Heat flushed my cheeks as we stepped out from the trees and Thierry's home came into view. "You know why I needed to do that, and you also went outside the walls."

"We're not talking about me."

"Oh, of course not."

Misha ignored that. "You're going to be the death of me."

"I think that's a wee bit dramatic," I said, even though I could be the death of him.

"Do you?"

"Yes."

He cursed under his breath. "So, were you eavesdropping on Thierry while was he was talking to them?"

"Will you get mad if I say yes?"

"Trinity."

I sighed. "Yes, I was eavesdropping. Zayne saw me and followed me outside. That's why we were talking."

"What did you hear?"

"They're here for reinforcements. Something is going on in DC."

"What?"

"They said something was killing demons and Wardens, and they don't think it's another demon," I explained. "They wanted to leave immediately with reinforcements, I guess, but Thierry is making them stay for the Accolade."

"Something that might not be a demon is killing Wardens?"

"Yep."

"That makes no sense."

"Yep," I repeated. "But maybe this is it, you know? There's some big baddie out there killing Wardens. Maybe we're going to get *called*."

He frowned at me. "I don't know about all of that."

Yeah, I doubted that was the case too, but at some point we *were* going to be called upon. We'd leave here. Together. And we'd leave here to *fight*. I shrugged. "Anyway, seems like they might be here for a week."

Misha was quiet for several moments. "I want you to stay in the house until they're gone."

"Are you for real?" I demanded as we crossed the driveway. Floodlights kicked on, alerted our presence; their brightness caused me to wince. "I can't stay in the house while they're here."

"Have you've forgotten why we don't have visitors here? Or are you just being recklessly selfish?"

"Is there a third option?"

Misha stopped in front of the wide steps and lit porch. He stared down at me as the tips of his fingers touched my cheeks, keeping my gaze focused on him. "Can you just do it? Stay hidden?"

Frustration pounded through me like a summer storm. "I can't just stay in the house, Misha. That's ridiculous. I'm not a prisoner."

A look of exasperation settled onto his face. "It's just for a week, and that's if they're really here for that long."

"A week is an eternity."

"A couple of days in a house that has virtually everything to keep you occupied is not an eternity, you little brat," he went on, dropping his hands. "You can sit and eat and marathon TV shows instead of training."

"I don't want to sit around and do nothing. That'll drive me to do something entirely irresponsible and reckless."

"Really?"

"Hey! I know my limits."

"You know most people would be happy that they're done with schooling and can just chill out."

"I'm not most people." Our classes ended mid-May, so Misha and I had gone from training four hours a day to about eight, which meant I was still incredibly bored an additional ten hours or so.

He ignored my very valid point. "You could treat it is a vacation."

"A vacation from what exactly?" I snapped, beyond irritated now. "What do I do that I need a vacation from?"

"Trin," Misha sighed.

"Don't talk to me like that, Misha. You can leave this community whenever you please—"

"That's not exactly true and you know it." Anger tightened Misha's jaw. "If you're suggesting that I have freedom when you don't, you're not being fair."

Guilt churned in the pit of my stomach, quickly followed by the all too bitter bite of heartache. He was right, and I was being a brat. Wasn't like Thierry had given him a choice, pairing him with me before either of us knew what that really meant, preparing both of us for the—

I sucked in a sharp breath as I stared at the boy I'd grown up with. The boy I'd watched turn into a young man, and for the first time, something struck me with the force of being hit by a semi-truck.

"Do you want this?" I whispered.

His brows knitted together. "Want what?"

"Us," I said. "Being bonded to me. This life."

Understanding flickered across his face. "Trin—"

I grabbed his hands with mine. "Be honest with me, Misha. I know it's not like we can change anything. It's already been done, but I...I just need to know."

He was silent, and the longer he was silent, the more my heart began to pound. "It's what I've been raised to do, Trin. It's all I know, and like you said, it's not like we can change anything."

Feeling a little sick, I looked away as I dropped his hands. "That isn't the same thing as wanting to do this."

Misha turned, and I looked at him, saw him thrust his

hand through his unruly curls. He hated them, but I'd always thought they were adorable, and as he stared up at the house we both lived in, the house where our bedrooms were separated only by a couple of walls, I suddenly felt like...crying.

Maybe it was my time of month, because I never cried.

But it wasn't.

The burn in the back of my throat was there, because I'd spent nearly my whole life beside Misha and our lives were irrevocably tied together. I hadn't thought about how he might feel about any of this, had I?

I had, but superficially, and mostly about how it impacted me.

"I am selfish," I whispered.

Misha's head whipped toward me. "Normally I'd appreciate this rare sense of self-awareness and not question it, but why do you think that?"

My lower lip trembled. "Because I never realized that you might not want this."

"Trin, stop." He was in front of me again, his hands on my shoulders. "I do want this. It's an honor to be your bonded Protector."

"Really?" I laughed hoarsely. "Because I don't—"

"It is an honor," he repeated, squeezing my shoulders, and the weight of his hands was both comforting and at the same time suffocating. "And I do mean that. What you are? What it means for me to be chosen to be there beside you? That is the highest honor."

He sounded like he meant that, he really did, but I sounded like I meant things all the time and I really didn't, especially when I wanted nothing more than to be what I was pretending I already was.

Misha pulled me to his chest and I went, loosely wrapping my arms around his waist as he folded his around my shoulders. When I was younger, I'd welcomed these hugs more than I could even understand, and even as I'd grown older, I could always find solace in his embrace. But now?

Now I felt itchy.

Misha was quiet for a long moment. "I was being ridiculous to suggest that you stay in the house. You'd end up burning it down or something."

I cracked a grin.

"But can you do me one favor?" he asked, and I nodded against his chest. "Can you stay away from Zayne?"

That I wasn't expecting.

I pulled back and stared up at him. "Not that I'm expecting to become his next best friend forever or anything, but what's the big deal?"

"I've… I've heard of him," he said, dropping his arms. "He's bad news, Trin. Zayne is not someone you want to be around."

4

I behaved and stayed in my room like a good little Trinity even though Misha had gone out after escorting me to my bedroom, because I felt bad after last night. I had stayed up pretty late waiting for him to return, but he hadn't, and I figured he'd run into Jada or her boyfriend, Ty.

So, I'd been left alone, which meant I spent a lot of time thinking, and I thought, well… I might owe Zayne an apology.

He hadn't grabbed me last night, and maybe he had called out to me and I hadn't heard him, *aaand* it was quite possible that my reaction had been a bit excessive and impulsive.

I probably should apologize when—if—I saw him again. Not that I was going to look for him. If Misha said he was bad news, he was bad news.

Then again, I was dying with curiosity to find out exactly why Zayne was such a big no-no.

Because I was *that* bored.

Rolling my eyes, I dropped my toothbrush into the holder,

then glanced at my reflection. Fine wisps of damp hair clung to my cheeks as I picked up my glasses from the sink and placed them on.

I shuffled over to my bed and flopped onto my back. My glasses slipped up the bridge of my nose as I stared at the glow in the dark stars splattered across my ceiling. They were barely visible now, as it was daytime.

At least Netflix had just dropped *The Fresh Prince of Bel-Air*, and there were, like, six seasons of Will Smith to enjoy.

As I rolled onto my side, my gaze fell to the framed photo on my nightstand and the old, tattered book that lay beside it. The photo was of my mom and me, taken two years ago. May 20. My sixteenth birthday. The photo was just a blob, but I knew what it looked like in my heart and in my mind.

The pic had been snapped by Thierry at the Pit, during the day. Mom and I were sitting on the stone bench, my cheek resting on her shoulder, and I was holding a pink Barbie car. I had jokingly asked for a car for my birthday. Jokingly for two reasons: no one had cars within the community. Everyone walked…or flew. And I would never drive. Didn't have the eyeballs for that. So, Mom being Mom, she had given me the car as one of my gifts.

That was…so her.

The book was also Mom's. Her favorite. An old paperback from the late '80s, with a couple on the cover embracing while the woman looked at the man with longing. Johanna Lindsey's *Hearts Aflame*. She'd been a huge historical romance fan, and she'd read that book a hundred times.

I'd read it at least a dozen times before the print became too small for me to read even with my glasses on.

God, I missed reading it, because it made me feel close to Mom in some way. I had downloaded the ebook on my iPad, but it wasn't the same as holding the paper copy.

It was never the same.

Sitting up, I straightened my glasses. The images on the TV were mostly a blur even after Thierry had upgraded my television from a thirty inch to a fifty inch. I picked up the remote—

"Who are the stranger dangers in the Great Hall? One of them just moved into my bedroom, Trinity. Into *my* bedroom."

I jumped at the question, dropping the remote on the bed as Peanut walked through my bedroom door—my *closed* bedroom door.

Peanut was a weird nickname, but he'd told me that was what his friends had called him, because he was barely taller than five feet. It was the name he preferred, and I had no idea what his real name was.

Peanut was... Well, he had passed away under bizarre circumstances—at a Whitesnake concert, of all things, sometime in the 1980s. He'd died after idiotically climbing one of the concert speaker towers during a storm, proving he hadn't been the brightest lightbulb in the bunch. The story goes, lightning struck near the tower, startling him, and he subsequently fell to his death.

It had been his seventeenth birthday.

Tragic.

I'd seen him for first time about eight years ago, when my mother and Thierry had taken me to an eye specialist in Morgantown, which was only about two hours from here. By the time I was ten, I had already seen enough ghosts and spirits to know what he was when I saw him standing on the sidewalk, looking bored and a bit lost.

The concert venue he'd died at had been nearby, and he'd spent God knows how long roaming the streets of Morgantown. He'd formed an attachment to me the moment he realized I could see and talk to him, and he'd done what some ghosts will do.

Peanut had followed me home.

I'd tried to get him to cross over, but he'd refused to move on. Meaning he was stuck in his death state and looked the way he had when he died instead of, like spirits, healthy and whole. He wore a shirt that was obviously vintage—the band's name written in white and the lead singer screened onto the shirt. His jeans were black and tight, and he wore a pair of red Chuck Taylors.

Ironically, what he wore was kind of in fashion now.

His hair was shaggy and black, which was a good thing, because it hid the slight indent on the back of his head that I'd had the misfortune of seeing once. Some massive head trauma had gone down.

So, yeah, Peanut was a ghost—a ghost who was so stuck in the '80s that half the time I didn't even know what he was trying to communicate to me.

He was a rarity—one who knew he was dead and could interact with his surroundings, had died decades ago and hadn't crossed over to the great beyond and still managed to be decent and kind.

Peanut was now kind of like a roommate, one that only I could see, who was supposed to knock before he floated through walls and doors.

Literally that was the only rule.

Well, that and not to mess with my stuff, especially since he'd learned how to access my iPad and my laptop and he also had this horrible habit of turning all my clothes inside out.

Which was notably weird.

"You're supposed to knock," I reminded him, heart slowing down. "Those are the rules."

"Sorry, my little dudette." Peanut raised transparent arms,

flipping the peace signs for some reason. "Do you want me to go back out into the hall and knock? I'll do it and I'll be perfect at it. I'll knock until the house—"

"No. I don't need you to do that now." I rolled my eyes. "Where have you been?"

"Chillin'…like a villain." He glided to the window—glided, because his feet didn't touch the floor. The upper half of his body disappeared through the curtain as he peered outside. "Who is the dude in my bedroom?"

I frowned at him. "What room do you think is your bedroom?"

"All the rooms in the Great Hall are my bedroom."

"Those rooms are not your bedrooms."

He pulled away from the window, his hands popping to his hips. "And why not?"

"You're a ghost, Peanut. You don't need a bedroom."

"I need space to roam and live and breathe and be creative—"

"You're not living or breathing, and there are extra, empty guest bedrooms here," I pointed out. "So, you can be creative in them."

"But I like that room in the Great Hall," Peanut whined. "The one that overlooks the garden. And it has its own bathroom."

I stared at him. "You're dead. You don't need a bathroom."

Peanut met my stare. "You don't know me. You don't know my life, my wants or needs."

"Oh my God, Peanut. Seriously." I scooted to the edge of the bed, dropping my feet to the floor. "The other bedrooms are just fine."

"I do not accept this."

I shook my head. "Who is in your room that's not really your room?"

"Some really big blond guy."

My heart skipped a beat. Had to be indigestion...even though I didn't have indigestion before. "Zayne?"

"Is that his name?" Peanut floated to me, his feet about six inches off the floor. "Is Thierry doing some kind of hot foreign Warden exchange student college edition thing now?"

I snorted. "Um, no. Those are the visiting Wardens from the capital."

"Oh, yeah. That's totes something different, isn't it? Like he's not accepting littlies into training right now."

"No, it's not time for new classes, and it is different that they're here." I paused. "I met one of them last night. The blond. Zayne."

"Do tell?" He popped his chin on his fist. "I have all the time in the world, but it better involve what kind of work-out that guy does to get those abs, because I just saw him in all his glory—"

"Wait. How did you see him in all his glory?" My face flushed at the thought of all Zayne's glory. I might find him exceedingly annoying and judgmental, but that did not change the fact that the guy was flush-inducing. "Please tell me you were not peeping on him."

"It was an accident!" He threw his hands up. "I was going into my room—"

"It's not your room."

"And he was coming out of the shower, in just a towel, and I was shocked. Shocked, I tell you." Peanut sat down on my bed and sank several inches, causing half his torso and legs to disappear.

It looked like my bed ate half of him.

"So, he started getting dressed, and I was like *hold me closer, tiny dancer*, this is not the America I was promised, but it is the afterlife I'm here for."

"I don't even know where to start with that."

"Start by giving me the 411 on this DC clan."

The 411? I shook my head. "I don't know much about them. They're here for reinforcements."

"That's boring. Why did they come all the way from DC to ask?" Peanut rose so that it looked like he was actually sitting on my bed. "I mean, hello, McFly, you have FaceTime and Skype."

I stared at him, and it took me a moment to refocus. "Yeah, it is weird that they came here—that they were even given permission."

"Huh." Peanut floated off the bed. "Maybe—"

A knock on the door interrupted us, and then I heard Misha call out, "Trin, you awake?"

"He knocked," Peanut pointed out.

"I am." I vaulted off the bed. "Come in!"

The door opened and Misha walked into my room, dressed in black nylon pants, tank top and sneakers. He looked like he'd just come back from a run.

He grinned as he closed the door. "You seem awfully chipper this morning."

"I'm just excited to see you," I said, and then winced as Misha walked straight through Peanut. "Uh…"

Peanut dispersed like smoke caught in a strong breeze and Misha jerked to a stop, his bright blue eyes widening. "Did I just walk through that ghost?"

"Yeeaah…" I drew the word out.

Piecing back together behind Misha, Peanut crossed his arms. "How rude!"

Misha shuddered. "That is so freaky and makes me so uncomfortable."

"How do you think I feel?" Peanut snapped back, even

though Misha couldn't hear him. "You were literally inside my body. Inside every part of me. Every. Part."

I wrinkled my nose.

"What is he saying?" Misha demanded.

"You do not want to know," I warned. "He's here because he's mad that our visitors are taking over 'his' bedrooms, and I tried to explain to him that since he's dead he doesn't need a bedroom, but he's not getting it."

"You dismiss my feelings." Flinging out his arms, Peanut flounced toward the door. "I'm going to go see if Zayne is getting undressed again. Tootles!"

My mouth dropped open.

"Is he still in here?" Misha asked, looking around the room.

"No. He's currently being a pervert."

His nose wrinkled. "You're right, I really don't want to know. I'm actually surprised."

"Why?"

"I didn't expect you to be here." He grinned when I rolled my eyes. "Are you actually laying low?"

"For now," I muttered. "Did you have fun last night hanging out in the Great Hall with everyone?"

He smirked as he turned away. "You sound jealous."

"I'm not jealous."

"Really?" He walked to my desk chair and sat. When he faced me, he gave me a look that said he knew better.

"Whatever." I folded my arms.

"I'm actually here to tell you that I finally got a chance to talk to Thierry last night about Clay."

"What did he say?"

"He's going to talk to him and his instructors." Misha moved himself around in a slow circle. "And I think his Ac-colade will be delayed a year to ensure that he's 'mature' and 'respectful' and can be trusted being assigned to one of the outposts."

"Wow." I'd known Thierry would do something, but I was surprised by how far he was going. There was a tiny part of me that worried I'd be in trouble somehow. That was dumb, but I couldn't help it even though I knew I'd done nothing wrong. The problem was that, upon birth, male Wardens were put on a pedestal, and the whole social structure was a breeding ground for misogyny. Sort of the same out in the human world. "Way to go, Thierry."

"Are you surprised?" The corners of his lips turned down.

"A little. I mean, you know how everything is." I sat down on the edge of the bed. "I knew he'd do something and I'm happy he's making sure Clay isn't some—"

"Creep who pushed too far?" he supplied for me.

I nodded.

Misha made another slow circle in the chair. "Just be alert. Clay's probably going to be pissed."

"Probably," I murmured.

"Not that you can't hold your own, but…"

"I know." I sighed, brushing a strand of hair out of my face. "Did you see our visitors?"

"Yeah, they were there, and they did not look happy about it." Misha smirked, and I frowned. "Anyway, get your butt into your workout clothes so we can get our training done for the day." Misha rose from the chair.

"I'll be there in ten," I told him.

He stopped at the door. "Oh, you won't be ready in ten minutes, but I'll wait for you outside."

"Why?" I blinked.

"I told Thierry you were eavesdropping on his meeting last night," he explained, and my mouth dropped open. Misha grinned. "I'm sure he's going to want to talk to you first."

"You jerk-face!" I shouted as Misha closed the door behind him. Falling back onto the bed, I groaned. I was going to be in so much trouble.

So much.

It was Jada who knocked on my door next, after I'd changed into a pair of black running tights and a loose white shirt that kept slipping off one shoulder and was surely going to annoy the crap out of me throughout the day.

I pulled my hair up into a ponytail as Jada waited for me on the corner of my bed. She was wearing a pretty, sky-blue, off-the-shoulder dress with a long, billowy skirt that looked amazing against her deep brown skin. Her black hair was buzzed close to the skull.

Sometimes I hated how effortlessly fabulous Jada was.

"I can't believe Misha told him I was in the hall," I muttered, tightening my ponytail.

"I guess he felt he needed to just in case someone else said something to Thierry," Jada reasoned.

I also sometimes hated how logical she was.

I shuffled out of the bathroom, tugging on my shirt so that it was on both my shoulders. "Let's get this over with."

Jada laughed as she rose to her feet. "Sorry. You look like you're about to walk the plank."

"Your uncle is scary when he's mad." I followed her from the room and closed the door behind me. I looked around as we went down the hall, not seeing Peanut.

"Yeah, he can be." She reached the top of the stairs. "You know, I expected you to make it at least a day before being seen by one of them."

"Well, you know me." We headed down the stairs. "I like to exceed expectations."

She snorted as we rounded the second-floor landing. "So, did you really swing at Zayne?"

"How did you know that? Did Misha tell you?"

"Yes." She giggled as I groaned. "So, you did. Why?"

"Have you met him?"

"Last night." She glanced over her shoulder at me, grinning. "He's...cute."

"I'm not sure *cute* is an effective adjective, and I wonder what Ty would think about you finding him cute."

Jada laughed. "I may be mating to Ty eventually, but that doesn't mean my eyes don't work anymore."

Mating was the archaic and gross way the Wardens referred to what normal people called marriage. They had a very similar ceremony, except the mating ritual lasted three days, and mating was... Well, it was for forever with the Wardens. They didn't recognize things such as divorce or separation, and I also found that archaic as all Hell gets out, because they still did the arranged mating thing quite a bit.

Ty and Jada were lucky, though. Honestly, truly in love. I didn't know what that felt like. To be loved like that or to love like that, in a passionate way that made you want to do ridiculous things like pledge your life to another person.

I would never know what it felt like, either, if I stayed here.

"You should write a book on how to impress and endear yourself to new people you meet," she said.

"Shut up." I laughed, pushing her in the back.

She stumbled a step. "Why in the world did you take a swing at him, though?" she asked as she led me through a maze of corridors that were all brightly lit. Thierry left the lights on, no matter if it were day or night. "He seems like a really cool guy."

"What?" My brows lifted. "He was kind of a jerk to me."

"Was that after you swung on him?"

"Well, yeah, but…" I snapped my mouth shut, not wanting to think or talk about Zayne. "You know what, whatever. Did you hear what their clan leader thinks about what's going on in the city?"

"The only thing they talked about while they had dinner was boring stuff, like the weather and which congresspersons they believed were being manipulated by demons," she said, and I didn't think the latter sounded boring at all. "But Misha mentioned something about it afterward. That they think something is killing Wardens and demons?"

"What do you think about that?" Surprise flickered through me as we walked past Thierry's office. I must not be in too much trouble, because if he was really angry, he liked to sit behind his big desk and lecture me.

"I don't know if there really is something else there, Trin. Seems crazy—watch out. Door." She caught my arm and pulled me to her side. I'd been so focused on her, I hadn't seen that it was open. "It has to be a demon, but displaying the bodies of the Wardens and the demons in such a public way? That sounds risky. If the general population finds out about the demons, all of them will be dead. The Alphas will wipe the demons out."

They'd wipe out all the Wardens, too, and a lot of innocent humans would end up being taken out right along with them.

At least, that's what we were told.

"Do you really think that would happen? I mean, I get that demons exist because of the whole need for balance between good and evil, but if the demons knew that the Alphas could wipe them out, why would they have had the uprising ten years ago?"

Jada's glance was sharp, like she couldn't believe I was questioning the fallacy of this long-held belief. "A lot of the demons involved in the uprising were lower level demons, ones too stupid to realize they were signing their own death warrants. They thought they could somehow take over the world and turn it into their own perfect Hellscape. You know that. We were taught that."

"We were also taught that there's always an Upper Level demon pulling the strings of a lower level one," I reminded her.

She eyed me as she pushed open the kitchen door. I knew that what I was saying was weird, but I had weird thoughts when I was confined to the house.

Even if it had been only twelve hours.

"Hi, Thierry," Jada called, and my gaze swiveled around the bright, airy kitchen until I saw him sitting at the island, coffee cup in front of him and his dark hands on the white marble countertop.

"Hey, girl." He smiled at his niece as she bent down and kissed his cheek, then went to the fridge. "I didn't know you were over here."

"Just came by. Mom wanted me to grab some Mississippi pot roast recipe from Matthew," she said. "Look who I found."

I waved awkwardly from the doorway.

Thierry's expression turned bland as he reached over and patted the bar stool. "Come sit with me."

Feeling like I was six years old and just got caught eating the marshmallows out of the Lucky Charms box, I dragged my feet over to him and sat down. "Hi," I said lamely, peeking over at him.

The skin around his eyes crinkled. "Hi."

"Want something to drink?" Jada asked as she poured herself a glass of apple juice.

I shook my head and decided to get this over with. "How much trouble am I in?"

Thierry cocked his head. "How much do you think you're in?"

Lifting my hands, I spaced them about a foot apart. "That much?"

"Not quite sure what that represents, but last night I briefly considered locking your doors and windows." Thierry picked up his mug. "You were in the Great Hall when you knew you shouldn't have been there. If the rest of the clan had seen you, what do you think they would've thought?"

I clasped my hands in my lap. "That I'm…nosy?"

"Yes, but more important, they would question why I did not know that a girl was eavesdropping on a very important conversation. Do you understand what that says about my control here, my authority? Our visitors could've been offended, knowing that I didn't have our meeting secured."

Glancing at Jada, I saw that she was studiously staring at her vibrant pink nails.

"I am the Duke, and there should never be a situation where I have someone eavesdropping on my meetings," he continued, and I felt about as tall as a banana, and I hated bananas. "You're lucky that it was Zayne who saw you and that he appears to be more amused than anything else."

Amused? He was *amused* by me? That—

"You know that my authority can be challenged at any time."

I gasped, looking at him sharply. I did know that, but would any Warden really see me eavesdropping as a massive failure on Thierry's part? One that was so bad that he should be removed as the Duke?

That seemed like an excessive response.

His bright blue eyes met and held mine. "Right now, there are too many things going on for any mistakes or mishaps."

Nibbling on my thumbnail, something I did whenever I was nervous, I shifted my gaze to the island.

"You know how important it is, for your own safety, to be smarter than you were last night." He touched my arm lightly, drawing my attention back to him. "Your father would not be thrilled to know about this. That you can count on."

Normally I would've laughed off the comment about my safety, but when Thierry referenced my father? Totally different story. Ice drenched my skin. I didn't need to look at Jada to know she felt the same chill. I couldn't help but ask. "You... Are you going to tell him?"

Thierry eyed me over the rim of his mug. It was then that I saw it read I Can't Adult Today. Matthew. That was such a Matthew saying. Thierry lowered the mug. "No."

Relief swept through the room like a summer's breeze.

"Only because I really don't want to talk to that sanctimonious son of a bitch today."

I blinked.

Thierry's lips twitched. "I'd rather have had our visitors come and leave never having seen you, but that's no longer in the cards. They know you're living here, or at least Zayne does, and if you were to suddenly never be seen again, they might think we're hiding something. That doesn't mean I want you seeking them out. I know how curious you get, often too curious for your own good. Nip that in the bud."

I figured this wasn't a good time to point out that we *were* hiding something. Me. But this was one of those rare moments that I knew not to say the first thing that came to my mind.

I said the second thing. "Should I not seek them out because Zayne is a bad dude?"

Thierry's dark brows rose. "What? Why would you think that?"

I glanced at Jada. "I...don't know?"

The corners of his lips turned down. "Zayne is...very honorable for such a young male. He is the opposite of a...bad dude."

Okay. Well, *that* was totally the opposite of what Misha had said, which was weird. How would Misha know something about Zayne that Thierry didn't?

I pushed the anomaly aside for the time being. "I won't seek them out or anything like that, but..." I took a deep breath. "If any of them ask questions about me and what I'm doing here, what do I tell them?"

"Tell them the truth."

Jada choked on her juice.

"Come again?" I squeaked.

"They'll sense the human part of you and nothing else."

"And if they ask how she ended up here?" Jada asked. "Do we tell them a pack of wolves dropped her off?"

I looked at her blandly.

"If they ask how you ended up here, you tell them the truth that the rest of those who live here know," he explained, resting his arms on the island. "Your mother and I met while I was in New York, when you were a young child. She was exposed to demons, wounded in a way that would have aroused human suspicion, so we brought her here. She stayed with us. Understand?"

That was...kind of the truth but not really. I nodded nonetheless.

Thierry's gaze met mine once more. "We do not know what they're capable of, Trinity. We already learned the hard way with people we thought we knew. Greed for power knows no discrimination, no boundaries."

The ice returned, seeping through my skin to my very marrow, and I suddenly felt sick to my stomach. I did know that. God, did I ever.

One of the prices paid for us to learn that…was my mom. "I know," I whispered.

"Good," Thierry replied. "Because they must never know what you are."

5

"I can't believe you didn't get into trouble." Misha handed the iron dagger to me.

I took it, wrapping my fingers around the leather-bound handle. "Sorry to disappoint you."

His brows, more brown than red, lowered. "I hope he at least yelled at you."

"No one asked to know what you hoped for, but yes, he did lecture me, thanks to you."

He snorted. "Sucks for you."

"It's your fault."

"How about I get you fries with extra cheese and bacon for your dinner to make up for it? The kind you like from that restaurant outside the walls?"

"Outback," I whispered. My eyes widened like an entire chorus of angels had begun singing in front of me. "Outback cheese fries?"

"Oh, wait. I have plans later. Can't do that for you."

I narrowed my eyes. "You're such a jerk."

He chuckled, but it was probably a good thing he wasn't going to get me the cheese fries. Wardens had a crazy fast metabolism, and the human DNA in me had the kind of metabolism that constantly thought I needed to store fat as if I were a bear about to enter hibernation.

Luckily—or unluckily—it stored a lot of it in the chest area. And in the hips.

And the thighs.

Whatever.

I'd still happily destroy that plate of cheese fries all by myself if given the chance. My stomach grumbled. I would do some really bad things for those fries actually.

Sighing, I looked around the massive room. Not like the fries were going to magically appear in the sprawling training facility where Wardens were educated in all manner of combat. Hand to hand. Grappling. Defensive and offensive takedowns. Mixed martial arts. There were even rooms for target practice with guns. Not that guns were particularly useful when it came to dispatching demons, but a head shot could slow them down and even knock them out for a while.

Some of the rooms did double duty, though. The one Misha and I were in was full of thick, blue mats to soften the blow of being pile-driven into the floor when learning how to do a takedown or recover from one. It was also used for knife play, which meant throwing very sharp daggers at very lifelike dummies.

Feeling the weight of the blade in my hand, I opened my fingers and then closed them. Iron was deadly to demons. So were Warden claws and teeth, but if you wanted to take out a demon without getting too close, an iron blade blessed in holy water was the way to go.

I eyed the hairless, expressionless creation across the room. It was too far away to see the many nicks that covered nearly every square inch of its very real-looking flesh. From where I stood, it was just a blob of a shape.

"I was thinking, you know, about you laying low while they're here." Misha moved with me, so he didn't stand too far in my peripheral. "Not to beat a dead horse or anything, but maybe just stay away from the Great Hall."

"I doubt I'll see them again," I said, lifting the blade as I thought about what Thierry had said about Zayne, which was vastly different from Misha's warning.

"You're not going to the Accolade tonight? They'll be there."

"That doesn't mean I'll see them. I doubt they'd notice me."

"I think you underestimate how much you stick out."

I looked over at him, frowning.

He lifted a brow. "It's the human thing. We can easily sense that."

"And honestly that's not a big deal, right? I'm not stupid. It's not like I'm going to walk up to one of them and be like, *Hey, nice to meet you, I'm a walking, breathing myth. Want the 411?*"

"The 411?"

I sighed. Peanut would be so disappointed. "Never mind."

Crossing his arms, he tilted his head to the side. "Actually, that wouldn't surprise me."

"Shut up."

He smirked.

I rolled my eyes.

"You going to get on with it?"

I refocused on the dummy. Taking one step forward, I angled my body slightly and then let the dagger fly.

It struck true, hitting the dummy in the center of the chest, sinking to the handle. Lowering my hand, I exhaled and glanced at Misha.

He was staring at the dummy. "I *still* don't understand how you do that."

I gave him my best cheeky grin. "I'm a special snowflake, unique and beautiful."

He snorted. "You're something."

Truth was, I was this good only because I had to practice and train harder than anyone else. I had to focus harder to compensate. I was this good because I couldn't let my failing eyes be a hindrance. At least not yet, not until they became too much to overcome, and even then, I would have to adapt.

And that meant training even harder.

Being able to use the daggers was important, just like knowing how to fight, and that wasn't just so I knew how to defend myself.

It was so I could *stop* myself.

What I'd done to the Ravers was not even a glimpse of what I was capable of if I didn't control myself.

"Don't you think it's weird that Thierry ordered the DC clan to stay for the Accolade?" I asked as nonchalantly as possible.

Misha didn't answer, but he frowned.

"I mean, since when did any of the clans come for it, even when they knew they were getting some of the new warriors?" I pointed out. "It's never happened before."

"What are you getting at?" he asked.

"I don't know, really. It's just weird. They don't want to stay." I shrugged. "And there's really no reason for them to be here."

He stared at me a long moment. "I think if you spend more than an hour in your bedroom a day, your brain starts to go to really weird places. Were you watching the ID channel again?"

"Whatever." I grinned. "I was watching *Fresh Prince*."

Misha crossed the room and gripped the handle of the

dagger. It made this gross sucking noise as he pulled it out. "Again?"

I nodded, and he walked it back to me. Taking the dagger, I glanced over to where he stood. "You said you knew of Zayne and that he's a bad dude. What did you hear about him?"

His head cocked. "Why are you asking?"

"Because I'm nosy," I replied, which was one hundred percent true.

Misha folded his arms over his chest. "His clan isn't exactly a fan of his. They don't trust him."

That was weird, considering the fact that his clan leader had brought him here with them. "Where are you hearing this stuff? Some kind of Warden message board?"

He snickered. "Yeah, exactly that. I knew one of the Wardens who was sent to his clan to help last year. He told me some stuff about him."

I stared down at the dagger, knowing that if I kept pestering him about Zayne, he would become suspicious. Misha knew me all too well. I trusted him with my life, but I had to wonder if his warning wasn't based in fact but rather due to some kind of brotherly love? Like no guy was good enough sort of thing. But I had only spoken to Zayne once, and it hadn't exactly been a love match. More like a hate match. I glanced at Misha again.

His gaze was swiveling to the door and back. I didn't have to look or see to know who was watching us. As he grew closer, the centers of his cheeks began to turn a faint pink.

"You're blushing." I grinned.

"Shut up," he grumbled, standing with his back to the door. Only a moment passed before he looked over his shoulder.

I shifted my weight from one foot to the next. "I think Alina likes you," I said, referencing the pretty dark-skinned female Warden who was definitely watching from the doorway.

Misha looked at me sharply.

"And I think you like Alina."

"Trin…" he began.

I thought about what he'd said to me last night. His life was irrevocably tied to mine. He hadn't said those words, but that was what they meant, and that wasn't fair. He was only a few months older than me, and like me, he'd carried a responsibility that few adults had. "You should go talk to her."

His eyes widened slightly at the prospect, as if it never occurred to him that he should speak to her. Then his expression locked down, devoid of any emotion. "I'm working."

"No, you're not." I laughed. "We're done training, for the most part, and I don't need you here to work with the daggers. Not like you can teach me anything when it comes to them. I'm like a million times better than you are."

"That's not what I meant. You shouldn't be—"

"I can be alone. I'm in no danger here."

"Safety anywhere isn't something we can be too sure of."

I ignored the way my skin chilled. "I'm fine. I'm just going to work with the blades for a little bit longer and then I'm going to head back to the house, see what Jada is up to. I don't need you acting as my Protector every waking second of the day—"

"That's not only what I do."

My gaze flew to his as the corners of my lips turned down as I lowered the blade. "Actually, isn't that exactly what you do?"

A moment passed as he held my gaze. "I meant I'm also your friend and not just your Protector."

"Okay." I stared at him, thinking he was being weird. "You're my friend, too, and I'm telling you, as your friend, that you should go talk to Alina."

He looked over his shoulder again, and I saw it flicker across of his face. *Yearning*. It was brief, but there was no mistaking it. I knew what it looked like.

I knew what it felt like.

That was what had led me to Clay's place. Too bad that had ended with him landing in a rosebush, but sometimes I was so bursting with yearning I couldn't take it.

"Look, you following me around like a shadow with our visitors here looks way more suspicious than I think you or Thierry realize." I shrugged. "Go talk to her. Take her to get a coffee or a smoothie or something. I'll text you later."

For a long moment I didn't think Misha was going to do it, but then his chest rose with a deep breath and he faced me. "How long are you going to be here?"

"No more than half an hour. Then I'm going back to the house."

"You're really going back to the house?"

I sighed. "Yes."

Misha seemed to have made up his mind. He nodded. "Okay. Text me later."

"Will do." I bit down on my lip and grinned. "Tell her she looks pretty today and actually listen to her when she talks."

"Shut up." He started to turn.

"And don't stare at her—"

"I know how to act around a girl."

"Do you?"

He looked like he was a second from throttling me, so I laughed. He shook his head as he turned around, and I watched him walk toward the doors, where Alina was standing. I waited until their shapes disappeared into the hall, then I walked to the small table against the wall. Lying on a leather satchel was the second iron dagger.

I picked it up, wondering just how long Misha would stay with Alina before he came running back to his *duty*.

I'm also your friend.

I didn't think he was lying, and neither had I been when I told him he was my friend. He *was* my friend, one of my very best friends, as was Jada and even Ty. So was Peanut. He was a ghost, but he still counted. Other than them? I wasn't close to anyone in the community.

I'd thought that Clay would be different. Not that he was madly in love or even in lust with me, but I'd thought he... He could've been something.

And that would be better than nothing.

I shoved away that thought, like I did whenever I thought too much about my future.

While the others accepted me, some were weary of a *human* in their midst. Some flat out ignored me. It was hard getting close to someone when they didn't know the truth about me.

And there were others who looked at me like I didn't deserve to be among them, to reap the fruit of their sacrifices. I knew enough about the world outside these walls to know that our communities were virtually utopias in comparison, completely self-sustaining with little of the issues faced by the world outside.

It was also hard to wonder whether Misha would be my friend if he hadn't been bonded to me. And even harder to wonder if Jada would be if it weren't for her uncle taking my mother and me in.

There were days and moments, like right now, when I felt utterly alone. But then I also felt silly feeling that way, because I did have friends—friends who were like family— better than most families. I loved Misha and Jada, but I missed my mom, and I...

I wanted *more.*

I wanted the yearning that had crossed over Misha's face when he saw Alina waiting for him at the door. I wanted the passion Jada and Ty shared. I wanted the love I saw in the looks Thierry and Matthew shared, in the words they often whispered to each other in hushed voices.

I wanted it *all*.

And I would get none of it here.

Feeling heavy, I walked back to where I'd been standing before and faced the dummy. I stared down at the daggers for what felt like a short eternity, telling myself there was no point in dwelling over hypotheticals or ruminating over what couldn't be changed.

I had a choice.

I could stay here. That would be the smart choice. I would be safe, and Thierry and my friends wouldn't have to worry about me. Or I could leave, and I could... I could live life, even if living meant looking over my shoulder every hour. But Misha and I would still be bonded. He'd be able to find me wherever I went, sensing me if he got within a handful of miles. And if something happened to me, it would happen to him. It wasn't fair to put him in danger by running off.

A tremor coursed down my arm. I knew what I *needed* to do. I knew what I *wanted* to do. And there was little room in this life for things that were wanted.

I drew in a breath, held it and then let the dagger fly. The satisfying *thunk* happened no more than a second later and pulled a faint grin from me. Switching the second blade to my right hand, I threw that blade and it sank deep, right below the other. Exhaling hard, I let my hand fall—

Several claps startled me, drawing my gaze to the doorway. It was empty. My gaze shifted to the right.

Oh crap.

It was him.

Zayne.

6

Leaning against the wall by the door, ankles crossed, Zayne was too far away for me to make out his expression. He was dressed a lot like he'd been the night before. Black henley paired with dark jeans, a startling contrast to his golden skin and hair.

"You're really good at that," he said, crossing his arms. "And I find myself thoroughly grateful that you did not have those daggers with you last night."

"Thanks," I said, heart thumping heavily as I glanced around the otherwise empty room and then back to him. "How long have you've been standing there?"

"Long enough to wonder if you were trying to memorize every centimeter of the blade before you threw it."

My cheeks heated. *Great.* "Do you normally watch people without alerting them to your presence?"

"I figured you saw me," he said, and I guessed that was true. He would figure that. "I wasn't exactly hiding behind a curtain or something."

I narrowed my eyes. "You could've said hi instead of watching me in silence."

"Well, the last time I tried to alert you to my presence, you tried to kill me."

My brows lifted. "I did not try to kill you."

"Not how it felt from my perspective."

"Then your perspective leans toward the overdramatic."

"You're hard to talk to," Zayne said after a moment.

Offended, I glared at him. "No, I'm not."

"Okay, let me rephrase that. You're argumentative."

"No, I'm not."

Zayne stared at me, as if me arguing with him just then was proof enough of what he claimed.

It *was* sort of proof of what he claimed, and that irritated me. "Why are you here?"

"Like on Earth, at this place, at this right moment and exact time—"

"That's not what I meant." I cut him off, and I swore I heard a smile in his voice. Was he...teasing me? "Why are you in this room, watching me?"

"You make it sound like I'm stalking you."

"You said it, not me."

He pushed off the wall but didn't come forward. "I'm sort of surprised to find you in here," he said, instead of answering why *he* was here.

"Why is that?" I started toward the dummy to retrieve the daggers. "Because I'm human?"

"Yeah, well, yes." There was a pause. "There are a lot of Wardens who can't hit a target as well as you just did."

I couldn't help it. That little compliment, intended or not, brought a smile to my face and a surge of pride.

"You really are trained, aren't you? That's why you reacted the way you did last night."

Stopping in front of the dummy, I pulled the first blade out. "I have some training." Out came the next blade, and I turned around. He wasn't by the wall anymore. He was in the center of the room. I drew in a shallow breath. Earlier I had told myself I needed to apologize to him, and now was a better time than ever I'd supposed. "About last night? I...think I owe you an apology."

"You think?"

"Well, I know I do."

He moved closer, and I saw that his hair was down, brushing the strong line of his jaw. "Really?" He sounded surprised, which was messed up since he didn't know me. "You're going to apologize?"

I walked toward him, shifting the blades to one hand, and as I drew closer, the striking details of his face became clearer. I sort of wished they'd stayed blurry. I dropped my gaze to his throat.

It was a nice throat.

Thinking his throat was nice was really weird.

"Now I feel like I shouldn't, because you're irritating me again."

"Don't let that get in the way."

"It's already in the way," I replied dryly. "But I...I overreacted. You didn't grab me." When I lifted my gaze to his, he was staring back at me, and I was finally close enough to see his eyes. They were... They were the palest shade of blue framed by the thickest lashes I'd ever seen on a guy. The color was odd, because all Wardens had bright blue eyes, but his were wolf eyes, cool as winter frost. Curiosity piqued.

I cleared my throat. "So, that was...wrong of me and stuff."

"And stuff?" A grin played over his full lips. "I accept your apology."

"Good." I shifted my gaze over his shoulder. If Misha returned and found Zayne here, he would have a minor stroke and never leave my side again.

"Actually, I was looking for you."

Surprise flickered through me and I took a small step back. The grin faded from his lips. "Why?"

"Because we got off on the wrong foot," he explained. "I'm a guest here, and usually I'm more…amicable than I was last night."

Some of the tension seeped out of my shoulders. "Well, I did swing at you, and that kind of set the tone."

"It did, but it was mostly on me. I was just so surprised to see a human at the regional seat." Thick lashes lowered, shielding those strange eyes. "May I?"

It took me a moment to realize he was talking about the daggers. "Sure."

His fingers brushed mine as he took one, causing that strange little jolt to travel up my arm. A sense of…familiarity swept over me, a feeling of *rightness*, of many moving pieces finally clicking into place.

I jerked my hand back.

I lifted my gaze to his and sucked in a sharp breath.

His eyes were wide, and his head was cocked slightly, like… Like he felt something he didn't understand.

Or he could just be looking at me because I was acting bizarrely.

Probably that.

Zayne cleared his throat. The dagger was so much smaller in his hand. "I didn't say anything to the Duke about you being in the Great Hall last night."

"Thanks." I watched him turn and walk toward where I'd been standing when I threw the blade. "Misha did, anyway, so…"

"The guy who was with you last night?" Zayne glanced over his shoulder. "He seems…uptight."

I snickered at that as I moved out of the path of the dummy. "It's kind of his job."

Facing the dummy, Zayne looked over at me. "His job is being uptight?"

Hell.

Why did I say that? I wanted to punch myself. "I meant, it's more like his personality. He meant no harm by it."

Except Misha did mean harm by it. He'd said Zayne was a bad guy, but Zayne really didn't need to know that.

Zayne stared down at the dagger, looking like he wanted to say something but was refraining.

"Are you going to throw it?" I asked.

Sending me a grin, he lifted a shoulder. "Maybe I just like holding it?"

My lips twitched. "Maybe." I thought about what I'd overheard last night. This was my chance to find out what the heck was going on. "Can I ask you something?"

"Sure."

"Do you really think it's not a demon killing the Wardens and other demons?"

"You were there." He paused. "Hiding behind the curtain, so you heard what I thought."

I ignored the curtain statement. "But what else could it be?"

Zayne was silent for a long moment. "I don't know. None of us do, and all of us have seen some strange stuff—not as strange as a fully trained human living at the regional seat—but very strange stuff. That's what concerns us."

Me living here was strange, but not *that* strange. "I…think I'd be concerned, too."

"You'd think the Duke would be also."

"I'm sure he is. Thierry hides what he's thinking pretty

well." I shifted my weight from one foot to the next. "Did you know that two days before you all showed up, there were Ravers in the woods outside our walls?"

His features sharpened. "No, I didn't know that. No one mentioned it to us."

I opened my mouth to respond, and then realized that if they hadn't been told yet, I probably should've kept my mouth shut. "Oh. Well, I'm sure it'll come up."

"Why in Hell would Ravers come all the way out here?"

"Good question," I murmured. "There wasn't an Upper Level demon with them. Just a horde of Ravers, sort of like what you said about DC."

He was quiet for a moment. "You know a lot about demons."

It wasn't poised as a question, so I shrugged. "Picked up quite a bit living here."

"Have you heard about the raids on other communities?"

"Yes, but Thierry doesn't know I've heard that."

"Snooping behind curtains again?"

I fought a grin. "More like standing outside closed doors."

"You do that a lot?"

"Enough to know better."

He inclined his head. "Doesn't make sense for any demon to try to invade this place, with the number of Wardens in various stages of training."

I agreed. The only way it made sense was if the demons knew what else was inside these walls. "Maybe they were lost. Or bored."

"Yeah." He didn't remotely sound like he agreed with that, and I really hoped he wouldn't mention to anyone else what I'd told him. "Besides the blade throwing and what I saw last night, what else are you trained in?"

I folded my arms and told a lie. "Not that much. Just little things that Misha has taught me."

"Did he teach you how to throw?"

Misha hadn't been the only one to train me. Thierry and Matthew had a huge part in it. "Yeah, but I'm better than him at it."

As he cocked his arm, Zayne chuckled, and the sound was still as nice as it had been last night. His movements were fast, and he let go of the dagger before I realized it. It struck the dummy, and I hurried over to see that it had hit the stomach.

"Was that where you were aiming?" I asked, wrapping my fingers around the still-thrumming handle.

"If I said it was, would you believe me?"

"No," I laughed, pulling the blade out.

"I was aiming for the chest."

"Then I'm better than you, too." I turned around.

"Looks that way." He dragged a hand through his hair. "I haven't used daggers in ages."

"You really don't need to."

"Do you?"

The question caught me off guard, and my mind raced to find a possible unsuspicious answer. "Um, you never know. I mean, I do live with a race demons like to target, and we did have Ravers outside the wall," I said. Okay. That was a smart answer, and I was rather proud of myself. "That's why I know basic training and how to throw a dagger."

"Smart. If you're ever out with one of them, you'll be able to defend yourself if you have daggers with you."

What he didn't know was that I really didn't need daggers. If push came to shove, I could take Zayne down. I could take every Warden here, and barely break a sweat.

He walked back to me, and when he handed me the blade, I made sure our fingers didn't touch.

"Have you seen a demon?" he asked.

"Yes. Have you?"

Zayne laughed then, and it was a real one. Deep. Throaty. Sexy as holy Hell. "You're kind of a smart-ass."

"Guilty as charged."

"What kind of demons have you've seen? Just the Ravers?"

"Why are you asking so many questions?" I started for the table.

"I'm curious as Hell about you."

"Because I live here?" I placed the daggers in their little slots. "If you saw me on the streets, you wouldn't look twice in my direction."

"That's not true."

My fingers lifted from the daggers as my gaze shot to where he now stood beside me.

"I always look twice or maybe even three times at a pretty girl," he said, and that easy grin was back, curving up one side of his lips. "I don't think we're supposed to admit that now, or do that, but it's the truth."

I was still staring at him.

The grin grew into a wide smile, warming those cool blue eyes. "Did I cross a line there?"

"No." I blinked, refocusing on the satchel. I closed the sides and tied them together. "Your curiosity is going to lead to one epic letdown."

"Why do you think that?"

"Because I'm not very interesting."

"That is probably the least correct thing I've heard all day."

I fought a grin, thinking if he only knew the truth. "My mom knew Thierry before he became a Duke, while he lived in New York. She was attacked by a demon, exposed to them when I was a kid, and the rest is history," I said, repeating what Thierry had told me to say. "When he became a Duke, we moved here with him."

"Your father didn't come?"

A near-hysterical-sounding laugh bubbled up my throat. "No. He's around, but he's not here."

His brows furrowed as if he was trying to work that one out. He never would. Not in his wildest imagination. "And your mother?"

I looked away as a sharp twinge of pain lit up the center of my chest. "She's gone."

Zayne didn't answer for a long moment. "Gone as in...no longer with us?"

Nodding, I swallowed the sudden knot that always appeared when I thought about Mom. "Yeah."

"I'm really sorry to hear that," he said, and when I looked at him, his gaze roamed over my face. "Losing a parent is... It's never easy."

His gaze caught mine and held, and I asked, "Do you... know how that feels?"

"My mother died giving birth to me, like many of our females do." He brushed a strand of hair back behind his ear. "My father died a few months back."

My heart squeezed at the unexpected piece of information. "I'm so sorry to hear that. God, that's...intense. I'm really sorry. My mom died about a year ago, so it's still fresh, but not...not like that."

"Thank you." He looked away.

Something clicked into place as I studied his profile. My stomach dipped. "Was your dad Abbot? The clan leader of DC?"

His head swiveled back to me. "Yes."

"I'm really sorry." I leaned to the side, catching his eyes. "He died a warrior's death."

"He did."

"I know that doesn't make it easier."

"It doesn't."

Wardens weren't easy to kill, but death was a shadow that always lingered a few steps behind them, as it was a horrific part of their everyday lives. That didn't make death any easier to process.

"I really am sorry," I repeated, feeling as if I needed to say it again. I cradled the leather satchel to my chest as something else started to click into place. Abbot, his father, had been the clan leader in DC, which meant, upon his death, Zayne should've ascended to the role. Had he been challenged by Nicolai and lost? Or had he refused to take the role? The latter seemed impossible to believe.

I thought about Misha's warning. Had the clan not accepted Zayne as a leader? He was young—he couldn't be more than a few years older than me—but was it more than that? Which didn't make sense, because if that was the case, Thierry would know and not say that Zayne was honorable.

"So," I said, running my fingers over the smooth leather. I knew what I was about to ask was grossly personal, but like Thierry had said earlier, I was often too curious for my own good. "Why aren't you the clan leader?"

Zayne looked down at me. "That's not something I can talk to you about."

Disappointment rose, even though it wasn't an unexpected response. "Because I'm not a Warden?"

He smiled tightly in response. "And because I don't know you."

Shame wiggled around in my stomach. "I'm sorry. I shouldn't have asked. I'm often…impulsive and nosy."

"Nosy? Never would've guessed that." His tone was light, teasing even, but I still felt the centers of my cheeks flush.

Glancing at the door, I decided it was time I do the smart thing and get my butt back to the house before I ended up saying something else that I shouldn't. "I need to go." I took a step back, feeling about ten kinds of awkward. "It was nice, um, clearing the air, and again, I'm sorry about last night."

The smile loosened. "Does this mean you don't hate me?"

I winced. "I said that last night, didn't I?"

"You did."

"I often say things I shouldn't. You can add that to impulsive and nosy."

He chuckled as he slipped his hands into the pockets of his jeans. "I'll make sure I'll add that to the glowing list of attributes."

"You do that." Taking a couple more steps backward, I said, "See you later, Zayne."

I pivoted around and took a several more steps.

"Trinity."

I stopped and closed my eyes. I had no idea what to do with the little shiver that curled its way through my core in response to the way he said my name. It was a strong reaction, but he spoke my name like he... Like he was *tasting* it.

"Yeah?" As if I had no control, I turned back to him.

He hadn't moved, and I was once again too far to see his eyes clearly, but I felt his gaze, intense and heavy. My heart rate kicked up. "How did your mother die? Was it a demon? Or something natural?"

Every muscle in my body tensed, and part of me knew I shouldn't answer truthfully, but the words rose to the tip of my tongue. A truth that was rarely given air.

"No," I said. "It was a Warden."

7

Jada let out a loud, weary sigh as she leaned back against the couch beside my chair. "He is so annoying."

"Yep." I took a sip of my strawberry smoothie as I watched Clay shove one of the younger males in the chest and laugh as the boy stumbled back against the stone of the Hummer-size fire pit.

Why hadn't I noticed this behavior before? Had I been blinded by the fact that he'd paid attention to me? I sighed. The answer was *probably*, which meant I needed to make better life choices.

"I really hope he gets assigned to someplace way, way far away from here." Jada wiggled her fingers, and I handed over the smoothie. "Like Antarctica."

"That's still too close." Ty was sitting on the other side of Jada, stretching out his long legs. He'd recently gotten his dark hair shorn, and I was still getting used to it. "Knowing my luck, he'll end up assigned to the same city as me."

By this time next year, he'd be going through the Accolade

himself, and then, like Clay and the others, he'd be relocated to a city. Jada would definitely go with him, and I...I would most likely still be here. Heaviness crept into my chest, and I tried to shrug it off.

Jada took a drink of my smoothie. "And yep, there goes his shirt."

Frowning, I turned back to the pit. Flames roared behind Clay as he pulled his shirt over his head and tossed it at the boy he'd just shoved as he shouted something. "Why does he do that?" I asked.

"I don't know," whispered Jada, shaking her head. "It's like his mating call or something."

"Ew." I shuddered.

"You should go talk to him, Trin." Ty lifted his brows when I sent him a sharp look. "He likes you."

Yeah, I'd already gone down that road.

"So," Ty said, leaning into Jada. "What's going on with your boy over there?"

My gaze shifted to where Misha sat next to Alina, and I clapped my hands together. "My little boy is growing up."

Jada giggled.

"Look at him," I whispered as I took the smoothie back. Misha was showing Alina something on his phone. "He's sharing. Bonding with her. The next thing I know, he'll be mating and—"

Misha's head swiveled in my direction. It was like he had some kind of sixth sense or something, because I know damn well he couldn't hear us.

The three of us waved at him.

Misha shook his head before turning back to Alina.

"Do you know Alina?" I asked them as I smothered a yawn.

"Not really well, but she's seems pretty cool." Jada rested

her cheek on Ty's shoulder. "Just kind of shy. Quiet. She's training to be a healer at the clinic."

I took another sip of my smoothie as I watched Misha and Alina, torn between wanting to bust up their conversation and be obnoxious like I normally was, and doing what I normally didn't do, which was to give them the space Misha deserved.

"Are those the guys from the DC clan?" Ty asked, and I followed his gaze.

My stupid stomach took a tumble as I searched out the blurred faces of two figures sitting not too far from us, under several strings of fairy lights.

"Yeah," I said. "That's Dez and Zayne."

Silence as both Jada and Ty looked at me. "What?" I asked.

Ty lifted his brows. "How do you know their names?"

"I didn't tell him you snuck into the Great Hall when they arrived." Jada lifted her head from Ty's shoulder, grinning.

I fixed a blank look on my face. "Yeah, I heard their names when I was eavesdropping."

Jada looked at me strangely, and as if I had no control, my gaze found its way back to Zayne and Dez. The latter looked like he was laughing at something Zayne had said, and I wondered what they were talking about and if Zayne was smiling.

Did Zayne even know I was here?

The moment that question formed in my thoughts, I wanted to smack myself. What a stupid thing to wonder. It wasn't like Zayne was out here looking or thinking about me. Sure, he'd been looking for me yesterday in the training facility, but he'd just been curious about why I lived here. I couldn't blame him for that.

And why was I even thinking about Zayne? There was no reason, and I wasn't thinking about him. Not at—

"You're staring at them." Jada leaned into me.

I blinked. I was, indeed, staring at them. Neither had looked over here, thank God. "I dazed out," I said, feeling my cheeks heat. "Wow."

Jada was looking at me strangely again.

"What?"

She looked over again to where they were sitting. "Nothing."

"Hey!" Clay shouted, and I looked up to see him heading in our direction, still shirtless.

"Hell," grumbled Ty under his breath.

I lowered my smoothie as he swaggered up to where we were sitting. There was no way he was going to talk to me, not after what had gone down between us.

None of us acknowledged him as he stood there. I just stared at him.

Undaunted, Clay looked at Jada and Ty and then refocused on me. "You know what you should be doing right now?"

I tensed.

"You should be getting me a drink," he said, loud enough that half the people around the Pit had to have heard him. "I'm empty-handed."

My jaw dropped. "Excuse me?"

"A drink." Clay's grin was slow, practiced in a way that showed he thought it was sexy and charming—a way I used to agree with. "You should get one for me."

I leaned forward. "Are you serious right now?"

His grin only got bigger. "Yeah, I am. Because what else are you doing?"

"Are you high?" Jada asked.

He looked at her as he ran a hand over his chest. "You don't get a body like this being high."

A laugh burst straight out of me. "I can't believe you just said that. Out loud. And in front of people."

"What?" Clay lowered his hand. "It's the truth."

Ty snorted as he shook his head.

"Come on, Trin. Get me a drink and we can talk." Clay ignored Ty and didn't dare step to Jada. He was a jerk, but he wasn't stupid enough to mouth off to the Duke's niece. "Because I think we really need to talk."

"I rather jump into that fire pit with a polyester suit on."

Ty outright laughed. "I think you got your answer."

"Why you gotta be like this?" Clay asked, ignoring Ty. "Look, I'm just trying to smooth things over. Especially since you messed things up for me."

I stiffened. "*I* messed things up for *you*? Are you sure you're not high?"

"What is he talking about?" Jada asked.

"Yeah, you would think you did nothing." Clay lifted his arms, bowing his back and cracking his spine. When he was done being his own chiropractor, he bent down and placed one hand on the arm of my chair and the other behind me on the back cushion.

He lined his face up with mine. "Are you going to kick me out a window again?"

"*What?*" Jada demanded.

"No." The fine hairs on the nape of my neck stood up as I tipped forward, making us nearly as close as we'd been when we'd kissed. "I'm going to kick you into the fire pit if you don't back up."

"Yeah." He spoke directly into my ear, for only me to hear. "I'd like to see you try."

Every cell in my body demanded that I put as much space as humanly possible between us, because I was a second away from turning him into a Warden tiki torch. "Really? Because I'm happy to oblige."

Clay smirked.

"I have a question for you," I said. "You've watched *Game of Thrones*, right?"

A flicker of confusion across his face was visible. "Yeah?"

"Remember King Joffrey?" I smiled sweetly. "You remind me of him."

Jada sounded like she was dying beside me.

The too-charming smile faltered. A long moment passed as Clay stared at me. "I get it."

"Get what?"

"You."

I lifted my brows.

"Is there a problem?" Misha was suddenly there, behind Clay. "Because I remember clearly the conversation you and I had."

"Yeah, I remember it." Clay was grinning again as he pivoted. He eyed Misha and then patted him on the shoulder. "One of these days."

With that, Clay walked off, throwing his arms up and out as he threw back his head and let out a roar that was definitely not human.

My gaze shifted to where Zayne and Dez were sitting. Both seemed to be looking over here, and my shoulders sagged. Of course they'd witnessed that.

"He's an ass," Misha grumbled, watching Clay over his shoulder. "I can't believe he had the nerve to talk to you."

"Okay, so what in the world happened?" Jada asked.

I answered before Misha could, giving them a quick rundown minus the whole kicking him through the window. "So, yeah, I'm kind of shocked he would even speak to me."

Jada was glaring in Clay's general direction. "And Thierry delayed his Accolade?"

I nodded.

"Good."

"That's huge." Ty leaned forward. "Don't get me wrong. Clay deserved it and more. But as much as it pains me to admit this, he's actually a really good Warden, skill-wise. He's almost impossible to take down in class. He's fast, and not just in his Warden form."

"Well, he brought it on himself." Smothering another yawn, I handed my smoothie to Jada to finish off and rose. "I'm going to head back."

"Why?" Concern pinched her features. "Is it because of Clay? Because, seriously, don't let him ruin your night."

"It's not because of him. I'm actually pretty tired," I said, telling the truth.

Jada looked at me as if she wasn't sure if I was telling the truth, but she dropped it.

"Okay," Misha said. "Just let me say goodbye to Alina—"

"No. Stay." I stretched up and patted his head, nimbly dancing out of the way of his hand as he swung at me. "I'm literally going back to the house. I don't need you to walk me."

Misha hesitated.

"I'll text you when I get back, okay?"

"Okay," he said after a moment.

I didn't waste time, because if I did, Misha would change his mind and leave Alina sitting by the fire. Saying goodbye, I dipped around the couch and then glanced over my shoulder toward the fairy lights.

Dez and Zayne were still there, and I quickly looked away.

I started toward the house. It was a good thing Misha didn't know about me running into Zayne yesterday.

Or what I'd told Zayne.

I was still smacking myself for that one, but if Misha knew about it, he'd be right here with me instead of hanging out with Alina and enjoying himself.

I thought about what Clay had said to me as I followed the

sidewalk back to the house. It had been...weird. *I get it.* What in the world had he meant? The thing was, he *didn't* get it.

Had Zayne heard Clay? I sighed. Probably. Not like that would be embarrassing or—

"Hey."

My heart jumped in my chest at the sound of Zayne's voice. It was like I'd conjured him from the shadows. I stopped and turned around, ignoring the way my pulse started pounding.

"You didn't try to hit me." Zayne halted a few feet from me, under the soft glow of a streetlamp, hands in his pockets. "Turning over a new leaf?"

"Ha. Ha," I grumbled. "Maybe you just called out loud enough for me to hear this time."

"Maybe." A small grin appeared. "So, what was going on back there?"

I knew exactly what he was talking about, but I played dumb. "What do you mean?"

"That guy," he answered. "Yelling about you getting him a drink or something."

"You heard." I sighed.

"Confident the entire state of West Virginia heard him."

Shaking my head, I lifted my hands. "It was nothing."

"Doesn't seem like nothing if you left immediately after that."

I lowered my hands. "Wow. You were really paying attention."

"I was."

Surprise stole my voice for a moment. "Why?"

"Because I saw you over there, so I was paying attention."

"You didn't even look at me until after Clay made an ass of himself."

That easy, teasing grin returned as he bit down on his lower lip. "So, you were also paying attention."

Warmth splashed across my cheeks. "No, I wasn't."

He chuckled as he tucked a strand of blond hair behind his ear. "You're ridiculous."

"And annoying?"

"That, too." He looked to his left and then back to me. "What's the deal with that Clay guy?"

"He's just... He's just a dickhead." A breeze lifted the ends of my hair. A weird little shiver curled its way down my spine. The wind picked up, tossing my hair over my face. I took a step back. "I need to get home."

"I can walk you."

There was a voice that whispered *yes*, a voice driven by an almost desperate need for something more than passing attention, but that need was irresponsible and reckless and *interesting*.

"I'm heading in that direction, anyway," he said, nodding toward my house and the Great Hall beyond it. "It's not a big deal."

Exhaling softly, I nodded. "Okay. Sure. Whatever floats your boat."

Zayne chuckled.

"Are you laughing at me?"

"Kind of."

"Then I revoke my acceptance of your offer." I turned and started walking.

Zayne easily caught up with me. "Nope. No take-backs."

I fought my grin and won.

We walked in silence for a while and then Zayne asked, "What's it been like, living here?"

"What do you mean?"

"Have other Wardens acted like Clay, or are they nice to you?"

I glanced at him. "Almost all of them have been accepting of me being here, if that's what you mean. Clay is just...

Well, he's an ass, but I grew up with a lot of the younger ones. Even Clay."

"And you were schooled with them? What was that like?"

"Okay, I guess. I learned about the Civil War in one class and the different species of demons in the next. Which means I probably had a more interesting educational experience than most humans," I said. All communities were outfitted with their own schools. They of course were much smaller than many schools in the human world. One building housed K-12, and each class typically had no more than ten to fifteen students. "What about you? Did you grow up in one of the communities?"

"I was born in one in Virginia, just outside Richmond, but I don't remember any of it."

"You've always lived at one of the outposts, then?" I asked, referencing the locations where trained Wardens who patrolled and hunted demons lived.

"Yep," he answered. "And you've never lived anywhere but here and...New York?"

I was surprised he remembered. "I came here when I was eight, with my mom." We crossed the street, heading toward the smaller stone wall that separated the main house from the community. "It's all I've known."

Zayne was quiet, and I stole a quick glance at him. He focused on the dimly lit path and then his chin tipped in my direction.

I looked away, sucking in a shallow breath of the cool, pine-scented night air. "What was it like in the outpost?"

"Nothing like this," he answered. "I grew up surrounded by trained Wardens and not away from...well, everything. I spent as much time in the city as I did in the compound. It's never this quiet there."

"I can imagine," I murmured, but I really couldn't. I didn't remember much about living in New York State. We'd been in a suburb outside of Albany, never anyplace like Washington, DC, or New York City. "You were homeschooled?"

"I was. My father brought in someone to handle my education, a human who wasn't too freaked out being surrounded by Wardens."

"That had to be hard, being the only kid."

"I wasn't the only kid," he said, and my curiosity piqued. Before I could I question that, he said, "Can I ask you something?"

"If I said no, you'd probably ask, anyway."

"I wouldn't. Not if you meant it."

The genuineness in his voice brought my gaze to him. I actually…believed that. "What do you want to know?"

"How old are you?"

I lifted a brow. "I'm eighteen. How old are you?"

"Twenty-one," he answered. "I'll be twenty-two in a few months. September."

I folded my arms over my stomach as we rounded the stone wall and neared the house.

"You're eighteen and your mom is gone—and I'm really sorry about that." He tacked on that last part quickly. "But why are you still here?"

8

Oh, damn, that was a hard question to answer, because I couldn't be honest. By the time we reached the house, I still didn't have a response. We stopped at the edge of the floodlight that shone down from the front porch.

"Is it because you don't have anywhere else to go?" he asked. "I don't mean anything rude by that. I can imagine it would be hard growing up here and then going out there, into the world."

"But I want to go out there." The moment I said it, I mentally cursed myself up and down the block. I really needed to get control of my mouth.

Zayne angled his body toward me. "Then why don't you?"

"It's not... It's not that simple," I admitted. "I mean, I don't have anyplace to go. Like you said. It's hard coming from this and going out there. The Board of Education now recognizes our diplomas, as do most colleges, but where would I get the money? Financial Aid would be tricky, because Wardens don't qualify for it, and even though I'm not a Warden, my education suggests that I am. It would be a mess, and everyone here has better things to do than help me figure it out."

"Sounds like you've looked into it."

I had. A lot. And all the looking I had done was pointless, because college wasn't in the cards for me. That wasn't what I'd been...born for. After Mom had been killed, I'd researched colleges, figuring there was no reason that I shouldn't be able to go to school and be ready for whenever I was summoned.

But how would I pay for it? Ask Thierry and Matthew for the funds? They already provided *everything* for me. I couldn't ask for that, too.

"I have another question," he said.

"Okay," I sighed, half-afraid of what this one would lead to.

"What happened to the Warden who killed your mother?"

The question was a jolt to the system, and I took a step away from Zayne. "I shouldn't have told you about that."

"Why?"

"Because I don't like talking or thinking about it."

"I'm sorry," he immediately said. "I shouldn't have brought it up."

Drawing in a shaky breath, I turned to head up the steps and then stopped, facing Zayne. "The Warden is dead. I wouldn't have stayed here if he wasn't."

"I wouldn't imagine that you would've," he said quietly. "I'm sorry, Trinity."

Air caught in my throat. There it was again. The way he said my name. A tight, hot shiver danced over my skin, and that shiver made me think of the yearning I'd seen on Misha's face when he saw Alina. That shiver made me think of warm summer nights, of skin against skin.

The heat inside me rose, rolling down my throat and over my chest, pushing down the bitter grief that always surrounded thoughts of my mother, and I knew it was time for me to go.

And that's what I did, without saying a word, without looking back.

★ ★ ★

The confused ghost was back again, pacing in the driveway outside the Great Hall, and it was far past time to talk to the poor guy and help move him on.

"This makes me uncomfortable," Misha muttered, trailing behind me as we walked along the paved path around the Great Hall.

I grinned.

Jada hated it when I dragged her along for these things, too. In all honesty, Misha should've been in the Great Hall for the Accolade along with everyone else, but as per usual, he was on Trinity Duty.

"You can't even see them, so I don't get why it makes you so uncomfortable."

"I may not be able to see them, but I know they're there." Misha caught the edge of my shirt, pulling me to the side before I sideswiped a baby fir tree I hadn't seen.

"Thanks," I murmured, stopping at the corner of the building. Night had fallen, and soft lights glowed from the entrance of the Great Hall.

Ghost Dude had stopped by the hedges, arms up and hands tugging at his hair. My heart squeezed with sympathy.

"What's he doing?" Misha whispered.

"Freaking out," I told him. There was enough light from the building to see where I was going. I started to step out but stopped and looked up the wide steps.

Muffled laughter and cheers floated from the hall, catching my attention. The Accolades were a good time. Dancing. Celebrating. Family. That was what it was like. Family.

I glanced at Misha. He was also staring at the hall, and I wondered if he was thinking about Alina. "Is Alina at the Accolade?"

"Yes," he answered, and I realized it had been a dumb

question. Any Warden of age who didn't have a youngling to watch over was at the Accolade.

He should be there, too. Not out here with me, creeping around in the darkness while I talked to ghosts.

Nibbling on my thumbnail, I faced him. "Why don't you go in and see what's going on? After I move Ghost Dude along, I'll join you."

Misha's face was shadowed. "Why would I want to go in there without you?"

"Because it's better than being out here with me while I talk to ghosts."

"I rather be out here with you even with the whole ghost thing."

My lips twitched. "That's a lie."

"Never," he replied. "Besides, I can't leave you alone when you're talking to a ghost. If someone came out and saw you, they'd think—"

"Something's wrong with me?" I supplied.

"I wasn't going to suggest that. I was going to say they'd think it was *odd* and they'd start asking questions."

Turning back to Ghost Dude, I saw he was still by the hedges. I walked toward the ghost, careful to stick close to the hedges. The ghost didn't seem to hear my approach, and now that I was closer, I could see that his shirt was the gold and blue of the WVU Mountaineers. I could also see that something was wrong with it.

The back of the shirt was torn and stained in a darker color. My heart gave a little jump, like it always did when I was this close to a ghost or spirit, no matter how many times I'd seen one.

I cleared my throat. "Hi."

The ghost dissipated like smoke in the wind. My mouth dropped open. "How rude."

A moment later, he began to take shape again, this time facing me. His head and shoulders formed first and then the rest of him came into view, but his body from the waist down was transparent.

"Holy crap," I gasped, my eyes widening as I got a good look at the man as I heard Misha stop a few feet behind me.

The ghost was young, maybe in his midtwenties, and his face was leached of all color. But that wasn't what turned my stomach with a sharp twist of nausea. The front of his shirt was ripped open, as was the flesh beyond it, his stomach torn into ragged strips.

I took a step back. I hadn't been able to see all of that when I'd been on the roof. Perhaps I was wrong about the car accident.

"You can see me?" the ghost asked, rushing toward me... and then through me.

Strands of hair blew back from my face as an icy wind whipped through me. I shuddered and swallowed hard, hating that feeling.

"Did he... Did he just walk through you?" Misha sounded sick.

"Unfortunately." I turned around and found the ghost staring down at himself. "Hey, let's not do that again."

"I'm sorry. I didn't mean to. I don't understand how that happened." Panic crept into the man's voice as he stepped toward me again but stopped. "You can see and talk to me?"

"I can." I glanced down and saw that his legs had solidified. "What is your name?"

"Wayne—Wayne Cohen. Can you help me? I can't seem to find my way home."

Oh God.

I started nibbling on my fingernail again as my gaze slid southward. He had to know he was dead. "I can help you,

Wayne, and I can help you go home, but it's not the home you're thinking of."

Wayne's dark brows furrowed. "I don't understand. I need to get home—"

"Do you know you're dead?" I asked. It was best not to drag it out.

Misha made a choking sound behind me. "Wow. Way to be gentle."

I ignored him. "Have you... Have you looked at yourself?"

"I have, but..." He placed two fingers against the side of his neck as he stared down at his body. "I'm... I can't be dead. I was on my way back to my house and then..." He dropped his hand, still staring at his ruined chest. "I was going to order pizza. Meat lovers and stuffed crust."

When people died, they were usually concerned with the most inane things alongside the most powerful things.

"Am I... Am I really dead?"

"You're definitely dead," I confirmed.

"I can't believe I'm dead," he whispered.

"I'm sorry." And I was, even though I'd never seen him before. Death was rarely easy to accept. "What happened to you, Wayne?"

"I don't... My car broke down. Flat tire." He turned to Misha. "Can he see me, too?"

"No, he can't see you."

"Is he looking at me?" Misha muttered. "Please tell me he's not looking at me."

Wayne cocked his head.

"He is and he can hear you," I said, shooting Misha a dark look that screamed *shut up*. "Wayne, what happened with your flat tire? That didn't do that to your...chest."

"Oh God," Misha mumbled. "What does his chest look like?"

Wayne stared at Misha, slowly shaking his head in confusion. "I was changing my tire and it came... It came out of nowhere."

"What did?" I asked. "A mountain lion?"

"Are you for real?" Misha exclaimed.

"There are mountain lions around here." I refocused on Wayne. "Is that what got ahold of you? Or maybe a bear?"

"How bad does he look?" Misha asked, lips curling.

I wasn't going to answer that question in front of poor Wayne, but it was bad, really bad, and even though Wayne had to know that already, I really didn't want to confirm it for him. Like the kind of bad that was sure to give me nightmares.

There were times, especially after seeing something like this, that I knew Misha or Jada would ask why I didn't just ignore the dead. It seemed like it would be easier to do that, but that wouldn't save me from seeing such haunting, gruesome death. There'd even been times when I asked myself that question, especially after I saw that little girl.

But I couldn't ignore these people.

I was always, *always* willing to help ghosts and spirits. Over the years, I'd gotten really smart about how to deal with them. As cliché as it sounded, being able to help them was... It was something *special*. And it wasn't like I was going to be able to see them forever. Time wasn't on my side.

So, I didn't run from what I could do.

I didn't hide from it.

"It was big, but not a large cat. It was on two feet." Wayne's gaze shifted to me. "It wasn't a bear, though."

A wave of goose bumps rippled down my arms as I checked out his chest again. "It wasn't an animal?"

"It was dark and it happened so fast, but it... Oh God, you know. I saw this show once about monsters. It looked like a monster, like something not real, and it...it had wings. Huge wings. I heard them. I saw them, even though I couldn't see anything else."

Tiny hairs rose all over my body. Monsters weren't real, not the kind he was thinking of, but if it wasn't a bear or a hungry mountain lion that did this to him, there was only one other thing.

And it wasn't a chupacabra.

Or bigfoot.

"I thought I got away. I mean, that's why I'm here. I got away," Wayne was saying. "Right?"

I shook my head. "Where were you when your tire got a flat?"

"Near the old fire tower. Maybe a mile away from it."

A chill swept through me. The abandoned fire tower wasn't far from here. Only a few miles. "Do you have any family?"

"I…uh, just my mother and a brother." His voice was hoarse. "How can you see me if I'm dead?"

"I just can."

He glanced down the driveway. It was too dark for me to make out his expression. I thought I knew what he might be seeing.

"Is there a light there?" I asked, hopeful. "A really bright, white light that might've followed you here?"

"Yeah." His laugh turned into a sob, and my heart squeezed once more. "There's a—there's a freaking light there. It's been there since I—since I got away from that thing."

"That's good. I know this sounds cliché, but you need to go into the light," I said, and thankfully Misha knew this was the part where he really needed to be quiet.

"Really?"

"Yes."

"I don't understand." His words cracked, and I winced.

"Everything will make sense to you once you go into the light. And you need to go," I told him. "You can't stay here."

"Why not?" His voice was a soft whine.

That was a common question. "Because you're meant to move on now, to what awaits you."

"H–how do you know what awaits me?"

Another common question. "I don't know exactly, but I do know that if you see a light, it's something good."

Never once had I come across a ghost that didn't see a light, even if they'd died long before I saw them. That light followed them around like a happy puppy.

Some people were just too scared or confused to go into it. Couldn't blame them for that. I'd be scared, too. Who wouldn't be? Death was the great unknown.

"Will I see my father?" He was still staring down the dark driveway, to where I now knew that light was waiting for him. "He died a year ago. Car accident on US50."

I tried not to lie to those passing over, because it felt wrong to do so. "I wish I could say yes, but I honestly don't know. I just know that you belong in that light. It's not going to hurt you."

Wayne was silent again and then he stepped forward, and that's when I moved closer to him. "Okay," he said. "All right. I can do this."

Lifting my thumbnail to my mouth once more, I squinted until his face became clearer. His image was more ghostly now than anything, but I still saw his expression the moment he decided to go into the light.

My lips parted on a soft inhale.

His eyes widened, and then warmth poured into his features as the look of a thousand Christmas mornings rolled into one settled into his expression. He began walking forward.

I asked then what I always asked when I saw that look settle onto their faces. "What do you see?"

Wayne didn't answer.

They never did.

Even spirits who'd passed on and come back didn't talk about what they'd seen. I guessed there was some kind of cosmic rule about it, like all the other stupid rules.

I did know that the light Wayne was about to enter would send him either upstairs...or downstairs. Heaven or Hell. They were both real, and based on the look on his face, I had a feeling he was about to experience something magical and pure. I'd never seen anyone scared once they decided to go into the light, and I theorized that meant all the ghosts I'd helped were bound for Heaven.

Wayne took one more step and then he was gone.

I let out a ragged breath, suddenly misty-eyed. I always felt that way after someone crossed over. I didn't even know why. Lifting a hand, I tucked my hair behind my ears.

"Is he gone?" Misha's voice was quiet.

"Yeah." I cleared my throat and slowly turned to Misha, pushing away the lingering sadness. "We need to see Thierry immediately."

"What?" Confusion filled his tone. "Why?"

I took a step toward him. "Because that man was killed near here...by an Upper Level demon."

9

Upper Level demons could look human, just like a Warden, and oddly enough, when they were in their true skin, they also tended to resemble a Warden, minus the slate-gray skin and horns.

That was one thing the depictions of demons always got wrong. They didn't have horns.

Wardens did.

"Stay here," Misha ordered as we stopped just outside of the main banquet hall, in the atrium adorned with statues of gargoyles that didn't turn into real, living creatures. They were spaced several feet apart, perched on the sides of the walls, wings spread wide.

Misha was gone before I could say a word, slipping through the open doors, and I was left alone with the statues.

I glanced to my left. The fanged open mouth of one of them was inches from my face.

They creeped me out.

Tossing my hair over my shoulder, I hurried toward the wide open doors and peered into the brightly lit hall.

My senses were immediately overwhelmed. So many people, many dressed in the bright ceremonial colors of stunning yellows and bright blues. The scent of roasted meat would've tempted me to rush in and grab a plate to go stuff my face in the corner somewhere if I hadn't just seen Wayne's chest and stomach.

Scanning the room, I couldn't see Misha, but I knew he was most likely heading to the raised dais, where Thierry would be sitting along with Jada and her mother, Aimee. Our guests would be seated with them in a position of honor, and if I had decided to attend tonight, that was where I'd be.

I didn't even know why I hadn't gone. I'd been feeling weird all day, barely going through the motions of training with Misha and turning down an offer to join Jada and Ty for a bite to eat afterward.

I'd spent most of the day holed up in my bedroom with Peanut, watching *Fresh Prince*.

I gripped the edges of the door as my gaze crawled over the dozens of rectangular tables, toward the sound of raucous male laughter.

A Warden stood in the center of the room, dressed in the ceremonial garb of one who is about to receive the Accolade—white linen pants and a sleeveless shirt. He was too far away for me to see who he was, and there were at least twenty graduating this round.

Antsy, I shifted my weight from one foot to the next. What Wayne had told me couldn't wait. We all knew that Ravers were often controlled by Upper Level demons, and what Wayne had described—

"Are you hiding again?"

I jumped at the sound of Zayne's voice and whipped around.

Good God, the guy was quieter than a ghost when he moved. He was standing only a few feet from me.

The first thing that I noticed was that his hair was pulled back once more, showcasing those high, broad cheekbones and the hard line of his jaw. I wasn't sure which way I liked it better. Not that I should have an opinion, but I was thinking I liked it better down.

And I was also thinking I needed to get a grip.

The second thing I noticed was that he wasn't dressed like the other Wardens attending the banquet. He was dressed as he usually was, in his black henley and jeans.

Was he not attending the banquet?

He lifted his brows, and I realized I'd been staring at him like a doofus.

I snapped out of my stupor with a jerk. A strand of hair fell across my cheek. "Are you stalking me? Because I'm beginning to wonder."

He smirked. "Yes. When I stalk someone, I always alert them to my presence."

"You could just be a crappy stalker."

"I could be." He paused as his pale gaze flickered over me. My hair was down, and without even touching it, I knew it looked like I could've doubled for some girl in an '80s music video. According to Peanut, anyway. My hair knotted pathetically easily. "I could just be as crappy at stalking as you are at hiding."

I folded my arms. "I'm not hiding."

"We really going to have this argument again?" Zayne stepped closer, dipping his chin as he spoke in a low voice. "Because it looks exactly like you're hiding again."

Stretching up on the tips of my toes, I met his stare. "If that's what it looks like I'm doing, you really don't have great observational skills."

"I don't know about that." He straightened. His gaze flickered over my head, to the open door. "You're not allowed in there? Is that why you're hiding?"

The question threw me off and I glanced behind me. "I'm not hiding, and yes, I'm welcome to attend the Accolade if I want." I turned back to him. "Why aren't you in there? You're the clan's guest."

"Not my kind of thing." His fingers brushed my cheek, catching the strand of hair and tucking it back behind my ear. I jerked in surprise, not having been able to see his hand move. He withdrew his touch, his brows knitting together. "I wouldn't hurt you."

Warmth crept into my cheeks. "No, you wouldn't, because I wouldn't let you."

That half grin appeared, but it didn't reach his gaze. "I wouldn't think you would."

Feeling oddly self-aware, I unfolded my arms and touched the tangled ends of my hair. "Why is the banquet not your kind of thing?"

He lifted a shoulder and dropped it. "It's boring."

"And lurking out here isn't?"

Those pale eyes warmed as they met mine. "There is absolutely nothing boring out here."

I jolted in surprise. "Are you...flirting with me?"

He bit down on his lower lip, dragging his teeth over the fleshy pink skin as he eyed me through thick lashes. "I'd never think of doing such a thing."

I had no idea if he was being honest or not. Wardens didn't flirt with anyone other than other Wardens. Well, with the exception of Clay, but look how that had turned out.

But what if he *was* flirting with me? What if he found me... attractive? Yearning blossomed inside me. Like a flower seeking sun and water, it spread its roots deep. What if he wanted to kiss me?

Whoa.

I needed to slow my roll. I was seriously getting carried away. My cheeks heated as I focused on one of the statues.

"What are you thinking about?" Zayne asked.

My eyes widened as my gaze shot back to his. There was no way he knew what my thoughts were. If he did, I would legit wither away and die right here.

That grin of his grew. "Your face is as red as a ripe tomato right now."

And I could feel it growing redder by the second.

"I imagine whatever is going through your head is something I'd thoroughly enjoy hearing about."

The flutter in my chest took flight. "I'm not thinking about anything."

"Uh-huh." He didn't sound like he believed me for one moment.

I desperately needed a change of subject. "Anyway, I'm not hiding. I'm waiting for Thierry."

"What for?"

"That's not something I can talk to you about," I said, repeating what he'd said to me the day in the training facility.

"Touché," he murmured. "Bet I'll find out sooner or later."

"I bet you won't."

"We'll see," he said. His gaze flicked above me. Zayne inclined his head.

I twisted at the waist, finding Misha.

"Zayne." Misha's tone was flat.

He smiled slightly. "Misha."

I frowned.

Misha turned to me. "Thierry wants us to meet him in the house. He'll be there in a few minutes."

"Okay." I glanced at Zayne, who was watching us curiously. That stupid, stupid flutter had moved to my stomach.

"See you around," he said, and I had a feeling I would.

Misha and I arrived at the house before Thierry and waited for him in his office. "We need to talk before Thierry gets here," he announced.

I plopped down in the thick cushioned chair directly across from the massive desk Thierry typically occupied. "About what?"

"You need to be careful around him."

"Who?" I asked even though I had a pretty good idea of who he was talking about.

"Zayne." He barked out the name.

Crossing my arms, I lifted an eyebrow. "Two things."

Misha's eyes narrowed as he leaned against Thierry's desk.

"First off, we already had this conversation. You don't need to warn me to be careful around him. It's not like we're going to be best friends or something. He'll be leaving in a couple days." A weird twinge of disappointment lit up my chest, and I didn't even remotely understand that, because we'd only talked a couple of times, and we'd spent most of that time insulting each other.

"That's a couple days too long."

"Okay, and that statement leads to my most important question of the evening. What is your problem with him? And it can't be because I've talked to him." I paused. "Unless you're secretly in love with me and you're jealous."

Misha's expression turned bland. "You don't know him."

"You don't, either. All you've said is that he's a bad guy and his clan doesn't trust him, but that doesn't make sense. If his clan didn't trust him, then why would they bring him here?"

Looking at the door, Misha dragged his hand through the

mop of reddish hair. "Haven't you noticed something odd about him?"

I've noticed a lot of things about him, but I kept that to myself. "Care to be a little more detailed?"

"His eyes." Misha dropped his hand. "You might not have been close enough to see his eyes—"

"I've seen his eyes." I cut him off, and his gaze sharpened. "They are a little different."

"A little different?"

I frowned. "They're a lighter blue."

"And have you ever seen a Warden's eyes that color before?" he questioned. "We all have the same eye color, Trin. That's just the way we're made."

"Okay. The fact that Zayne's eyes are different is odd, but what's the big deal? Are we discriminatory toward light-eyed Wardens now?"

"Don't be dumb," he snapped. "There is no other Warden like him."

"There is no other being like me," I pointed out.

"It's not the same. Far from it," Misha argued. "Look, his eyes are like that because he… He's lost a part of his soul."

Out of everything I might have expected Misha to say, that wasn't it. I leaned forward, nearly toppling out of the chair. "What?"

Misha glanced at the door before continuing. "I don't know the details, but their clan raised a girl who was half Warden, half demon."

"*What?*" I whisper-yelled. "How had I not heard about this until now?"

He blinked. "Why would anyone tell you?"

"Because I… Okay, I don't have a good reason," I relented, and I immediately remembered Zayne saying he wasn't the only kid raised in his compound. Had he been talking about this girl? "Please continue."

"The girl was Lilith's daughter."

I sucked in a sharp breath. "Like *the* Lilith?"

Misha nodded, and I blinked slowly. Lilith was the mother of a lot of very dangerous demons—creatures that could take a soul with a touch. They were called the Lilin, and something was vaguely familiar about that. Several months ago, I'd overheard Matthew and Thierry speaking about those creatures. It had been right around the time Zayne's father had died.

"I don't know the circumstances around how, but he lost a part of his soul," Misha continued.

Falling back against the chair, I had no idea what to think. "Are you saying he's…soulless?"

He shook his head. "I'm not saying that, because if he was, I doubt he'd still be alive. His clan would have put him down."

Put him down.

Like a rabid animal.

I shuddered as I gripped the arms of the chair. "Then what are you saying, Misha?"

"Why do you think he's not the clan leader? He was the last leader's son, groomed to take over, and he didn't."

I'd asked him that question and still felt like a nosy brat for doing so. "Maybe he just chose not to."

Misha looked at me like I was half-stupid. "Doubtful. It's obvious that the clan doesn't trust him in that kind of role, especially since he's still friends with that demon."

"The half demon, half Warden?" I couldn't wrap my head around that. I didn't even know that inserting tab A into slot B between a Warden and a demon could produce a child.

"Lilith's daughter," he corrected me. "And he's been known to work with demons."

"Really?" I laughed at the absurdity of that claim. Not just because it was insane to think of a Warden doing that, but also because a demon wouldn't get close to a Warden if they had a choice. This half demon, Lilith's daughter, was obviously the exception and that was because she was half Warden too. "Where are you even hearing this nonsense?"

"I'm not the only one who overhears stuff. I heard Matthew and Thierry discussing it months ago, apparently when all of this went down. And it's not nonsense, Trin."

I started nibbling on my thumbnail. "He doesn't seem like he's missing a part of his soul."

"And how does one seem like when they're missing a part of their soul?"

"Evil?" I suggested. "And Zayne doesn't seem evil."

Misha met my gaze. "Isn't that evil's greatest achievement? It often hides itself in innocence?"

Well, he kind of had a point there.

I had no idea what to think about Misha's warning. Maybe a part of Zayne's soul *was* missing. Maybe he couldn't be trusted to be clan leader, and maybe even more crazily, he'd worked with demons.

Misha was right. Evil often cloaked itself in innocence.

I should be careful around Zayne, especially given the risks, but the truth was, what Misha had shared only made me more curious about him.

Thierry showed up shortly after that, and he wasn't alone. He'd brought a whole crew with him that didn't just include Matthew, whom I wasn't surprised to see. It was the last one who walked through the door that shocked me.

Nicolai.

I glanced at Misha with wide eyes. Hadn't he made it clear to Thierry what this conversation would entail? Misha looked just as confused as I felt.

"Can you close the door, Nicolai?" Thierry asked as he crossed the room and sat behind his desk. Matthew joined him, standing to his right. "Misha told me that there is something you needed to share that can't wait until after the banquet."

"Yeah, but…" I trailed off as Nicolai sat in the chair next to me.

"I don't believe Trinity has met Nicolai." Matthew stepped in smoothly, his red hair falling forward, brushing his forehead.

"No, we haven't met." Nicolai smiled in my direction. "Pleased to meet you."

"Same." My confusion was nearing epic levels as my gaze swung back to Thierry. "I don't understand…"

"It's okay. You can speak openly in front of Nicolai." Thierry smiled faintly.

Misha's brows rose.

I had no idea what was going on. "Um, I'm not sure—"

"You can. Nicolai understands that what he hears in this room cannot go beyond it."

Nicolai nodded. "Of course."

"What do you need to tell us?" Mathew prodded.

I glanced at Misha, who was frowning so severely I thought his face might crack. "I saw…" I took a deep breath as my heart started pounding. "I saw a ghost outside of the Great Hall tonight."

Nicolai's head swung in my direction. "Excuse me?"

I stared at Thierry, having no idea what to say.

"Trinity can see ghosts and spirits," Thierry explained rather calmly, as if he were telling Nicolai I was able to walk backward while patting my belly and rubbing the top of my head. "That's all."

I got the unspoken message there.

"You can?" Nicolai was staring at me, and I didn't need to look at him to know that.

"Yeah." I sank down in my chair, feeling like a strange insect under a microscope.

"I've never met someone who could do that."

Feeling about seven different kinds of self-conscious, I gave a close-lipped smile.

"Yes, I imagine you haven't," Matthew murmured.

My wide eyes swung to him, and he winked. I had no idea what was going on, but I knew in an instant that something was, and something big had changed for Thierry to go from *they must not know anything* to revealing one of my abilities to Nicolai.

Nibbling on my thumbnail, I glanced at Nicolai, and yep, he was still staring at me.

"Please, Trinity, continue," Thierry urged.

I tugged my gaze away from Nicolai. "The ghost—the man? He was killed by a demon," I said. "And it wasn't a Raver demon."

Tension poured into the room as Thierry said, "Tell us everything."

And I did, telling them what Wayne had shared with me.

"How can you be sure it was a demon and not an animal?" Matthew asked. "There are bears in these mountains."

"The only animal I can imagine doing that to him would be a chupacabra, and the last time I checked, they weren't real."

"Chupacabra," Nicolai repeated, shaking his head.

Matthew leaned forward, planting his hands on the desk. "How long ago did he pass?"

"I'm not sure. He was too confused to tell me, but I first saw him the day they arrived." I glanced at Nicolai. "And he disappeared before I could talk to him, but I don't think it's been that long. Maybe a few days."

"Long enough for a demon to have discovered the community." Matthew looked at Thierry.

"And the abandoned fire tower is only a few miles from here," Misha reminded them. "But this could've happened around the time the Ravers were here."

Nicolai didn't seem surprised whatsoever by the mention of Ravers, so either Thierry had filled him in or Zayne had.

"Is it possible this man had been dead that long?" Thierry asked.

"I'm not a forensic pathologist nor do I play one on television, so I can't tell you the time of death. It could've happened before the Ravers or after," I told them.

"We'll send a team out today to scout the area." Thierry began to rise. "I don't want either of you two speaking about this to anyone, not even Jada. Do you understand me? I don't want to cause unnecessary alarm."

"Understood," Misha said, and I nodded.

We were dismissed after that, and I went upstairs to my bedroom. Misha followed, and as soon as I opened my door, I knew something was off.

The room was an icebox.

I scanned the room, seeing the curtains billowing over the cream-colored chaise lounge.

"Peanut," I grumbled, hurrying to the window. Pushing the curtains aside, I closed the window and then turned back to Misha.

"That ghost is really weird."

"Not as weird as what just went on downstairs. I can't believe Thierry had me talk in front of Nicolai." I walked over to my bed and plopped down. "Something is going on, Misha."

"Normally I would tell you that you're being paranoid, but you're right." He leaned against the door. "That was freaking weird."

"Yeah, it was." I stared at him as I rubbed my palms over my thighs. "Knowing that I can see ghosts and spirits isn't that big of a deal, but…"

"But knowing that is one step closer to finding out what you are."

I couldn't sleep.

Probably because it was only, like, eleven at night and normally I didn't even think about climbing into bed until midnight, but I was feeling…weird.

Again.

Restless. Antsy. Irritated.

I didn't even know why I was irritated, but I was.

I hadn't even taken Misha up on his offer to go down to the Pit. I was kind of surprised to hear that people were there, but maybe the Accolade had ended early? Who knew? All I did know was that Misha wanted to go the Pit because Alina would likely also be there, so here I was, feeling…

Antsy.

Restless.

Nervous.

Irritated.

Expectant.

I didn't understand that last one, or any of it, but that was how I felt—like I was waiting for something to happen. Like everything was about to change.

Or that something *had* changed.

Lying in bed, I stared up at the softly glowing stars as I drew one leg up. My heart was pounding too fast, like I was in the middle of a training session with Misha, but all I'd been doing for the past hour was lying here. Before that I'd gone looking for Peanut, but I guessed he was in the Great Hall peeping on Zayne.

Zayne.

Ugh.

I smacked my hands over my face and dragged my palms down. Had be been flirting with me? Like for real? Not that it mattered. When he left, he'd be gone, and he'd been leaving soon. The final ceremony was in three days.

And there were way more important things to be thinking about.

I rolled onto my side, eyes peeled wide open. A thousand different things were circling around in my head. I was worried about what had killed Wayne and if the group that had gone out scouting would find anything. I couldn't sense a demon, but all that meant was that one wasn't close to the walls.

I couldn't stop thinking about how Thierry and Matthew had brought Nicolai into that meeting, letting him know what I could see, which was beyond freaking strange.

And yeah, I was also wondering if Zayne really was missing a part of his soul.

I was so not going to sleep anytime soon.

Nope.

Sitting up, I swung my legs off the bed, then reached over to turn on the bedside lamp. I blinked until my eyes adjusted and then rose. I grabbed a pair of leggings and pulled them on, along with a sports bra, before snatching up a thermal I'd stolen from Misha ages ago. It was baggy, almost a tunic on me, and I loved it because it was cozy and smelled like cloves no matter how many times I washed it.

I left the bedroom and made my way downstairs. As I walked past Thierry's office, I saw a faint light seeping underneath the paneled double doors. There were voices. Matthew's. Thierry's. A third voice, also, but I couldn't make out what they were saying.

More closed-door meetings.

If Peanut was around, I'd send him inside to spy for me, something he'd love doing. Said it made him feel like Davey Osborne, and I had no idea who that was. I was guessing it was something '80s related, but he was so curious about the visitors, all he was doing was hanging out at the Great Hall.

Ducking my chin, I headed out the back door and across the patio, following the worn path I didn't need to see to walk since I'd traveled this route hundreds of times over. I tugged the long sleeves over my hands and crossed my arms against the still-chilly night air as I reached the stone wall that was smaller than the one that surrounded the whole community. This wall circled one of the larger, wooded parks.

All the way at the end of the stone wall was the Pit.

I made my way to the opening to the Pit. The scent of burning wood surrounded me. Laughter and the hum of conversation mixed with the soft lull of music.

I stopped at the opening, watching the flames dance against the night sky. What was I doing? Was I about to insert myself between Misha and Alina? If I did that, he'd be focused on me instead of Alina. Instead of enjoying himself.

What if Misha hadn't wanted to be bonded?

The moment that thought entered my head, I wanted to scrub it out with a wire brush. Neither of us had a choice, not me from birth and not Misha from the moment he met me. Misha had said it was an honor, and I believed him, but just because something was an honor didn't mean it was something someone wanted.

Feeling sick to my stomach, I pivoted and started back to the house. Maybe Thierry and Matthew would be done in their office, and I could bother them.

Maybe I'd crawl into bed and force myself to go to sleep. That sounded like a ton of fun.

Halfway back from the Pit, I stopped and looked up at the sky. It was a pretty clear night. I could see four faint twinkles. Stars. I closed my right eye. Correction. I could see three faint twinkles. There were probably more. The whole sky was probably full of stars, and maybe if I stared long enough—

I heard the footsteps behind me, and instead of swinging like I had done several nights before, I started to turn.

Pain exploded along the back of my head, powering down my spine, short-circuiting my senses, stunning me.

And then I was falling.

10

My knees cracked on the pavement as my palms scraped across the rough surface.

Breathe.

That's what I told myself as I forced my eyes to stay open and sharp, throbbing pain and nausea nearly overwhelming me. *Breathe through it. Don't pass out. Breathe.* My vision tunneled more than it normally did, and I struggled not to cave to the encroaching darkness and the pulsing pain.

An arm circled my waist, a whoosh of air stirred around me and I was lifted clear off the ground. In the back of my mind, I knew… I *knew* what it was that grabbed me. I didn't sense a demon, and no human could pick me up like that.

Warden.

Memories from a year ago surfaced. Mom's wide brown eyes, full of horror, as she realized what was about to happen. We'd been caught off guard, betrayed.

No. No way.

This was *not* happening again.

A bolt of fear blasted through me like a gunshot, kicking years of training into gear, pushing me past the panic and pain. Dropping one foot to the ground, I swung the other one back, my foot connecting with my attacker's calf.

I was rewarded with a grunt of pain and the arm loosened around me. I went limp in his grip, my sudden deadweight throwing him off. He dropped me, and I hit the ground, rattling my teeth. I pushed through it again—through the woozy pain in my head and the roaring confusion. I rolled and then sprang up, whirling around.

And saw a mask—one of those white, plastic doll masks with the painted red cheeks and wide, pink smile.

"That's therapy-inducing." I stumbled back a step, shuddering.

The Warden was in his human form. I could tell, because he began to shift as he charged me. His dark shirt ripped along the shoulders as wings unfurled, revealing dark gray skin.

This was bad—so bad. Even if I had my blades, which I didn't, I would be in for a whole different kind of fight once his skin hardened.

I feinted to the left as he grabbed for me. Spinning, I bent at the waist and kicked out. My foot connected with the side of his face, snapping his head back and cracking the plastic mask. It started to slip, but I couldn't see anything other than shadows under the mask.

He stumbled back a step and then swung out. It was too much and too fast, coming from the periphery in my blind spot. I jumped back as his hand shifted, forming razor-sharp claws. The Warden caught the sleeve of my shirt. Clothing ripped and then fiery pain lit up my shoulder.

Wet warmth poured down my arm as I spun out of his grasp, sending a bolt of pure, raw terror through me. The fear did not come from the wound or the fact that a Warden was after me—it sprang forth because of the blood.

My *blood*.

Its aroma filled the air and rose with the wind, a metallic, sweet scent that could not be hidden.

It would draw them, and that knowledge triggered the thing that rested deep inside me, a power that I'd been taught since birth to keep under control, to keep hidden until the time my father unleashed it—unleashed *me*.

"No," I whispered, even though it was pointless. It was triggered, and there was no stopping it.

Heat flared in my chest, the power and the warmth of a thousand suns. It rushed through my veins like a storm and heated lightning.

My *grace* rose to the surface, took over even as I fought it, even as I tried to think of winter, of cold mornings and icy rain. It was no use.

I felt it.

Heat rippled down my arm and white light filled the corners of my eyes. "You should run."

The Warden didn't listen.

White fire erupted from my arm and exploded from my hand, shooting out in a spitting flame as my fingers curled around the heated handle already forming against my palm. The weight of the sword was heavy, inherently familiar even though I'd called upon it only once before. Fire flared from the razor-sharp edges as the very air crackled and hissed.

His wings unfurled as I lifted the sword high. Flames arced as I swung it down, catching the Warden in the shoulder. A Warden's skin was almost impenetrable. *Almost.* The sword cleaved into him like a hot knife sliding through butter, burning away skin and blood before it could even spill into the air, carving him in half as the righteous fire rippled through him, consuming every inch of the Warden before he could even scream.

Within seconds, nothing was left of the Warden but a pile of ashes, lit by the spitting, burning sword. Only the half-melted mask remained.

The *grace* recoiled and the sword collapsed into itself, becoming wisps of smoke and a fine dusting of golden light that evaporated in the wind.

A thin stream of blood trickled from my nose.

Slowly, I crouched and picked up the ruined mask. The moment my fingers touched it, the plastic fell apart, joining the dust on the ground.

"Whoops," I whispered, and straightened.

Breathing heavily, I shuddered and stepped back. Blood... It was running down my left arm, dripping from the tips of my fingers, smacking onto the sidewalk.

This was bad, so bad.

I needed to get to Thierry, stat. This mess needed to be cleaned up before it was too late. That was the priority, more important than trying to figure out why a Warden had tried to kill me again.

Spinning around, I took off, and I ran—ran faster than I had ever run before, and I didn't slow down, even though every step caused the pounding in my head to feel like a drummer had taken up residency inside my skull. I didn't slow down and give in to the darkness chasing me. If I passed out and didn't get to Thierry, and I kept bleeding, *they'd* come.

Especially if what killed Wayne was still nearby. They'd come in droves.

I reached the edge of the wall surrounding my house, hung a right—

I slammed into something warm and hard—something that smelled like...winter mint.

Zayne.

I pinwheeled backward, losing my balance.

"What the Hell?" Zayne exclaimed, catching my arm—the wounded arm. I sucked in a sharp cry, swallowing it as the pain flared hotly. "Trinity?"

He pulled me forward so fast there was no stopping me. I bounced off his chest and then I didn't make it very far. He caught my other arm, steadying me. Winter mint crowded out the metallic scent of my own blood. My wild gaze landed on his face, but it was too dark back here to see him.

"Holy crap," I whispered, feeling nauseous. "You're like a wall—a warm, hard wall."

"A warm, hard wall? Wait." Concern filled his voice as his hands shifted on me. "You're bleeding. Hell. You're bleeding bad."

I was vaguely aware of his touch gentling as my heartbeat thrummed. "Kind of."

"Kind of? What happened to you?" Zayne kept ahold of one of my arms, anger joining the concern, sharpening his tone as he spoke. "Who did this to you?"

I started to answer, but stopped myself. "I...I don't know."

"You don't know?"

"No." I swallowed down the rise of bile. God, I was going to puke. Or pass out. Maybe both. "I need to... I need to see Thierry."

"I think you need a doctor." A hand touched my cheek, and there was the weird jolt again—the sense of acute awareness. I jerked back at the contact. "Sorry," came the gruff reply. "It's okay. Everything is okay."

I wasn't sure about that.

"Nicolai," he called out, and my stomach sank. He wasn't alone. Great. How were we going to explain any of this to them? "We have a problem."

"Not a problem," I murmured, aware of the DC clan leader joining us.

"What the Hell happened?" Nicolai demanded.

"I had an accident," I said.

"With a chain saw?" Zayne asked. "Are you hurt anywhere else?"

"I'm fine." I leaned away from his touch. My legs...felt weird. "I just need to get to the house. Matthew is... He can help me."

"Trinity—"

"I need to see..." The world wobbled a little. "Whoa."

"Whoa what?" The hand was back on my cheek, fingers spreading and sliding down the side of my neck, through my hair. Despite the fact I felt like I might vomit, I shivered in response of the slow glide of his skin over mine. "Your head is bleeding, too."

It was? I shouldn't be surprised. The Warden did try to smash my skull in. "I just need to..."

"I don't think she's doing well," Nicolai said, voice urgent.

Zayne stepped into me, and the warmth of his body was luring. The weird feeling in my legs increased, and whatever light I could see blinked out. I thought he shouted my name.

The next thing I knew I wasn't on my feet anymore. I was... I was being carried. My cheek was resting against a chest—against *Zayne's* chest.

Oh, what the Hell?

"Put me down," I said, trying to lift my head, but it felt funny. Like it weighed a ton.

"Oh, I'm not putting you down." His steps were long and quick. "You just passed out and I really don't want to have to catch you again."

Confusion swamped me. "I...I didn't pass out."

"You really going to argue with me when you just dropped like a sack of potatoes?"

Sack of potatoes? That was…flattering. "I've never passed out in my entire life."

"Well, there's a first time for everything."

I tried to see where we were, but there weren't enough lights. "Where are we? Where's Nicolai?"

"He went ahead to get Thierry. I have no idea where a hospital is in this place. If I did, that's where your ass would be."

Squeezing my eyes shut, I tried to not think about the fact that I was being carried by Zayne, who wasn't just the most attractive guy I'd ever seen but also—

"You…smell."

"What?" I gasped through gritted teeth as my eyes flew open. We were under lights now—floodlights—and Zayne was staring down at me as he strode forward. "I'm bleeding to death and you're taking the time to tell me I smell?"

"I thought you were fine?" he said.

"I don't… I don't smell."

"You do." He sounded confused. "You smell like…ice cream."

I blinked, thinking the blow to my head had messed up my hearing. "What?"

"You do." A short, unsure laugh shook Zayne. "I didn't even know it had a smell, but it does. Vanilla and sugar," he went on, and I couldn't tell if he was being serious or not.

"I do not smell like ice cream," I grumbled. "And put me—"

"Trinity!" Thierry roared my name so loudly I was sure the heavens heard him, and then he was there, beside us. He touched my cheek. "Dear God, bring her inside now."

Zayne didn't need to be told twice. He climbed the steps and we went through the open door, into the well-lit house.

I caught a brief glimpse of Matthew. He was rushing forward with his bag of hopefully really, *really* strong meds.

"Was it Clay?" Thierry asked.

Zayne tensed. "Who in the Hell is Clay?"

My heart jumped in my chest. Would he have done this because of me kicking him through a window? I thought about what he'd said at the pit. *One of these days.* That was kind of a warning.

"I...I don't know." I wasn't sure how much I could answer in front of Zayne, and I had no idea where Nicolai was. "I didn't see who it was, but he's not..." I trailed off, meeting Thierry's stare, willing him to understand what I couldn't say.

There was a slight widening of his eyes, and I knew Thierry understood. "Oh, Trinity," he whispered. "Where did this happen?"

I told him where and then whispered, "I'm sorry."

"What did I tell you before?" he said, touching my brow.

"I don't know," I whispered. "You've told me a lot."

Thierry's chuckle was hoarse. "I'll ask you again later, the next time you apologize for what you cannot help."

Then Matthew was there, edging Thierry aside. His gaze roamed over me, lingering on the arm smushed against Zayne's chest. "What have you gotten yourself into this time, Trin?"

"A little trouble."

The corners of Matthew's lips curved. "A little trouble just finds you, doesn't it?"

"Always," I whispered.

"You can help her?" Zayne interrupted, and my gaze shifted to him. I looked up and I couldn't... I couldn't look away. He was staring down at me, the strong line of his jaw hard. "Because I really think she's bleeding to death all over me."

I started to frown. He didn't need to sound so...put out about it. "I didn't make you pick me up."

"Should I have just left you out there, lying on the ground?"

"Yeah," I said defiantly. "And I wasn't lying on the ground. You nearly knocked me over."

"You ran into me."

"Because you were hiding behind a wall!"

"Now, you know I'm not the one who hides behind things." Zayne's striking face was perplexed. "So, you'd prefer me to have left you there?"

"It beats you bitching about me bleeding on you."

"You're so…annoying."

I glared back at him. "I hope I stained your clothes."

His lips twitched as the cool eyes warmed. "Confident that's been accomplished."

"Perfect," I muttered.

"Well, I can see she's not at death's door if she's arguing. Bring her into the kitchen," Matthew ordered. "Easier to clean up in there."

Zayne followed Matthew down the hall, and I still… I was still staring up at him. And he was… He was still staring back down at me. I had no idea how he didn't walk into a wall or anything.

"Where's Misha?" Thierry demanded from somewhere behind Zayne.

Zayne blinked and his gaze shifted up.

"He's…he's busy," I said.

"That's unacceptable." Thierry stormed ahead.

I finally dragged my gaze away from Zayne. "It's not his fault—"

"He's supposed to be with you," Thierry roared, causing me to jerk. "He has *one* job." He slashed his hand through the air. "One! That is all."

Zayne's arms tightened. "Maybe take it down a notch?"

The Duke's head swiveled toward him. "Excuse me?"

"I don't think yelling is helping Trinity right now." Zayne held the Duke's disbelieving stare, and I decided in that moment that he wasn't as irritating as I'd formerly thought. "You have her flopping around like a dying fish."

Okay. He was still freaking irritating.

Matthew was suddenly in my line of vision, shoving two chairs out of the way. "Zayne's right, Thierry. There's time for yelling later. Place her down here."

"On the floor?" Zayne hesitated. "A bed or at least a couch would be more comfortable."

"It would be, but I need her on the floor," Matthew reasoned. "Now."

"It's okay. The floor is fine," I said, my eyes glued to the medical bag on the chair.

For a moment I thought Zayne wasn't going to listen, but then he was kneeling. He carefully placed me on what felt like a blanket. I expected him to back off at that point, but he didn't. Surprise flickered through me as he stayed kneeling at my side.

"Okay. I'm going to try not to hurt you, Trin," Matthew said, but I was back to staring at Zayne's face again. "I just need to check out your arm and then...?"

"Her head," Zayne answered for me, and then I was falling into those pale blue eyes. There were fathomless, and they... they suddenly reminded me of someone else's eyes. I couldn't quite grasp whose, but I realized I'd seen eyes like his before. Or it was blood loss making me think that. "Her head is bleeding and so is her nose."

"Thank you." Matthew's fingers were gentle and quick, peeling away the ruined sleeve. "Oh, hon. This is going to need stitches."

Zayne's gaze lifted mine. "God. She's been... She's been *clawed*." A muscle popped along his jaw as he looked up to where Thierry stood by my head. "Why would she have been *clawed* here?"

"Call Misha," Thierry ordered to someone I couldn't see. "Find out what in the Hell he's so busy doing. I need someone to find Clay and make sure he's still…here. And get a team out there, by the park, to clean up the blood *now*."

"Clay?" Zayne demanded again, his gaze narrowing on mine. "Was he that Warden at the Pit giving you a hard time?"

I didn't answer.

"If it was him, he's no longer anyone's concern," Matthew commented quietly.

Zayne didn't respond to that, because I think he knew what that meant. If it had been Clay, he was deader than dead. Matthew slipped his fingers under my head and felt around. I winced and squeezed my eyes shut as pain flared.

Thierry ordered, "And you. I need your clothes now."

"What?" Zayne exclaimed.

"I really don't want to repeat myself. I need the clothes off you now. They must be destroyed."

Oh, wow. I opened my eyes, because if he was going to disrobe, I was going to be just like Peanut. No shame. If I died from blood loss, at least I'd die getting to look at whatever was underneath that shirt.

I was a horrible person.

"Why do my clothes need to be destroyed?" Zayne asked.

"Do as he said," Nicolai interrupted, and wow, I'd forgotten he was here to witness all of this. "I'm sure he'll provide you with something to wear and some answers."

I didn't think they were going to get the answers they sought.

"I don't feel anything too concerning in your injuries, but I'm going to need to stitch this arm." Matthew eased my head back down and reached for his bag. "I'm going to give you something that will knock you out, all right? You don't need to be awake for this."

"Okay." I stared at Zayne, because I really didn't want to see that needle. Not at all. "I don't like needles."

Zayne's hands were resting on his knees and they were tinged in red—covered with my blood. "I don't think most people do."

I swallowed as Matthew's fingers brushed over the center of my arm. "You seem like someone who likes needles."

"Because I'm a pain in the ass?"

My laugh ended in a sharp gasp as the needle stung my arm. "You said it. Not me."

One side of his lips kicked up. "You doing okay?"

"Yeah." I blinked slowly, feeling the buzzing warmth travel up the back of my neck and splash over my skull. "Are you?"

The other side of those lips tipped. "Yeah."

"That's good, because if you pass out, you might fall on me," I said. "And you look really heavy."

"I am really heavy." His gaze flicked to Matthew and then his gaze came back to mine and held it just as I'd started to look to see what Matthew was doing with that needle. "You want to hear something strange?"

I swallowed as I felt the warmth flood my chest. "Sure."

Zayne leaned in, and when he spoke, his voice was so low. "I feel like…like we've met before," he said, and I vaguely became aware of Matthew's fingers stilling. "I felt that way the first time we spoke, but we haven't. I would've remembered."

My heart rate sluggishly picked up, because I… I'd felt that way, too. "Same," I murmured. "That's weird, isn't it?"

"It is," he replied.

"Thierry," Matthew said in a hushed whisper, but I didn't hear what he said, if he said anything else. The last thing I saw was those pale blue eyes, and then I saw nothing at all.

11

When I opened my eyes again, Peanut's transparent face was right above mine.

"I thought you were dead," he said.

Gasping, I shrank back into bed, away from Peanut. "Oh my God, don't *ever* do that again."

His head tilted. "Do what?"

"That!" I shrieked. "Hover over me while I sleep."

"I do it all the time."

My eyes widened. *"What?"*

"Sorry. Forget I said that." He drifted to the side, somewhere out of the line of my vision. "Glad you're not dead."

"Me, too." Mouth and throat incredibly dry, I sat up and looked around. I was in my bedroom and the bedside lamp was on, casting a soft glow into the darkness. Above me, the stars on the ceiling were gleaming. "Do you really do that while I sleep?"

"Do you really want me to answer that?"

I thought about that. "No."

He giggled.

Pushing the blanket down, I checked myself out. "How did I get into my pajamas?"

"Some lady cleaned you up and changed you. I think they set your clothes on fire or something. You were out cold." Peanut floated to the center of the room. "I didn't peek. I swear. I only peek at strangers."

"That's…that's not any better."

"Don't judge me and my life and my choices."

I stared at him and then I lay back down, feeling like there were no tendons between my bones and muscles. I knew the deep exhaustion had nothing to do with whatever meds Matthew'd shot me up with.

Speaking of meds… I pulled up the sleeve on my left arm. Three angry red marks stretched about four inches over my skin. The stitching was fine and neat, but that was… That was definitely going to scar.

A scar wasn't a big deal.

What happened and why was a big deal. If it hadn't been Clay, then it had… It had to be like what happened to my mother, and that meant I wasn't safe here.

I wasn't really safe anywhere.

If it had been Clay? I had no idea what that would mean. I'd defended myself, but Wardens were… Well, they were sometimes above what I believed was right and wrong.

Worse, I'd bled everywhere. If there were more Ravers nearby, or if that Upper Level demon was close, they'd turn into big, raging and ravenous bloodhounds. They'd scent that blood and come here.

Demons tended to get a wee bit…cannibalistic when they got ahold of someone like me. That was one of the reasons I was the last of my kind.

All of that was a big deal, so a scar was nothing.

I let go of my sleeve and dropped my hand to my stomach as what happened to me really sank in.

Everything was about to change.

"Someone's coming," Peanut said, and a second later, my door cracked open.

I rose onto my elbows, squinting. It was Thierry. "Trin?"

"I'm awake," I croaked out.

The door opened the rest of the way, and I saw he wasn't alone. Matthew followed, carrying what I hoped was a glass of water. I expected to see Misha right behind them, but Matthew closed the door.

That was...odd.

"How are you feeling?" Thierry asked, nearly walking through Peanut on the way to the chair at my desk.

"Okay." I watched Peanut wave his arm in front of Thierry's face to no avail. "Just tired."

Matthew sat beside my legs. "Do you think you can sit up and stomach some water?"

"I would jump out of that window for some water," I said, pushing up. The stitches tugged at my arm.

"That would be interesting," Peanut said as Thierry rolled the chair over to the bed.

"Let's not go that far." Thierry reached behind me and fluffed up the pillows so that I could lean back against them. "How exhausted are you?"

Thierry knew what happened after I used my *grace*. There was little he didn't know. "The same as before."

"The nosebleed doesn't seem as bad this time." Matthew offered the glass.

It wasn't. Last time, I'd bled for hours afterward.

I took the glass from Matthew and drank greedily until his fingers covered mine, tipping the glass away from my lips.

"Slowly. You don't want to get sick."

"And hurl all over yourself." Peanut was behind Thierry now.

"Can you talk about what happened?" Thierry asked.

Reluctantly I lowered the almost-empty glass. "I was here, but I...I couldn't sleep, so I got up and went to the Pit, but when I got there, I changed my mind. On the walk back, I heard someone behind me. Before I could look, I was hit on the back of my head. It stunned me."

"You didn't see who it was?" Thierry asked.

I finished off the rest of the water and murmured my thanks when Matthew took the glass from me. "He was wearing a mask."

Matthew straightened, his blue-eyed gaze darting from me to Thierry. "What kind of mask?"

"A really creepy doll mask. The kind with the painted red cheeks." I shuddered. "I never saw his face, but I know it was a Warden." I prepared myself for the possible answer to my next question. "Was it Clay?"

"We haven't found him yet," Thierry answered. "He wasn't at home or at the Pit."

I looked between the two. "So, it could be him?"

"Could be," Thierry said.

I didn't know what to think. Would Clay really have attacked me because he'd gotten in trouble for what happened between us? That was horrible to even consider, but at the same time, was it better than the attacker being an unknown enemy?

"Everyone is being checked to see if we're missing anyone," Thierry continued as if he could read my thoughts. "We'll know shortly who it was."

Drawing in a shallow breath, I focused on Thierry. "I'm so sorry. I tried to stop it, and I fought back, but I was...unprepared." Embarrassment clogged my throat. "He came at me from behind and he clawed me. I guess instinct took over. I couldn't—"

"Stop." Thierry covered my hand with his. "You have nothing to apologize for. You did what you needed to do to survive."

A knot formed in the back of my throat. "But—"

"There are no buts. What happened is not your fault. If it's anyone's, it is the bastard who attacked you, and Misha—"

"It's not Misha's fault."

"I've already spoken to him." Thierry leaned back. "Misha knows he's partly responsible. He should've been with you—"

"I told him I was staying in all night, and I was. He didn't know I was going to leave," I reasoned, not wanting Misha to be in trouble. "I thought I was safe here."

Thierry's jaw hardened. "His duty is not to do as you tell him or to assume that you're going to do one thing or another, Trinity. You know that."

"He can't watch over me 24/7. He needs to have a life."

"*You* are his life," Thierry responded. "That might sound extreme, but it's true."

"She knows that, as does Misha," Matthew interjected smoothly. "But they're young. Both of them. Mistakes are going to happen. God knows we've made plenty ourselves." He looked at Thierry. "We've made big ones that inevitably have led to other ones."

I had no idea what he was referencing.

Thierry's dark brows snapped together and he sat back. A long moment passed. "Is there anything else you can tell us about who attacked you?"

I still wanted to make sure that Misha wasn't in a lot of trouble, but I also knew I needed to answer as many questions as I could. "He said nothing. He just snuck up on me and hit me over the back of the head. I fought back, and I think he was surprised by that. I don't know, but all I can tell you about is the mask."

Thierry fell quiet, and I noticed that Peanut had disappeared. I settled back against my stacked pillows. "Do you think this is like what happened…when my mother was killed?"

Matthew's head bowed, but Thierry leaned in. "I don't know, Trin. After what happened with your mother, we flushed out all the Wardens who were working with Ryker."

My skin chilled at the mention of his name. It was never spoken out loud. I couldn't even remember the last time I had heard it.

"We could've missed one," Thierry said with a sigh. "That's always possible."

I didn't think Clay had been close to Ryker. "If it's someone who was following Ryker, then why now? Why come at me after all this time?"

Thierry and Matthew exchanged a long look, one that perked my curiosity like no other. It was Matthew who answered. "Someone could've figured out what you were. I don't know how. We've been so careful."

I was thinking that telling the DC clan leader that I could see ghosts and spirits wasn't being all that careful, but I hadn't been all that careful, either, when I kicked Clay through a window.

Granted, it wasn't like Clay would've figured out what I was, but he had to realize something was up with me.

"I just… I don't understand why a Warden would want to hurt me," I said after a moment. "I didn't understand it back then, either. I'm not a danger."

Both men fell quiet, and it was Matthew who broke the silence again. "But you are."

My heart skipped a beat as my gaze found his.

He smiled faintly. "Thierry and I know you would never be a danger to a Warden, but you are a weapon, Trinity, and when someone who isn't supposed to know what you are finds out, they react in the way all of us are trained to react to a weapon that could end our lives in seconds."

Hearing that made me feel like there was something wrong with me. Like I wasn't a...person capable of restraining myself from caving in to wild, violent tendencies.

"That doesn't make what Ryker did or what this Warden attempted to do okay," Matthew continued.

Thierry rubbed a hand over his head and clasped the back of his neck. "Hopefully by morning we know who this was and who they were close to so that we can flush out anyone else who may know."

Trepidation had never blossomed to life quicker than it did in that moment. What if there were more?

Thierry pushed back the chair and stood. "I do have some good news to share. The scouts reported back. No demons were found anywhere near the community."

That was good news, but we weren't in the clear. Not with me bleeding like a stuck pig.

"I want you to get some rest." Thierry bent over and pressed a quick kiss to the center of my forehead. "Okay?"

"Okay," I promised.

Thierry left then, closing the door, and it was just Matthew and me.

"What else is going on?" I asked. "You were all acting so weird, even before this happened. All the closed-door meetings. You let Nicolai stay in the room and were totes cool with him knowing I can see ghosts and spirits."

He shook his head slowly as he stared at the chair Thierry had been sitting in. "Nothing is going on, Trin."

"Really?"

Matthew leaned over, moving slowly so that I could see him coming. He smoothed his fingers through the mess of my hair, tucking the strands back. "Nicolai learning that you can see spirits and ghosts doesn't tell him what you are. There are plenty of humans out there that can do the same thing."

Yeah, but those humans were watered waaay down, and they just had no idea how they got their otherworldly gifts.

Matthew rose fluidly. "By the way, you have a visitor."

"Misha?"

Matthew grinned at me. "It seems you've made a friend with the young Warden from the capital."

"What?" My eyes nearly popped out of my bed.

"Yes. He's been waiting to see you." Matthew paused. "Out in the hallway actually. Refuses to leave until he can see for himself that you didn't bleed to death all over him. I'm pretty sure that was his exact wording."

Of course it was.

Matthew opened his mouth and then closed it. "Where was he when you ran into him?"

"He was coming around the interior wall, by this house. He was with Nicolai," I answered. "Why?"

"He didn't say what he was doing out there?"

"No. Why?" I stiffened. "You don't think he had something to do with...with what happened to me?" It didn't even feel right, suggesting that. "Matthew?"

"No. Not at all." Matthew's smile was brief. "He just had... really good timing."

He had.

"You up to seeing him for a moment?"

I was still somewhat dumbstruck over the fact that Zayne wanted to see me, and that Thierry and Matthew were allowing it.

And that Misha wasn't out in that hallway kicking a fit over it.

So, I nodded and hoped I looked better than I felt, and then immediately told myself how I looked honestly did not matter.

Matthew opened the door and slipped into the hall. I heard him speak, and then a second later, Zayne was standing in my doorway. He'd changed into what I swore was a pair of Thierry's nylon workout pants and white shirt. His hair was damp and shoved back from his face.

I suddenly remembered what he'd said to me before I passed out. *I feel like we've met before.* Had he really said that? Or was that the drugs Matthew had been pumping in my veins? I wasn't sure, but as he walked forward, not once talking his eyes off me, I knew that was what I'd been feeling all along, too.

It *was* like I knew him.

Zayne stopped by the foot of my bed. "Glad to see you're not dead."

My lips twitched. "I'm hard to kill."

"Good to know." He turned to the chair Thierry had occupied. "May I?"

"Sure." I ignored the nervous little buzz in my veins as he folded into the chair. I glanced at the door, still expecting Misha to appear.

"How are you feeling?"

I looked at Zayne, and my antsy restlessness returned with a vengeance. I'd been wrong about what it was. It wasn't nervousness. It was like taking a shot of a really potent energy drink, like the jitters from too much caffeine.

"Trinity?" His head cocked.

"Sorry." I blinked. "I feel okay. Just a little sore."

His gaze moved to my shoulder, where I knew only the edges of the claw marks were visible. I also knew that in a day or so, those marks would be nearly healed. "What happened to you out there?"

"I really don't know." And that was the truth.

Rolling the chair closer to the bed, he tipped forward, resting his elbows on his knees. A strand of damp hair fell forward, brushing against his cheek. "Thierry and Matthew didn't tell me much, but I'm under the impression that whoever attacked you is dead?"

"He is," I admitted.

"Good."

I jolted in surprise.

"He was trying to hurt you." He gestured at my arm with his chin. "He did hurt you. He got what he deserved."

Wow.

Zayne was a little bloodthirsty.

I kind of liked it.

"And you did it? Killed a Warden?" he continued, and I didn't answer. "How?"

I slowly shook my head.

"The blades?" he asked, and then said, "Or you're a Hell of lot more trained than you let on."

A smile tugged at the corners of my lips. Time to change the subject. "Did you really wait in the hallway this whole time?"

"With the exception of getting changed and taking a shower? Yes." He tucked the piece of hair back behind his ear, and I hoped that Peanut hadn't spied on him again. "Your shadow wasn't too thrilled about that."

"You saw Misha?"

"Briefly." He tugged at the collar of the shirt. "Is he your... boyfriend?"

"What?" I laughed. "He's a Warden."

"So?"

"So?" I repeated, eyes widening. "Wardens don't date anyone other than other Wardens."

His brows knitted together. "That's not true."

"You've dated humans?"

"I've dated outside of Wardens."

"Oh." I didn't know what to do with that information other than cuddle it really close and fantasize over it later. "Misha and I kissed once. Well, actually, I kissed him, and it was really weird since he's like my brother—it felt supergross." I didn't know why I was telling him this, but he was listening. "Anyway, he really is like my brother, minus the one kiss... that felt like incest."

Zayne pressed his lips together.

"That was an overshare moment, wasn't it?"

"A little. I'll add that to your list of attributes." The grin broke free. "He was really worried about you, though."

I glanced at the door. Where *was* Misha?

"I was worried about you, too."

My gaze shot back to his. "Why?"

His brows lifted as that grin disappeared. "Are you really asking me why?"

"Yeah. Thought you found me annoying and frustrating."

"I do." A quick smile appeared and then disappeared. "Doesn't mean I can't worry."

"Well, you can see I'm just fine."

"No one is just fine after bleeding that much," he commented, and, well, I couldn't argue that point. "Thierry and Matthew reacted a little oddly to the whole blood thing."

Crap. They should've thought about that before flipping out over the blood. "They are...really squeamish about blood and stuff."

"Uh-huh."

There wasn't a single part him of that believed me.

"I've seen a lot of weird stuff. I've told you that before." He paused. "Been through a lot of weird stuff."

Well, if he'd lost a part of his soul, that would definitely be considered weird. Probably would be on the top of the list of weird stuff.

Zayne wasn't done. "You, this clan and every damn thing that's happened since I arrived is competing for the top spot of weirdness. We didn't come here for the Accolade. We came for reinforcements, and Thierry demanded that we stay, which is bizarre because it's rare that anyone is even given permission to come here, let alone stay for a while. And then there's you."

"Me?" I squeaked.

"You're a human living in the regional seat of power—a human who can kill a Warden. And the whole blood thing? Yeah. This shit is bizarre to the max."

"I have no idea what to say to that."

"Well, get ready, because I know something else about you," he said, and I tensed up so badly a dull burst of pain radiated down my arm. "Nicolai said you can see ghosts."

My mouth opened and then closed. It took me a moment to speak. "He wasn't supposed to repeat that."

"There's very little Nicolai doesn't share with me," he replied, tilting his head. "So, it's true?"

I gave a little shake of my head as I said what Matthew had said to me. "I'm not the only person out there who can see ghosts and spirits, Zayne. A lot of people can. It's not a big deal."

He chuckled softly as he let his hands hang between his knees. "Only you would think that's not a big deal. It is. I don't know anyone else who can do that."

"Maybe you do and they just haven't told you."

"Doubtful," he murmured. "You've always been able to see them?"

"Yeah," I admitted, and it was odd but nice to be talking to Zayne about what I could see. "Always."

"What's it like?" he asked, curiosity threading his voice.

I lifted my brows. "It's hard to explain. I mean, ghosts and spirits are different. Did you know that?"

He shook his head.

"Yeah, ghosts haven't moved on. They either don't know they're dead or refuse to accept it. They're usually in their death states, so sometimes they can be kind of gross. Spirits have passed on, gone wherever they're supposed to go, but are back either to check on loved ones or deliver a message."

"And that's what you do? Give people messages?"

"When I see spirits, yes, but I haven't see one in ages," I admitted, fiddling with my blanket. "When I see ghosts, I...I help them move into the light. So they can find peace."

"That's sounds difficult, but also...amazing," he said, and when I lifted my gaze, I found that he was staring at me intently. "Some people would probably choose to ignore them or be afraid."

"I couldn't do that. They need help, and if you saw them, especially the ghosts...they're so confused. They shouldn't be left like that," I told him, falling quiet as I dragged my teeth over my lower lip. "There are other things, though, that I won't interact with."

"Wraiths?"

Surprise shot through me. "How did you know?"

"Unfortunately, I have experience with them."

Wraiths were humans who'd had their souls stripped from them before they died. They couldn't pass on, either to Heaven or Hell. They were stuck, and the longer they were stuck, the farther from human they became. "There are also...shadow people," I said, curling my fingers around the edge of the blanket. "Have you heard of them?"

"Lower level demons," he said, and I nodded. "They're not ghosts or spirits."

"I know, but they're often mistaken for them. I've only seen one once. It was superfreaky." I paused. "How do you have experience with the wraiths?"

Zayne sighed heavily and stared down at his hands. "In all the snooping you do, you didn't hear about this?"

"I don't snoop," I muttered. "That much."

His lashes lifted and a ghost of smile touched his lips. "It's a long story."

"We have time."

"It's late and you should be resting."

"I am resting." I gestured at myself with a flick of the wrists. "I'm in bed." When he said nothing, my eyes narrowed. "Or is it a story you don't think I should hear because I'm not a Warden? Because you don't know me?"

Zayne was stubbornly quiet.

Irritation pulsed. "You ask me a ton of questions and yet refuse to answer ninety percent of mine. That's not cool."

He dragged his bottom lip through his teeth. "We had a Lilin in DC."

If I had been sitting up, I would've toppled over. "You're for real?"

He nodded. "There was a demon who wanted to free Lilith," he explained, and I immediately thought of the half demon his clan had raised. Lilith's daughter, supposedly.

"Convinced himself he was in love with her and tried to carry out this ritual to free her. His name was Paimon."

Now my eyes felt like they were going to pop out of my head. Paimon was an ancient Upper Level demon, like one of the biblically old demons. A King of Hell, he ruled over hundreds of demons. "Paimon was topside?"

"We actually get a few of the big players in DC. With all

the politicians to corrupt, they're sort of lured there," he said. "Anyway, we thought we'd stopped him in time, but little did we know, the ritual had been completed." His jaw hardened as a beat of silence passed. "A Lilin was created, and it unfortunately got ahold of a few humans. Some, it stripped the souls immediately. Others, it toyed with, taking a little here and a little there, which left us with wraiths to deal with."

Processing this, I wanted to ask if that was what had happened to his soul, or if it really did have something to do with Lilith's daughter, but I didn't even know if it was true. And while I was impulsive and often spoke before thinking, I wasn't so much of a jerk that I'd flat out ask someone if they'd lost a part of their soul.

So I asked instead, "How did you deal with the Lilin?"

"It wasn't easy. Took a lot to take it down. A lot of sacrifice," he said. "The Lilin had created an army of wraiths, and it somehow got them inside these old statues of gargoyles and they came to life. It was… It was crazy. One of them got ahold of my father. That's how he died, fighting the Lilin. I was there, but I couldn't get to him."

"It's not your fault," I said.

"How do you know that?" That gaze met mine.

"Because I'm sure you did everything you could," I said, and even though I hardly knew him, everything in me believed what I said. "I'm sorry, Zayne. I know that what you… you experienced wasn't easy."

Jaw working, he nodded. "He died fighting, but he also died to protect someone he cared very much for. Knowing that does… It does make it easier to process. To deal."

"I'm sure it does," I said, wishing I had something better to say, something more powerful.

"You know, you're the first person outside of those who were there that I've talked to about my father," Zayne said, shocking me yet again. A winsome smile appeared as he shook his head. "Surprises me."

"Why? I'm easy to talk to."

He smirked. "Seriously?"

"Seriously." I let a grin sneak through. "It's another one of my attributes."

"I'll have to remember that," he said, and I knew it didn't matter, because he'd be leaving. "You told me something, when we were at the training center. You said your mother was killed by a Warden."

Oh God, I really shouldn't have said that. "She was."

"And now, you've been attacked by a Warden. Are those two things related?"

I wanted to smack myself, but my head had already been through enough so I resisted. "I don't know."

Zayne stared at his hands again. "Can I ask you something, and you answer me honestly?"

"Yeah?" I hoped it was a question I could answer honestly, but I was betting it wasn't.

Thick lashes lifted. "Are you safe here?"

I opened my mouth, but closed it, because I had no idea how to answer that and for some reason I...I didn't want to lie to him.

And that was dumb, because I'd been lying to him in many ways since I'd first spoken to him.

A muscle feathered along his jaw. "If you're not safe here, we can take you with us when we leave. Help you in any way you need."

Shock rendered me silent as a swelling motion rose in my chest like a balloon about to float to the ceiling. "That...that is sweet of you to offer."

"I'm not being sweet," he replied, his gaze holding mine.

"I'm serious. If you're not safe here, we can take you some-place where you will be."

Looking away, I focused on my bedspread, finding it hard to not be completely honest with him while meeting his gaze. "I'm all right here, but thank you."

He fell silent for so long that I had to look at him again. He was watching me. "Okay."

"Okay," I repeated.

He gripped the arms of the chair and rose with the kind of inherent grace all Wardens possessed. "I should go now."

I didn't say anything, because I wanted him to stay.

As if he could somehow read my mind, Zayne stopped, and I don't even know why, but my breath caught, and I was *waiting* again.

"What were you doing outside tonight?" I blurted out.

Zayne's brows snapped together. "You know, it was the strangest damn thing. I'd been feeling keyed up all evening. Restless, even though I was with Dez and Nicolai, and this... this is going to sound bizarre, but I just had this sudden... urge to get some fresh air." He coughed out a laugh. "Good timing, huh?"

"Yeah," I said. "Perfect timing."

12

"I have a job for you," I said to Peanut.

Seconds after Zayne left, the ghost had drifted through the bedroom wall. Of course he didn't knock, but I was too tired to have that conversation with him.

"I'm down for whatever. You know why? *'Life moves pretty fast. If you don't stop and look around once in a while, you could miss it.'*"

I blinked slowly. "What?"

Peanut's transparent expression fell. "Ferris? Ferris Bueller?"

"Yeah. Okay. Anyway, can you pay attention to Matthew and Thierry? See if you can hear anything they're talking about?"

"Like what?"

Good question, because I wasn't exactly sure, either. "Like, if they are talking about our guests or…or about what happened to me. I don't know. Just anything weird."

Peanut nodded. "I can do that. I can do that all night long.

Actually, I can do that right now. They were just downstairs whispering between themselves and the other guy. Nicolai."

"Okay. Yes. Now would be a good time to spy for me."

"Awesome!" He gave two thumbs-up and then simply evaporated.

My head fell back on the pillow. I didn't think I'd be able to fall asleep, but it was like whatever burst of energy I'd experienced when Zayne had entered the room had left with him.

Which was notably odd.

I ended up passing out pretty quickly.

I'd slept for what felt like an eternity, waking up a little after ten in the morning. The first thing I wanted to do was find Misha, but I took a shower first, towel dried my hair and combed out all the knots. My arm was a little sore, but the redness had already started to go down. Like Wardens, I healed pretty quickly. By tomorrow the stitches would probably dissolve, and by the weekend the scars would be a faint pink.

After pulling on a pair of dark denim jeans and a T-shirt, I toed on a pair of flip-flops and left to find Misha. I didn't have to look far. He answered when I knocked on his door.

"Hey," I said, entering and then closing the door behind me.

His room was dimly lit, curtains drawn and only a small lamp on by the bed. He was sitting at his desk, closing his laptop. "Hey." He didn't turn to face me.

I stopped just inside of his room, suddenly...feeling weirded out. I glanced around. His bed was so neatly made that I knew he hadn't slept in it, because it was always a mess. I waited for him to turn around, and when he didn't, trepidation formed in the pit of my stomach. I opened my mouth, closed it and then tried again. "Is everything okay?"

"Yeah," came the gruff, short reply.

I clasped my hands together. "Then why are you sitting with your back to me?"

Misha finally turned the chair around. He didn't say anything, and it was too dimly lit for me to make out his expression.

My stomach dropped. "Are you... Are you mad at me?"

"Why would I be mad at you, Trin?"

I wasn't sure. "Because of last night? I told you I was staying in—"

"I'm not mad at you."

"Really?"

"Really. I wish you would've stayed in like you said, or texted me that you wanted to come out, but you didn't do this to yourself."

Feeling a little relieved, I inched closer. "Then why..." I trailed off, unsure of how to ask what I wanted to know.

"Why what?"

I drew in a deep breath. I never held back with Misha before. "Why didn't you come see me last night?"

"I wanted to, but after getting my ass chewed out by Thierry, I didn't think I'd be good company."

I guessed that made sense, but still. "I'm sorry you got in trouble. I told Thierry it wasn't your fault."

"I know, but Thierry was still right. I should've stayed in," he said, letting his head fall back. "And don't argue with me about it. You're not going to change the way I feel."

"Misha—"

"Look, my job is to make sure you're safe. I failed last night."

I crossed my arms as I bit down on my lip to keep my mouth shut, but I couldn't hold it in. "You know, I didn't need you last night."

Misha's head straightened.

"I took care of myself. I saved myself."

"You used your *grace*, Trin. That's how you took care of yourself."

Irritation pricked at my skin. "I know I shouldn't have used it, but I did, and it was fine. And if I'd used it last time—"

"You still wouldn't have saved your mom, Trin." His voice was quiet. "Even if you used your *grace*, it wouldn't have changed anything. Don't put that on yourself."

I pressed my lips together. The guilt surrounding my mother's death was...beyond complicated, but Misha was wrong. Her death was my fault for multiple reasons.

He leaned forward in the chair. "So, you're saying you don't need me anymore?"

"That's not what I'm saying and you know it." I walked to his bed and plopped down on the edge. "We're a team, but there's no reason for you sit in your room pouting because someone else tried to hurt me."

Misha stiffened.

"And there was also no reason for Thierry to chew your ass out, either. Instead of him yelling at you and you pouting, we should be figuring out who tried to kill me last night."

Looking away, he dragged a hand over his head, and a long moment passed. "You're right."

"Damn straight I am."

He snorted. "It's just..." He leaned back in the chair. "It doesn't matter. How are you feeling?"

"Fine." I pulled up the sleeve of my shirt, knowing he'd be able to see it. "See? Not a big deal."

He rubbed his fingers over his forehead. "That's going to scar."

Letting go of my sleeve, I lifted the other shoulder.

"It was Clay," he said.

My breath caught. "For real?"

"I talked to Thierry this morning. Everyone is accounted

for except him," he said. "And Thierry doesn't think he left the community."

I didn't know what to say. "How can they be sure he didn't leave? He could've just flown right over the walls."

"Yeah, he could've, but we have cameras. The footage has been looked at and, so far, they haven't seen anyone jump ship."

Unsettled, I stared down at my hands. "You think... You think he came after me because he got into trouble with Thierry?"

"Yes."

I gave a little shake of my head. "What an idiot."

"No truer words have been spoken," Misha said.

My stomach twisted. It wasn't guilt. I had defended myself. If I hadn't fought back and killed Clay, I could've died, and that meant Misha would have, too. But I felt strange.

It wasn't the first time I'd killed.

And it probably wouldn't be the last.

I lifted my head. "I honestly didn't think it was him. I mean, it made sense, but... How long has Clay been here? Since he was a kid, right?"

Misha frowned. "Right."

"So, he would've known Ryker."

"Yeah, of course, but that doesn't mean he shared Ryker's...beliefs."

I wasn't sure. Misha was right. It made sense. Clay was pissed, and he'd said things to me that could be taken as a threat, but something about it didn't seem right.

"You know, I've been thinking." Misha tipped his head back. "I didn't feel anything last night. Nothing when you were hurt, and I think I should have."

Unsure what to say, I lifted my hands and then dropped them. "The bond doesn't work that way."

"The bond is designed to alert me to when you're in danger," he said, looking at me. "You were in danger, and I felt nothing."

I was supposed to be resting, but that wasn't what I was doing. I wasn't even in the house, and if Misha or anyone else discovered that I wasn't in my bed, there'd be Hell to pay.

But I was on a mission—a mission to locate and retrieve Peanut.

Call it a seventh sense, but I just knew that pervy little ghost was hiding out in Zayne's room.

I hadn't seen him since he'd left the night before to spy on Matthew and Thierry, and I was guessing he hadn't heard anything of note to report.

And yeah, maybe I wanted to talk to Zayne, tell him thank you for getting me to Thierry so quickly last night and for checking on me. I didn't think I'd thanked him.

And maybe I didn't want to be alone with my conversation with Misha playing over and over in my head. Between learning that it had been Clay trying to kill me and that Misha hadn't felt anything signaling that I was in danger through the bond, I needed a distraction.

Wearing my favorite pair of oversize dark sunglasses that still didn't block out enough of the sun's bright rays for me, I made my way to the Great Hall and slipped in through the side entrance. Climbing the back stairs, I wondered how I was going to figure out which room Zayne was staying in. I hadn't thought that far ahead and knocking on every door wasn't the brightest plan.

Probably should've thought about that.

Too late now. I pushed open the stairwell door and stepped in the wide second-floor hallway, right into the path of Nicolai and Dez.

"Whoa." I drew up short with a little laugh. "Sorry. Wasn't expecting to see either of you."

Nicolai immediately stepped forward. "What are you doing out of bed? How are you feeling? Should you be—?"

"I'm fine," I said, cutting off his rapid-fire questions. "Just a little sore. Thank you so much for helping last night."

"No need to thank me at all," he replied, concern pinching his brow as I glanced at Dez. "I'm glad to see that you're up and moving about."

"I feel the same." Dez smiled. "Dez. I don't think we've met." He paused. "I'm also glad to see you're up and moving about."

"Thank you."

The smile on Dez's face kicked up an inch. "This is the part where you shake my hand."

"Oh. Sorry." Flushing, I looked down and, sure enough, Dez had offered his hand and I hadn't seen it. I shook it. "I'm actually here to, um, thank Zayne. I didn't get a chance last night. Do you know if he's in his room?"

"I believe he is." Dez looked over his shoulder. "His room is the fifth on the right."

I smiled, thanking the little dose of serendipity. "Thanks."

Both men nodded, and just after I stepped around them, Nicolai spoke. "Trinity?"

I turned. "Yes?"

His gaze searched mine as he stepped forward, lowering his voice. "Zayne told us that he offered you the opportunity to leave with us if you find that necessary. I just want you to know that I completely support his offer."

The shock I'd felt when Zayne made that offer returned as I looked between the two Wardens.

"As do I," Dez said. "We know you said you were safe here,

but if that changes, even after we leave, you have friends in DC that can help you."

A knot formed in my chest. "Thank you," I said, meaning it. "I'll...I'll remember that."

Nicolai nodded and then both men left, disappearing down the stairwell I'd just come up. I stood there for a moment. They were... They were good people.

Smiling, I walked down the hall, squinting as I counted the doors. I stopped in front of the fifth on the right and the smile faltered and then failed.

What was I going to say to Zayne? *Hey, there may be a creepy peeping ghost in your room?* Well, I did need to thank him, but it could've waited.

"Damn. Damn. Damn." Taking a step back, I started to turn—

The door opened before I could move an inch. "Trinity?"

Turning back as I desperately tried to come up with a good reason for being there that had nothing to do with him, I came to a complete, utter stop.

Zayne was naked—naked *and* wet.

My eyes widened. Okay, he wasn't completely naked. He did have a dark blue towel wrapped around his lean hips, but that towel hung indecently low. There were indents on either side of his hips, and I had no idea how he got muscles there.

Misha was ripped, but he didn't have those. I knew. I'd seen him half-naked a million times.

There was also this very interesting fine dusting of hair a little darker than blond that trailed from his navel and farther down...

Heat blossomed in my stomach and flushed my skin. It felt like it was the dead of summer, not early June, and I was wearing a turtleneck and a jacket.

And a blanket.

God, he was... He was stunning, and I needed to stop gawking at him, but I couldn't seem to help myself. I also knew, deep in my bones, it was more than a visceral reaction. But he wasn't the first guy I'd ever been attracted to, so I didn't understand why he affected me so much.

Those hips shifted and he seemed to spread his thighs. "I'm starting to feel a little violated over here."

"Huh?" I blinked, dragging my gaze to his face. "What?"

Fresh from a shower, his wet hair was slicked back from his face. "You're staring at me."

Warmth flared even hotter in my cheeks. I was just as bad as Peanut. "No, I'm not."

"You're staring at me like you've never seen a guy before."

"I am not! And I've seen guys—lots of them."

One eyebrow rose perfectly. "So, you see a lot of naked guys?"

My eyes narrowed. "No, that's not what I meant."

"That's what you implied."

Truth was I'd never seen a guy completely naked...or this undressed. "Why are you almost naked?"

He cocked his head. "I just took a shower."

That much was evident. "So, you always open the door like this?"

"I heard footsteps and thought I'd better check it out."

"But you have a towel on," I pointed out. "And how in the world did you hear me? I wasn't out here stomping around."

"I have really good hearing," he replied. "You should know that, as you live with a bunch of Wardens."

He was right. Wardens had astonishingly good hearing and sight. Hated them.

"Do you always answer the door in a towel when you hear someone?"

"Not typically." He reached down, curling his fingers

around where the towel folded together. "But *you* were standing outside my door cussing, so I figured I should see what you needed."

What I needed? Mouth suddenly dry, I swallowed. I wasn't sure what I needed.

"And I thought to myself, when I heard you repeatedly muttering *damn* under your breath, surely that could not be Trinity."

I refocused. "Why not?"

"Because I was thinking that after nearly bleeding to death—"

"On you?"

"Yes, thanks for the reminder. I thought after what happened last night, you'd be in your room resting and not roaming around by yourself."

Annoyance flared. "Well, it is me out of my bed and roaming around, which I'm allowed to do." Not exactly true. "And what happened last night isn't going to make me hide away in my bedroom."

"Apparently it also doesn't make you use common sense." Zayne sighed. "What do you want, Trinity? I'd like to dry off and put some clothes on."

Just because he had to point out that he was in nothing but a towel again, I had to look. This time my gaze ended up on his chest, and we were close enough that even with my vision I saw the bead of water coursing between his pecs, down the tightly packed muscles of his stomach.

"You're staring again."

"I wasn't..." Okay, at this point lying was stupid. "Whatever."

He stared at me for a moment and then bit down on his lip. "Hold on a sec."

Zayne didn't give me a choice. He stepped back, opening the door the rest of the way. I didn't see Peanut, but it wasn't like I could see the whole room. Zayne turned, giving me a glimpse of his back before he disappeared from view. In under ten seconds he returned, having donned a pair of nylon workout pants. That was measurably better than just a towel, but if he had found a shirt, that would've been a hundred percent better.

"What's going on?" he asked, still standing inside the room.

"Nothing's going on. I just wanted to thank you for last night, but I'm reconsidering that."

"Why would you thank me for last night?"

"Because you helped me. Made sure I was okay and got back to Thierry and Matthew." *And you waited to see if I was okay.* But I didn't say that.

"You don't need to thank me," he replied. "I was just doing what was right."

He was.

But was it more?

Ugh.

That was such a stupid thought. Of course it wasn't more.

"Why are you reconsidering it?" he asked.

"Huh?"

"You said you were reconsidering thanking me."

"Oh. Yeah." I shrugged my uninjured arm. "Because I'm annoyed at you again."

Zayne chuckled, and I shivered, hating and loving the sound all the same.

"It's not funny," I grumbled.

He sat down on the bed. "How are you feeling?"

"Almost perfect," I answered truthfully. "My arm barely hurts."

"That's surprising." He was far away enough now that his face was a blur. "Those claw marks were pretty deep."

Crap on a cookie.

"Well, Matthew did give me some good meds, so that's probably why it doesn't hurt so badly." Shifting my weight from one foot to the next, I shook my head. "Ask me again when they wear off."

He was quiet for a moment. "You were lucky last night."

I wasn't lucky.

I was just powerful, but I nodded nonetheless. "I was."

"Have you heard anything about who could've been behind it?" He leaned back on one elbow and the sight of him twisted up my stomach.

I nodded.

Zayne stared at me from his reclined position. "You know, you're welcome to come in here. You don't have to stand out in the hall."

"I know." I didn't move.

"I mean, you're more than welcome to stand out there if that's what you like to do. Just figured you're be more comfortable coming in here, since you want to talk."

Did I want to talk? I'd come here looking for Peanut, but was that the only reason I came here? No. I was woman enough to admit that, but I was also here to make sure Peanut wasn't peeping.

I didn't know why I was still standing in the hall. Zayne was just a guy. Okay, he was also a Warden and he was mind-blowingly beautiful, but he was just a guy who annoyed the living daylights out of me.

He'd also told me about his father and offered to take me with him if I wasn't safe here.

I walked into the bedroom and studiously looked away from Zayne, because the closer I got, the more I noticed that the muscles in the arm he was leaning on were doing interesting things.

I looked around and found a certain pain in my behind.

Peanut was in the corner of the room, sitting on top of the dresser with a huge grin on his stupid face.

"You okay?" Zayne asked.

Lifting a finger to his mouth, Peanut winked.

My eyes narrowed on him. "Yeah. *I'm* fine."

"Oh, so scary," Peanut said, shaking his arms and legs.

"Oooh-kay." Zayne drew the word out. "Is there a reason you're staring at the dresser?"

"Good question," Peanut chimed in.

I dragged my gaze from Peanut. "I thought I saw a bug."

Peanut gasped. "Are you calling me a pest?"

"Do you guys have bug problems?" Zayne asked.

"Sometimes," I muttered. "But if the bug knows what's best, it'll be gone from here."

Peanut snorted.

Zayne blinked slowly. "You...you are so very odd."

"This is awkward to listen to," Peanut commented.

I ignored Peanut.

"So, what did you learn about who attacked you?" he asked.

"It was Clay," I said with a sigh. "Or at least that's what they think."

"The guy from the Pit?" he asked, and I nodded. "Do you know why?"

Part of me didn't want to go into it, but I did. "Clay was always...nicer to me than most here. I mean, the Wardens aren't rude or anything, but they don't pay attention to me. Last week I was hanging out with him...and we kissed."

"Okay, this is more awkward," Peanut said.

I shot him a dark look. "Anyway, I was cool with it at first, but he got supergrabby, and when I told him to stop, he didn't at first. I mean, I made him stop. If I couldn't have done that,

I don't know if he would've..." I stared at the beige carpet. "I told Thierry, and Thierry delayed his Accolade for a year."

"Well," Zayne said after a moment. "That would definitely piss him off."

My gaze flew to his.

"You did the right thing by telling Thierry. Clay needed to know there were consequences for his actions, to learn not to do something like that again." His shoulders lifted with a deep inhale. "I knew a guy like that once. He's dead, too."

I hadn't been expecting him to say that.

Zayne continued. "You know, people think that Wardens are above evil because of the purity of our souls. Even other Wardens think that, but the one thing no one takes into consideration is that, just like humans, we have free will, too. Wardens aren't above acts of great evil, and what we are shouldn't protect us from consequences."

I stared at him for what felt like five minutes. "I've never heard anyone say that."

"Yeah, well, it needs to be said more often."

He was right. "Who killed the Warden you knew?"

"A demon," he answered. "A demon killed him for what he tried to do to someone."

"I have no idea what to say to that." Which was true. Especially when Misha claimed Zayne worked with demons.

"Most wouldn't. I have a question for you. How did you kill Clay?"

"The blades," I lied. "I got him...in the neck." A vulnerable spot, even for Wardens. "It was quick."

"Yeah," Zayne murmured, studying me.

I lowered my gaze. "I...I killed him, and I don't feel bad, because I was defending myself." I didn't know why I was telling him this, but I couldn't seem to stop myself. "But I'd rather not have had to kill him."

Zayne didn't respond for a long moment and then he sat up fluidly, resting his arms on his legs. "You did what you needed to do. That's all you need to tell yourself."

Being a Warden, he'd killed many times. All demons. Not the same as killing a Warden or a human, though. "Have you...?"

"Have I what?" he echoed, splaying his fingers against his knees.

I shook my head. "Never mind. It's stupid."

"Let me decide if it's stupid."

Crossing my arms, I drew in a shallow breath. "You've killed demons. Probably hundreds if not thousands of them, but have you ever had to kill a Warden or...a human?"

Zayne stared into my eyes. "I haven't, but I've come extremely close, and there have been times that I wanted to."

"Really?" I thought about the Warden he knew, the one killed by a demon.

He nodded. "If I'd succeeded, I wouldn't have felt a damn moment of guilt over it. Wardens aren't inherently good," he repeated. "That was something it took me a long time to realize, but obviously it didn't take you that long."

"No, they're not," I whispered, feeling like I was committing an act of treason.

"I like him," Peanut spoke up, reminding me that he was still there.

I remembered what Misha had told me, about the half-demon girl and him working with demons. "Can I ask you something?"

Zayne leaned back again, and once more, the muscles across his shoulders and stomach did interesting things I wished I could see more clearly. "Sure."

"Is it true...that you've worked with demons in the past?"

Something flickered over his face, but it was gone too

quickly for me to decipher what it was. "Someone has been whispering in your ear."

"Perhaps."

He tilted his head to the side. "What would you think if I said it was true?"

Good question. "I don't know. I would think it was unbelievable."

"Most would."

"But?"

"But I guess most would think seeing ghosts and spirits is also unbelievable," he said.

My brows knitted as I glanced at Peanut, who flipped me off. My lips twitched. "Seeing ghosts and spirits is not the same as working with demons."

"It's not, but to some people, ghosts and spirits *are* demons."

"How dare they!" gasped Peanut.

"But that's not true," I argued.

"I'm not saying it is, but there are humans out there who believe that."

I frowned at him. "What point are you trying to make with your Chewbacca argument?"

"Chewbacca argument?"

"Yeah, you're just saying a bunch of nonsensical words and stringing them together like they mean something."

He looked like he was fighting a laugh. "What I'm saying is that Wardens are not pure and innocent just because of our birth. The same could be said about some demons not being evil and corrupt."

My mouth dropped open. He was saying there were some demons that weren't evil? That was utter crazy pants with a side of dangerous sauce.

"Do you think that because of the half demon your clan took in?" I asked.

Everything about him changed in an instant. His jaw hardened and those eyes turned to frost. "That's none of your concern. Is there anything else you need? If not, I have stuff to do."

I jerked back, stung at the unexpected shutdown and obvious dismissal. "Okay, then. There's nothing else I need." I moved to leave, then stopped. "By the way, there's a ghost sitting on your dresser," I told him, and smiled evilly when I saw the blood drain from his face. "He's name is Peanut, and he's taken quite a liking to you. Have fun with that!"

13

The conversation with Zayne lingered in my mind the rest of the morning and into the afternoon, making it hard to focus on anything else.

The way Zayne had shut down after I'd brought up the half demon was telling, but so was the fact that he'd insinuated not all demons were evil. I couldn't even process that.

Just like I couldn't process that I'd actually talked to him about how I felt after killing Clay. It made me feel scratchy and uncomfortable in my own skin, because I shouldn't feel anything after what I'd done last night other than acceptance. After all, Matthew and Thierry were right.

I was a weapon.

And a weapon didn't feel bad for killing in self-defense.

I sighed as I rubbed my hands under my glasses. I had more important things to worry about than Zayne's reactions or my suddenly sensitive feelings. Like the fact that Clay had been able to claw me. I needed to train harder and prepare better. I needed to figure out how to work without relying on my eyes, because I should've been faster than Clay. I should've been careful enough to keep space between us.

Peanut drifted over my bed, snagging my attention. He was swimming backward across the room. I really had no idea what to say about that.

"What are you doing?" I asked Peanut.

"Getting in my daily exercise." He reached the curtained window. "I have to stay trim and fit."

I lowered my hands. "Do ghosts gain weight?"

"Yes." He started swimming back to me.

"I don't think that's true."

"Are you a ghost?" he asked.

"No," I sighed.

"Then how do you know?"

"I don't need to be dead to understand that ghosts needing to stay in shape doesn't logically or scientifically make sense."

Peanut swam above my head. "Didn't know you were a scientist. Should I start calling you Dr. Marrow?"

I rolled my eyes.

"I'm going to get abs like Hot Guy." Stopping in the middle of my room, right under the ceiling fan, he started to do crunches.

"His name is Zayne." My eyes widened with each crunch. Every time he sat up, the blade of the ceiling fan cut through his head.

"I'm going to be ripped," Peanut continued, grunting with each sit-up. "I'll have abs of steel. I'm going to be as big as Hulk Hogan and Randy Savage."

I stared at him.

"No pain, no gain," he went on. "Sweat is glory."

"Are you sweating?"

Peanut stopped and looked at me like I was half-dumb. "Ghosts don't sweat."

My mouth dropped open. "Do you even listen to yourself when you speak?"

"Not really," he replied. "I can't believe you told him I was in his room when you left."

I smiled happily at the memory.

"I thought he was going to salt and sage the room."

"Does that work?"

"It works when the Winchester brothers do it."

I stared at him. "You're a mess."

Half of Peanut's body disappeared as he grinned at me. "A hot mess." He came down from the ceiling, stopping about a foot off the floor. "By the way, I did hear Thierry and Matthew talking about something weird."

"And you're now just saying something?"

"I've been busy, Trin. My scheduled is packed. As you just saw, I had to get my workout in—"

"What did you hear?" I interrupted.

"Not much." His feet touched the floor. "I mean, it was this morning, when they were in their bedroom."

"Peanut, I didn't mean for you to go into their bedroom."

He lifted his shoulders. "If anyone is going to have a secret squirrel conversation, they're going to have it in their bedroom." Peanut had a point, but still. "As I was saying, I heard them talking about making some kind of mistake. Matthew said that, but then Thierry was like, we weren't the only ones that made a mistake."

My brows knitted together. "Matthew said something similar last night. They didn't say what the mistake was?"

He shook his head. "No, but then Thierry said there was nothing that can be done now. That it was already 'righting' itself. No clue what that means. You?"

"No," I whispered, shaking my head. "I have no idea."

★ ★ ★

"Are you going to the final ceremony tomorrow?" Jada asked as she walked toward the training facilities with me.

Squinting against the bright glare of the early-morning sun from behind my sunglasses, I shrugged. "I don't know."

"Thierry will want you there." She looped her arm through mine. "And I want you there."

"So you're not suffering in boredom alone?"

Jada laughed. "Maybe."

I shot her a long look, which just made her laugh harder. The final ceremony of the Accolade lasted hours. Between the speeches and the dinner, I would go stir-crazy, but since I hadn't gone to any of the Accolade yet, I should probably show my face.

"I don't have anything to wear," I told her.

She snorted. "I have a dress you can borrow—and don't look at me like that. I have plenty of dresses that will fit you."

I groaned as I opened the door and we stepped out of the warm sun and into the cool interior hall.

"Where's Misha, by the way?" Jada asked.

Pushing the sunglasses onto my head, I led the way. "He's with Matthew. They're interviewing the trainers to see if they can get any information…on Clay. See if he said anything about what he…he was planning to do."

Jada shook her head as she slipped her arm free. "I still can't believe it. Neither can Ty. I mean, the guy was a jerk, but I wouldn't have suspected this."

"Me, neither. I just… I don't think we ever know what people are capable of."

Jada fell quiet as she followed me past the numerous rooms that were occupied by Wardens. I was heading for the one Misha and I normally trained in, since it was usually open.

"Do you think you should be out here? Without Misha? Not that you can't defend yourself, obviously, but..."

"But Misha is busy, I'm tired of being in my room and the thing with Clay was isolated. At least, that's what we think. And do you know what Peanut was doing all day yesterday?"

"God only knows."

"He was swimming back and forth across my ceiling 'working out.'" Shifting the leather satchel into the crook of my arm, I walked toward the windowless blue door. "He was doing sit-ups and jumping jacks while singing Michael Jackson's 'Beat It.' If I spend one more moment in there, I'm going to lose my mind."

"What?" Jada choked on another laugh. "Oh my God, that is the most bizarre thing I've heard in a while."

"Welcome to my life," I muttered, yanking open the door and coming to a complete stop. "Oh."

Jada bumped into me from behind. "Why are you...?" She trailed off as she saw what I saw, which was Zayne and Dez training.

They were unaware of us as Dez charged Zayne. The blond Warden spun out of his grasp with the agile grace of a dancer, darting under Dez's outstretched arm. He popped up behind him, catching the older Warden by his shoulders as he dipped down. I had no idea how he did what he did next, because he was nothing but a blur of speed. In a heartbeat, he had Dez completely off the ground and held above his head. A second later, Zayne slammed Dez into the mat.

"Good Lord," murmured Jada.

"Uh-huh." I nodded, tensing when Zayne straightened, shoving the strand of hair that had fallen free out of his face as he looked over to where we stood.

Dez groaned as he rolled onto his side. "That didn't hurt at all."

Zayne chuckled as he turned back to Dez, extending a hand. "We have company."

"I see." He took Zayne's hand and was hauled to his feet. He gave us a wave, which we returned. "Good to see I have an audience while I get my ass handed to me." He placed a hand on his lower back. "You guys should've showed up fifteen minutes ago when I had Zayne on the mats."

Zayne smirked. "That only happened in his imagination."

"Not true." Dez cracked his back like a skilled chiropractor. "Do you all need anything?"

"Nope," I answered, still seeing Zayne lifting Dez clear in the air like the Warden weighed nothing more than a sack of grain.

Zayne cocked his head.

"Well, we were looking for an available room," I corrected.

"We didn't know you guys were in here," Jada added.

"We're done," Dez said. "Well, *I'm* done." He shot Zayne a look before he focused on Jada and me. "Are you here to practice with the blades?"

Surprise caused me to tighten my grip on my leather satchel.

"Zayne told me you were really good with them," Dez added as Zayne moved off to a corner of the room, arms folded over his chest.

"I'm okay with them."

"Okay?" Jada laughed, shoving me forward. "She's better than most Wardens."

Not given a choice, I went forward, sneaking glances at Zayne as I stopped beside him. We hadn't exactly parted ways all warm and fuzzy the last time we'd spoken, and he was being abnormally quiet.

"Would you give me a little demonstration?" Dez requested.

"Of course," Jada answered for me, and I turned to glare at

her. She snatched the satchel from my hands and strode across the room to the table. "She loves showing off."

That was…true.

Normally.

Right now, I sort of wanted to just go back to my room, because when I looked at Zayne, I was no longer seeing him slam Dez into the mat.

I was seeing him as clear as day in nothing more than a towel, chest damp and—

"You're staring at me again." Zayne leaned in, whispering in my ear. "Just thought you should know."

"Am not," I snapped back, cheeks flushing as I turned away from him. Dez was watching us curiously. So was Jada, who was doing a really poor job of not smiling as she handed my blades to me.

"How's your arm?" Zayne asked as I stepped to the side, lining up with the blob of human-looking flesh at the other end of the room.

"Fine." I curled my fingers around the familiar weight of the handle. "How's your mood?"

"What?"

"Is it better than the last time I saw you?" I queried, fighting a grin when I saw him frown.

"It *was* better," he said after a moment.

I smirked at that as I lifted the blade. "Tell me where to hit."

"Anywhere?" Dez turned to the dummy. "How about the… chest?"

"That's too easy," Jada said. "Pick another area."

"Okay." Dez chuckled. "The head?"

The head was a smaller blur of beige, but muscle memory took over, and I let the blade fly. It struck true, hitting the center of the dummy's face.

"Damn," Dez said.

"Get the neck," Jada ordered.

Smiling, I switched the blade to my throwing hand. The blade also struck where I aimed, right in the middle of the throat.

Dez turned to me. "I think we could use you to teach our warriors."

My smile spread as Jada hurried over to the dummy, retrieving the blades.

"You're good, real good." A half grin appeared on Zayne's striking face when I looked at him. "But it's a bit harder when the target isn't standing still."

"I know," I snapped. "You want to give it a try?"

"Nah." He unfolded his arms. "I'm more skilled at the hand-to-hand stuff."

I told myself to shut up, but my mouth started moving before I could stop myself. "I bet I'm better at that, too."

Zayne snorted. "Trinity, you know better than that."

"Oh, I do know better." I squared off with him. "Do you think you're better just because you're a Warden?"

"I know I'm better, because I've had years of training and you've had the basics," he said, an assumption that was not remotely correct. "Not to mention, I'm bigger and stronger than you."

I gave him the kind of smile that irritated the Hell out of Misha. "Speed and intelligence will always prevail over strength and weight." I paused. "Shouldn't you know that?"

His jaw hardened as he glared down at me. "I have a feeling you just insulted my intelligence."

"Never," I demurred.

Zayne's brows lifted. "You really think you can take me?"

"I don't *think* anything. I know."

His eyes narrowed.

"You know, I'm suddenly very hungry," Jada announced, placing my blades on the satchel.

"What?" I turned to her, hands on my hips. "We just ate."

"Yeah, but I'm in the mood for dessert." Eyes twinkling with mischief, she grinned at Dez. "Have you had a chance to try the red velvet cupcakes that the café has?"

"No, I haven't." Dez smiled so widely it was a wonder it didn't crack his face. "I'd love to try one."

"Perfect." Jada sent a passing glance to Zayne. "Can you make sure she gets back to the house in one piece, Zayne?"

I opened my mouth but Zayne answered, derision dripping from his tone. "It would be my pleasure."

Forgetting Jada and Dez, I whipped back toward Zayne. "Oh, wow. You could at least sound like you want to."

"I said it would be my pleasure." Those pale eyes fixed on mine.

"Then your idea of pleasure must really differ from mine."

"You know…" He rolled his lower lip between his teeth. "I'm going to have to agree with that. Come on, get your blades and I'll walk you back."

I had a feeling what he said was a dig, and asking if hanging out with demons was something he found pleasurable rose to the tip of my tongue, but I managed to not give it voice. I was a brat, but not that much of one.

But I wasn't ready to go back to the house.

I was antsy and energized and feeling the need to prove myself. "So, you're admitting that I can take you. You know that, right?"

Zayne stared at me like I spoke an ancient, unknown language. "I've admitted no such thing."

"Then come on." I stepped back, motioning at him with my hand. "Bring it."

He laughed—straight up laughed a deep, belly laugh that

flipped my bitch switch into power on like a mofo mode. "You can't be serious."

"I am perfectly serious."

"Look, I'm not into overpowering girls to prove my technique or skill, especially girls who were just injured," he said, turning away. "I'll grab your blades—"

I waited until he was only a foot away before I sprang forward, fast and light on my feet. I jumped, grasping his shoulders as I brought a knee into his back, digging it deep. Zayne went down, mostly out of surprise, but I was anticipating that. Using his shoulders, I launched myself over him, landing in a roll that caused my injured arm to ache as I popped up on my feet and spun to face him.

Zayne was already back on his feet, gaping at me. "What the Hell?"

"What was that again about overpowering girls?"

A slow, smoky smile pulled at his mouth. "You're out of your mind."

"Just don't think you need to go easy on me," I said, and then I charged him.

Zayne feinted in one direction to avoid a sharp thrust, but I expected that. Spinning, I caught him in the midsection with a sideways kick that caused him to grunt. He spun, catching my uninjured arm as I gripped his. Using him for balance, I leaped and turned, delivering a fierce spin kick that knocked him back several feet.

"Are you sure you've had years of training?" I taunted, steadily approaching him.

Several strands of hair had fallen free, brushing his cheeks as he faced me. "Are you sure you've just had a few training sessions?"

"Guess what?" I darted under his swing and hit the floor,

planting my palms on the mat as I kicked out, taking his legs out from underneath him. "I lied."

"I can see that," he grunted.

"Admit it. I'm better than you."

Expelling harshly, he jumped onto the balls of his feet. "I'm not admitting that yet, princess."

"Princess?" I repeated, blinking. "I'm not a princess."

"You're something." He smirked, and then flew into a butterfly kick I almost didn't see in time.

I met him with a wild laugh. Blow after blow, we went after each other. In the beginning, when I first went at him, he was holding back, but with each punch and kick I got through his defenses, he stopped messing around.

Zayne blocked a series of kicks and jabs that would have knocked a human on their ass. He kept up with the moves easily. "Come on, *Trinity*, can you do better than this? I'm getting bored."

The way his mouth curled my name sent a shiver down my spine and a flush to my skin. I hated it.

Sneering, I spun on my heel and turned into a roundhouse kick that knocked both of his stupid legs out from underneath him. He went down hard onto his back, grunting. Panting, I stalked over to where he lay prone. "You bored now, douche nozzle?"

Zayne coughed as he rolled onto his side and looked up at me. "Douche nozzle? What generation do you live in?" Moving lightning fast, he had my legs before I could see him move. He snagged the edge of my foot and yanked.

Unable to catch myself, I landed across his lean body. I recovered quickly, clasping my hand around his throat as I straddled him. "If I had my blades, you'd be dead right now."

He lowered his chin, and then his gaze lifted to mine. Those pale eyes weren't so frosty now. They were full of fire, and I got a little hung up, staring into them. The pupils had started to stretch vertically, a sure sign he was close to shifting.

"I win."

"Not quite," he said.

I blinked. "I won. There's no way——"

My words ended in a squeal as he rocked up, folded his legs over my waist and flipped me onto my back with a roll of his hips. Within a heartbeat, he had me pinned underneath him.

"You won?" He grinned down at me.

I tried to kick out with my legs, but the iron strength of his thighs pinned them to the floor. When I lifted my upper body to throw him off balance, he quickly forced me back with pure brute strength, catching and trapping my wrists on the mat above my head.

"Speed and intelligence will get you far," he said, lowering his head so close to mine that the edges of his hair brushed my cheek. "But speed, intelligence *and* strength always wins in the end."

Not ready to admit defeat, I threw my head back as I managed to wiggle one leg out from underneath him. I was ready to plant my foot somewhere sensitive, but getting my leg free caused something entirely unexpected to happen. His body shifted and settled between my legs, lining our bodies up in a very interesting place. His lean torso and legs pressed against mine in a way that made me think of other things—things that didn't involve fighting, but did include less clothing.

With his face inches from mine, our eyes met. I stopped moving. I might've stopped breathing.

There was a swift change in the atmosphere around us, a sudden charge of heady tension as a wild rush of desire swirled through me, clawing to break free. It reminded me of my *grace* when it lit up my veins, burning through skin and tissue.

Breathing became difficult as we continued to stare at one

another. Zayne didn't move off me, and I thought he would've by now, but he was still above me, those pupils continuing to stretch. His full lips parted.

I...I *wanted* him.

I'd never really felt desire before, but it was burning me up from the inside. Want. Need. *This* was what had been missing when I'd kissed someone before. *This* was what yearning really felt like, and as I lifted my head off the mat, bringing our mouths so close that I could taste his breath on my lips, I thought I might drown in it. Zayne didn't pull away. Instead, it seemed as if he became even more still.

I kissed him.

It wasn't much of a kiss at first, just a brushing of my lips against his, and when he didn't move, I pressed harder, feeling a shivery rush at the touch of our mouths all the way to the tips of my toes. I touched his lips with the tip of my tongue, licking him.

His hands tightened around my wrists and then loosened. A stuttered heartbeat later, his hands moved, sliding down my arms, the rough calluses along his palms causing my breath to catch.

And then I wasn't the only one doing the kissing.

Zayne pressed down, his warm lips moving against mine for the briefest, hottest second, and then he was *gone*.

Zayne tore himself away from me, crouching on the balls of his feet, breathing heavy as his skin darkened, hardened. I couldn't see his eyes any longer, but I knew the pupils of his eyes were vertical.

He was beginning to shift, and I...

Sitting up, I scooted back as I dragged in deep breaths. What had I just done? I'd kissed him. Well, actually, I sort of licked him, and he was staring at me like I'd done just that.

Holy crap.

My entire body felt like it turned beet red as I sprang to my feet, unsteady and dizzy. "I'm sorry," I said, backing up. "I...I didn't mean to do that."

He rose slowly, watching me like I was a wild animal capable of pouncing on him at any given second.

"I really am sorry—" I spun around, and to my horror, I saw Misha standing in the doorway, one hand holding open the door.

I darted across the mats to the door without looking back, not even once as I slipped past Misha and into the much cooler hallway.

Holy crap, I kissed Zayne.

I kissed him, and he'd launched himself off me like a rocket was secured to his waist.

"Trinity," Misha called out to me.

I kept walking fast, hands opening and closing at my sides. What had I been thinking?

Misha caught up to me. "What was that all about?"

"Nothing," I said, drawing in a shaky breath. "Absolutely nothing."

14

"You...you kissed him?" Jada asked, her voice muffled from the other side of the bathroom door. "When I left you guys yesterday, I figured you two would just, I don't know, continue to argue-flirt. You've exceeded my expectations yet again."

Standing in front of the mirror, I tried to tug the bodice of the borrowed dress up, but the moment I let go, it slipped down, giving me cleavage for days and then some.

I sighed, giving up. The white dress was also a little snug in the hips, but it was the perfect length and fit everyplace else. It was going to have to do since Jada was threatening to drag me to the final ceremony no matter what I wore.

Reaching behind me, I scooped up my hair and brought the thick strands over my bare shoulders. Not bad. That hid the fact that my arm was nearly healed, which was suspicious as all Hell, plus the hair kind of covered up the chest area.

Kind of.

"Trinity?"

I squeezed my eyes shut, probably smudging the mascara

I'd stolen from Jada's room. A huge part of me wished I hadn't said anything to Jada, but I'd had to tell someone.

I'd have self-imploded if I hadn't told her.

"I kissed him," I said, opening my eyes and reaching for a tube of peach-colored lipstick.

"And did he kiss you back?" she asked.

"I...don't know." I slid off the cap.

There was a pause. "How do you not know that, Trin?"

"Well, at first, I thought he did, but now, the more I think about it, I'm not sure." I smoothed the lipstick on and pressed my lips together. "I mean, it was a quick kiss." Entirely too brief, but I could still remember the feel of his mouth against mine. "And he sort of launched himself off me."

There was a long quiet moment. "Did he say anything?"

"No." I sighed again, feeling confused and ashamed and angry, which really wasn't a good combination.

I hadn't seen Zayne since yesterday afternoon. The blades and the sunglasses I'd left in the training room had magically appeared this morning on the kitchen island. Either Zayne had returned them or Misha had retrieved them.

"I don't know what to say," Jada said finally.

"Yeah, me, neither." I opened the bathroom door. "How do I look?"

"Amazing." Jada was the one who looked stunning in a white Grecian gown with a golden ribbon tied around her slim waist. "Good enough to actually kiss you back."

I blinked slowly at her.

"Can you guys stop talking about kissing?"

Gasping, I sidestepped Jada and saw Misha sitting on the edge of my bed, dressed in black linen pants and a matching sleeveless tunic-style shirt. "How long have you been in here?"

"Long enough to know why you ran out of the training room with your face on fire."

"I hate you," I muttered, crossing my arms.

"You might not want to do that," Jada advised, eyeing my chest. "You'll burst a seam or two."

Rolling my eyes, I unfolded my arms. "I hate both of you."

"We're not the one running around randomly kissing guys," Misha remarked.

"I'm not, either!"

"Look, this is not the same thing as with Clay," Jada said, defendeding me. "She didn't kick Zayne through a window afterward."

I opened my mouth, then snapped it shut. "Well, I kind of kicked him several times before the kiss."

Misha's brows lifted. "Why are you so violent?"

I raised my hands, then dropped them. "I need serious help."

Still sitting on my bed, Misha nodded somberly.

"You guys don't understand, though," I said, feeling whiny beyond belief as I looked at Jada. "You have Ty." And then I turned to Misha. "And you're starting something with Alina. Thierry has Matthew, and I know you think Zayne's a bad dude," I said to Misha, "but I don't think he is, and I just want... I just want a smidgen of that. I want to be..."

You're a weapon, Trinity.

"What?" Jada asked quietly.

"Nothing." I shook my head. "Shouldn't we get going?"

"No, it's not nothing." Jada blocked my path, becoming an immovable force. "What do you want?"

I was trained to fight—to kill when necessary. I had the *grace*, a powerful weapon that could slay demons and Wardens and everything in between. I'd been a weapon since birth, and very few things scared me, but I didn't have the courage to say what I wanted.

Which was to *be* wanted for anything other than what I was born for.

Misha rose from the bed, swinging an arm over my shoulders. "Come on, let's go or we're going to be late."

For a moment, I didn't think Jada was going to relent, but she nodded and turned with a graceful swirl of her skirts. After guiding me out of my room, Misha stopped us at the top of the stairs and I prepared myself for a massive lecture. When he spoke, his voice was a whisper against my ear.

"I know what you want," he said, squeezing me against his side. "You want to be wanted, and there's nothing wrong with that, Trin. Not at all."

There was a spirit in the Great Hall.

I knew he was definitely not on Team Alive and Breathing because his body was doing the whole flicker in and out thing, and although he was standing directly behind Dez and Nicolai, they were unaware of the man, going so far as to push their chairs through the spirit more than once.

Dez and Nicolai sat directly across from us, on the opposite side of the wide table. There was a chair empty on the other side of Nicolai, and if I'd had any hopes that Zayne would show—which I didn't—I would've been disappointed.

He wasn't coming to the ceremony.

Not that I was surprised. He'd said this wasn't his kind of thing, and if he'd caught wind of me showing, I couldn't blame him for being anywhere but here.

I felt like such an idiot—an idiot who didn't understand personal boundaries. Blowing out an exaggerated breath, I told myself it didn't matter.

The Wardens from DC would be gone tomorrow, leaving with the reinforcements they needed. Everything would return to normal in the morning—well, as normal as things could be, but with Zayne gone, I'd stop... I'd stop wanting what I couldn't have.

As I toyed with the edge of my napkin, my gaze shifted back to the spirit. He was still standing behind Dez and Nicolai, as if he were a part of their conversation.

It was so bizarre. The spirit had a vague sense of familiarity about him, but I'd never seen the older man before. Was he connected to Dez and Nicolai somehow? Or was it someone else here?

Either way, as I cautiously watched him, I knew that he'd definitely seen the light and crossed over. His skin tone was a healthy gold, and if he wasn't doing that flickering thing, he'd look human, which was why, sometimes with my eyes, I often mistook spirits for living, breathing people.

He was a handsome man with a head full of reddish-blond hair that reminded me of a lion. He was big and broad of shoulder, and I imagined if he were alive, he would've drawn the attention of everyone here.

Had he been a Warden? It wasn't impossible. I'd seen a few Warden spirits before.

Someone laughed.

Pulling my gaze from the spirit, I glanced at the head of the table. Thierry was meeting with someone, so the seat was empty. Matthew was sitting there beside Jada and her mother, his reddish hair a fiery sight in the bright lights of the hall.

I looked back at the spirit. He was staring at the entrance, brows knitted.

"What do you keep looking at, Trinity?" Dez asked.

Oh, crap.

Apparently I wasn't being as inconspicuous as I thought. Since I didn't know if Nicolai or Zayne had filled Dez in the whole *I see dead people* thing, I forced a smile. "Nothing. Just dazed out."

He lifted an eyebrow. "Is the dinner that boring?"

I pursed my lips. "Would you believe me if I said no?"

Dez chuckled as he leaned back in his chair. "Not in the slightest."

Grinning, I glanced at the stage. Thierry had already given his speech, toting the skills and successes of those Wardens receiving the Accolade. We still had the trainers' speeches to sit through, and then there'd be dancing.

Misha draped his arm along the back of my chair and angled his body toward mine, lowering his chin. "What *are* you looking at?" he whispered.

I lowered my gaze. "You don't want to know."

"A ghost? Peanut?"

I shook my head.

He was quiet for a moment. "A spirit?"

"Yep."

"Interesting," he murmured, looking to where the spirit had been but now was gone.

What the…?

Scanning the large, brightly lit room and the marble-adorned, cream-colored walls, I finally spotted him in the center of the room.

Seizing the opportunity for distraction, I scooted my chair out. "I'll be right back."

Misha gripped the arms of his chair, about to rise, but I stopped him.

"You don't need to come," I told him, aware that both Dez and Nicolai were watching us. "I'm going to the restroom."

A look of doubt crossed his face, but he sat back down, knowing if he followed now, it would look superweird. I grinned at him, imagining the string of curses he was coming up with as I nodded at the two Wardens across from me.

I was careful not to walk into the tables the spirit drifted *through* while the occupants were straightening their dishes and candles, expressing their confusion in exclamations.

I picked up my pace, passing two warriors in training waiting by the doors. Out in the much more softly lit hallway, I looked both ways. There were people out here chatting in small groups. It took a few moments, but I saw the spirit once more at the end of the hall, by the doors that led to the garden. A second later, he drifted right through them.

Clutching the skirt of my dress so I didn't trip, I made my way down the hall and stopped at the doors. The garden was lit only by warm string lights and torches. What was worse for my eyesight than an extremely bright room?

Minimal to no light.

I sighed, using my hip to open the door, and stepped onto the veranda into the warm, early-June air. My steps were cautious, as I remembered that there were stairs. My depth perception wasn't the greatest at night. Slowly, I made my way down to the paved walkway.

I didn't hear anyone outside as I followed the path, wondering if I would even be able to see the spirit out here.

Passing what appeared to be several empty benches, I followed the curve of the path and was surprised when I discovered it flowed into an open area that was well-lit by several old-fashioned-looking lamps. There was a statue in the middle, a battle angel lifting a sword high with one arm and gripping the head of a demon in the other hand.

I walked around the statue only to draw up short when I spotted the spirit on the other side. My heart gave a little jump, like it always did when I was this close to a ghost or spirit, no matter how many times I'd seen one.

He was staring at the statue, and now that we were closer, I couldn't shake the familiarity of his features. Maybe I had seen him before, when he'd been alive.

Letting go of the skirt of my gown, I glanced around. I

didn't hear anyone else out here, but that didn't mean someone wasn't.

I bit down on my thumbnail, curiosity leading me into a state of recklessness.

I ignored the way my stomach churned. It was an odd reaction to the presence of the spirit, one I didn't understand, so I shoved that aside to dwell on later—

"Hello," the spirit said.

Jolted, I took a step back as the spirit turned to me and, from the waist down, became transparent. I felt my eyes go wide. "You know I can see you?"

"Why would you think that I wouldn't?"

"Because you're dead?" I suggested.

One side of his lips twitched into a half grin that raised tiny goose bumps all over my arms. "Yes, but I'm not the first spirit you've seen."

"No," I said. "Not even remotely. How do you know that?"

The spirit studied me for a moment. "I just do."

"That's a vague answer," I said. "How about I ask you another. You've crossed over, right?" When he nodded, I wrapped my arms around my waist against the cool mountain breeze rolling through the garden, stirring the leaves. "But you're back."

"I am."

I waited for him to elaborate, but when he didn't, I prodded. "Why are you back?"

The faint smile faded as he looked up at the statue. "I wanted to see."

My brows knitted together. "See what?"

Several moments passed before he said, "See how badly I messed up."

Understanding flickered through me. This spirit was back

because he regretted something he'd done or should've done, or something he'd said or wished he'd said.

I could help him with this.

"You're a Warden, aren't you?" I asked.

The spirit nodded. "And you…you are not a Warden."

"No."

He looked down at me, his face almost going transparent. "I know who you are."

Startled by that statement, I didn't know what to say. I'd never come across a spirit or a ghost who knew who I was. Had he lived here? Maybe when I was younger? "You do?"

"Being dead makes some things so much clearer while other things not so much." He faced me fully, his features becoming sharper, clearer. "Now I know why I came back right now, at this moment."

A shiver curled its way down my spine.

"Funny how fate has a way of righting itself against all odds, isn't it?"

Okay, this was the most bizarre conversation I'd ever had with a spirit, and I'd had some really out-there conversations, but even more out there—wasn't that what Peanut had overheard Thierry saying?

Before I could ask him what he meant, his features were suddenly marked with such heavy sadness that I could feel it in my own chest. A second later, he scattered into thin air. My brows rose as the breeze lifted a strand of my hair and tossed it across my face.

I waited.

He didn't piece back together.

Frowning, I unfolded my arms. "Why did you disappear?"

"I cannot fathom why anyone would disappear on you."

15

My heart nearly jumped out of my chest at the sound of a deep voice laden with amusement and a hint of sarcasm. The hem of my gown whirled around my ankles as I spun around.

"Zayne," I said, my eyes going so wide I was sure I looked like a squeezed bug.

He looked regal, standing a few feet from me, dressed in the ceremonial garb of a warrior. White linen pants and matching, sleeveless tunic. His hair was loose, brushing his shoulders.

I was so shocked by his sudden presence that I just stood there, staring at him, and all I could think about was the fact that I'd kissed him. And maybe—maybe he had kissed me back, but even if that was true, he most definitely had torn himself away from me as if I were on fire. He hadn't lost himself to the whirling, chaotic desire that had been pounding through me.

One side of his mouth curved up as I continued to openly

gawk at him. "Are you okay?" A moment passed. "I'm starting to get a little concerned."

Heat swept across my face as I snapped out of my stupor. I found my voice. "I'm sorry. You startled me."

That half grin ticked up. "I can tell. I didn't mean to." He glanced at the statue and then looked back at me. "Then again, I was kind of quiet."

"Obviously," I replied, hands fidgeting at my sides.

A moment passed as he looked around the garden. "So, someone...disappeared on you?"

I nodded. I'd found it amusing earlier to taunt him about Peanut's presence, but not so much now. "You're dressed as if you're attending the Accolade."

"I am."

"You weren't inside."

"I decided to attend last-minute." A lock of blond hair fell against his cheek and he reached up to brush it back behind his ear. "I'm surprised to see that you're here."

Was he? And was that why he'd decided to attend, because he thought I wasn't going to be here? I clasped my hands together and lifted my chin. "I'm here against my will, basically."

Zayne chuckled. "I can't imagine anyone making you do anything against your will."

My lips twitched in response. "Well, as you can see, I'm not really attending the ceremony, and it doesn't look like you are, either." I looked around, not seeing the spirit. "I'm not even sure if I'm supposed to be out here, to be honest."

"Why not?" he asked.

"These gardens are supposedly sacred," I explained. "Only trained warriors are allowed."

He tilted his head and appeared to study me. "I can't imagine that this is the first time you haven't followed the rules."

I shrugged.

"Can't really blame you," he said. "I'd rather be out here staring at trees and this statue than inside that hall."

Unable to help myself, I laughed.

Zayne stepped closer. "But this is definitely a marked improvement over staring at the statues and trees."

There was tiny flutter in the center of my chest that I ignored. "That's not saying much."

"I'm going to have to disagree." That grin kicked up another notch. "That's saying a lot."

I didn't know how to respond to that.

"It's a beautiful night." He lifted his gaze. "Clear skies and all the stars."

Following his gaze, I squinted and was able to see the faint twinkles. I knew they were brighter to him and he could probably see a lot more. I could see…four. I closed my right eye. Correction. I could see three. My shoulders tightened.

"It is," I murmured, pushing away the oppressive feeling of finality.

"And you…you look like a goddess, Trinity. Beautiful."

I felt my breath catch in my throat as my gaze shot to his. Was he being serious? I was confident very few people, if any, would look at me and think *goddess*. Jada? Yes. Me? More like the dirty tree nymph running from the gods.

Zayne looked away, clearing his throat, and I wanted to hear him say those words again as a different kind of warmth swept across my cheeks and down my throat.

"Really?" I whispered, and the moment that word left my mouth, I wanted to take it back.

He dipped his chin and I thought his grin might've curved into a full smile. "Yeah, really."

I bit down on my lip to keep myself from grinning like an idiot. "Thank you," I said. "You don't look so bad yourself."

He chuckled as he looked back to me. "I actually was hoping to speak to you. I wanted to talk to you about yesterday."

Every muscle in my body tensed as I closed my eyes. "About yesterday. I'm...I'm sorry for the way I behaved."

"Which part of your behavior are you apologizing for?" he asked, sounding closer.

I opened my eyes, discovering he was only about a foot away. "Well, there are probably multiple aspects of my behavior yesterday that I could apologize for."

"Like goading me into fighting you?" he suggested.

Pressing my lips together, I nodded. "Yes, that, but—"

"Or suggesting that I wasn't trained well enough?"

"I don't think I suggested that."

"Oh, I think you did."

My fingers dug into my skirt. "Okay, so maybe I did, but I was apologizing for—"

"For calling me a douche nozzle?"

I had called him that.

"Or are you apologizing for lying about having minimal training?" he continued smoothly.

I started to frown.

"Oh, wait." His gaze lifted to mine. "Are you apologizing for refusing to admit defeat when I won?"

I drew in a deep breath. "Are you done yet?"

"I don't know." The slow, teasing grin both irritated and excited me, and the last emotion frustrated me even more. "Have I forgotten anything?"

"Yes," I snapped. "The one thing I was actually going to apologize for."

"Which was?"

He was going to make me say it. Bastard. "For kissing you." My face burned like an unholy fire.

Zayne tilted his head to the side and a long moment passed. "That's the one thing you don't need to apologize for."

"What?"

He lifted a shoulder. "It happened. You don't need to apologize."

"Yeah, but I shouldn't have done it," I said. "I mean, no one should run around kissing people and it wasn't like you were into it—"

"You don't know what I am and am not into."

I quieted, unsure how to take that. What did that even mean? I was confident I couldn't be the only person who would be thoroughly confused by that statement.

"It happened," Zayne said quietly.

"It happened?" I repeated. "You're making it sound like I slipped and my mouth fell on yours."

Zayne laughed, and it was a real one, nice and deep.

"It's not funny."

"The way you just described it was pretty funny."

"Glad you think so." I sighed, angling my body away from his.

"Trinity, you're not the first girl to kiss me."

"Wow." My gaze slid back to his. "Do you have that problem often? Girls just randomly throw themselves at you?"

"I wouldn't say you threw yourself at me, nor do I have that problem. What I meant is that you…felt something and acted on it. That happens."

Feeling more inexperienced than I'd ever felt in my entire life, I had no idea what to say. It wasn't remotely acceptable to feel something and simply act on it, and I had a strong suspicion that he was saying that to make me feel better. While I appreciated it, it actually made me feel worse.

"Well, anyway, I'm sorry and I wanted to say that," I said, clearing my throat. "I should probably get back inside—"

"How long have you've been training?" he asked, stopping me. "There's no way you picked up all of that with just a few sessions with Misha or any of the trainers here."

Because I'd felt the need yesterday to show off, I was now backed into a corner by my own actions. "I've had a...substantial amount of training. Probably as much as any of the Wardens going through the Accolade."

Zayne probably had already figured that out, but there was still a margin of surprise settling into his features. "Why would they train a human like that?"

And that was the million-dollar question, but it was one I couldn't answer. Not truthfully.

Zayne shook his head. "This is what I don't understand about you. You're human, but you can see ghosts and spirits, and yes, I know other humans can do that, but you're living with Wardens and you've trained with them to the point you can hold your own against one of us."

"I like to think I did more than hold my own against you," I pointed out, not really helping myself at all.

"You're right. You've killed one of us in self-defense," he said, and a cold slice of dismay cut through my stomach. "You were attacked, and not a damn person here, including you, seems at all that worried about it."

"People are worried. I'm worried—"

"Are you?" he challenged. "Because you're roaming around alone like you're not remotely worried that someone here wished you harm."

"I'm not exactly supposed to be roaming around, and the threat to me, well, it's been dealt with. It's not like I'm out here just lollygagging around."

"That's exactly what you're doing," Zayne replied dryly. "What were you doing out here, by the way? You were talking to someone."

I sighed. "I was."

His brows lifted as he crossed his arms.

"I saw a...spirit."

There was a slight widening of his eyes. "Here? At the Accolade?"

He sounded so much like Misha that I had to laugh. "Yes, spirits are everywhere. Even here. It was strange, though." I glanced back at the statue. "I'd never seen him before, but he seemed to know who I was." I shrugged. "I guess he was a Warden here."

"You...you see spirits of Wardens?"

I nodded, relieved to be on safer, not so embarrassing grounds. "I don't see them often, and I've never seen a ghost of one, but I have seen a few spirits."

Zayne seemed to mull that over. "Why do you think you've never seen a ghost of a Warden?"

"I guess they all cross over," I explained. "Unlike humans, they have very little to fear upon death."

"I guess so..." The corners of his mouth turned down. Tension rolled off Zayne as he stared into the trees and bushes surrounding us. He became so still that I wasn't even sure he was breathing. Then his arms unfolded.

A knot of unease grew in my stomach, spreading like a virus, and then I felt it—like a hot breath against the nape of my neck, a sudden heaviness at the bottom of my spine—

My wild gaze bounced around the garden, from Zayne to the statue and all the shadowy recesses around us.

Demons.

Demons were near.

My breath caught in surprise as Zayne's hand curled around my arm. A jolt of electricity danced from his fingers to my skin and traveled up my arm, followed by an odd sense of acute awareness, but the feeling was quick and then I wasn't thinking about it anymore.

One second I was standing by the statue, talking about ghosts and spirits, and the next I was spinning through the air as he thrust me behind him and held me there, *off* the ground by a good six inches.

Something…something happened—happened to Zayne. The arm around my waist was like a steel band and the back my chest was plastered to became as hard as stone and as hot as basking in the sun. There was a ripping sound, a tearing of cloth, and then a rapid stirring of air that lifted the strands of hair around my face as Zayne's wings unfurled.

Zayne was shifting.

I drew in a shuddering breath as the air around us seemed to explode.

16

A startled scream lodged in my throat as Zayne doubled over, taking me to the ground, to my knees.

What in the holy Hell was happening?

My brain couldn't process the shouts coming from every direction, the roar of the sirens going off and the sound of glass shattering, and the screaming—the high-pitched screams of terror. We'd gone from talking about spirits to the entire world exploding all around us. No amount of training could've prepared me for this, to react as fast as I needed to.

Something slammed into the ground near us, pinging off the marble and embedding deep into the soil.

Bullets.

There were bullets, and that made no sense. Demons didn't use guns.

Cement chipped and tiny rocks flew upward, pelting the sides of my face and arms. I bit down on my lip until I tasted blood, squeezing my eyes shut. No matter how awesome I was, my body was part-human. Bullets were not my friend, and they were raining down around us.

Inside me, the buzzing, powerful warmth of my *grace* stirred to life.

Zayne's arm tightened around my waist and I felt the next breath he took as if it were my own. "Stay down."

I didn't get a chance to respond. A second later, his arm slid from my waist and his hand planted on the center of my back. Pushed flat to the ground, I felt my fingers splay against the broken asphalt. Then the weight and the warmth left my body in a rush of wind and the sound of wings beating the air.

Some kind of inane, primal instinct took over, silencing the voice of common sense that told me to keep my head down. My chin lifted. I blinked and then squinted, trying to see through the strands of hair that already obscured most of my already less than stellar vision.

I saw...*legs*—legs coming toward me.

Zayne landed in front of me in a crouch that rattled the ground. My heart leaped as I rose onto an elbow, pushed the hair out of my face and saw him.

Saw Zayne for who he really was.

As he rose to his full height, he was the same shape and size that he'd been moments ago, but now the white tunic shirt hung in torn strips from his waist. Muscles tensed along his bare back, moving under deep slate-gray skin, and his...

Holy crap on a cracker the size of Texas, his wings were spread out on either side of him, a span of at least eight feet, maybe ten? Parting his blond hair, two fierce horns curled back.

I'd always though Misha was large for a Warden, but he had nothing on Zayne.

He shot forward, and there was a sharp yelp of pain. Something fell to the ground. A moment later I realized it was some sort of rifle. The next thing that hit the ground was a body, its neck falling in an odd, twisted angle. My stomach churned as Zayne spun to the right, lifting off the ground and coming down again. There was a fleshy smack, a sound of skin and muscle giving away. The sound of more gunshots rang out as my fingers dug in the ground.

I didn't understand this—any of this. Demons didn't use guns, and the bullets were virtually useless against Wardens. Once they shifted, their skin couldn't be pierced by a bullet.

Mine could, so I stayed low and turned my head to the right, toward the Great Hall. The rapid fire sounded like it was coming from everywhere at once, and Jada was in there. So were Misha and Matthew and everyone.

I couldn't just lie here. Pushing up with my arms, I—

A loud boom pierced my ears, and then there was no sound. Night suddenly turned to day in a flash of ultrabright, orange-white light. A blast of hot, scorching air followed with a force that kicked me back down, knocking the air from my lungs. Stunned, I was frozen for a moment, and then debris started to hit the ground. Large chucks of cement crashed all around me. Throwing my arms over my head, I grunted as the world seemed to fall apart.

Then the world stopped ending.

Sound came back in a rushing force, and screams—all I heard was screams and people calling out names.

Arms and legs shaking, I pushed up to my knees and saw a thick white cloud billowing out from the side of the building. Where a wall used to be, there was now a gaping hole with wires hanging free. Floodlights turned on with a series of clunking noises, and bright light poured into the garden, cutting through the smoke. The smell of burned metal and plastic and something that reminded me of a…a barbecue surrounded me as I reached out to steady myself. Whatever

I gripped broke off as I rose to my feet. I looked down, seeing that I was holding the sword from the statue, and a near-hysterical giggle rose in my throat.

Struggling to breathe as the cloud of heavy, white dust flowed into the garden, I stumbled over debris and tried to find shelter. I didn't see Zayne or anyone. The blast had been close, and I had no idea what kind of damage it could do to a Warden or how close he'd been to it.

"Zayne?" I called out, wincing at the dryness in my throat. I tried again.

Panic dug in with razor-sharp claws as I tried to see through the thick smoke. I clutched the iron arm as I called out. "Zayne?"

I didn't think anyone could hear me over the shouting and the wailing of the sirens that alerted everyone in the community there had been a breach and to shelter in a safe place.

The cloud of white smoke stirred in front of me, spreading and clearing. I saw a man—a man in a tuxedo and a white mask. Another of those creepy, porcelain-like doll masks with the pink circles painted on the cheeks and the bright red smile.

The same one Clay had been wearing.

"What the Hell?" I whispered.

My gaze dropped. He was holding something, and my body reacted before my brain caught up with what I saw.

Swinging the stone sword as hard I could, I brought it down on his arm, knocking the thing—the rifle—from his hands. There was a yelp of pain that briefly reminded me of a noise an animal would make. I didn't stop there. I brought the arm back up, catching the masked man under the chin, knocking his head back. He dropped to the ground, twitching.

Letting go of the stone sword, I snapped forward and straddled the attacker. I didn't think as I gripped the creature's head and twisted sharply. It shuddered under me before going still.

Folding my fingers under the mask, I pulled until the strap that held it in place snapped free. I found myself staring down into the face of a...

"Human." I rocked back, stunned. This man... He was a human. I slowly shook my head as I rose to my feet and backed away.

Realization rose. I sensed demons, but this man wasn't a demon, and it suddenly made sense. I could feel demons sometimes minutes before Wardens could. I hadn't felt the men in the garden, or heard them like Zayne had. Demons weren't here.

Yet.

A hand landed on my shoulder, and I gasped. Spinning around, I came face-to-face with Zayne in his Warden form.

It was his face, but it wasn't. The cheekbones were still high, but the forehead was broader, the nose flatter and jaw wider.

He was beautiful in the most primitive way possible.

"What did I tell you?" Zayne demanded in a deeper, rougher voice. I saw two white fangs. "I know you can fight, but they have guns. I told you to stay down."

"They're human," I said, taking deep breaths. "They're human and I...I killed one of them."

The line of his jaw appeared to soften, but his voice was gruff as his gaze flickered to the man behind me, on the ground. "It's okay. You did what you had to do."

I opened my mouth to agree, to say that yes, he deserved it if he was part of what was happening here, but I'd killed a human, and I'd never killed a human before.

"Are you okay?" he asked, those odd eyes searching my face and then, as he stepped back, looking over the rest of me. "Are you hurt? Trinity?"

I pulled it together. "I'm fine. You?"

"I'm okay."

"Are…?" I looked around, beyond the dead man to the doors I'd walked out of earlier. There were… There were shapes on the floor, on the ground. "Are they—?"

"Don't." His other hand curled around the back of my head, turning my gaze back to his. "Don't look."

My heart lodged in my throat. "They're more humans, aren't they? There's more of them—"

"Trinity! Are you out here? Trinity!"

Recognizing the sound of Misha's voice, I tore free from Zayne's grasp. I searched the fading smoke desperately, needing to see him, to know that he was okay even though I already knew, because I would've felt it through the bond if something horrific had happened, but I still needed that reassurance.

I saw him. Finally. He was striding through the hole in the side of the building, shoving the wires aside.

"Misha!" I shouted, starting toward him. He was too far for me to see if he was hurt. "Misha!"

Zayne hooked me with his arm before I made it a foot. I grabbed his arm, his skin hard and hot under my fingers.

"Let go," I said, and he tugged me back. "Let go of me!"

"I can't do that."

"What?" I shrieked, pulling against his hold. "I need to go—"

Zayne's wings swept in from the side, folding over me and blocking out Misha, the garden—the entire world.

"Holy crap," I gasped, falling back against his chest. I couldn't see *anything*. I was in complete darkness, like…like I was blind. A knot of bitter, raw panic formed in the back of my throat.

"Listen to me." Zayne's breath stirred the hair around my ear. "It's not safe for you to go charging across the garden. There could be more humans with guns."

"I can't see," I whispered, trying to get air, but the knot was expanding in my throat.

"There could be more bombs," Zayne continued as if he hadn't heard me. "I can't have you running off."

"I can't see," I repeated, chest rising and falling heavily.

"You're fine. You're—"

"I can't see!" I shrieked, scratching my throat.

His wings flew open so suddenly that my vision didn't have time to adjust. I winced as the bright light hit my eyes. I blinked several times, my vision focusing just as Misha scrambled over a stone sitting wall.

"Trin," he exclaimed. His face was covered with soot. There was a red smudge under his nose. "Are you okay?"

"She is," Zayne answered, dropping his arm from my waist.

I pulled free and met Misha halfway. "How's Jada? Ty? Thierry and Matthew—"

"They're okay." His gaze shot to Zayne. "What happened out here?"

"They came in—humans," I told him, looking over my shoulder. "They came in with guns, firing, and I killed one of them."

Misha cupped my face, his gaze searching mine. "Did you...?"

I knew what he was asking. "No, I didn't."

"Good." He dropped his hands, turning to Zayne. "She shouldn't have been out here."

That statement caught me off guard. "He didn't make me come out here. I was out here by myself and we ran into each other."

Misha glared at Zayne like all of this was his fault, which was ridiculous, and right now, his misplaced anger wasn't important.

"What in the Hell just happened? They were humans," I

said, pointing out the obvious. "But I felt—" I stopped myself before I blurted out that I'd felt a demon. As a human, that was impossible.

Zayne stared down at me, his hard, brutal face calculating. "Felt what?"

"I felt scared," I lied, whipping back toward Misha. "Were there demons?"

"No, just humans," he growled, turning to Zayne. "Were there any demons out here?"

"No." Zayne was still staring at me, his heavy wings twitching and stirring the air around us. "Just humans."

"But there *could* still be demons," I said, clutching Misha's arms.

Misha got what I couldn't say. I could feel them. They were near. He nodded, and I let go of his arm. "I don't understand what happened here." I shook my head, stunned as I turned back to the Great Hall. I didn't even want to think about how the humans got past the walls. They were *always* guarded, and that meant...

That meant there were dead Wardens.

17

Misha had taken me back to the main house, and it was just us. I was pacing the length of the foyer, still in the stupid gown, but I had rushed upstairs to grab my blades just in case.

"Where is Jada?" I asked, stomach churning.

"I think she went with Ty to his place to lock down," he said, standing sentry by the front windows. "I know she's safe, Trin. As soon as the guns started firing, she shifted, as did Ty, and then he made her leave with him."

A little bit of relief seeped into my tight muscles. "And you're sure Thierry and Matthew were okay?"

"Yes. The only injuries I saw were very minor." He glanced over his shoulder at me. "Are you sure *you're* okay?"

"Yes. Just scratches." I passed him, the skirt swishing along my calves. "I can't believe they were humans working with demons. I thought at first they might be those Church of God's Children people, but if they hate Wardens, why would they work with demons?"

Misha's back was rigid. "Because those idiots don't realize

demons are real. They'd be easily manipulated by demons or by anyone who provided them a chance to dole out violence against us."

That was true, but...

"But they were wearing the masks, Misha." I shuddered. "The same masks Clay was wearing and...and Wayne was killed by a demon nearby. The scouting party said there were no signs, but they were obviously wrong. And I can still sense demons."

"I told Thierry. They're looking." Misha turned from the window. "Something is definitely going on."

Understatement of the year.

"Where do you think Thierry and Matthew are?" I asked, stressing like a...like a human.

"They're probably at the walls."

The walls were less than a mile from here, and the Great Hall was in between. There were several football-field lengths separating the main house from the community and the other, much smaller wall, but if the demons or wayward, idiotic humans made it here, to this house, they'd run through this community like a blade through tissue.

Most of the Wardens here, besides those who guarded the walls and trained the classes, weren't skilled warriors. There were more women and children than men, and due to the ridiculous, sexist as Hell structure, female Wardens weren't trained.

Not even Jada.

I turned, pivoted on my heel and then stopped as the siren went off again. Misha and I stopped moving, stopped breathing, as we listened. If it went off twice, it was the all clear. Three times meant bad, bad news.

The siren blared once, twice, as the familiar oppressive

feeling settled on my shoulders…and then a third time before casting the large, rambling house into eerie silence.

A chill swept down my spine as I turned to Misha. In the bright light of the foyer, his reddish curls looked like autumn flames. "The demons are here."

"They are." The pupils of his bright blue eyes began to stretch vertically. His jaw was hard as he turned to the large iron-cast doors.

In all the years I'd lived among the Wardens in the Potomac Highlands, there'd never been a breach, let alone something like this.

A tremor coursed through my arms as I walked toward the door, finding it unlocked.

"Trin, don't—"

I opened the door and dark night air rushed in, sweeping over my bare arms. "Do you really think a door is going to stop them if they make it this far?"

"It would at least slow them down."

The cold cement of the porch chilled my feet as I stepped outside. I could hear nothing. Not even a bird or the chirp of an insect, as if they could sense the unnaturalness in the air.

It was quiet—too quiet as I stared over the driveway lit by the powerful floodlights and beyond, into the darkness no light could penetrate.

"Can you see anything?" I asked.

Misha came to stand beside me at the top of the steps. Even if my eyes weren't crap, his vision would still be a million times better than mine.

"I don't see anything," Misha reported, glancing down at me. "Except that dress. You could've changed. All a demon is going to see is your—"

"Shut up," I grumbled.

"You know, maybe you should go to the wall," he went

on. "Pretty sure if any demon saw you in that dress, they'd think twice before trying to lay siege."

I shoved him. "You're stupid. Zayne said I looked like a goddess."

He snorted. "Really?"

"And he said I looked beautiful." I elbowed him this time.

"The same guy who didn't kiss you back? The same guy I warned you to stay away from?" Misha shoved me back and I bumped into the railing. "You think I wasn't going to bring that back up?"

I rolled my eyes. "Now really isn't time to lecture me about that. Why don't you wait until we're not under siege by humans and demons?"

He sighed. "You should go back inside, Trin."

I ignored what he said, as I did most of the things he ordered or bellowed at me. "Do you think Jada is okay?" I asked for what had to be the fifth time.

"She's with Ty. I'm sure she is," he reassured me yet again. "Besides, all the homes have panic rooms just in case something like this happens, and that's where you should be, but that's not happening. They'll be fine. All of them will be."

Unless the demons breached the walls and laid waste to the community, burning the homes like I'd heard had happened to a community west of us several months ago, and those panic rooms hadn't saved them all. Some of the panic rooms hadn't withstood the abnormal fire the demons had wielded.

"And if that happened here?"

I closed my eyes as a shudder rolled through me. "This is my fault."

"What? No, it's not." Misha's response was quick, almost too quick. "This is *not* your fault."

Feeling the burn travel up my throat, I shook my head.

"But it is. I got caught off guard by Clay and bled all over the place, Misha. I used my *grace* when I should've just run—"

"If you hadn't used your *grace*, you could've died." Misha's warm fingers touched my cheeks. "I could've died. You protected yourself. You did everything you could do."

Opening my eyes, I met his gaze. Under the porch light, his eyes were pools of midnight blue. "Why do you always have to sound so logical?"

Misha lowered his head so we were eye level as his thumbs slid over my cheekbones. "Because you're always so illogical."

A ragged laugh parted my laugh. "That's a fair point."

"A fair point is—"

The sudden eruption of tingles along the nape of my neck and between my shoulder blades stole my breath. Squeezing the blades until the handles imprinted on my flesh, I whispered, "They're coming."

Misha lowered his hands and faced the driveway. "Get back."

This time I listened, taking a few steps away to give him space. Misha was about to shift into his true form, and I couldn't take my eyes away from him when he did. I'd never been able to, and I wished I'd seen the actual moment Zayne had shifted.

Misha's pale, pinkish skin was the first thing to change. It deepened in hue as his skin hardened, becoming a deep slate gray. His hands bent into claws sharp enough to cut through stone. Bold horns sprouted between the mess of reddish-brown curls. The bones of his shoulders shifted under the skin and the blades protruded out. Wings formed, spreading out behind him on either side.

I'd be right. Misha was huge, but Zayne was even bigger.

He looked over his shoulder at me, and I saw that his face had changed. Nostrils had flattened into thin slits. His mouth had widened, giving room to fangs that could tear through flesh and metal. Only those eyes remained the same: Warden blue.

"You going to listen to me for once and go into the house?" he asked, his voice thicker, richer, now.

I snorted. "And let you have all the fun of killing demons alone? Ha. No."

"There's something wrong with you, something terribly wrong." He turned back to the driveway, and I grinned despite all of this. "What if there are more humans?"

My skin chilled as my grin faded. "I can do it."

"Just try to keep it under control, Trin."

I knew what he was referencing. "Sure thing, boss."

The sound of pounding feet echoed up the driveway and Misha jumped, landing in a crouch several feet from the steps. My breath caught as something bulky raced under the floodlight, and I saw it.

Dear God, it was a Nightcrawler.

I was stunned as I recognized the moonstone-colored skin. I'd never seen one in person. Only in the texts we read in school, alongside normal things like English and calculus. Like Ravers, Nightcrawlers weren't supposed to be topside, on Earth, because they couldn't remotely blend in with humans. Their venom was toxic, paralyzing its victims within minutes, sometimes even less. This one was too far away for me to see the details of its face, even with the bright lights, but I was thinking that was a blessing.

They were notoriously ugly.

Misha lifted off the ground, but I could be faster. Cocking back my arm, I focused and the world around me fell away. I let the blade fly.

It struck true, driving deep into the Nightcrawler's chest before Misha could even take flight.

The Nightcrawler's steps faltered as it let out a roar of pain and fury, a sound so horrific it rattled my insides. Flames erupted from its chest, encompassing its body within seconds.

Iron was deadly to a demon and striking one in a vital place, like the chest, rendered them pretty damn useless immediately.

My iron blade clattered onto the driveway, settling in a pile of demon dust.

Landing a foot from where the Nightcrawler had been, Misha looked back at me. "You can't see me if I step one foot to the left, but you nailed that bastard in the blink of an eye."

Another Nightcrawler appeared at the edge of the flood-light.

"This one is mine." Misha took off, his wings cutting wide through the air. A second later, he crashed into the Night-crawler, knocking it several feet back, into the darkness and the void I couldn't see through.

I hurried to my blade and snatched it up, ignoring how warm the metal was. I became very still, scanning the darkness as I heard the grunts echoing from where Misha was fight-ing the Nightcrawler. How many more might there be that made it past the Wardens on the walls? A trickle of fear in-vaded my blood, but I ignored it, pushing it down so I didn't give in. Fear could be useful. It could hone the senses, but it could also overwhelm. It was a dangerous, fine line to walk, and I wasn't willing to walk it at the moment.

Something shifted to my right, moving too fast in my pe-ripheral vision for me to focus. I spun just in time as a tall, lithe form rushed me. It looked human. Beautiful like an angel, a gorgeous woman whose beauty surely had lured many a man and woman to some terrible fate.

An Upper Level demon.

I caught sight of her yellowish eyes as her mouth gaped open, jaw unhinging in the most unnatural way as she let out a low growl that reminded me of a very large, very angry cat. Fine hair rose all over my body.

I darted to the left, but she was fast—faster than anything I'd ever faced. A whoosh of air whirled around me as she grabbed a handful of my dress and tossed me aside. I slammed into the side of the porch. Bright bursts of lights dotted my vision as I scrambled to my feet, still holding the blades.

The demon was on me in a nanosecond, grabbing my shoulder and pulling me toward her. I had no idea what she planned to do, and I didn't wait to find out.

I let instinct take over. I twisted around, catching the surprise flickering across her face a second before I kicked. My foot connected with the side of her pretty face, snapping her head back with a sickening crack. She wheeled around, spinning back toward me, her head hanging at a very unnatural angle, and her neck…

"Dude," I whispered, eyes going wide. "Your neck is superbroken."

She let out a huffing laugh. "That wasn't very nice of you."

It was a sight I wouldn't be able to carve out of my memories for many years to come.

The female demon shifted, her skin turning a shade of deep orange. Her wings unfurled, and for a brief moment, I allowed myself to be struck by how much Upper Level demons looked like Wardens. Then I shot forward—

A clawed hand thrust through her chest, sending inky, dark blood spitting into the air. The hand jerk back and the demon staggered sideways. Surprise turned to horror as she looked down at herself.

"I think that was your heart," I said.

The female demon lifted her chin and then burst into flames, incinerated on the spot.

I lifted my gaze to where Misha stood, wiping his hand on the black ceremonial pants. "That was gross."

"You didn't just have your hand inside her."

"Well, I'm smart enough to let the blades do their job."

"More like you need blades because you don't have these bad mamajamas." Misha wiggled his bloodstained fingers at me. "And didn't I tell you—"

The ground trembled as something large and heavy landed behind Misha. I caught the glimpse of black wings and then Misha had ahold of my arm, pulling me along behind him as we raced back up the steps and into the house.

If something was making Misha run, then it was bad, really bad. I looked over my shoulder as we crossed the porch, and all I saw was a black form slowly coming up the steps, strolling as one would in a park—

Misha shoved me into the foyer, letting go of my arm as he spun, slamming the door shut behind him.

I faced him. "What was th—?"

The steel door blew off its hinges, flying backward and slamming into Misha. I shouted, starting toward him as he crashed into the wall. The door shattered on impact. Misha collapsed onto the floor. Reaching his side, I shifted the blades into one hand and grabbed him by the arm as I looked up and froze.

Inky, oily darkness filed the ruined doorway, licking over the walls with thick tendrils. A wave of heat followed as I let go of Misha's arm and straightened.

I'd never seen anything like it. I'd never even heard of anything like it.

The smoky blackness whipped out, striking me in the midsection. Lifted off my feet, I flew backward and hit the floor in the hallway. Rolling into a wall, I lost my grip on one of the blades. Stunned and disorientated, I struggled to my feet as the mass filled the foyer.

Letting instinct take over, I took aim and the dagger flew, going for the center of the mass.

The darkness blinked out of existence and my blade impaled the wall behind where it had been. A startled heartbeat later, the mass appeared directly in front of me.

"Holy shit," I whispered.

The thing took form rapidly. One second it was nothing but a collection of pulsing, thrumming shadows and then it was a man staring down at me, eyes golden and lips curved into a cruel little smile.

"Hello there," he said. "I've been looking for you."

I swung, but he caught my arm with one hand and slammed his fist into the center of my chest, knocking the air out of me and my feet out from under me. I skidded backward, past the offices and into the kitchen, crashing into the bar stools.

The power of my *grace* wiggled alive, but I fought it back as I wheezed for air. Spinning around, I grabbed a bar stool as I felt the heat hit my veins. I couldn't let the demon know what I was. I *couldn't*—

Misha was coming down the hallway with one hand on the wall, still in his Warden form.

The Upper Level demon turned to Misha, and I swung the stool as hard as I could.

It never connected.

One hand shot out, and the demon caught the leg of the stool. He looked over his shoulder at me and smiled. The scent of burning wood filled the kitchen. A second later the stool went up in flames, becoming dust in a heartbeat.

"Jesus," I whispered, jerking my arm back. This demon could control fire.

"Not quite, darling."

Screw not tapping into the *grace*. I spread my arms, letting the warmth in the pit of my stomach grow.

"Do it!" Misha shouted as something heavy hit the kitchen door and landed in the kitchen, the impact like an earthquake. Without looking, I knew in my bones it was Zayne, and he was about to get the show of his life—

Everything happened so fast, too quickly for me to react.

Something akin to recognition flickered over the Upper Level's demon's face when it locked eyes with Zayne. Then it spun and shot toward Misha. It crashed into him and then they were both in the air, flying back toward the front entrance.

I shot forward, chasing after them as panic snuffed out the fire building inside me. My feet slipped over the shattered hardwoods and I tripped over the broken door as I rushed toward the front door.

"Misha!"

Zayne caught me, his warm hand heavy on my shoulders. "Trinity—"

"No! Get Misha!" I struggled against Zayne's hold, straining to break free. "Let me go! We have to—"

"It's too late."

"No!" I screamed, kicking back and hitting his legs. "Let me go!"

"I can't." His arms folded around me, drawing me against his chest. "I can't let them have you. I can't. They're already gone."

I stopped fighting, staring at the sky, unable to see the stars as horror dawned. Zayne was right. Misha was gone, into the night, into the darkness.

18

I sat on the couch, knees pressed together and my hands clasped in my lap. I was still wearing the borrowed dress.

It was ruined.

The front of the dress was torn over my knees. Soot and demon blood dotted the bodice and waist. I needed to change and shower, because I felt like there was a layer of grime and gore covering me, but I couldn't leave until the group that had left to search for Misha came back.

A huge group had gone, including Dez and Zayne. Even Matthew had joined them, and now Nicolai and Thierry were in a corner of the room, speaking in low voices. Jada had arrived with Ty once the all clear had been sounded. She sat beside me, her nervous glances bouncing between Ty and me. She'd given up on trying to talk to me about half an hour ago. I was strung too tight to form words.

"What happened? I don't understand what happened," Peanut repeated over and over as he drifted near the couch. I'd already explained to him what I knew, but he still didn't understand, because none of it seemed real.

The Upper Level demon had taken Misha. Anger was a storm in my gut, a fury directed at Thierry and Matthew and everyone in the world, but mostly at myself, because I could've done something to stop this. If I had used my *grace* instead of fighting it, I would've been able to stop this demon before he took Misha.

But instead, like all the damn times before, I had done what had been expected of me. I'd hidden my true power. Just like I had when my mom was murdered.

It was more than my inaction. This demon, he'd come for me.

My fingers curled around my knees as I closed my eyes. If something happened to Misha... God, I would never be able to forgive myself. I would never—

Voices from the front of the house snapped me out of my thoughts. My eyes opened and I was on my feet, coming to stand beside Nicolai.

Zayne and Dez entered first, in their human form, and behind them was Matthew. The moment my gaze met Matthew's, I knew—they hadn't found Misha.

Dez reached me first, his gaze somber. Sympathy etched into his handsome features as he placed his hand on my shoulder. "I'm sorry."

"He's not dead," I said, breathing deeply as I stepped out of his grasp. "I know he's not dead."

Dez glanced at Zayne and then to where Thierry and Nicolai stood. They didn't understand that I would know if Misha was dead. The bond would tell me if he died, and I hadn't felt that.

I turned to Thierry. "Misha is still alive."

He nodded and then focused on the group. "Did you find anything?"

"We did," Zayne answered. "About two miles from here there was a large passenger van on the side of the road. The driver was still there, but he was dead."

"Human?" Nicolai asked.

Zayne nodded. "Dead. Throat slit. We took care of it."

Taking care of it meant they most likely got rid of the van and the body.

"There was nothing else," Matthew said wearily, sitting beside Jada as I stood in the center of the room. "Nothing that told us if they belonged to the church, but it would be safe to assume that they did."

That didn't make sense to me. "Demons are manipulative, but there were Nightcrawlers with them. How in the world would the demons have been able to hide them?"

"They may never have seen them," Zayne answered. "They could've traveled here separately, but I recognized the demon who took Misha." His stare flickered from me to his clan leader. "I've seen him before in DC. Engaged him a couple of times. He's a fast one, strong, and can control fire, which he usually uses for the perfect distraction to make his escape. His name is Bael."

Bael?

My knees felt weak. Bael wasn't just another ancient, powerful demon.

"Bael?" Jada asked, looking around. "Everyone just got superquiet. I get that he's an Upper Level demon, but I sense there's more?"

Wardens that weren't being trained were given only a cursory education in demonology. They didn't get all the gory details.

"Bael is a King of Hell," Nicolai explained. "Back in the

old days, he used to roam topside as a false god. One of our Wardens first saw him around January, but Bael didn't want to engage. We thought he was in the city messing with one of the politicians. Bael is known for his ability to sway minds. Every time we saw him, he kept his distance, giving us a Hell of a chase through the city. Like Zayne said, he uses fire to help make his escape. Burned down a ton of buildings in the process, but we haven't seen him... Hell, in three months?"

"The last time I saw him was at the end of March," Zayne answered. "He was the last Upper Level demon I saw in the city."

"Do you think he followed your clan here?" Ty asked, standing behind Jada. He placed his hands on her shoulders.

Nicolai didn't answer for a long moment. "Anything is possible, but if he did, why would they wait until now to attack? We've been here nearly a week."

Part of me couldn't believe it had only been a week. It felt like so much longer.

"The Wardens at the wall were killed in a way that suggests they didn't see it coming," Dez explained, crossing his arms. "All of them were shot in their human form, direct hits to the chest or the head."

"What happened tonight has to be connected to Clay," I said, shaking my head. "And the Ravers? We know that you never see them without an Upper Level demon near. They were right outside these walls, and that poor human guy Wayne was killed by an Upper Level demon. And the attacks on the other communities? They were searching—"

"We are looking into every possible connection," Thierry cut in before I could say what they could've been searching for.

"I know Clay was an utter dickhead, but working with demons? How would he have been in contact with them?" Ty thrust a hand over his short hair. "I don't know about that, Trin."

But some Wardens *did* work with demons.

My gaze slid to Zayne and I felt my stomach pitch. Zayne had worked with demons and had even suggested that he didn't believe all demons were evil. An uncomfortable heaviness settled over me, and I stared at him while the rest of the group talked about upping the security at the wall and sending out scouting groups more regularly in case there were plans for a second attack.

None of this had started until he arrived. Clay hadn't tried to attack me until they'd been here for a few days, but why would Zayne or any of them be behind this? It wasn't like they knew what I was.

At least, that was what I thought.

My heart started pounding in my chest. The DC clan knew I could see ghosts and spirits, and Zayne realized I was stronger than I looked, faster than he'd expected. I hadn't exactly tried to hide that from him, and the whole time he'd been here, he seemed to be everywhere I was.

Zayne slowly looked over at me, his striking face unreadable as our gazes connected. A chill skated down my arms, leaving tiny bumps behind.

If I was any bit right, I still didn't know why Zayne or his clan would be behind this, which was why I didn't say anything. I might be impulsive, but I was smart enough to not suggest such a thing without hard-core evidence.

But was there already evidence?

Zayne was missing a part of his soul, and that could be reason enough to do evil things.

Jada had fallen asleep on the couch and the DC clan had retreated with Thierry and Matthew into the office. Ty had carried Jada upstairs to one of the extra bedrooms and I'd followed, going into my room. I finally stripped off the ruined dress, leaving it on the floor of the bathroom, a crumpled mess of gauze and cotton.

I never wanted to see it again.

I swooped down and picked up the ruined dress. Balling it up, I shoved it into the trash can and then backed up, looking down at myself.

My knees looked angry and spotted, like a strawberry. Twisting at the waist, I saw that my elbows did, too. That wasn't bad. Not at all, because it could've been so significantly much worse.

What was happening to Misha right now?

Horrible, horrific things.

I couldn't process what happened. This wasn't a nightmare. This was real. Misha had been taken, and if the demon didn't happen to know who or what Misha was to me, he would be killed.

And if Bael knew, and that was why he'd grabbed Misha?

Then there was a chance that he'd keep Misha alive. I had to think that he took Misha to use him as collateral. At least that was what I hoped, because that meant there was a chance I could get Misha back.

Steam filled the space and I stepped into the shower, hissing as the hot water pelted the raw spots on my skin. The water felt like it was only a few degrees short of scalding, but it did nothing to ease the coldness that had settled deep in my bones and marrow.

I showered in a hurry, watching the sooty water circle the drain. By the time I stepped out of the tub on shaky legs, I was exhausted. I didn't stop to look at myself again as I dried off and changed into the clothing I'd brought into the bathroom with me. The leggings were a little hard to get on with my skin still damp, adding to my angry frustration. The shirt was easier, thank God, and when I stormed out of the bathroom, I'd already broken a sweat. All I wanted to do was lie down, but there was no time for that.

Peanut was hovering by my bed as I stalked toward the bedroom door. "What are you doing, Trinnie?"

"Going back downstairs to see what they're doing to get Misha back," I told him, opening the door and stepping into the quiet hallway.

Peanut followed me to the closed office door on the first floor. I knocked and Thierry's muffled voice answered. Opening the door, I found that everyone was still in his office. The DC Wardens had found shirts, replacing the ones ruined when they'd shifted. Thierry was behind his desk and Matthew leaned against the edge of it, face weary.

Thierry didn't look surprised to see me as I entered the office. "What is it, Trinity?"

"I want to know how we're going to get Misha back," I said, stopping behind where Nicolai and Dez were seated. I didn't look at Zayne, but I knew he was standing by the window. I kept my gaze trained on Thierry.

He leaned back, the chair creaking under his weight. "We're sending more scouts out in the morning," he said.

"What if they're no longer nearby?" I asked. "When the scouts went out earlier, they saw no sign of Misha or the demon."

"That's a good question," Peanut chimed in.

"That doesn't mean they haven't holed up somewhere," Matthew reasoned. "We will leave no square foot unchecked."

That...that wasn't good enough for me.

I wanted people out there right now, looking for him. "You know what Misha means to me," I said, struggling to keep my voice level. "He's still alive, but the longer we wait—"

"Why do you think he's still alive?" Zayne asked from where he stood, drawing my gaze. "I hope he is and that would be great news, Trinity, but demons don't keep Wardens alive unless..."

"They want to play with their prey first?" I finished for him, feeling my stomach twist. "Or use them to draw out more Wardens? I know what demons do to Wardens."

"I hope they're not torturing Misha," Peanut whispered. "He's always so freaked out when he knows I'm around, but I like the dude."

Nicolai twisted around, facing me. "I know this may be hard to hear, but the likelihood of him being alive—"

"He's not dead," I said. "I would kn—"

"We're not giving up on him," Thierry said, interrupting me. "We are still going to look for him."

A *but* hung in the air between us. A *but* that meant they would look for him, but they wouldn't endanger other Wardens to do so. *But* meant that, in the end, Misha was disposable, because if he was killed, the bond would be broken but would be reassigned by my father.

But meant that Misha was as good as dead.

"We're leaving in the morning to return home," Nicolai was saying. "We will look for him in DC, as well."

"So, you've got your reinforcements and that's it?" I snapped, unable to stop myself. "You come here asking for our help, but when we give it, you're just going to bail?"

"You tell them, Trinnie!" Peanut shoved his fist into the air.

"Trinity," Thierry warned.

"We're actually not getting reinforcements." Zayne spoke up once more. "After the massive size of this attack, there's no way the community can afford to send any new trainees with us."

"Well, that sucks," I grumbled, and he cocked his head. "Sorry to hear that."

"Wow," Peanut murmured. "You could sound a little more convincing."

Then it struck me.

Zayne had said he recognized the demon, so there was a good chance that this demon *would* be taking Misha to DC. And now that they weren't getting reinforcements, they still had their own problem to deal with—the problem of something killing demons and Wardens.

Nothing against Zayne or his clan—I was not going to rely on them searching for Misha, and I couldn't go to DC by myself. I'd never been, and I had no idea where to look. Add into that the problems with my vision? I'd need help.

"I want to go to DC," I said, and got nowhere quick.

Peanut gasped.

"Absolutely not," Thierry said, placing his hands on the desk. "That is not going to happen."

I ignored him, turning to Nicolai. "I can help you."

Nicolai looked visibly uncomfortable as he met my gaze. "Trinity, I know you're worried about Misha, but—"

"I *am* worried about him. He's like a brother to me, and I'm not okay with letting everyone else look for him while I stay sheltered here," I said, ignoring the way Thierry's jaw hardened.

"I know you're trained and you can hold your own," Zayne began, walking away from the window. "And I'm sorry for what has happened to Misha. We will look for him. I promise you that. But we don't have the resources to babysit you while you run around DC looking for him."

"*Babysit* me?" I laughed, my hands curling into fists. "Are you serious?"

"Oh, no." Peanut popped his hands on his hips. "Boy is about to get a smackdown."

"I don't think he meant to say it the way it came across," Dez said.

"Actually, I did mean it that way," Zayne said.

"I didn't ask for your opinion," I said.

"I'm freely giving it to you," he replied.

"While Zayne could have phrased that much better, he is right," Dez continued, his voice rising above ours. "We have a significant issue at home and without reinforcements—"

"Without reinforcements, you and I both know you won't be going out of your way to look for Misha, and there's a good chance this demon will take him to DC. You all said you'd seen him there." My heart started pounding as I turned to Nicolai, who would ultimately have to agree for me to be able to go with them. "You have a problem, and I can help you better than any Warden can."

"Trinity." Thierry started to rise. "Don't—"

Matthew reached behind him, placing his hand on Thierry's arm, halting him.

"I have no choice," I said, voice thready. "I will not stand by and let something happen to Misha when I can do something about it."

"Oh, no…" Peanut drifted to the ceiling. "Oh, no, Trinnie, what are you gonna do?"

I was going to show them exactly how I could help them.

Thierry saw it written on my face as I took a step back. He lifted his hands as if he could stop me. "Your father—"

"I don't care what he thinks. You can't stop me, Thierry. Neither can he. I'm eighteen and there is no law that supersedes the fact that I'm an adult," I said, welcoming the warm glow sparking alive deep in my stomach. "I love you—I love both of you, but I have to do something."

Then I let the *grace* take over.

19

Warm, heady power lit up my veins and turned the corners of my vision from darkness to light, and I saw the exact moment those in the room saw that I wasn't who they thought I was. For some reason, I focused on Zayne.

His eyes widened as he took a step back from the glow that was starting to radiate from my skin. His arms unfolded to hang limp at his sides.

"What in the Hell…?" someone whispered.

"More like the opposite," I said as I extended my right hand and felt the whirl of white fire erupt and swirl down my arm, forming the sword that had been very much like the one the statue of the battle angel had held.

"Holy smackeroos," Peanut whispered from somewhere above me.

The sword was heavy and warm in my palm, spitting and dripping white fire as I pulled my gaze away from the awe-struck expression that had planted itself on Zayne's face to those of the older Wardens from DC. The glow from my *grace* danced over their faces.

"I can help you defeat whatever thing is killing Wardens," I said, fully aware of the fact that Thierry and Matthew looked like they were seconds away from having a heart attack. "This sword can cut down a fully shifted Warden within a heartbeat, leaving nothing behind. The same for a demon—*any* demon." I lifted the sword, bringing it near my chest, causing both Wardens to flinch. I turned my head to where Zayne stood. "So, as you can see, I do not need a babysitter. You all need *me*."

"That's enough." Thierry's voice was weary as he sat back down in his chair.

"Is it?" I challenged, scanning the room. "Because I just want to make sure everyone in here realizes I'm not a liability. I'm an asset."

"I'm confident everyone in here now realizes that," Matthew said, sighing. "Please, Trinity, pull it back. I think you're starting to frighten them."

Smirking, I drew in a deep breath and forced my muscles to relax. The white fire around the sword flared and then flickered before the sword collapsed into itself, leaving a fine shimmer of golden dust that evaporated before it touched the floors. I knew the exact moment they could no longer see what existed in me when the corners of my vision returned to the vague, muddy darkness.

Feeling itchy in my own skin, I crossed my arms and lifted my chin. "You help me find Misha and I'll help you deal with your problem."

"What...?" Zayne cleared his throat, and when I looked at him, I inherently knew he had no idea what I was. No one could fake the shock settling into his face. That didn't mean I trusted any of them entirely, but he truly hadn't known. "What are you?"

"She's a Trueborn," Thierry answered, sounding more tired than I'd ever heard. "Half human—"

"Half angel?" Nicolai finished, his eyes wide as he stared at me with a mixture of wonder and…something else, something far more potent. Fear. "You're a nephilim."

"I prefer to be called Trueborn," I said. "Nephilim is so… outdated."

Peanut snorted, reminding me that he was still lingering in the room.

"How?" Zayne reached out, clasping the back of an empty chair. "How is this possible? I thought that…"

"You thought that all Trueborns were gone? Hunted out of existence by demons and Wardens alike and nothing but myth and legend?" Matthew supplied for him. "That is true."

"But…but she's standing right here." Zayne took a step toward me and then stopped short. "How?"

"She is the last of her kind," Matthew explained. "And we've been charged with keeping her hidden and safe in our community since she was a young child. That is how she's lasted this long."

"That's not the only reason," I said, feeling the wet warmth start to drip from my nose. Reaching up, I wiped my hand under my nose. When I looked down, my finger was dotted with blood. I sighed. "It's why I've been trained."

"And…you've just been kept here?" Zayne asked.

"Until my father summons me." I shrugged as Matthew strode toward me, pulling a handkerchief from his pocket. "End times, I guess, or something like that. But I've been safe because of Misha."

Matthew slowly lifted his hand, making sure I saw him before he dabbed the handkerchief under my nose. "Oh, Trinity," he murmured, handing me the fabric.

"Why is she bleeding?" Zayne demanded.

"It's the *grace*," Matthew said, stepping back. "She's always had nosebleeds afterward and it weakens her. Trinity may be a walking, breathing myth, but she is still half-human. Using the *grace* is hard on the human side of her. She'll be curled up asleep somewhere soon."

I smiled a little at that, because he made it sound like I was a child who tuckered herself out.

"I think I know Misha's role in this," Dez said, speaking for the first time since I'd decided to do the whole show-and-tell routine. "If I remember correctly, when there were many more Trueborns, they were...bonded to Wardens. Their strength helps... How do I say it? Cancel out some of the human setbacks? And vice versa? The angelic side powers the Warden, makes them stronger and faster?"

I nodded. "He's my Protector. If you take me with you and help me look for him, I will help you with your problem. I will stay with you as long as it takes, even after we find Misha."

"That's how you know he's not dead," Zayne said. "Because you're bonded to him?"

"Yes. I'd feel it." I put my fist to my chest, crumpling the handkerchief in my grasp. "And I haven't felt it. Not yet. Until I feel that, I cannot give up on him. I won't. Would you?"

A muscle flexed along Zayne's jaw as he looked away.

"Unbelievable," Nicolai murmured. "Who all knows what she is?"

"Very few," answered Matthew, dropping down in the unoccupied seat. "If it were to get out, demons would be trying to breach these walls every day to get to her. Demons think she's human unless they smell her blood."

"That's why you all reacted the way you did to her blood," Zayne said, cursing under his breath. "They can sense it and it will tell them she's half-angel? Hell. They wouldn't be able to stop themselves from coming after her. She's the closest thing to Heaven that they'd ever get to."

"Yeah, and they tend to get a wee bit nom-nom," I said, shivering. "Demons believe that if they consume a Trueborn, they'll be able to enter Heaven."

"Holy Hell," whispered Dez. "Is that true?"

"We have no idea," Matthew said. "But the demons believe it, and as long as they believe it, it's a threat."

"And not the only one," Thierry said. "Trueborn blood, bone, hair and even their muscles are coveted for incantations and spells. Every part of her is considered valuable in the dark market."

The dark market was sort of like the black market for organ donors…except the dark market was frequented by witches and demons and a whole slew of supernatural baddies.

"I'm special." I lifted my shoulders again. "Very special."

Zayne stared at me, opening his mouth and then closing it.

"Is that why you can see ghosts?" Nicolai asked.

"Oh, now people care about seeing me?" Peanut sighed dramatically from his position near the ceiling fan.

I shook my head at him. "Yes, it's because angels can see spirits and the souls of those who have died. And other humans that can do it, they have watered-down angelic blood. Probably from a great-great-great-grandmother times a thousand who got a little freaky with an angel."

"I think it goes without saying that you must not tell anyone what Trinity is, not even your other clansmen," Thierry said, and something flickered across Zayne's face, like he was putting a puzzle together in his head and he'd found the missing piece. "We were charged with keeping her safe until she is needed—"

"And I'm needed now," I told Thierry.

"I know Misha is like a brother to you, but you cannot expose yourself to demons," Thierry tried again, speaking softly. "You going after him is a risk that he wouldn't even want you to take, and this could be a trap."

"I don't care," I said. "I could've stopped that demon. I should've used my *grace* to do so, but I didn't. I can control it. You know that. I cannot sit around and do nothing, Thierry. I'm sorry. And if you forbid it or forbid them helping me, I swear to God, I will leave on my own. You will not be able to stop me. You know that."

Thierry did know that.

Sitting back, he ran his palm over his face as he slowly shook his head.

"This was coming," Matthew said to him. "We knew this deep down. She's right. We can't stop her. Only her father can."

"Who is her father?" Zayne asked.

"You don't want to know," Thierry muttered under his breath, and I snorted at that. They really didn't. He lifted his head as he dropped his hand. "Trinity is a weapon, and whatever problem you're having in DC, she will be able to help you. That is true. But are you willing to help her?"

My breath caught as understanding roared through me. Thierry was relenting. Holy crap, he was.

"Yes." It was Zayne who answered, surprising me. "Yes, we will help her. You're right," he then said to me. "I couldn't walk away from this, either, if this was someone I knew and cared about. So, I understand that. I do."

Feeling a little bad for being suspicious of him, I ducked my chin. "Thank you."

Nicolai's gaze shifted from me to Zayne and then to Thierry. "Yes, we will help her."

I almost fainted, right then and there. Part of me couldn't believe this was happening. They would help me find Misha and I...I was leaving the community, really leaving it, for the first time since I was a small child. We'd be leaving in the morning and I would need to pack.

I was still stunned when Peanut spoke. "I'm going with you."

Surprised by Peanut's statement, I forgot that I was around other people when I turned to him. "What?"

Peanut was fully corporal, his eyes wide. "I'm going with you. To DC."

"But you haven't left the community since you came here with me."

"Who...who is she talking to?" asked Dez.

"Probably Peanut." Thierry sighed. "He's a ghost."

"You have a ghost here?" Nicolai's voice was strangely pitched.

"Yes," answered Matthew. "Apparently he followed her here about ten years ago..."

As Matthew explained who and what Peanut was, I focused on my ghostie roommate. "Are you sure?"

"Yes." He nodded. "I'm positive. If you're leaving, I'm going."

"But I'll be coming back," I told him.

A look of doubt crossed his pale face. "If you're leaving, I'm going with you. Don't even try to argue with me. You know it's pointless. I'll just follow you, anyway, and haunt you. You know I will."

I did. He would totally do that.

"Okay." I turned back to everyone. "Well, apparently you're getting a two-for-one special. Peanut's coming with."

Saying goodbye to Jada and Ty the following morning was harder than I ever could have imagined, even if it was temporary.

"I wish we were going with you," Jada said, her beautiful vivid blue eyes glimmering. "I'm going to be so stressed out with you being out there and me stuck here."

"Don't," I told her, squeezing her hands. "You know I can take care of myself and I'm not going to be alone."

"I know, but that doesn't mean we're going to worry any less." Ty reached over and placed his hand on my shoulder. "You promise to call us every day."

I nodded. "Of course."

"FaceTime," Jada said. "You have to FaceTime us even though I know you hate it."

"I will even though I completely hate it," I said, laughing. "I won't be gone that long, and I'll be back before you know it, with Misha."

"Yes." Jada squeezed my hands. "With Misha."

Jada and Ty hung out while I finished packing, which consisted of me throwing all the leggings and tops, along with a few lightweight sweaters, I could pack in an oversize luggage. It was just the start of summer, so I figured there could still be some cool nights. Upon Jada's suggestion, I added a few pairs of jeans. After they left, I shoved all the undies and bras I owned into a small suitcase, because I really didn't know how long I was going to be. I was trying to be optimistic, but even with the DC clan's help, it wasn't like I was going to show up and find Misha immediately, and that was if—

"Stop," I whispered, closing my eyes. Misha was still alive, and he would stay that way. I refused to believe anything else.

Opening my eyes, I zipped up the bag and then grabbed my laptop, shoving that into a tote along with my glasses and the satchel with my blades in them. Then I went to my nightstand and picked up the photograph of my mom and her paperback. Carefully I tucked them away in a tote bag, placing them in between the sweaters that didn't fit in the suitcase so they'd be safe. I was scanning my room for anything else I might need when there was a knock on my open door. I turned, finding Zayne.

A mixed bag of emotions roared through me upon seeing him. Suspicion lingered, but it was overshadowed by anticipation and something sharper, heavier.

"May I come in?"

I nodded. "I'm almost done. Just making sure I'm not forgetting anything."

"It's okay. We have time." Zayne sat on the edge of my bed, his pale blue gaze fixed on me. "I didn't sleep well last night. I'm sure you didn't, either."

"I slept maybe an hour." My fingers lingered on the strap of my tote.

He did look tired. Faint shadows had blossomed under his eyes. "Nicolai, Dez and I were up, discussing how we were going to do this without letting the rest of the clan know."

I sat beside him and placed the tote on the floor. "So, what's the plan?"

"Keeping what you are a secret is going to be too hard at the compound," he said, scratching one hand through his loose hair. "It's going to be hard enough to explain your presence in the city, but since I...I haven't been living at the compound for several months now, we figured it would be best if you stayed with me."

"What?" I gasped, not at the fact that I'd be staying with him alone—and that was a whoa, big deal—but more for the fact he was living by himself. "You're not living at the compound?"

"No."

"Why? That's so dangerous, being by yourself. Demons can sense what you are," I said, donning my Captain Obvious hat.

"The place I have is in a good neighborhood and so far has

been relatively demon free." He smiled. "It'll be easier and will hopefully delay explaining your presence."

"But how are we going to delay it? If we're looking for Misha and this thing you guys are worried about, the whole clan will be involved, yes?"

He angled his body toward me. "The whole clan can't be involved in looking for Misha. Not if we need to hide what you are. Dez is going to help, but it's going to be mostly you and me. That's the best option."

I mulled that over. I really didn't have a choice, and it made sense. "Okay. That will work." When Zayne didn't respond, I looked at him. He was staring at me. "What?"

"Now I know why you smelled like ice cream to me."

I flushed. "That was random."

A quick smile appeared and then vanished. "You have to know that Heaven has a smell, right? That for everyone it's different, but it's always something that they enjoy or makes them feel good. My favorite food is ice cream."

"It is?"

"You sound so surprised."

"I guess I am. I don't know. I picture your favorite food being steak and potatoes."

"That would be my second favorite food," he replied. "But now I understand why I smelled that on you when you were hurt."

"It was my blood," I finished for him. "I didn't know that. I mean, I knew demons could smell it."

"But you didn't know that the light has a scent?"

I shook my head, thinking I'd never smelled anything all the times I'd seen the light. "And you know this how?"

"Whenever the Alphas come to see us, there's always this thick, golden light that comes first. I'm not even sure it is light, because it reminds me of liquid. Whenever I've been around them, I've smelled it." He shook his head. "So much makes sense now, and I almost can't believe I didn't figure it out."

"How could you, though? Trueborns are thought to be things of the past." I rested my hands on my thighs. "I don't want you to treat me differently now that you know what I am."

Zayne laughed softly under his breath. "I'm not sure I can do that."

"Why?"

"Because I know what you are, Trinity."

"So?"

"So?" He laughed again. "Were you taking it easy on me the day in the training room?"

Pleased by that question, I didn't even try to fight my grin. I was too tired to. "Actually, no. You're really good, but I'm just…"

"Better?"

I laughed a little under my breath. "Don't let it get you down too much. Even Misha—" I sucked in a breath and tried again. "Even he can't get the best of me."

His gaze flickered over my face. "I don't know what it's like to be bonded to someone you care about, but I do know what it's like to grow up with someone and then have them virtually vanish from your life."

"You do?"

Zayne nodded. "Not for the same reasons. Nothing like this, but it's hard being around someone almost every day and then having them not be a part of your life and…and have no idea what their life is like now."

I wanted to prod him for more information, but he rose from the bed.

"Ready?" Zayne asked quietly, extending his hand.

Turning from Zayne, I took one more look at my bedroom—at the bed, and the stars tacked to my ceiling, at the desk I rarely used, and the chair in the corner. A sudden sensation of uncertainty swept over me. I had told Jada and Ty that I wouldn't be gone long, but as I looked around my bedroom, I couldn't stop the feeling that this would be the last time I saw this room—that I was leaving and I wouldn't be returning.

Unsettled, I placed my hand in Zayne's and felt that jolt dance over my fingers as they closed around his. "Ready."

20

Due to the lack of sleep and the late start we got, because I had to make sure Peanut was with us—and he was—and because Thierry and Matthew had treated me like I imagined parents did when their child left for college, I ended up passing out thirty minutes into the drive. I tried to fight the lull of the humming SUV and the quietness inside the car, because where we were heading was someplace I'd never been and I wanted to see everything, but I lost the battle.

Trinity?

My brow pinched at the sound of my name breaking through the layers of sleep. I ignored it, because my bed was toasty. I snugged back down, and my...my bed shifted slightly under me. Weird.

"Trinity?" The voice came again, and the cobwebs of sleep started to clear. "We're here."

Something touched my cheek, catching the strands of hair resting there and tucking them behind my ear. I smacked at it, hitting nothing but my own face. Then my bed chuckled.

It *chuckled*.

Beds didn't do that.

"You sleep like the dead." A hand curled around my shoulder, gently shaking me. "Come on, Trinity, wake up, we're here."

We're here.

The two words cut through the haze of sleep. My eyes snapped open, and the moment my vision adjusted to the dim interior, I saw a leg encased in dark jeans—a thigh actually.

Oh my God. I hit a Defcon level of WTFery.

Jerking upright, I swung my wide gaze toward Zayne, whom I'd apparently been using as a pillow.

"Nice of you to finally join me. I was getting worried." Zayne watched me with his small, teasing half grin. "Especially when you started drooling."

I snapped out of the fog. "Drooling?"

Warmth entered those frosty eyes. "Just a little."

"I was not." I hastily wiped my mouth with the back of my hand.

The back of my hand was damp.

"Jerk," I muttered.

He chuckled and then nodded toward the front of the car. Dez and Nicolai were watching us from the front seats.

"Hi," Dez said, grinning.

"Hey," I grumbled, feeling my face heat. "So, we're here?"

Dez nodded.

"Perfect." I found the door handle and pulled, found that it was locked. I sighed heavily and waited for Dez to unlock the doors, and then was free. Stepping out of the car, I was ready to see Washington, DC, for the very first time and I saw—

Nothing but shadows.

What the...? I turned around. I expected to see the Washington Monument and buildings and people, and while I could hear horns honking, I saw...

Wait. We were in a parking garage, near a set of elevator bays. Duh.

The guys were out in a jiffy, unloading my suitcase and tote bag...and Peanut, who was sitting on my suitcase, unbeknownst to Zayne.

I blinked slowly. Peanut smiled so widely that he looked a little crazed as Zayne took my suitcase by the handle and rolled it...and Peanut...over to where I stood.

"You okay?" Zayne asked.

Peanut giggled creepily.

"Yeah, I'm...still out of it a little."

Zayne stopped, his gaze flickering from me to the suitcase. "Is it the ghost?"

"Yee-aah." I drew the word out, and Peanut clapped his hands together like a happy little seal.

"Do I want to know?" he asked.

"Nope." I walked to the back of the SUV and grabbed my tote bag. We parted ways with Dez and Nicolai, and I followed Zayne to the elevator doors. Zayne hit the last button and had to enter a code. I didn't see how many floors it was, but based on the way my ears popped halfway through the ride, I figured we were going high. The ride was smooth and quick, and when the elevator stopped, the doors slid open to reveal a huge room lit by sunlight streaming in through a wall of glass windows that appeared to be tinted, because the glare didn't knock me over.

Peanut hopped off the suitcase. "I'm off to investigate!"

I didn't say anything as he blinked out of existence.

"Come on." Zayne held the doors for me, and I shuffled inside, looking around and finding myself...thoroughly confused.

The floors were exposed cement, ceilings were high and large fans dropped from them, churning slowly. To my left was a kitchen area. A row of white cabinets was parted by a gas stovetop and stainless steel exhaust fan. There was a long, rectangular island, large enough to seat several people, but only two black, sturdy-looking metal stools sat on one side. Across from the kitchen area was a large sectional couch, wide enough for two Wardens to lie on side by side, and it sat in front of a large television. To the left of that was an open space. I could make out a punching bag and what appeared to be blue mats tucked against the wall, the kind that were in our training facilities back home. There were several closed doors and that…that was all.

Everything was very industrial, very bare.

"Are you sure you live here?" I asked, still surprised that Zayne was living on his own. It was just unheard of.

Zayne slid me a long, sideways glance. "Yes. Why?"

"Doesn't look like anyone lives here." I put my tote on the island.

"It has what I need." He walked to the fridge, opened the door and pulled out two bottles of water. He placed one of the bottles on the island and then he grabbed my luggage, rolling it behind him. "Follow me."

Taking the water bottle, I followed him across the wide room, looking for something that proved he lived here. Like a left-out pair of shoes or a magazine or a half-drank can of soda. There was nothing.

"This is one of the bathrooms. No shower in there, though." He nodded to our right as he led me toward the middle door. "This is the bedroom."

He opened the door and turned on a light. My gaze flicked from the floor-to-ceiling windows that were covered with blackout blinds to the large bed in the center, next to the nightstand. There was nothing else in the room. No dressers. No TV. Not even an area rug.

Walking past me, he opened one of the doors, revealing another bathroom while I was frozen just inside the bedroom. "This is the master bathroom. Has a shower and a tub."

The plastic of the water bottle crinkled beneath my fingers as I stared at the bed—the only bed I saw in this whole place. How was this going to work? Were we going to share a bed? An uncomfortable amount of warmth infused my body at the thought.

I shook my head, because there was no way Zayne intended that. This was the guy who'd jumped off me when I kissed him, and telling me I was beautiful and that I reminded him of a goddess did not erase that.

I stepped out of the bedroom doorway, into the room, as Zayne walked past me. I didn't see Peanut, but that didn't mean he wasn't around. I walked over to the windows. The closer I got, the more intense the glare was, but I peered out, seeing brick buildings across the street. I looked down—I'd been right about being on a high floor. Everything on the ground was a moving blob.

Turning from the windows, I faced Zayne. "So, what do we do now?"

"We rest," he said. "You have the bed and I'll take the couch."

I stared at him as he opened a linen closet and grabbed a pillow and a thin blanket. "Shouldn't we start looking for Misha?"

"If you know anything about demons, you know they're not that active during the afternoon." He tossed the blanket onto the back of the couch.

"But that doesn't mean we can't start looking for them."

"No, it doesn't, but you only got about an hour of sleep last night and another on the drive here," he pointed out.

"I'm fine. I'm wide awake." That wasn't exactly untrue. If I lay down, I probably would go back to sleep, but I wanted to get started.

And I wanted to see the city.

"I also barely got any sleep last night and, unlike you, I didn't have a comfortable leg to nap on," he reminded me, tossing the pillow onto the couch. "Look, you can sit around and chill for the next couple of hours or you can be smart and get some rest."

"You can get some rest and I can start looking for Misha—"

"Look for him where?" Zayne faced me then, brows raised. "Do you know how big this city is? How many people live in it? How many people work here and don't live here?" He fired off the questions at a rapid pace. "Do you know where demons hang out? Where you can typically find one?"

"Well, no, but—"

"There's no *but*, Trinity. You have no idea where to go." He shoved a hand through his hair, then clasped the back of his neck. "Look, I said I would help you look for Misha, and I will. I don't make promises I don't keep, but we're going to be smart about this, Trinity. We don't know if the demon that took Misha knows what you are, but if that demon does, he's going to be looking for you."

"Good," I snapped. "That makes my job so much easier, because this time, I will use my *grace*."

"You're not leaving this place without me, and if you attempt it, I'll know."

My eyes widened. "I'm a prisoner now?"

"You're a guest who will use common sense," he shot back. "So, you can feel like a prisoner or you can feel like a well-rested guest. Either way, I'm sleeping, because I'm going to need some sleep before we do what we're going to do this evening."

"And what is that?" Frustrated, I crossed my arms. "Do each other's hair and try out face masks?"

"Oh, will you braid my hair for me?" He lowered his hand and it closed into a fist at his side. He looked like he wanted to throttle me, and I knew I was being annoying, but this demon had Misha and I was supposed to take an afternoon siesta?

"Do you know what it feels like to know someone is in danger and to just stand by and do nothing?" I asked, feeling my throat thicken. "Do you?"

Zayne's expression softened as he stepped toward me. "Yes, I do know, Trinity. I know what it's like to be forced to watch someone you care about be hurt and be completely unable to do *anything* about it."

I snapped my mouth shut as his words got past my irritation.

"We may think we know each other, and I know you've heard stuff about me, but you don't know me. You don't know what I've experienced and what I haven't," he continued. "Just like I don't know all that you've been through. But what I do know about you is that you're strong and you're tough, and you're loyal. And I also know you're smart enough to realize that both of us need to be well rested so that we're prepared for anything."

I drew in a shaky breath, closing my eyes against the sudden burn of tears. "You're right," I admitted, pushing the tears back down. "And I'm…I'm sorry. I'm just…"

"You're worried." His voice was closer, and when I opened my eyes, he was not even a foot from me. I had no idea how he could move so quietly. I saw him lift his hand and catch a strand of my hair that had fallen forward. He tucked it behind my ear, his hand lingering. "I understand, Trinity. I really do."

My body took control. Closing my eyes, I pressed my cheek

against his warm palm. I shouldn't do that. I knew that, but there was something soothing about his touch, comforting. It was as if he was built simply for that, and that was a weird feeling to have.

"You are tired," he said. "Just rest for a couple of hours."

"Do I look that bad?" I asked.

"No. You look perfect."

I opened my eyes, and my gaze was snared by his. Something darkly possessive flickered across his face before he dropped his hand and took a step back.

Feeling off-kilter, I folded my arms over my chest. "Okay. So, we sleep and then...?"

"I know a person, and I can't believe I'm even considering this, but if anyone knows where Bael could be, it'll be him. He should be around by this evening. He doesn't exactly keep a normal schedule."

"Who is he? Another Warden?"

Zayne laughed again, the sound without much humor. "No. He's not a Warden. He's probably the biggest pain in my ass that has ever existed." Zayne paused. "Which means you'll probably get along with him."

21

I came awake with a gasp, jerking upright and coming face-to-face with Peanut...

Who was blowing on my face.

"What are you doing?" I asked, heart thumping.

"Making sure you aren't dead." He drifted to the other side of the bed. "Guess what?"

"What?" I shoved a chunk of hair out of my face as an unseen weight settled on my shoulders. I knew what that feeling meant. "Demons," I whispered, shoving the thick blanket off me and swinging my legs off the bed. "There are demons nearby."

"What?" Peanut screeched.

Launching off the bed, I raced to the bedroom door and threw it open. My bare feet skidded over the cool cement floors as I scanned the room for Zayne. I saw a rather large, still shape on the couch and I hurried around it.

Zayne was asleep on his back, his head turned toward the

back of the couch. One arm was under his head and the other hand rested in a loose fist on his chest.

His bare chest.

The gray blanket had pooled around his lean hips, and I really hoped he was not completely naked under there. I wouldn't think that he would be, considering that I was here, but most Wardens slept in their true form. It was how they got their deepest sleep, so it was strange to see Zayne sleeping like this.

"Zayne," I said, voice thick was sleep. "Wake up."

He didn't move.

I reached for him, gently touching his shoulder. There was an odd static charge that radiated up my fingers and made no sense. "Zayne—"

He moved so fast that I didn't even know what was happening until I was on my back and he was above me, one hand planted on my shoulder, pressing me down into the thick cushions of the couch. My wide-eyed gaze swung to his face, and I saw that his pupils were vertical.

"Jesus," I gasped, frozen.

It seemed to take a moment for him to recognize me and realize that he had me pinned underneath him. The pupils were first to shift back to normal, human-looking eyes. "Trinity, what are you doing?"

"What am I doing?" I blinked once and then twice. "You're asking me what I'm doing when you just flipped me in midair?"

"Yes." He was still above me, but his hand came off my shoulder, landing in the cushion next to my head. "I was asleep."

"I know." I dared to glance down and saw that he wasn't nude, thank baby gargoyles everywhere. He was wearing what appeared to be gray sweatpants. "I tried to wake you up. I called your name, but you didn't respond."

"Sorry," he grunted. "Not used to people being here."

"I can tell."

"What time is it?" He looked toward the kitchen. "It's only four, Trinity. You should still be asleep."

"I know, but I woke up." I kept my arms still at my sides. "I sensed demons. It woke me up."

"I don't feel them." His head cocked, and several strands of golden hair fell across his cheek.

"I'm more sensitive to them," I explained. "I can usually sense them minutes before a Warden does, and I can feel them now. There are demons here, Zayne. Not in your apartment but close. Probably outside, on the streets or—"

"They probably are outside on the streets," he interrupted with a sigh.

"Okay. Then we need to get up and go—"

"There are demons everywhere here," he said, his eyes meeting mine. Well, only one eye. His hair shielded the other. "Probably just Fiends out walking around. They're the only ones active in the day, usually in the late afternoon."

"And we're still lying here because…?"

"Fiends are relatively harmless, Trinity. All they do is mess around with electronics and crap. They don't really bother humans."

I knew that Fiends were somewhat harmless and that they appeared as human as he and I unless you looked really closely at their eyes. Light reflected off them weirdly. Fiends were pretty much why Murphy's Law existed. If everything went wrong for you in one day—your car breaking down, stoplights out of service, your favorite coffee shop closed and your office without power—a Fiend was most likely behind it.

"You don't…hunt them?" I asked, confused.

He didn't answer for a long moment. "I used to hunt demons indiscriminately, no matter what they were guilty of."

"Isn't that kind of your job as a Warden?"

"Yeah."

When he said nothing else, all I could do was stare at him and wonder what in the Hell had I gotten myself into. No wonder he wasn't the clan leader. How could he be when he didn't hunt Fiends? And I couldn't forget he'd worked with demons before. But his clan appeared to trust him, at least enough to allow me to stay with him even knowing what I was.

"You're a strange Warden," I whispered.

One side of his lips kicked up. "And you're just...strange."

"I think I'm offended."

The half grin slid into a smile. "You're going to need to get used to sensing demons. I wasn't joking when I said they're everywhere here, especially the lower level ones like Fiends."

"Okay," I said, because I didn't know what else to say. I was wholly aware of the fact that I was still lying underneath him, and even though our bodies weren't touching, I could feel the heat rolling off his skin. The last time we were in this position, I'd kissed him, and we'd both had a Hell of a lot more clothes on then. "So, um, are you going to let me up?"

Zayne blinked as if he just realized I was under him, and for some reason, that felt more offensive than him saying I was strange. Like, was he *that* physically ambivalent toward me?

Damn.

"Yeah, I guess I can do that." Zayne rocked back smoothly, and I rolled out from underneath him and then off the couch. I came to my feet. His chin dipped as he dragged his lower lip between his teeth. Shoulders tensing, he looked away. "You should probably try to get another hour or so of sleep."

I started to protest since we both were already awake, but

it was at that exact moment I realized I hadn't changed into my pajamas before my nap. All I'd done was take off my jeans, which meant I was in my shirt and undies, and my shirt was not a long one.

He could see my undies.

My black-and-white skull-print undies.

Oh my God.

Face burning, I spun and darted back across the room and into the bedroom, closing the door behind me. I leaned against it, eyes closed.

I was such a mess.

It was close to six when Zayne and I left his place to go speak to this friend…who didn't sound like much of a friend.

Before I left Zayne's bedroom for the second time, I made sure I actually had pants on and had dug out the hip holster that secured the blades. It was another gift from Jada, one that I'd actually never used, but was relieved to see it fit and was well hidden under a much longer shirt.

Now I found myself in the garage staring at a black, sleek Chevy Impala parked next to some kind of fast-looking motorcycle, trying desperately not to think about the fact Zayne had seen me in my undies.

I was impressed as I eyed the Impala, having not seen one this vintage in person before. "Are you a *Supernatural* fan?" I asked.

Zayne stepped around me and opened the passenger door. "Not until recently. Had the car before I was introduced to the world of the Winchesters."

"Oh."

He turned to me, holding the door. Like me, he was wearing sunglasses. His were silver aviators and the lenses were reflective. Mine were oversize to the point that they probably made me look like an insect and the lenses were as black as I could get them.

Those full lips tilted up on one side. "Are you going to get in?"

"Oh," I repeated. "Yeah."

Zayne was behind the wheel in a nanosecond, it seemed, turning the key. The engine rumbled to life.

"So, where are we going?" I asked.

"Across the river. Shouldn't take too long to get there," he said, pulling out of the parking spot as he glanced over at me. "Buckle up."

I hadn't even realized I hadn't done that. I snapped myself in and then all but planted my face to the window as he pulled out of the garage and stopped when we were greeted with bumper-to-bumper traffic. My wide gaze tried to take in everything that I was seeing.

It was nothing like earlier, when I was looking out the window from high above.

Buildings of every size and color seemed to be crammed on top of one another like thick fingers stretching into the early-evening sky, blocking out most of the fading sunlight. There were people everywhere.

Everywhere.

I'd never seen so many people on a sidewalk before. Even in Morgantown when I was younger, it was never like this. There had to be hundreds of people, their forms and faces nothing but blurs to me as they hurried around slower-walking people and cut in front of traffic. Horns blared. People shouted. Not only that, I still sensed demons, and knew that some of those people weren't exactly people. Sound poured in from every direction, and it was all a little overwhelming. I could barely tell the difference between humans and ghosts as it was. How was I going to be able to tell now?

"There are a lot of people," I stated.

"This is actually not that bad," Zayne replied, and my wide-eyed gaze turned to him.

"Really?" I whispered.

He nodded. "It's after rush hour. If we came out about three hours earlier, it would have been double this amount."

"Holy crap." I was glad I hadn't come out here by myself. I wasn't afraid of large crowds, or at least I hadn't thought I was. Now, I wasn't sure.

I turned to the passenger window. My thoughts wandered as I stared out, seeing a hazy view of buildings that eventually became a kaleidoscope of elms and parks. I started to think about Misha, about what could be happening to him, and I had to force my thoughts elsewhere. I couldn't let myself fall down that rabbit hole. I hadn't felt the loss of the bond, so he was still alive and that was what mattered.

I found myself thinking about what Zayne had said earlier about being forced to watch someone he cared for being hurt and not being able to help them. He'd been right yet again. I didn't know a lot about him, and I wanted... I wanted to know more.

"We're here," Zayne announced, startling me from my thoughts.

I focused on our surroundings and was surprised to find that we were on some kind of private road, pulling up in front of a...mansion?

Plastering my face to the window, I squinted at the massive two-story brick structure with freaking white pillars lining a wide porch that appeared to circle the entire home.

Yep, that was definitely a mansion.

I didn't move, even when Zayne killed the engine, and as I drew in a shallow breath, I felt the heavy presence of... demons. They could be literally anywhere. I'd felt them nearly the whole way here with the exception of when we were crossing a bridge.

"You okay?" Zayne asked.

"Yeah," I whispered. "Where are we?"

"Just over the river in Maryland. It's the... It's a private home," he said, tone distant enough that it pulled my gaze to him. He was staring at the house also, his expression tight. "Two people live here, but I think others come and go."

"Wow. Only two people live here?"

"Yeah," he murmured, taking off his sunglasses and placing them in the visor. "But look at Thierry's home. That was double this size, and how many people lived there? Four?"

He had a point. "Are you okay?"

Zayne blinked and looked back at me, his expression smoothing out. "Always."

My brows lifted, but he opened the door and climbed out, and I decided it was time for me to do the same. Leaving my bag on the seat, I brought my phone with me.

As I walked across gray pavers, I noticed that it was warmer here even though the sun was behind the house. The breeze wasn't as cool as it had been in the mountains.

"Hey."

I stopped, turning to Zayne.

He stared down at me, the wind tossing that strand of hair across his cheek. Then his chest rose with a deep breath. "Just a heads-up. The guy you're about to meet? He is...different."

"Different as in?"

"He's a demon."

"What?" I gasped, reaching for my blades out of habit.

"Bad Trinity," Zayne murmured, catching my wrists before I could grab the blades. "Hear me out. There's no reason to be murderous. None of the people here—"

"You mean none of the *demons* here—"

"None of the *people* here are going to hurt you or me." Zayne kept his voice low and calm, but his eyes narrowed.

Holy crap, Zayne really did work with demons. I don't know what I'd thought. That it was something he'd done only in the past? That he didn't actively work with demons now?

Zayne stepped in front of me, still holding my wrists. "I know this is odd, but I'm telling you that they are okay. I've known one of them half my life, and if we want help finding Misha, these are the people who can provide it."

I immediately knew who he was talking about.

The girl—the half Warden and half demon that had been raised with him. That was who lived here? Biting down on my lip, I looked over my shoulder to the huge house. Could I do it? Walk into a house that demons lived in and ask for their help?

What would my father think?

Hell, he'd have a fit. Part of me expected him to appear and strike Zayne down and then cart me off back to Thierry's.

"We are safe here," Zayne continued, letting go of my wrists to raise the sunglasses to the top of my head so he could see my eyes. "Do you trust me, Trinity?"

"I…" I wasn't sure how to answer that question. Part of me did, because he'd given me no true reason not to trust him, but I was still wary of him, of all of this. I drew in a shallow breath. "You really think they can help us?"

Zayne nodded. "I do."

This was huge and potentially crazy, but I would do anything to find Misha, even if that meant going against everything I'd ever learned.

"Okay," I said.

Letting go of my wrist, he turned with me to the house and we started toward it.

The double bronze doors were already open and a man

stood there. He had icy blond hair that hung past his shoulders, and he was wearing a…romper?

Yep.

Definitely a black romper.

The hot breath on my neck and the heaviness increased. My steps locked up, and I immediately reached for my blades.

The man in the romper was a demon.

Zayne placed his hand on my lower back, giving me a gentle nudge forward as the demon stopped at the top of the steps.

"This is a surprise," he said.

I stopped at the base of the steps, glancing at Zayne.

"It's okay." Zayne took my hand in his warm one. He led me up the steps. "This is Cayman."

Cayman tilted his head as his gaze flickered between us. "Long time no see, Zayne."

"It has been a while." He stopped before Cayman, and since we were close, I noticed that the demon's eyes were the color of rich honey. He wasn't a lower level demon. "Is he here? I need to see him."

"They're both here."

Zayne's jaw clenched. "Great."

Cayman looked down at our joined hands and slowly looked up. "It is." He turned on bare feet. "Follow me."

A wave of goose bumps erupted over my skin as we followed, stepping into a large foyer. I looked up, saw a huge crystal chandelier. Fancy. Zayne let go of my hand as we walked under a wide spiral staircase. Looking around, I noticed some…odd paintings on the wall. Some were muted shades of red and black, paintings of fire next to large, blown-up black-and-white photographs of skyscrapers.

"So, Zayne, my man, when you going to let me take the sweet ride for a drive?" Cayman asked, glancing over his shoulder. His brows were nearly black, and the contrast was striking on him.

"When you stop making deals, Cayman."

My gaze sharpened. Was Cayman a demon broker? They were Upper Level, but sort of like…middle management, making deals with humans for their soul. They were known in pop culture as crossroad demons, but you didn't need to find a road somewhere deep in the south to summon one. Often, you could find them at bars and other places where humans who were full of angst were drawn.

"Well, that's never going to happen," the demon said.

"I know," Zayne replied, and I couldn't fathom how he could chit chat with a demon that stole people's souls.

"Sorry about the living room. It's kind of a mess. We were marathoning *Avenger* movies and we kind of built a pillow fort in the process."

A…pillow fort?

The demon in front of me wore rompers, wanted to drive Zayne's car and also built pillow forts?

Had I fallen outside and hit my head?

Zayne didn't respond, but then Cayman hung a left and I saw what he was talking about. The living room was huge with floor-to-ceiling bookcases on either side of a television so big that I hadn't even known they made them in that size. A large sectional sat in the center of the room, and on the floor in front of the TV was exactly what Cayman had stated.

A fort made of colorful throw pillows, long narrow body ones and fluffy white ones.

It looked so comfortable.

I pulled my gaze from the fort. The largest bowl of popcorn I'd ever seen sat on an end table, next to a half-eaten roll of…cookie dough?…and about three bottles of orange juice.

What an odd combination.

Cayman plopped down in the center of the sectional while I stopped just inside the room. "He'll be back shortly." Those odd eyes slid in my direction. "You can come in and sit. I don't bite." A slow grin curled his lips. "Unless you like that."

I tensed.

"Cayman," Zayne growled out in warning.

The demon ignored him, and I decided I was okay where I was standing. He pouted. "What about you, Zayne?"

"I'm fine. Thanks," he said, leaning against the wall a few feet from me, hands in the pockets of his jeans and ankles crossed. He looked like he didn't want to get any closer, and that didn't make me feel any more comfortable.

"Sorry," a deep voice interrupted. "Had to take care of a few things."

My eyes widened as a tall, dark-haired guy entered the room from what I was guessing was the kitchen. He was dressed all in black—black jeans and black shirt. There was a good chance he was even taller than Zayne. Definitely not as broad, but taller. He was too far away for me to make out much of his features.

"Stony, what up?" he asked.

Stony?

I looked at Zayne.

He shot the demon a dark look.

Undaunted by the rather cold greeting, the guy strolled behind the couch and then came to a complete stop as his gaze landed on me.

His head tilted as he took a step closer to me, and then suddenly he was right in front of me, and his features pieced together. He was... He was stunningly attractive, with sharp, angular features and eyes that were golden in color, like Cayman's, luminous and slightly curved, giving him a feline-like appearance. His lips parted on a sharp, audible inhale.

"What are you doing?" Zayne asked, pushing off the wall.

The guy didn't answer. He lifted his arm like he was in a trance, his fingers stretching out toward me.

"Don't touch me." I staggered to the side, bumping into Zayne.

Zayne hauled me back against him, and within in a heartbeat, I was sandwiched between the two of them, my back warming from the heat Zayne was throwing off, and the same from the guy who stood in front of me. "Remember what I told you. He's not going to hurt you," Zayne said. "I was telling you the truth. He's just being weirder than normal."

"This is getting bizarre," Cayman commented from the couch. "And kind of hot, which is not remotely what I expected."

I blinked.

"What?" The guy in front of me blinked and then looked down at his hand. A look of surprise flickered across his face, as if he just realized what he was doing. His hand curled as he lowered his arm. "Whoa."

"Whoa what?" Zayne shifted me so that I was somewhat behind him. "What are you doing?"

"I'm coming!" a female voice rang out, and I heard Zayne curse under his breath. "Sorry—"

"Everything is fine," the new guy called out to her, taking a step back from us. "Don't come in here, Layla. I mean it. Give me a few seconds."

My stomach hollowed as the muscles along Zayne's back tensed. "Shit."

That also didn't reassure me.

The demon lifted his chin. "Where did you find her? In a church or something?"

I started to frown. Did Zayne often find people in churches?

"No. I didn't find her in a church. What kind of question is that?"

"Okay. Well, wherever you found her, you need to put her back, Stony."

"I'm not a toy," I snapped, stepping away from Zayne. "Or an inanimate object to be picked up and put back."

Those fierce amber eyes landed on me. "Oh, I know exactly what you are."

I went ramrod straight.

"How?" Zayne demanded. "How do you know what she is?"

"I'm not some basic demon, Stony." His skin seemed to thin and dark shadows blossomed underneath. "I am Astaroth, the Crown Prince of Hell. I *know*."

22

Holy canola oil, Zayne brought me to see the *Crown Prince of Hell*?

What in the holy Hell?

My fingers itched to feel the weight of my blades, but worse yet, I could feel the *grace* stirring alive in the center of my stomach. I beat it down, but it was still there, demanding to be let loose.

"You're an actual prince?" I asked.

He inclined his head. "I'm *the* Crown Prince of Hell."

My lips parted as I turned to Zayne. "When you dropped the bomb that we were going to see demons, you failed to mention one of them was the Crown Prince."

"Sorry, I'd hoped Roth would keep that little fact to himself," Zayne growled. "But he's…unique like that."

"That I am," Roth replied.

"Uniquely annoying," Zayne added, and when my gaze shot back to Roth, he pouted. "He is the Crown Prince, but he isn't…all that bad."

Roth sucked in a breath as he placed his hand over his heart. "Stony, did you just compliment me?"

Zayne ignored him. "He's not a bad guy," he repeated.

"Another compliment? Oh, wow, I'm going to blush," Roth said. "But that doesn't change the fact that I'm very, very displeased that you brought *that* into my home."

Zayne was suddenly in front of me, blocking me completely. "I came to you for help, Roth."

"You brought *that* into my house with Layla here?" Roth repeated. "Are you out of your mind?"

"Okay," Cayman said from somewhere behind them. "I am *so* curious as to what is going on here."

Zayne ignored Cayman as I peeked out from behind him. "I know what she is—she knows what she is, but she is no threat to you. We're here because we need your help."

"Okay, I'm not waiting any longer, because I swear I hear Zayne's voice and that—" the female who was probably in the kitchen announced. Roth shouted something before blinking out of existence in front of us. I gasped as he reappeared on the other side of the couch just as Zayne stiffened beside me so much that I thought he'd shifted.

I looked up at him. It was like a veil had slipped over his face. If I thought he'd looked devoid of emotion before, I'd been wrong. He looked like a statue now. My gaze followed his to a girl who now stood close to the end of the couch.

The moment I saw her, I couldn't look away. She was... beautiful in an unreal, ethereal sort of way, and if I hadn't known what I was and what she was, I would've thought she was the Trueborn. With her long, white-blond hair and big, pale blue eyes, she looked like she had more angel blood in her than I did, but I knew what she was.

She was half demon, half Warden, and she had no angelic blood in her.

"Zayne," she spoke, a smile racing across her face. "I am...
I am so happy to see you. It's been way too long."

"Yeah. It has been." His voice was gruff, strangely so.
"Trinity? This is Layla. We, uh, grew up together."

"Her name is *Trinity*?" Roth sounded like he'd choked,
and I ignored that as I focused on someone who was just as
rare as I was.

Layla was still staring at Zayne, and I had a feeling she hadn't
even looked at me yet. She reminded me of one of those por-
celain dolls, the kind that was beautiful but also slightly creepy
and possibly haunted. My gaze shifted to Roth.

What else was creepy was the way Roth was staring at me
from where he stood beside Layla. He was looking at me like...
like I looked at a plate of cheese fries.

I was really starting to feel superuncomfortable.

Layla finally dragged her gaze from Zayne and looked at
me. Her smile faltered and her blue eyes grew wide. "Holy
shit," she whispered.

I froze. "Uh..."

"What do you see?" Roth asked, placing a hand on
Layla's arm.

Wait a second. I could maybe believe that the Crown Prince
of Hell could sense what I was, but a half Warden, half demon?
That didn't make any sense to me.

"I don't know," Layla said, stepping around Roth, but he
didn't let her get very far, holding on to her arm. "I've never
seen anything like it."

My brows inched up my forehead.

"I really wish someone would fill me in." Cayman sighed.
"I'm feeling left out over here."

"Why did you bring me here?" I asked Zayne.

"That's an incredibly good question I've been asking," Roth
remarked, still holding on to Layla, and...and now *she* was

looking at me like I was cheese fries *with* buttermilk ranch dressing.

"They shouldn't know what I am," I continued. "But those two are staring at me in a way that makes me very uncomfortable."

"They shouldn't be able to, but Roth is...just *so* special," Zayne said. "Apparently."

"Are you flirting with me, Stony?" Roth asked.

"Yeah, that's what I'm doing, Roth." Zayne turned to me, his gaze searching mine as he spoke, voice low. "I don't think Layla knows what you are, but..." He glanced over at her. "She's seeing your soul."

"What?" My voice turned shrill as I looked back at them. Layla was now straining against Roth's arm. "Are you really sure they're good guys?"

Zayne shot Roth a look of warning as he said, "They are. You can trust me. And you can trust them."

"I don't know about that." I stared at them. "They're looking at me like they want to eat me."

"Hopefully they'll stop doing that," Zayne advised. "Like *right now.*"

"I see that look," Cayman commented. "I see it now. Layla, you might want to, you know, pull it back."

"What?" Layla blinked and looked around the room, her cheeks flushing as she realized how far she'd stretched Roth's arm. "Oh, wow. Sorry."

"It's okay." Roth pulled her into his arms, holding her close—the way I'd seen Ty hold Jada. I didn't understand that, the way he was embracing her. I didn't understand any of this. "I had the same reaction."

Layla placed her hands on Roth's arm. She kept looking around me, seeing...my soul?

"What do you see, Layla?" Zayne asked.

"I see..." She rubbed one hand over Roth's arm. "I see pure white...and pure black."

Zayne looked at me, and I had no idea what that meant, but he looked surprised.

"The best of both worlds," Layla murmured, and I shivered. "What is she?" she repeated, asking in a way that reminded me of a child asking for a snack.

"She's a Trueborn," Roth answered, and I felt my stomach pitch. He really did know what I was. "More commonly known as a nephilim."

Layla's mouth dropped open.

"Holy shitballs." Cayman jumped up and vaulted over the couch—actually *vaulted* to the other side.

I felt rather proud of that reaction, considering the other two looked like they wanted to get really, really close and personal.

Zayne smirked. "Wow, Cayman, I don't think I've ever seen you move that fast."

"What the Hell, Zayne? I told her to sit next to me. Actually sit next to me. That's messed up," Cayman said, shaking his head. "I've never seen a Trueborn. Jesus." He backed up, eyes wide. "I am not about this kind of life."

"I'm...I'm not going to hurt you guys," I said, feeling sort of like a badass and sort of like a freak. "I mean, I don't want to." I looked at Zayne, unsettled by all of this. "Right?"

One side of his lips kicked up. "Right."

"But you can," Roth said, resting his chin atop Layla's head. "There are only two things in this world that even I don't want to come face-to-face with. Neither of them are a Warden."

Zayne sighed.

"And one of them is a Trueborn," Roth said.

I couldn't stop myself from asking, "What's the second thing?"

Roth's smile was like smoke as he stared back at me, causing me to shiver.

"She has no reason to hurt you all," Zayne said. "So, let's not give her one, because if you know anything about a Trueborn, you know I'm not going to be able to stop her if you tick her off."

Roth's lips thinned. "And yet again, you'd bring her here, putting Layla at risk—"

"We came here for your help—"

"I like when you need me, Stony." Roth grinned.

"God, I hate you," Zayne grumbled.

"Hey! That's the first time you used my name."

Zayne rolled his eyes. "*Anyway*, we're here because I trust that you guys can look past the fact that she's part angel, especially if she's looking past the fact that you all are demons." Zayne's voice hardened. "So, can we please get back on track?"

No one spoke, so I raised my hand. "I have a question."

"What?" Zayne let out another sigh that reminded me so much of Misha that it caused my chest to hurt.

I looked over at Layla. "How do you see souls?"

She glanced at Roth before she spoke. "Do you know what I am?"

"Half Warden and half demon?"

"Okay. Do you know who my mother was—and I use the word *mother* lightly?"

"Lilith?" I said, remembering what Misha had told me. I could feel Zayne's surprised jerk, but I ignored it. "Your mother is Lilith?"

"Yes, and my mother's gifts manifested differently in me because of my Warden blood," she explained, still rubbing Roth's arms with her two small hands. "I can see souls. They're like auras to me. White souls are the purest—Wardens and angels and humans without sin have pure souls." She paused, her gaze flickering around me. "You have a pure soul and…"

"And what?" I squinted, wishing I could see what she saw.

"I don't know. I've never seen a soul so dark," she said, and I blinked. "I mean, like demons don't have a soul, so there's nothing there."

Roth pouted behind her.

"And really bad, really evil humans have very dark souls, but pure black? Pure black and pure white?" A look of wonder crossed her face. "I guess it's because of what you are and that's why I've never seen anything like it."

"But why would it also be black?" I asked. "I mean, if the darker the soul means the more evil the person is…"

"I can answer that for you," Roth offered helpfully. "Probably paying for the sins of your father. Don't really think angels are supposed to be hooking up with humans."

"Nah," Cayman murmured.

"They did for a long time," I pointed out. "There used to be thousands of my kind."

"And that was how many hundreds of years ago? Things have changed since then. Procreation between angels and humans has been forbidden," Roth replied.

"How do you know that?" Zayne asked.

"I'm a demon. I'm the Crown Prince. I know what is forbidden and what's not." His smile was smug. "Which makes me wonder why an angel would break that cardinal rule, create you and let you live."

I lifted a brow at the whole *let you live* part.

"And it also begs the question of who your father is," Roth said.

"Do you have other abilities like your mother?" I asked Layla, ignoring Roth's question. "Like, can you take souls?"

"I can, but I don't do it," she said, meeting my gaze and obviously seeing the doubt there. "I mean, I try not to. There've been a few missteps in the past..." Her gaze flicked to Zayne, and I knew it in my bones. Misha had been right about Zayne missing a part of his soul. And I knew it had been Layla who had taken it. "But I do everything in my power not to do it."

"And she's almost always successful." Roth dropped a kiss on top of Layla's head. "And even when she's not," Roth continued, "she's still perfect."

A soft smile pulled at Layla's lips as she tipped her head back. The kiss Roth dropped was light and quick, but still floored me. I was thrown by the affection, at the obvious love between them. I was so confused.

I'd never been taught that demons could...love. Yes, they could experience lust, but love? Every lesson I'd had implied that they were incapable of such a human emotion.

Angels, pure-blooded ones, couldn't love like humans. Hell, in the very beginning, Wardens couldn't even experience it. They'd learned to love through interaction with humans. Over hundreds of years, it became a learned behavior. Had it been the same for demons?

I glanced at Zayne and he was quiet and tense, watching them through thick, lowered lashes.

A long moment passed and the demon prince led Layla over to the couch and pulled her down so she was sitting beside him. "Sit, Trinity. Apparently we all need to chat."

I didn't want to sit.

Zayne nudged me gently. "Go ahead."

Resisting the urge to protest, I shuffled over to the couch and sat while Cayman stopped looking like he was trying to disappear into the wall. Instead, he appeared curious again.

Roth leaned forward, his gaze flicking from me to Zayne. "So, Trinity who may or may not be holy, how did you meet Stony over there? I am dying to hear the story."

"Me, too," murmured Layla.

I glanced at Zayne. His chin had dipped and he looked like he was a second from ripping the bookcase off the wall and launching it at Roth's head.

"How we met isn't really important at the moment," Zayne said, his voice tight with impatience.

"Actually, I think it is important. I want to know how you two met," Layla chimed in, her gaze shifting to mine.

I took a shallow breath. "He…he came to the community where I live."

"You live in a community—a Warden community?" Surprise colored her tone.

"At the regional seat," I said, not elaborating further, but Layla seemed to know what that meant.

Her eyes got even bigger. "And how long have you lived there?"

"Since I was young—seven or eight," I admitted, unsure of what I could share that wouldn't be betraying the clan that had protected me. "I was…hidden there. Very few knew what I am."

"Interesting," Roth murmured in a way that told me he thought the exact opposite. "But I'm more interested to learn why Zayne needs our help?"

"The community was attacked last night and someone… close to Trinity was taken by a demon I recognized. An Upper Level that I've seen in DC," Zayne explained. "We need to find him, and it's very possible that the demon came back here."

Roth leaned back, resting an ankle in his knee. "And this someone who is close to Trinity is a Warden?"

"Yes," I answered.

"Why do you think this someone is still alive?" Roth asked,

tugging on Layla's hair. "With the exception of pretty half Wardens, demons don't usually keep captives alive."

"I know he's alive," I said. "He's my bonded Protector. I'd know if he were dead, and he's not."

"Bonded protector?" Layla mumbled to herself.

"So, that is true?" Roth wiggled his foot. "Trueborns were bonded to Wardens?"

I nodded.

"And if he's still alive, then there's probably a reason," Cayman spoke up, coming to stand behind Roth and Layla. "And it's not a good reason. They'll be—"

"Using him to either get information on the community or to draw me out, if they know what he is and what I am," I interrupted. "I know, but we don't know if this demon knows what I am."

"I think we can safely assume he does, if he went into a community of Wardens and only took your Protector," Cayman said.

Roth raised his hand. "Since we're doing the hand-raising thing…" He winked at me. "I have a question. How did a demon get into this community and manage to escape with its life and a Warden—a bonded Protector?"

Good question, and Zayne took over, explaining what happened, including the earlier Raver attack, the humans with the creepy masks and the Nightcrawlers. The only thing left out was Clay's attack on me.

While he talked, still leaning against the wall, arms crossed, I realized that while he was in the room, he didn't want to be part of this group.

"If humans were working with this demon, there's a good possibility they're possessed," Layla said, glancing at Zayne. "We've seen that happen. You get a demon talented in possession, and they can create a nice little army."

I hadn't considered that and now I felt silly for not thinking of it.

"What else do you know?" Roth asked.

"Trinity was also attacked while I was at the community," Zayne answered.

Well, there went not sharing that.

Roth's gaze sharped. "Pray tell, that also may be useful information."

"A Warden attacked you?" Layla blinked rapidly.

I nodded.

"And what happened to this Warden?"

"He's dead," I said, suppressing the shudder. "I killed him."

"Good girl." Roth smiled his approval.

A shiver danced over my skin as I stared at him. Boy, wasn't that smile unnerving?

"The earlier attack has to be related, because the Warden who went after Trinity was wearing the same kind of mask the humans wore during the invasion," Zayne was saying. There was a pause. "There is one other thing."

"What's that?" Layla asked.

Zayne looked at me, and it took me a moment to figure out what he was referencing. Tension crept into my muscles. "It's not related to that," I told him. "Not at all."

"What isn't?" Layla asked.

Pressing my lips together, I shook my head. Never in my life had I expected to explain what had happened to my mother to demons, but here I was. "My mother was killed about a year ago by a Warden we trusted."

"Oh my God." Layla pressed her hand to the center of the black shirt she wore. "I'm so sorry to hear that."

"Thank you," I murmured, clasping my hands over my knees.

"And why are you sure that's not related?" Zayne asked quietly.

"Because the Warden who killed my mother tried to kill me, because he…he believed I was an abomination," I said, staring down at my fingers. "That I was threat against Wardens, more so than any demon. He caught us off guard, and my mom—she was really brave. She got between us and that… Yeah, that was it."

"Jesus," Zayne said.

"Yeah, so it doesn't have to do with that." Drawing in a shallow breath, I lifted my gaze to the demons across from me. "Misha is more than my Protector. He's like my brother. We were raised together, and even though we annoy the living crap out of one another, I don't know what I'll do if something happens to him."

A sad smile tugged at Layla's lips as she glanced from me to Zayne. "I know how that feels."

Didn't take a genius to figure out she was talking about Zayne, and these two had obviously had a major falling-out. Was it over her taking a part of his soul? That would do it. Or was it more? I looked at Roth. Did it have to do with him?

"I see," Roth said, and I had no idea what he saw. He looked over his shoulder at Cayman. "Do you happen to know who this demon is?"

"Bael," Zayne answered.

"Hell," Roth muttered as Layla seemed to pale. "He's back in town?"

"Well, I'm thinking so. He was running around the city for a while, and it was definitely him who took Misha."

"You know Bael?" I asked.

"Why, yes. All of us demons are friends on Facebook," Roth replied, and my eyes narrowed. He grinned. "I know him, and I don't like him."

"The feeling is mutual," Cayman added. "Bael has always been jealous of Roth."

"Because I have better hair," Roth explained.

I started to frown.

"Actually, because Roth's always been the Boss's favorite," Cayman clarified, and I had a sinking suspicion the Boss was Lucifer, and I really had no idea what to say about that. "Well, *was* the Boss's favorite. Not so much anymore."

Roth nodded slowly. "That's true, but if you're right, and Bael has your Protector, that's bad news."

"I figured that out already," I said.

The demon prince tipped forward. "No, I don't think you do, Trinity. Bael is just not some Upper Level demon with a mean jealousy streak. He only comes out to play when the payoff is big. He wouldn't just take a Warden for shits and giggles. He took *your* Warden, and if there was any doubt in your mind that he doesn't know what you are, what your Warden is, erase that now. He took him to get to you, which means you should cut your losses and get as far away from here as possible."

I sucked in a shrill breath. "Cut my losses? I can't do that. I *won't* do that."

Roth tilted his head. "What do you think will happen if Bael gets his hands on you?"

"I know exactly what will happen," I snapped. "I will kill him."

His jaw hardened as he continued to stare at me and then he rocked back. He looked over his shoulder. "See what you can find out about Bael."

"Of course." Cayman turned back to Zayne and me. "Always good seeing you." Then he looked at me. "You scare me."

And then Cayman blinked out of existence.

Roth said, "Give him a couple days—"

"A couple *days*?" My breath caught as I scooted forward. "Misha may not have a couple days."

"He may not," Roth said. "But let's try to stay positive here. We have to be smart about this. Demons like Bael aren't stupid. We start carpet-bombing every dark corner in this city, and anyone who knows anything will become scarce."

Pressing my lips together, I shook my head as I struggled with the rising frustration.

"We'll find out where your Protector is," Roth said. "I'm like the A-Team."

"Yeah, if *A* stood for *asshole*," Zayne commented, and my eyes popped open wide.

"That was actually pretty funny." Roth laughed as he rose and walked over to where the cookie dough was sitting. He handed it to Layla and then moved to stand in front of the fort.

One big question remained. "Why are you willing to help me?"

"Because I always wanted a Trueborn to owe me a favor." Roth smiled.

I shuddered, thinking maybe I didn't need to know why.

"And because Zayne brought you here," Layla added. "That tells me you're important to him."

I opened my mouth, but I had no idea what to say about that. Peeking at Zayne, I couldn't make out his expression.

"He's helping me, because I promised to help them," I said, watching Zayne. Still no reaction.

"Help them with what?" Layla asked, breaking off a piece of dough.

"You know there's something in this city killing Wardens and Upper Level demons," Zayne answered after a moment. "Whatever it is, it's powerful, but I doubt it's as powerful as a Trueborn."

A weird sense of disappointment swept over me. I was the

one who'd suggested that Zayne was only helping me because of the deal we'd made, but…I wanted him to deny that and say it was because we were friends.

But I wasn't sure we were friends.

"Can we talk?" Layla asked, looking at Zayne. "Just for a moment?"

"Now's not a good time," he replied quickly. "We have to get going."

"It'll just take a couple minutes," she said. "That's all."

"I don't really have time."

Layla leaned forward and opened her mouth, closed it and then tried again. "I haven't seen you in months, Zayne. Months. I've called and I've texted, and you haven't responded to me, and then you show up here, unannounced, with *this*."

With this? The corners of my lips started to turn down. The way she said that made me feel like I was an STD—the kind you couldn't get rid of.

"Layla," Roth started.

"No." She pointed the roll of cookie dough at Roth.

He lifted his hands in a quick surrender.

Layla shot to her feet and then swung toward Zayne. "I saw Dez a couple of weeks ago. Did you know that?"

Zayne didn't reply, but even I could see the muscle ticking along his jaw like a time bomb.

"And do you know what Dez told me?" Layla ranted, her cheeks flushing pink. "You've moved out. On your own! No clan member does that and survives—" She cut herself off, drawing in a deep breath, groaning with exasperation. "Why did you move out?"

"It's none of your business."

"None of my business? You show up after months of silence with a nephilim, after I learned you moved out, and then tell me this is *none of my business*? Who are you?"

"Obviously not who you thought I was," Zayne snapped back. "Does that answer your question?"

Layla stiffened, lowering the tube of cookie dough. A mixture of hurt and anger flashed across her face and then she swung toward me with that roll of cookie dough, and I could tell that whatever was about to come out of her mouth wasn't going to be nice.

I was so done being quiet. "Okay. I don't know what is going on here, and frankly, I couldn't care less. Honestly. My best friend has been taken by a demon, and he's possibly being tortured while we're sitting here yelling at one another over unreturned phone calls!"

Layla snapped her mouth shut.

On a roll now, I wasn't stopping. "And on top of all that, I was raised to believe that demons were evil, no gray area, and here I am with the Crown Prince of Hell who builds pillow forts like that's normal—"

"It's normal for me," Roth murmured. "I like pillow forts."

I ignored that. "And I'm sitting in front of a half Warden, half demon who has eaten, like, twenty pounds of cookie dough in ten seconds flat! I get that you guys have issues, but they cannot be more important than what could be happening to Misha. I need to find him before he is killed."

"And what if you don't get to him in time?" Roth asked, and the room fell silent.

"If he's dead?" My heart cracked and I couldn't bear to think of that. "Then I'll deal."

"There are worse things than being dead, Trinity."

A shiver danced over my skin as I met his amber-colored gaze. "I'll have to take your word on that."

"You should." Roth crossed his arms. "I think it's time for you two to leave. We'll be in touch." He glared at Zayne. "And next time we call, try answering the phone."

23

"Well, that was fun, wasn't it? Can't wait to do it again," I said when Zayne climbed behind the wheel of the Impala. I waited until he closed the door and then I leaned over, socking him in the arm.

"Ouch." He looked over at me, eyes wide. "What was that for?"

"That was for not telling me that we were going to see the freaking Crown Prince of Hell." I punched his arm again.

Leaning away from me, he rubbed his arm. "What was *that* for?"

"That was for being a dick to Layla." I cocked back my arm one more time.

Zayne's hand shot out, catching my fist. "Hitting isn't nice," he said. "And I wasn't a dick to her."

"Yes, you were." I tried to pull my hand free, but he held on.

"Look at you. After one meeting with demons, you're now

defending them." Zayne lowered my hand to the space be-tween us.

"No, I'm not." I totally was. "What the heck was up with you and her?"

Zayne's pale eyes met mine. "You're not going to hit me again if I let go? I'm fragile."

I snorted. "I won't hit you again."

He let go and then turned the key in the ignition. The en-gine rumbled to life.

"So?" I asked.

Zayne sighed as he shifted the Impala into gear. "Things with Layla are…complicated and that's all I can really say about that."

"That doesn't reveal much more than I already know."

When he didn't respond, irritation spiked and, underneath it, a thin slice of disappointment lit up my chest. Why wouldn't he tell me what had happened between them? There was a massive wall around Zayne, made of granite and stubbornness.

Zayne was quiet as he drove. The sun had set, so I pulled the sunglasses off the top of my head and placed them in the sun visor.

"Do you think they're going to help?" I asked, focusing on important things that weren't his personal issues.

"Yes, I do." Zayne kept one hand on the steering wheel and rested his right arm along the back of our seats. "If any-one can find information on where Bael holed up or what he's planning, it'll be Cayman."

I thought about the demon in the romper. "He seemed re-ally scared of me."

"Yeah." Zayne chuckled. "He was."

It was a weird thing to smile about, but I grinned. "So, he's a deal broker?"

Zayne nodded. "He doesn't seek humans out. They tend

to find their way to him, wanting or needing something that they'd give up anything for, including their soul. Messed-up thing is that most humans want utterly inconsequential things. They give up a part of their soul for a promotion, or to be with someone who probably doesn't even deserve them."

"Just a part?" I asked. "I thought they gave up their whole soul?"

"No, just a small part of it."

"And...you think that's okay?" I asked.

"I think that when humans use their free will and jeopardize where they end up when they die, that's on them. We do everything we can to keep them safe from demons who break the rules, and you know there are rules. There must be a balance of good and evil," Zayne said as we neared the bridge that led back into the city. "Cayman follows those rules."

I knew there were rules and that the balance of good and evil stemmed from the concept of free will.

"I don't know what to think about all that," I admitted, staring at his shadowy profile.

Zayne was quiet for a long moment. "You know, I was a lot like you for, Hell, my entire life. I saw things in black and white. No gray—except for Layla." He was staring straight ahead as he spoke. "I used to think that the Warden part of who she was canceled out the part of her that was a demon. I would even tell her that, when she was younger and would come to me, worried about what she was, upset that the clan never would accept her or worried that something was wrong with her. I always stressed to her that she was part-Warden and that was all that mattered. I was wrong."

I kept my mouth shut, listening to him as some instinctual sense told me this was something he didn't talk about a lot.

"I should've told her to accept the part of her that was demon, and *I* should've accepted it, because what she showed me…what I was a little late in realizing…was that what you are at birth does not define who you become." His jaw tightened. "Did you know until today that demons could love?"

"No," I whispered. "I didn't know."

"Yeah, well, I didn't know that until I met Roth. He's one of the most powerful demons you will ever come across, and he is still deadly when provoked. But the fact that he is capable of the kind of love he feels for Layla tells me that what we've been taught isn't necessarily the truth at the end of the day."

Fiddling with the strap of my seat belt, I still had no idea what to say. Agreeing with him went against everything I'd ever been taught, too, but he was right about Roth loving Layla. I'd seen that with my own eyes, heard it in the way he spoke to her.

What if we were inherently wrong about some demons? And if that was the case, how would one even begin to decipher how to proceed with them? Were some of them out there, trying to live their best life, and were Wardens supposed to just ignore them? How would Wardens even tell?

Zayne seemed to sense my thoughts. "Not many demons are like the ones you just met, and it's fairly easy to tell which ones are."

"How?"

"You can usually tell by one simple fact." Zayne grinned at me. "They don't try to kill you on sight."

Zayne and I were patrolling and it involved a lot of…walking.

A lot of walking.

And it wasn't particularly the easiest thing with my eyesight. I wished it was dusk, which was the best time of day for me to see. If it was, I'd be able to actually check out the city. The sidewalks were lit well enough for me to walk without stumbling, but my depth perception was off and I was having a hard time not walking into people while trying to decipher if the people on the busy sidewalks were all alive or if some of them were dead, or if they were demons.

We'd returned to the condo Zayne was staying in, grabbed a quick bite to eat at a diner down the street and then I held up my end of the bargain.

I patrolled with Zayne, keeping an eye out for the mysterious being that was slaughtering Wardens and demons alike.

We'd been at it for at least two hours, and so far, all we'd seen was a handful of Fiends who'd hightailed their butts in the opposite direction the moment they saw Zayne.

"Is that normal?" I asked as we neared an entrance to a subway. "The Fiends running the moment they see you?"

"Yep. They don't ever engage." Zayne led me down the subway stairs. My heart skipped a beat. Steps were the *worst* in poor lighting. I clasped the railing, taking my steps cautiously. "I leave them alone. Some of the other Wardens don't, but like I said before, they're relatively harmless."

A part of me was relieved to hear that, because a lot of the Fiends I'd seen tonight had looked young, like teenagers, and I wasn't sure if that was their true age or not.

"I have another question," I said as I made it down the stairs without dying and we reached the dank, musty-smelling platform.

Zayne sighed. "Of course you do."

I'd been peppering him with questions all evening, and I knew I was at the height of annoying, but now I had a more serious question for him. "So, does your moving out and being all independent have to do with Layla?"

He walked ahead of me. "Why do you care?"

"Because I do." I hurried to catch up to him. "And because

the fact that you live by yourself is odd and, hey, if you'd answered the question before, I wouldn't be continuing to ask it."

Zayne's exhale was loud as he stopped under the glare of a fluorescent light. "I just needed space, Trinity. After my father died, and after things with…with Layla, I turned down taking over the clan, because I needed space."

For a moment I was shocked that he was actually answering the question. "What happened with Layla?"

He looked away. "It's a long and convoluted story, but the gist of it is that the clan turned on Layla. Not all of them, but enough. After watching her grow from a little girl to a young woman, knowing what she was and wasn't capable of, they assumed the worst about her and nearly killed her. My father led the charge against her," he said, and I felt my stomach twist. "And it was my fault."

"How was it your fault? What—?" I stopped, squinting, and stared at the space behind Zayne. "Um, my eyes may be messing with me, but…"

We were about five feet from the stairs, and the dark space between us and the steps was…shimmering and vibrating. The breath I'd been holding expelled harshly, forming puffs of small, misty white clouds. Icy wind barreled down the tunnel, blowing my hair straight back.

"What the Hell?" I muttered.

Zayne turned, backing me up. "Damn."

"What?" I asked, peering around him, and then the low hum of warning exploded into pressure at the base of my neck.

The shape took form within seconds. A manlike creature, standing nearly seven feet tall. Muscles rippled under shiny, onyx-colored skin. Two thick horns jutted from the top of his head, curving inward. The points were sharp, and I had no doubt that if this creature head butted someone, he'd impale them.

Pupils shaped like a feline's were set among irises the color of blood. Then it smiled, flashing two razor-sharp-looking fangs.

A Hellion.

Created by pain and misery, these creatures did not walk the earth. I'd read about them in one of the massive books Misha and I had studied. They existed in the bowels of Hell, there to torture the souls of the damned. They were forbidden to be topside, and yet one stood in front of the steps leading up to the world—to where people were strolling about.

But that wasn't the most disturbing thing about it.

"It's naked. Like really naked," I said, reaching for my blades.

"I can see that."

"Like I can't unsee this, Zayne. It's really supernaked," I said, shaking my head. "I can't focus. Oh my God. Everything is just dangling out there for the world to see."

"Would you stop pointing it out, please and thank you?"

"But why is it naked? Is there no clothing in Hell?" I thought that was a valid question.

"Maybe it wanted to impress you."

I gagged. "I'm going to puke."

"Try not to do it on me."

Zayne shot forward then, shifting as he ran at the Hellion. He was in full Warden form as he slammed into the creature. The Hellion roared, knocking him to the side. He hit the wall with a grunt. Chunks of cement gave way under his impact.

I cursed, starting toward Zayne as he picked himself up. Relieved to see that he was okay, I spun on the Hellion.

Adrenaline kicked my senses alive as the Hellion eyed me. It tilted its head, sniffing the air through bull-shaped nostrils. Ignoring the fact that it was very, totally naked, I cocked back my arm, prepared to let one of my blades go, when the Hellion simply vanished. A second later, I felt its breath on my neck. I spun around. Two puncture holes bled, due to Zayne's claws piercing his heavily muscled stomach.

I swung on the Hellion with my iron blade. It popped out of existence and reappeared a few steps to my left. Dropping down, I went for the legs of the creature, cringing because, yeah, it was naked. Before my kick could connect, the Hellion vanished again.

"Dammit!" I shouted, annoyed.

The sound of its deep, throaty chuckle alerted me to where the Hellion now stood. Jumping to my feet, I aimed the blade for the midsection—

Moving disturbingly fast, it caught my arm and then it had its hand around my throat, lifting me clear off the ground. Its body vibrated, and then a man stood before me, almost too beautiful to look at. The horns were still there, as were the fangs, but he looked as if he'd stepped out of a calendar of naked hot dudes.

Naked hot dudes with horns.

It sniffed the air again and growled. "He said it would be easy to find you. I didn't think it would be *this* easy."

"Who?" I gasped.

The dark-haired Hellion smiled, flashing fangs that did not remotely look human as he drew me forward, toward his mouth. "The one who is making your Protector *bleed*."

Fury exploded inside me. My *grace* burned through my veins, but I pushed it down. Even though they knew what I was, I didn't need to broadcast it to any other nearby demons. Gripping the meaty wrists, I pulled my legs up and used the Hellion's chest as a springboard. The action broke the creature's hold, and I rolled into the fall, springing back to my feet.

Zayne rushed across the platform, jumping over the guardrail. He hit the stunned Hellion in the back, knocking it down.

They both fell to the hard cement floor and rolled, coming dangerously close to the edge of the platform and the tracks below.

"Don't kill it!" I shouted. "He knows about Misha!"

"No promises." Zayne swung, catching the Hellion in the jaw.

For a moment, I was a bit entranced by the brutality etched into Zayne's striking face as he reared back to deliver another punch. Maybe it was because this was the first time I'd been out here, fighting like this. Misha and I had trained for this day, but outside of the Ravers and the attack when he was taken, I'd never experienced this.

The Hellion popped out of existence, and Zayne hit the floor, catching himself before he face-planted on the cement.

Reappearing above him, the Hellion grabbed him by the scruff of his neck and lifted him. Arching his back, Zayne swung his legs backward, locking them around the Hellion's waist as he used both arms to break the Hellion's hold. He swung down and planted both hands on the dirty floor. Using momentum and the Hellion's weight, he flipped the creature head over heels.

An icy cold breath danced along my bare neck. Swinging around, I found myself face-to-face with another Hellion.

This one had skin the color of red coals. It shimmered and turned into another inhumanly stunning man—who was also supernaked.

"Grab her!" yelled the first Hellion.

"Done," the one in front of me replied, its voice also deep and guttural.

"Do you guys not have clothes in Hell?" Letting instinct take over, I ducked under the Hellion's arm and wrapped my arm around its neck, squeezing as one of the subway trains blasted its horn in the distance.

The Hellion laughed. "You like what you see?"

"Sorry," I grunted. "Not interested."

"Oh, but I am." The Hellion swooped down, tossing me over its shoulder.

I hit the edge of the platform back first. Pain exploded through me, momentarily stunning me. In an instant, the Hellion was standing above me. I rolled, but not fast enough. Its foot landed a direct hit to my back, and before I could catch myself, I toppled over the edge of the platform.

The fall was only about four feet, but the landing still hurt like Hell. It wasn't the third rail, however, and the blaring horn from the quickly approaching train washed away the pain. Springing to my feet, I ignored the pain and gripped the edge.

"Where do you think you're going?" The Hellion was behind me, pulling me away from the platform. "Thought we were going to play?"

I briefly caught sight of Zayne moving behind the other Hellion, shoving his clawed fist deep into its back. Dark, oily blood gushed from the Hellion's chest as a hole formed where the heart—I assumed they had one—would be.

The Hellion's roar of agony told me that I'd been correct, and, well, I wasn't going to get any info out of that one.

Zayne released the Hellion as it burst into flames. Within seconds nothing remained but scorched cement and a smell of sulfur.

He lifted his head and saw me. "Shit!"

A second later, he landed on the tracks beside me in a crouch. "Back the Hell off," he warned.

The Hellion shifted back into its true form and laughed. "Step aside or I will spread your entrails over this yard and feast upon your heart, Warden."

"I'd like to see you try."

"I'd like to see you die," the Hellion snarled, baring fangs.

Light swallowed them as the train rounded the bend about half a mile down the tracks. My heart rate spiked as the Hellion disappeared.

"Behind you!" Zayne shouted.

I whirled around and swung, but the Hellion caught my fist. It tipped its head to the side. "Or perhaps I will just make *you* relive your worst memory over and over again until you claw at your own skin and beg for death. Ah, yes… Mommy? Care for me to remind you how she died? How you—?"

Rage, potent and lethal, rolled through me in poisonous waves and I felt my *grace* burning at my skin. "Screw you."

I stopped thinking. Twisting, I bent at the waist as the Hellion closed in and kicked out, my boot catching the creature just below the chin. Its neck snapped back, and I spun around, slamming the blade through its neck first, just to hear its guttural scream. "Where is Bael?"

"Kill me now." Blood sputtered from its mouth. "Because I'll never tell."

I lowered the dagger and pressed the weapon into its chest, piercing it. "Tell me where in the Hell is Bael!"

The Hellion lowered its head, let out a bloody laugh and then shoved itself fully onto my dagger. As sharp as it was, it sank deep into its chest.

"Dammit!" I shouted, yanking my hand back. It, too, burst into flames and then was no more. I started to turn toward Zayne—

He shot forward, pressing his body to mine and holding me against the stone wall. There was no space between us. A deafening roar filled my ears as the train barreled past us. The high-pitched shriek of the wheels rolling over the tracks pierced me. I could feel Zayne's body tensing around me as my fingers dug into his arms. It felt liked the train would never end. The wind from its speed beat down on us, whipping at our clothing and hair.

Finally, the last car passed us, and with the threat of being run over by the train gone, I became aware of every place that part of his body touched mine. Neither of us moved. I couldn't. Not with his body pressed so tightly against me.

Not that I really wanted to.

Zayne was still in his Warden form, his shirt shredded from the change, and the heat of his body seared through my clothes. The skin of his arms under my hands was rock hard and smooth, just like the skin of his chest pressed to my cheek. His head was still pressed against mine, his hand still around the back of my head. I hadn't realized he'd done it when he leaped toward me, but he had gotten his hand between my skull and the wall, protecting me as he'd forced me against it.

He smelled... God, he smelled amazing. That winter mint scent invaded every pore of me, and with each breath I took, I could taste it on the tip of my tongue.

My lips parted as I shut my eyes, surprised that he was still holding me and suddenly, desperately, afraid that if I moved or did anything, he'd let go.

I didn't want that.

I wanted him close. I wanted him *closer*. My pulse started thrumming wildly as I became aware of his heart pounding against my cheek. The hand at the back of my head spasmed, his fingers tangling in my hair, and a shiver rolled down my spine.

Zayne's warm breath skated over the side of my neck as he slowly lifted his head. I forced myself to be as still as possible as his breath now danced over my cheek, and then I couldn't be still any longer.

I shifted my head, chasing his warm breath and stopping only when I felt it on my lips. My eyes opened, and all I could see was those pale wolf eyes, heated and consuming. My gaze dropped, and I saw the thin slice of fangs parting his lips, but I wasn't afraid.

I was enthralled.

I wondered what it would feel like to kiss him in his true form, and something I'd never, ever experienced before swept through me. Potent, paralyzing desire blossomed, leaving me feeling out of control and dazed and like...

Like I'd been waiting forever for this—for *him*.

Zayne suddenly broke contact and leaped onto the platform, leaving me cold in the absence of his body heat and wondering what just happened.

"Trinity," he said, extending an arm as he crouched down. He hauled me up, and we ended up on our sides, facing one another.

I rolled onto my aching back and bent my knees. "Sweet Jesus."

"Yeah." He exhaled heavily. "Did it bite you?"

"No," I answered. Hellion bites were extremely venomous. They would kill a human within seconds and could paralyze a Warden for days. "You?"

"No. You okay?"

"Just dandy." I winced as I sat up. "Well, that was fun. They were looking for me. The first one said..."

"I heard what he said. He could've been lying." He turned his head and looked at me. "Just to mess with your head."

"Maybe," I whispered, but I knew better than that. So did Zayne. "Did you see what that Hellion did? He impaled himself on my dagger."

"I saw it."

"He killed himself rather than tell us where Bael is."

"Not at all surprised." Zayne knocked a strand of hair back from his face. "You know what that means, right?"

"What?" I groaned, trying to knock the dust off me with no luck. I looked like I'd fallen into a pile of powdered sugar. "Bael knows you're here."

24

"He knows I'm here," I told Jada as I lay in bed the following morning. As promised, my phone was propped against an extra pillow and we were FaceTiming. She looked amazing, all bright-eyed and snuggled into her pink-and-gray paisley comforter. I, on the other hand, was half-hidden by Zayne's blanket and was beyond grateful that I couldn't see myself in that tiny square at the top of my phone. "Bael sent two Hellions after me."

"Holy crap," she said.

"Yeah." I held the blanket against my chin. "I didn't even feel them until they popped out of thin air. I forgot that they could do that. We tried to keep them alive, but Zayne had to kill one and the other impaled itself on my dagger."

"God, Trin, that's not good for your first night out there." She reached out and adjusted her phone, bringing it closer to her face. "He has to know what you and Misha are."

"I know." I shuddered. "I mean, I guess that's good news."

I saw her mouth drop open. "Why would you think that's good news?"

"Because it means he's keeping Misha alive." I paused. "Probably as bait, which sucks, but he's alive and that's all that matters."

Jada was quiet for a long moment and then she asked, "Is it?"

I frowned. "What do you mean?"

Her sigh was audible. "I don't want to even think about this, and I know you don't, but God only knows what they're doing to Misha and how that is going to affect him. I'm not saying that being dead is better, but…it's probably going to be really rough when you get him back."

"I know." Tears burned my eyes. "I don't… I can't think about it. No matter what…condition he's in, we'll make him okay again."

"We will," she agreed, blinking rapidly and then wiping under her eyes with her palm. "Okay. Tell me something else. Have you gotten to see the city?"

Welcoming the change of subject, I let out a shaky breath. "Not really. We stayed in and got rest yesterday during the day and then went out last night," I told her, skipping over the meeting with Roth and Layla. I didn't think Jada would understand seeking help from demons when I didn't understand it myself.

"Are you going to make time to see some stuff?" she asked.

"I want to, but it seems kind of weird to be out sightseeing while Misha is…" I gave a little shake of my head.

"Yeah, you have a point." A faint smile came and went. "I would love to see the museums. Always wanted to, but not like that's going to happen."

Sympathy rose as I watched her. Female Wardens were kept in jeweled cages. "Maybe Ty will get assigned here next year? They obviously need the help."

"Maybe," she said with a sigh. "You know, I get why I can't just come and see you or help, but it…"

"It sucks," I told her. "If they'd just train the females to fight, you guys wouldn't be so…" I trailed off, trying to think of the right word.

"Stuck," Jada answered for me. "That's how I feel. Stuck."

I didn't know what to say.

"Don't get me wrong. I'm lucky, you know? I love Ty and I know I'll be happy with him, but…knowing that my friends are out there and they need help and I can't do anything just sucks." She exhaled heavily. "It pisses me off, too, because it doesn't have to be this way."

"Then change it," I told her.

"How?"

"Thierry listens to you. If anyone can help you change things, it'll be him." Thinking I heard Zayne in the living room, I shifted slightly and glanced at the closed bedroom door. I groaned as pain flared along my back.

"I saw that!" Jada exclaimed. "Are you hurt?"

"Not really. Just my back is sore," I told her. "The Hellion tossed me around like I was a misbehaving toddler. Hey, let me call you back—"

"Wait! Real quick, how are things with Zayne?"

My gaze slid back to my phone. "Fine. I guess. I mean, we haven't tried to kill each other yet."

"Have you kissed him again?"

"Oh my God," I moaned, thinking of last night. "No, but thanks for reminding me. I'm hanging up now."

She laughed. "Call me later, okay?"

"Will do. Love you."

"Love you more," she said, disconnecting the call.

No sooner had I rolled onto my aching back and looked at the picture on the nightstand, tucked close to the book, than

Zayne spoke from the other side of the door. "Trinity? Can you come out here?"

Groaning under my breath, I pulled myself out of bed and shuffled out of the bedroom, immediately taking in the scent of coffee and…bacon? My stomach grumbled as I saw Zayne at the stovetop. His hair was pulled back at the nape of his neck. I didn't realize until that very moment that I did appreciate a well-done man bun.

Jada would laugh her butt off hearing that.

"Come on." He glanced over to where I lingered in the middle of the room. "Figured you'd be hungry."

I didn't realize how hungry I was until that moment. "I am."

"Then take a seat and let me feed you."

I did just that, hopping up on the stool. Zayne was turning off the stove. There were already two plates ready, both covered with a paper towel.

"Do you drink coffee?" he asked, looking over his shoulder at me. I shook my head. "I have some orange juice."

"That's perfect." I started to get down. "I can get it if you just—"

"Stay seated." He went to a cabinet and grabbed a glass, then made his way to the fridge. "Figured after watching you get chased around by naked Hellion demons, breakfast was the least I could do."

I shuddered. "I'm going to need years of intensive therapy to erase the memories."

"You and me both." He placed the plate and glass of OJ in front of me, and I made quick work of the bacon. It was delicious, salty and yet sweet. Maple flavored, and I had to stop myself from licking my fingers when the bacon was gone.

Zayne finished his off with a cup of black coffee as he eyed me over the rim of his mug.

"What?" I demanded, running my finger along the edge of my plate.

"You're doing really good."

"At what? Eating bacon? I'm extremely skilled at that."

He grinned. "At all of this. You've never been patrolling before, and while you have fought demons, it's not an everyday thing for you and you did really well last night."

Pleased by the compliment, I forced a shrug. "That was what I was trained for, you know? Maybe not fighting naked Hellions, but I've spent my whole life training with…" I trailed off, my gaze following to my empty plate. I wished I had more bacon and maybe chocolate.

Lots of chocolate.

"Misha?" he said quietly.

I nodded. "We've been training forever for the day we'd be called upon."

"Called upon for what?"

"You know, that was never really specified," I told him, sliding off the stool and wincing when it jolted my back. "Only that we'd be summoned by my father at some point, to fight."

Zayne lowered his mug. "What was that?"

"What was what?"

"You just flinched." Understanding flickered over his striking face. "Are you hurt?"

"I'm fine," I said as I took my dish over to his sink, and technically I *was* fine.

He was still and then he was suddenly behind me, moving faster than I could track.

"I hate when you do that!" I snapped.

"Uh-huh." He grabbed my shirt, ignoring my protests as he lifted it up. He swore under his breath, and I knew what he saw. I'd checked it out in the bathroom mirror when I got up this morning to use the bathroom. "Why didn't you say something, Trinity?"

Pulling my shirt free from his grasp, I walked over to where my OJ was sitting. I snatched it up. "It's fine."

"It's not fine," he shot back. "Your back looks like a worn-out punching bag."

I frowned. "Nice description."

"This happened with the Hellions? Or has it been like this for a while?"

"From the Hellions. Probably when I got thrown off the platform."

"You should've said something."

Taking a drink, I lifted a shoulder as he stalked around me, his bare feet whispering over the cement.

"Why would you not say something?" He walked behind the island and opened one of the drawers, grabbing a small jar.

"I don't know." Honestly, I didn't want him to think that I was whining.

"You may be this badass Trueborn, but you're still half-human. You bruise easier than Wardens do, and if you had been fully human, you'd would've been killed a dozen times over last night." He looked at me from where he stood, his stare piercing even if his features were a blur at this distance.

I rolled my eyes. "I just didn't want to come across like I was complaining and it's…it's really not that bad. They're just bruises and they'll fade soon."

"Just bruises?" As he came back over to me, I realized he had something in is hand. "I'm not used to…patrolling with half humans, so I don't know your limits, and I need to know them so that you don't hurt yourself."

"I'm not hurt."

"I beg to differ." He took my free hand in his. "And this

is the first time you've engaged with demons on a daily basis. *You* don't even know your limits."

"You're overreacting."

"Have you seen your back?" he demanded, dragging me into the bedroom and then into the bathroom, flipping on the bright lights.

I winced. "I've seen it and it's not a big deal."

Zayne let go of my hand. "Only you would argue with me over the condition of your back." He placed the jar on the counter. "I need you undressed from the waist up."

"What?" I gaped at him. "Usually a guy tells me I'm pretty before he demands that I take my shirt off."

He shot me a bland look. "Is that all it takes for you to take your shirt off? You're very pretty, Trinity."

My eyes narrowed as I placed my OJ on the sink so that I wouldn't throw it in his face. "That's not all that it takes, thank you very much, and you didn't even sound like you meant that."

"Oh, I meant it."

"Whatever. Why do I need to take my shirt off?"

"So I can put this—" he picked up the jar "—on your back. It'll make the bruises heal faster, and unless you're double-jointed, you're going to need help putting it on. I need to see your back."

I stared at him.

He held my glare. "You're being ridiculous, Trinity. I'm not trying to see you half-naked. I'm trying to make sure you're not hurt more than I can tell, and also make sure you heal so that we can continue patrolling."

There was a tiny part of me that was...disappointed he wasn't trying to get me naked because he was attracted to me. How messed up was that? I had no idea why that disappointed me. It shouldn't. Zayne was the perpetual gentleman—annoying and a smart-ass, but a gentleman to the bone. However, the weird twinge of disappointment twisted into something explosive.

I don't know precisely why I did what I did next, but there was a whole list of reasons for me to lose control, so I could blame any one of them for what I did.

Holding his stare, I reached down and whipped my shirt off, then let it drop to the floor. "Happy now?"

Zayne was incredibly still as he continued to hold my stare and he did so for so long that I thought he might've fallen asleep standing up with his eyes open, but then his gaze lowered from mine, and now I was holding my breath. I wasn't wearing anything sexy. Just a normal bra, a plain black one with scalloped edging over the cups.

A muscle feathered along his jaw as his gaze slowly lifted to mine. Without breaking eye contact, he reached over and handed me the towel.

I took it from him, but I didn't cover myself. "Does the bra need to come off, too?"

Zayne lifted a single brow and a long moment passed. "Probably be easier."

For a tiny second, I imagined whipping off the bra, too, right in front of him. Zayne would probably die, right then and there. The look on his face would be worth it, but I chickened out before I even gave it serious thought. "Can you turn around?"

Zayne arched a brow and made a show of turning toward the shower, out of the path of the mirror.

Twisting at the waist, I placed the towel on the sink and then unhooked my bra. It slipped down my arms to the floor. I toed it under my fallen shirt and then picked up the towel and held it over my chest. I could see my back in the mirror, and it did look like a chessboard of pink and blue.

"I'm decent-ish," I said, and I saw Zayne turn around behind me.

"Jesus," he grunted, and not in response to my near-nakedness. "I can't believe you haven't said anything, and don't tell me it doesn't hurt. That has to hurt, Trinity."

It did. "I'm tougher than I look."

"You are, but I should've kept a better eye on you."

"It's not your fault," I said, sniffing the air as he unscrewed the lid on the jar. The scent reminded me of Icy Hot, but there was something else under that. "What is that?"

"A salve that Jasmine made. That's Dez's wife. She's really good at this kind of stuff. It's a mixture of arnica, turmeric and menthol. I think there may even be some witch hazel in it. It's an anti-inflammatory and it reduces pain and swelling," he told me. "The stuff is a miracle worker."

Zayne then placed his fingers against my skin, and I jolted at the contact.

"Sorry," he muttered. The salve was cold and slimy, but it was his fingers that caused the reaction. Other than occasionally taking my hand or knocking me over, Zayne didn't make a habit of touching me.

And he was really touching me now.

He worked the thick balm across my skin and then up and around. His fingers brushed the side of my breast, and my skin felt strangely warm as I lifted my gaze to the mirror.

All I could see was him standing behind me, so incredibly tall and broad, his golden head bowed as he concentrated on what he was doing.

Seeing him behind me so didn't help cool my skin down.

"What is Jasmine like?" I asked, trying not to think about the fact I was utterly topless.

He chuckled. "She and her sister, Danika, sort of buck the system whenever they can, but she and Dez are lucky. They love each other, the real-deal kind of thing, and they have two young ones. They're both a trip. Their girl, Izzy? She's just learning to shift and fly. Keeps going right to the ceiling fan."

"Oh, my," I murmured, my body jerking all on its own, thinking of Peanut when he was near fans. Which made me pray that Peanut didn't suddenly appear. "I always like to watch the little ones in the community when they begin to shift. It's adorable watching them learn how to walk and use their wings."

"Sorry," he murmured when I jerked again.

"It's okay." I felt really, strangely hot, which was weird, because the balm was so cold.

Zayne continued quietly, his fingers skimming under the edges of the towel and along my ribs, causing me to shiver, and I wasn't sure if there were bruises there or not. When his hands slid back, I wasn't sure if I should be relieved or disappointed.

"Do you think I'll get to meet Danika and Jasmine?" I asked, desperately trying to distract myself.

"If you want to, I don't see why not." His quiet answer warmed me inside, too.

"I'd like that."

His gaze flickered up, meeting mine in the mirror for a second. "Then I'll make sure that happens."

Several more seconds passed and I started thinking about strange things—anything, really—to keep my mind away from his hands. "Before I knew what I was...or I guess, before I understood what I was, I thought I was normal and I wanted to be a thousand different things when I was a kid. None of them was this, but..."

"What were some of the things you wanted to be?"

"Oh, some of them were really stupid."

"I doubt that."

I snorted. "After watching *Jurassic Park*, I wanted to be an archaeologist."

"I don't think that's dumb," he said, and even though I couldn't see his smile, I could feel it.

"And I wanted to raise llamas."

Zayne's hand stilled again. "Llamas?"

"Yeah." I giggled. "And don't even ask why. I have no idea. I just wanted a llama farm. I think they're the most amazing animals ever. Did you know children can ride them? Adults can't. It wouldn't be very comfortable for you or the llama."

"No, I didn't." He chuckled. "That is probably the strangest thing I've heard in a while." His deft fingers slid over my spine. "Did you want to go to college?"

"I did." I took a steadying breath, and the cool scent of menthol reached me. "But my mom was always against it, you know, before I understood what I was," I admitted, closing my eyes. "I wanted to see the world a little and it's weird, because the first time I got to see DC, when we went to Roth's place, it freaked me out. That sounds stupid, doesn't it?"

Zayne's hand stilled. "No, it doesn't. The city is a lot to take in if you're not used to seeing all the people."

A wry grin pulled at my lips. "It was overwhelming. So many people. I can't tell you how many times I couldn't tell if a person was dead or alive when we passed them on the street."

"That has to be inconvenient." His hand started moving again, and my back arched a little.

It took me a moment to collect my thoughts. "It is a little."

"Speaking of ghosts, the one that came with you?"

"Peanut?"

"Yeah." A pause. "Him. Can he…move things?"

I grinned. "Yes. Did he move something?"

"This morning my shoes were in the fridge."

A giggle snuck out of me. "Sorry. Peanut is very…very

weird, but he's harmless. He just wants your attention and has a weird way of showing it."

"Can I be honest?"

"Yeah?"

"I'm trying to ignore the fact that he's now haunting my place."

"He's not really haunting it," I said. "Think of it as co-habitation."

Zayne snorted. "I'm almost done." His hand was on the other side, smoothing the salve up my side. "You should already be starting to feel better."

"I am."

And that was true, but as we both fell silent, I could no longer ignore Zayne's hands on my skin and how they were making me feel. It was like electricity flowed from his fingers over my skin, and when those long fingers brushed the sensitive swell near my ribs, I sucked in a soft breath.

"Sorry." His voice sounded different, thicker even. "You okay?"

"Yeah." I cleared my throat. "Yes." I tried to find another distraction. "You know what I'm jealous of the most when it comes to Wardens?"

"What?"

"Your ability to fly. I'm this badass Trueborn, but I don't have wings. That sucks."

He chuckled.

"It's not funny." I pouted. "I'd love to fly and get close to the stars. I used to try to get Misha to take me up in the sky, but he'd never do it even though you guys could probably carry a car into the air. Such a punk."

Zayne carefully turned me around and then his hands left me. I looked into his eyes. I was immediately snared, feeling hot and dizzy, like I'd been sitting out, sunning on the sandy white beaches, and even though he wasn't touching me any longer, I could still feel his palms and fingers. I couldn't stop wondering what would happen if I dropped the towel.

Every muscle in my body locked up. Drop my towel and be topless in front of Zayne? My God, he'd have a stroke. What was I thinking?

But I wanted to, because I wanted… I wanted to feel his hands on my skin again. I wanted to feel his mouth on mine, and this time I wanted him to kiss me.

Something changed in his expression.

Those pale eyes, usually so chilly, were full of fire, and that jaw was a hard, straight line. His features were both beautiful and brutal, a raw combination.

"We may have to do this again," he said, and his voice sounded off, deeper and rougher.

I was *so* looking forward to that.

His lips parted as if he were about to say something else, but his phone rang in the other room. He hesitated, his gaze still latched to mine, and then he put the jar on the counter before pivoting on his heel and walking out.

"God," I whispered, turning back to the mirror.

Still feeling way too hot, I drew in another shaky breath. I really needed to put my shirt and my bra back on. That was the appropriate thing to do, especially before Zayne returned, but I stood there, staring at my reflection in the mirror.

I didn't look like myself.

Well, the messy, half-fallen topknot was all me, but the glassy eyes, parted lips and flushed skin looked nothing like me. Another fine shiver danced its way over my skin as heat pooled low in my core. Zayne wasn't even in the bathroom with me anymore, but I could still feel his hands on the skin of my back, along my sides to where just the tips of his fingers had grazed the sides of my breasts.

A sharp buzz hit my veins as I sucked in air, and a warm, pleasant heaviness settled over me.

It's normal.

That's what I kept telling myself. What I was feeling was just my body reacting to the touch of someone I was attracted to, and I was attracted to Zayne, but that was all, just a…a carnal attraction, one that I was positive wasn't two-sided.

But if it were?

My breath hitched. That would complicate things, wouldn't it? My body didn't care about that at all, though. Neither did that primal part of my brain that was suddenly flashing images to accompany the memory of his bare hands, slippery and smooth against my skin, and those images were as clear as reality.

Zayne's reflection appeared in the mirror, causing me to gasp. His gaze met mine in the mirror. "I thought you'd be dressed," he said.

"I…" I really had no idea what to say as I turned to him, figuring the towel was more discreet than my bare back. "I, um, I'm still wet."

Those pale eyes flared with wintry heat as his gaze dipped. "Really?" he said, and I swore it sounded like a purr against my skin.

My face burned as I realized what I'd said and how that could be perceived. "The salve—the salve is still wet and I thought I'd let it dry a little."

Zayne nodded slowly as he bit down on his lower lip. Those thick lashes lowered, shielding his gaze.

"Who just called?" I asked.

"Roth," he answered, and my skin immediately chilled. "He wants to meet with us. Tonight."

25

The place we were meeting Roth turned out to be a restaurant called Zeke's. We had to park in a garage down the street, and it was a little weird walking beside Zayne, wondering if any of the people we were passing on the street had any idea what he was.

I liked the restaurant from the moment we walked in. Softly lit, the interior was a mixture of exposed wood and steel. The booths looked comfortable with thick cushions and lush pillows. It had a rustic-modern feel that reminded me of mountains and Colorado.

Which was weird, because I'd never been to Colorado, but for some dumb reason, I imagined there were a lot of places like this in Colorado.

The hostess appeared to recognize Zayne. With a genuine smile and lingering gaze I couldn't blame her for, she seated us in a surprisingly private booth near a large stone fireplace. There was a romantic vibe to the place that made me overly aware of Zayne and made me feel like I should be wearing something...cuter than jeans and a T-shirt.

Whatever.

I was comfortable and that was all that mattered.

The moment the waitress left after placing our drinks on the table—a Coke for me and a water for Zayne—I asked, "Is it okay for us to meet here?"

The candlelight from the center of the table flickered over his face as he nodded. "People that come here mind their own business."

"Oh." I toyed with the napkin as I glanced around. "Do they know what you are?"

"They know I'm a Warden, but they don't know what Roth is," he explained. "How's your back feeling?"

"Perfect." And it really was. It didn't ache or throb at all when I made sharp movements. Pulling my hands into my lap, I glanced around the restaurant before my gaze found its way back to his. "Thank you for doing that."

His chin dipped, causing a strand of hair to slip against his cheek. "It was my pleasure."

A humming warmth traveled through my veins. "I'm sure there're better things you could be doing than rubbing gunk all over my back."

"You're right. I could be doing better things with my time," he replied.

Ouch.

The warmth vanished.

"But that doesn't mean I wasn't enjoying myself," he added, and my gaze shot to his. A half grin played at his lips.

Before I could come up with a response, I felt the sudden increase in my shoulders. "I think he's here," I said. "Or another demon is here."

A moment later, Zayne said, "I feel it now. Crazy how you can feel it before me."

Zayne rose and moved to my side of the table. He sat beside me, thigh pressed against thigh. "What does it feel like to you?" he asked.

"Like a hot breath on the nape of my neck," I told him, voice low. "And a heaviness in the shoulders. Same for you?"

He nodded.

Roth arrived, dressed very much like he'd been the first time I saw him. All black. He wasn't alone. The icy blond demon was with him, his hair braided in pigtails, which looked weirdly good on him.

"I hope we kept you guys waiting." Roth slid into the booth across from us, followed by Cayman. "And yes, I meant that just the way it came out."

"We just got here," Zayne answered, stretching his arm along the back of the booth. "We weren't waiting long."

"That's disappointing," Roth replied, his bright amber gaze fixed on me as he got himself situated. "So weird."

"What?"

He tipped forward. "I still want to touch you."

My eyes widened. "You're an odd, creepy demon prince."

Roth grinned.

"Well, you still creep me out," Cayman announced as Roth leaned farther toward me, one hand sliding across the table.

"No touching," Zayne warned.

The demon prince pouted as he pulled his hand back. "That's no fun."

"Where's Layla?" I asked, changing the subject from the whole touching-me thing.

Roth smiled tightly. "She decided it would be best if she sat this one out."

I glanced at Zayne. There wasn't even a hint of emotion on his face.

"Don't you two look supercozy and cute." Cayman eyed us intently.

"Do we?" Zayne murmured.

"You do," Roth answered. "I like it. A lot."

Zayne's finger began tapping along the back of the booth. "I'm so glad to hear that, as I've been waiting on bated breath for your thoughts and feelings."

Roth smirked.

"Did you guys order anything?" Cayman asked, scanning the menu. "I'm starving."

We hadn't, and I didn't get the chance to redirect the conversation to why we were here, because the waitress showed up and took Roth and Cayman's drink orders, along with requests for an array of appetizers.

When the waitress hurried off, I leaned forward. "Have you guys found out anything?"

It was Cayman who answered. "I have not so great news and bad news."

I stiffened as my stomach pitched. "Okay?"

"I put my ear to every ground possible, and no one is talking about your Misha, about Bael...or about you," Cayman explained.

"I don't know if that's the not so great news or the bad news," I said, glancing at Zayne.

"It's the not so great news. It means Bael doesn't want anyone to know about it, and that's strange, because us demons are the bragging sort," Cayman said with a grin. "And I'm not talking about humble bragging like the Wardens do."

Zayne snorted. "Two Hellions came after us last night. They were sent by Bael."

"Bael has a damn army of Hellions at his disposal, so you

should expect to continue to see them if he's got them look-ing for you."

"And what's the bad news?" I asked, and Zayne touched the back of my shoulder, sifting through my hair to reach the muscles tensing there.

Roth met my gaze and his features softened a little. "No one knows where he's holed up, but I think he's the reason we've been seeing an increase in lower level demon activity. Since he's topside, they're going to follow."

Zayne shifted beside me, keeping his hand on my shoulder. "What are you saying?"

"I'm saying that when we do locate Bael, it's not going to be just him. He's obviously got a ton of Hellions with him, but you can expect to see a lot more."

"Great," I murmured.

"And Bael isn't known for his hospitality," Cayman re-marked, picking up his wineglass. "Not even when he's try-ing to be nice."

My gaze shot to Roth, and he lifted his shoulder in agree-ment. "But I know you already realize that, and you already know that he's keeping Misha alive for a reason, which is backed up by your run-in with the Hellions the night prior. He's using Misha to draw you out and sending Hellions after you."

"They're not going to get her," Zayne said.

I shot him a look, oddly...complimented by the certainty in his tone.

"But this brings us to the portion of the weird news," Roth continued. "No one is talking about her. There's no whisper-ing of a Trueborn on the scene."

"Well, that's not bad, right?" I asked.

"It's not good, either." Zayne's fingers were still on the back of my shoulder, light but oddly comforting. "Because it doesn't tell us what Bael is trying to accomplish here, other than wanting you."

"Getting his hands on you can be reason enough for him." Roth drew his finger around the rim of his glass. "You know what demons will do to a Trueborn."

I suppressed the shudder as I reached for my drink. "Could Bael be behind what's attacking the Wardens and other demons?"

Roth shrugged. "Bael is a big deal. He's powerful enough, but…"

"You don't think it's him, do you?" Zayne asked.

The demon prince didn't answer immediately. "Why would it be? What does he have to gain by risking exposure? Nah, Bael is ballsy but he's not stupid."

An array of appetizers arrived—crab cakes, cocktail shrimp, crab dip and fries. The food looked and smelled amazing, but I didn't touch it.

"Did you know several Infernal Rulers have left the city or are planning to?" Roth plucked up a shrimp, glancing at Zayne. "Isn't that…suspicious?"

Infernal Rulers were Upper Level demons that controlled legions of lesser demons. They were sort of like executives, and I guessed that would make someone like Roth a CEO with his boss, Lucifer, being the president, but that would mean Bael was also like a CEO…?

My head hurt.

Zayne's fingers splayed out across my shoulder. "So, whatever is out there on the streets has them scared, too?"

"The Wardens aren't the only ones turning up dead in very graphic ways," Roth reminded him.

"That's something I don't get," I said, glancing down at the plated crab cake Zayne had slid in front of me. "If it's a demon, why would it go after other demons?"

Shaking his head, Roth unloaded a spoonful of dip on his plate. "Wants to be the biggest fish in the sea, I suppose."

"And you two aren't worried?" I asked, frowning again as a fork ended up between my fingers. "Scared? You're both big...demon fishes."

Zayne chuckled under his breath.

"Never been called a demon fish, but yes, I like to think we're big deals." Cayman popped a fry into his mouth.

Roth's smile was slow and wicked. "Concerned? Yes. Afraid? Never."

"Arrogant," Zayne murmured as I cut into my crab cake and he picked up a steamed shrimp. "You should be somewhat afraid, if not for yourself, then for Layla."

The lazy amusement vanished from Roth's features as his gaze flicked to the Warden beside me. "Did I ask for your advice on what to worry or be afraid of?"

"No, but it sure as Hell sounds like you need it."

Busying myself, I took a bite of my crab cake and almost moaned in pleasure. It was amazing. Mostly meat seasoned with Old Bay. I took another bite, close to shoving my whole face into the cake, while Zayne and Roth eye-screwed one another.

"Get used to it, Trinity."

I looked up at Cayman. "Used to what?"

"Them arguing and trying to out-snark one another." Cayman winked. "Some people find it tiresome, but I find it wildly entertaining. I'm just waiting for the moment when their passionate arguing turns into passionate lovemaking."

My lips twitched as Roth snarled something under his breath. I finished off the delicious crab cake. "I was thinking. Bael has the ability to control humans, right?"

"Beyond what all of us typically can do? Yes. But on the kind of level you saw during the attack on the community? I would be surprised," Roth said. "Bael is particularly skilled at influencing humans, but to pull off that amount of possessions, I'm thinking something else was involved."

"What?" I glanced down at my plate when some dip and chips ended up on it. The melted cheese and crab looked tasty.

"A spell," Roth answered.

"Witches," Zayne said, nodding. "That would make sense."

"Witches?" I turned to him, surprised. Witches, *real* witches, were humans whose ancestors at some point had hooked up with a demon, and that watered-down demonic blood had gifted them with certain abilities that usually involved the four elements—earth, wind, water and fire. They also had a knack for spells and enchantments. "You have covens here?"

"We do. Some really active ones. They tend to hide from both demons and Wardens, which is why they've managed to stay alive and off the Wardens' radar mostly," Roth said, sliding a glance in Zayne's direction. "Because you know, Wardens do like to kill indiscriminately."

Zayne sighed.

"Do Trueborns like to kill indiscriminately?" Roth cocked his head as that amber gaze slid to me.

"At this moment? Yes," I said, annoyed.

Zayne chuckled under his breath while Roth grinned and leaned forward. "I like you."

"That's awesome to hear," I murmured.

His grin grew. "There's a chance that witches could've been used, and while most of them stay as far away from my kind as they do Wardens, there are a few covens who like to get down and dirty with demons. I know of one in particular." Roth leaned back. "Of course, Zayne wouldn't be able to talk to them. They aren't fans of Wardens."

"But they're fans of yours?" I asked.

"Everyone is a fan of me," he replied. "You could meet

with them. They won't be able to tell what you are, and I can take you. There's a huge group of them that usually meet on Saturdays."

Saturday was like another week from now. Seven whole freaking days. Impatience blossomed, tinged with frustration. Would Misha survive another week?

Zayne stiffened. "I don't know about this."

The demon prince's gaze shifted to Zayne. "I thought you trusted me?"

"I trust you, but I don't trust you to make wise life choices." Zayne pulled his arm off the back of the booth.

Roth pressed his hand against his chest. "I'm offended."

"I'm down for it." I ignored the look Zayne sent me. "If there's even a small chance they can give us any information, I'm willing to go with you and meet with them."

"Perfect," Roth purred, and Zayne didn't look remotely happy.

"Good." I leaned back against the booth. "You just have to promise me that you're not going to try to…eat me or something."

That devilish smile of Roth's returned. "Now, that might be asking too much."

26

"I don't like this," Zayne was saying as we left the restaurant. I kept close to him since the lighting on the sidewalk was poor.

"Like what?"

"You going with Roth to see the witches."

"I thought you trusted Roth—" The toe of my boot caught the curb I didn't see and I stumbled. "Dammit."

Zayne caught my arm. "You okay?"

"Yeah." I tugged my arm free as I glared down at the sidewalk I couldn't see. "I just tripped. I'm fine."

A moment passed. "I trust Roth, but I don't trust the witches. Anything they do, they do to gain something in return. You need to be very careful around them."

"So no letting them take clippings of my hair or nails?"

Zayne snorted as we headed into the parking garage. "Yeah, try to avoid that, but also don't make any deals with them to get information. Sometimes they will help, but the price you pay is never what you expect."

"I'll pay any price."

Zayne stopped so quickly I walked into him and bounced back a step. Irritation flared to life as Zayne faced me. "See, that's why I'm worried."

I stared up at him, able to make out his features in the harsh white light of the parking garage. "You shouldn't be."

"I shouldn't be? You being willing to do anything to get the littlest piece of information regarding Misha is dangerous. Especially when you're going to meet a coven of witches, who are notorious for taking people's desperation and manipulating it to their benefit."

I crossed my arms. "I'm not easily manipulated."

"I didn't say you were, but I also know that you're desperate, and I get it—"

"Do you really?" I demanded. "I don't know. You keep making vague statements on how you know what it's like to see someone you care about in trouble but not be able to do anything. If that's true, then you would understand. You would do *anything*—"

"I know this is dangerous, because I *do* understand." Zayne took a step forward, crowding me, but I held my ground. "I've been desperate enough to do anything, and that never ends well, Trinity."

The constant feeling of helplessness surged and it stripped the filter right off my mouth. "Is that how you lost a part of your soul?"

Zayne drew back as if I'd hit him. A veil slipped over his face and his features became devoid of emotion. "Who told you that?"

I snapped my mouth shut.

"Who?" Zayne demanded, reaching for me but stopping short. "Who told you that?"

Wishing I had kept my mouth shut, I unfolded my arms and looked away. "Misha told me. He said... He said he'd heard that you'd lost a part of your soul and that's…that's why your eyes are different."

"Is that what he said?" He cocked his head.

Heart thumping, I nodded. "Is it…true?"

Zayne didn't answer for a long moment, and then he did. "Yeah, it's true."

I'm going to die.

Cowering on the subway platform, I knew the beautiful demon, with his golden eyes and cruel smile, was going to kill me. He was supposed to help me, but the room was bathed in blood and the broken, huddled mass on the floor was Zayne.

"He can't save you," the demon growled between jagged teeth. "No one can."

A scream rose in my throat as the demon lurched toward me with razor-sharp claws—

Jerking awake, I gasped for air as I tried to get a sense of my surroundings. Where was I? I didn't recognize the darkness of the bedroom. There were no stars on the ceiling and the bed…was far too big to be mine.

It took me moment to remember that I was at Zayne's place, in his bed, and he was alive and I was alive.

It was just a nightmare.

Groaning, I pulled my hands out from under the comforter and pushed several strands of hair out of my face.

The bedroom door cracked open, startling me. I held my breath as I strained to see the shape filling the darkness of the doorway.

"You okay?" Zayne's voice was rough from sleep. "I thought I heard you scream."

The warmth of embarrassment crept across my face. "Sorry. I didn't mean to wake you."

"It's all right," he replied, and I didn't see him move but I felt him draw closer. My vision still hadn't adjusted when the lamp on the bedside table turned on, causing me to wince. His gaze drifted over me, lingering on where I was clenching the edges of the blanket, my knuckles bleached white. "Can't sleep?"

I shook my head, surprised that Zayne was checking in on me. After the whole showdown in the parking garage, things had been…awkward between us. We'd barely spoken, even when we came across a pack of Ravers in the back alley of one of the major theaters downtown. We'd come back to his place a few hours ago and parted ways without saying much of anything to each other.

I dared to peek up at him.

A look of understanding flickered across his face as he glanced at the door he just came through. Then, wordlessly, as my heart started beating crazily fast, he gestured toward the bed.

"May I?"

I wasn't sure if this would help our current standoff, but I didn't want to be alone, so I nodded and scooted over, keeping ahold of my blanket like it was lifeline.

"Nightmares?" he asked, his voice low as he sat beside me and leaned against the headboard.

I nodded as I watched him stretch out his long legs, crossing them at the ankles.

Tipping his head back, he looked over at me. "I'm sorry."

"About what?"

He was quiet for a long moment. "About everything, really. You've been through a lot, and that's emotionally and mentally tiring. Your mind is going to make it rough on you, even when you're at rest."

"You don't have to apologize. It's not your fault," I said.

"You're actually doing everything you can. It's just... I don't know. I feel like I don't have control in any of this and I'm..."

"What?"

Confused. Antsy. Uncertain. "I'm just... I'm scared. I know I shouldn't admit that, but I'm scared that I won't find Misha in time or, when I do, it will be too late, because he must be going through things I can't even imagine."

He folded his arms loosely over his chest. "It's okay to be scared, Trinity. It's okay to worry."

"I know." I held my blanket tighter.

"Then stop giving yourself such a hard time."

I exhaled heavily. "And I...I should apologize to you. I shouldn't have asked you what I did earlier. It was none of my business and I was just— I was being an ass, and you were trying to help me."

"It's okay. You don't have to apologize." He drew one leg up. "It just caught me off guard. Sort of surprised me that you haven't said anything until tonight, considering all the questions you ask."

I snorted. "Yeah, I'm kind of surprised myself."

"I just... I want you to know that I do understand why you need to do everything you can," he said while I wrestled with the desire to ask him what happened.

I pulled my knees up under the blanket and rested my chin on them. Easier said than done. "So, you're okay with me meeting with the witches?"

"Going to have to be."

"You're...not used to having to sit things out, are you?"

"Not even remotely."

I smiled at that, feeling a little better about what had happened in the garage. "Do you think these witches Roth was talking about are going to be able to tell us anything?"

"At this point, who the Hell knows?" He nudged my knees

with his. "But if those humans who attacked the community alongside Bael were under a spell, they should know who did it, or at least who's capable of it, and through them, we may find where Bael is and if he still has Misha."

"And what if the witches we go to are the ones who helped Bael?" I asked.

"Then things are going to go south." A pause. "I know you've been taught to not use your *grace*, because it weakens you and it can draw other demons to you, but if you ever find yourself in a situation you can't get out of by fighting, use it."

I didn't know how to respond at first. "You know, you're the first person to say that to me. Neither Misha nor Thierry has ever said that."

"I know it's a risk for you to do it, but I'd rather deal with the risk and the consequences than have you end up hurt or worse," he told me, and my chest got all warm and fuzzy. "If the witches try anything, take them out."

"You're kind of bloodthirsty."

"I've learned to be."

That he had. Shifting my gaze from his, I looked up at the ceiling and wished I could see stars. "I miss my ceiling."

"What?" Zayne laughed.

A faint smile tugged at my lips. "At home I have these amazingly tacky glow in the dark stars on my ceiling. They're white. Not green. I'm not *that* tacky."

"Never," Zayne murmured. "I remember seeing them."

"Anyway, I like staring up at them." I lifted a shoulder in a shrug that caused my back to ache a little. "Kind of stupid, I know."

"It's not," he replied. "It's familiar."

I couldn't help but wonder if I would ever lie under them again.

"Can I ask you a question?"

I nodded. "Sure?"

"What happened with your mother exactly?" he asked. "I hate to bring it up and I felt like shit for doing so when we were at Roth and Layla's place, but you said that this Warden thought you were..."

"An abomination?" I supplied for him, sighing. I didn't talk about my mom a lot, because it always ended with me wondering why I'd never seen her ghost or spirit, but I wanted to talk to Zayne about her. Maybe because he hadn't known me when it happened, and that made opening up easier? Or maybe because, unlike Jada or Ty, he knew what it felt like to lose a parent? I wasn't sure. "My mom was trained. Did you know that?"

"No, I didn't."

A small smile pulled at my lips. "She wanted to be trained just in case something happened. She was strong like that, didn't want anyone to take care of her while she sat around like a frail flower."

"Sounds an awful lot like her daughter."

That made my smile grow. "That's a compliment."

"I would hope so. Who trained her?"

"Thierry and Matthew. They...they loved her," I said, rolling onto my side, facing Zayne. "And I think... I think they still mourn her death as much as I do." I drew in a shallow breath. "Ryker was a Warden my mom trusted, as did Matthew and Thierry. They were friends and...he was always kind to me, but I...I messed up."

"How do you think you messed up?"

I closed my eyes. "It happened about a year before my mom was killed. I was sixteen, and I was training with Misha. He'd gotten the upper hand on me." I paused. "He got the upper hand on me a lot, because he knew my weaknesses and he exploited them to try to get me to improve."

"That makes sense."

"Yeah, it does." I thought about the way Misha would purposely stay in my blind spots to train me to react even when I couldn't see what was going on. "Anyway, I got mad…and as you've already realized, I can be a wee bit impulsive."

"Just a little," he said, and I could hear the gentleness in his voice.

"Well, Misha was really getting on me, just messing around, but I lost my temper—my control. I let the *grace* take over to remind him that at end of the day, he couldn't beat me. Not that he needed to be reminded, but I was being a brat and… and Ryker saw me. I didn't realize at the time that he had, and I don't even understand how he did, because he never came to the training facilities, but…he figured out from there what I was. He saw me as an abomination and a threat to other Wardens. He also knew that I could attract demons to the community, so it was a double-edged threat. He told a few other clansmen, and they decided that I should be…put down."

"Jesus." Zayne sounded horrified.

"The messed-up thing is that he waited nearly a year to come after me. A year of pretending to be my friend, being kind to my mom and hiding the fact that he hated me." I let out a shaky breath. "Anyway, I used to go see a doctor in Morgantown for something that I couldn't get treatment for in the community, and Ryker had accompanied us before, a lot of times actually, but…that time was different. After the appointment, on the way home, he pulled over and said there was a problem with the car. Mom and I got out, and that's when he made his move. He shifted and came at me, and I was so shocked. I just stood there like a dumbass, and Mom—she jumped in front of me, and that was…that was it."

I flipped onto my back while Zayne remained quiet, and somehow, when I straightened my legs, we were closer. My leg rested next to his. "I have been taught nearly all my life to control my *grace*. To not use it until it's time. But if I had used my *grace*, I could've stopped him—stopped him like I did Clay. I could've saved my mom—"

"Trinity, don't go down that road any farther. Without even knowing you this whole time, I know you've been blaming yourself for two years. You are not responsible for your mom's death."

I swallowed, still utterly thrown by the fact I was talking about this. Jada would be so shocked she'd want to record this moment. "I'm not? Because what if that was the time I was supposed to use it? What if we were taking the whole 'being called by my father' thing too literally? What if—?"

"Stop. You're not responsible. You didn't hurt her. That was on this Warden. Him. Not you."

I knew I hadn't hurt her with my hands, but I couldn't help but think I had hurt her with my actions. It was hard getting past the fact that, at the end of the day, my behavior had played into a chain of events that led to her death.

Zayne was quiet for a long moment. "I think... Sometimes I think my father is still here."

I looked up at him, pressing my lips together.

"Almost like I can...feel him? I know he's not here, and it's probably because there are times I forget he's gone. I find myself thinking about telling him something and then it hits me. He's *gone*."

"I still have those days," I admitted. "I don't think we'll ever stop having those days."

"No, we probably won't." He took a deep breath, and I felt it. "Things weren't good between us toward the end. We were barely speaking to one another."

I was able to put two and two together from what he'd told me previously. "Because of Layla?"

"Yeah, because of her." He fell quiet again, so long that my eyes began to drift shut, and then he spoke. "But before he died, he'd begun to realize that how someone was born and what they are didn't dictate whether they were good or bad. Life, even for creatures we think don't have the free will to choose between good and evil, isn't the sum of DNA. Everyone is…a lot more complicated than that."

"Did you guys get a chance to talk it out before he died?" I asked.

"A little." Zayne went silent, and it seemed like an eternity stretched out between us before he said, "You okay with me turning off the light?"

My eyes opened. "Are you leaving?"

"If you want me to, I will."

"I don't want you to."

"Then I won't for now." He paused.

For now lingered in the space between us as I looked to where my hand fell. "Can you stay for a little while?"

"Yeah." The bed moved a little as he reached for the light. A moment later the room plunged into darkness. "The picture? You look like your mom."

I smiled into the darkness. "I do."

"Nice reading material by the way."

"Shut up." My smile grew. He'd must've seen it before he turned off the lights. "That was my mom's favorite book—and mine."

"Maybe I'll have to read it."

"Not sure Vikings are going to be your thing."

"You never know." There was a pause. "I think my ceiling could use some stars."

It took me a moment to realize what he was saying. "Do you really?"

"Yes." He chuckled softly. "You sound like you don't believe me."

"I thought you'd find them childish or something, and I cannot picture you with stars all over your ceiling."

"I'm full of surprises, Trinity."

My toes curled at the way he said my name.

I don't know how much time passed after that, but I was still awake and I...I wanted to know more about Zayne. "I have questions."

A soft chuckle radiated from him and shook the bed. "There isn't a single part of me that is surprised."

My smile returned. "Why don't you have a girlfriend?"

"What?" Zayne huffed quietly. "I'm not sure how to answer that question." He paused. "Why don't you have a boyfriend?"

"That's easy to answer," I said, wanting to bury my face in the pillow. "I'm a Trueborn who lives with Wardens who think I'm a human. Not exactly a lot of dating options."

"Good point." He shifted, and I felt his leg move just the slightest against mine. "And you and Misha never had anything?"

"No. Seriously. I already told you that I had a crush on him for, like, five seconds. I've had a lot of crushes, but Misha and I have never looked at each other like that. Plus Trueborns aren't supposed to hook up with their Protectors," I told him.

"Why?" he asked.

I half shrugged. "It goes against the rules and supposedly messes with the bond. I don't know how. It was never really explained to me." I paused. "And you didn't answer my question."

"Mainly because I really don't know how to answer that."

"You're good-looking. You're funny and charming when you're not being annoying."

"Thanks." A pause. "I think."

"You're...a good guy," I said. "So, just surprised that you're single."

Zayne seemed to ponder that. "You know Wardens are expected to mate. I'm almost twenty-two. Most males of my age are already mated with one child on the way."

"Yes. So, why haven't you mated and got to baby making?"

He shifted beside me. "If you ask my clansmen, they'll say I have little respect for tradition, but no one is going to force me into a lifelong commitment, even if that life isn't going to be that long."

My heart dropped. "Are you planning to die soon?"

"I wake up every day knowing it could be the last. I don't plan for it. I just accept it," he answered. "It was what I was trained from birth to do."

I mulled that over, realizing that what he spoke was the truth. Not a lot of Wardens made it to retirement age. It was one of the reasons they mated and had children so quickly. "Have you ever wanted to do anything else?"

He sighed. "You do ask a lot of questions."

"I do." My hands relaxed on my stomach. "I understand you have this huge, important duty, but was there ever a time when you didn't want to be out there? That you wanted to do something else? Is being a warrior what you want?"

"Whoa. Okay. That was a lot of questions. Do I want to be out there? Is this what I want?" He repeated my questions and then let out a little laugh. "You know, no one has ever asked me that. Not even—" He cut himself off, and I wondered how he would've finished that sentence. "It's all I know, Trinity."

I bit down on my lip. "That doesn't answer my questions."

"I know," he replied.

The pressure on my chest increased. "What...what would you do if you weren't a Warden?"

"I can't answer that."

"Try." I nudged his leg with my knee.

"I really can't." His arm moved out of my reach. "I've never thought about it. I've never even considered it."

What kind of life was that without any options, even impossible dreams? I'd had them before I knew what I was. I still had dreams of doing more than what I was born to do, even if my options were seriously limited.

Silence fell between us, and after a moment, I asked, "Tell me... Tell me what it's like growing up here, in the city." I paused. "Please?"

There was that rough chuckle again and then he told me what it was like growing up as the only child in a large house with nothing but trained warriors to keep him company until Layla came along. He didn't talk about her much, though. Instead, he spoke about how he spent afternoons shadowing his father, learning all the streets and the different buildings. I don't know how long we talked, but after a while, I started to feel myself slip under.

I fell asleep with a smile.

27

I sat on the bed, cross-legged, and stared at the photo of Mom and me. I'd just gotten off the phone with Jada and Ty. Peanut was in the living room, jamming out to music only he could hear while Zayne spoke to someone on the phone. It was in the afternoon, around three, and we still had several hours before we would start patrolling.

Over the last several days, we hadn't seen anything but Fiends. No Hellions. No Ravers. No strange creature killing both Wardens and demons. The nights had been rather long and boring, but when we got back to his place, usually close to three in the morning? Anything but boring. Ever since the night my nightmare had wakened him, he had been coming into the bedroom and staying up with me until I fell asleep. He was always gone in the morning, and although we talked about everything in the sometimes minutes, sometimes hours it took me to fall asleep, when we were awake and the sun was out, he didn't mention visiting with me and I didn't bring it up.

I didn't know what it was, Zayne just being kind and keeping me distracted or something else, but I'd quickly found myself looking forward to it and the end of each patrol.

I missed Misha with every fiber of my being and there were only a few minutes of every day that I didn't think about him, but once I found him, things would change between Zayne and me. I wouldn't leave the city, not until I held up my end of the bargain, but I doubted I'd be staying with Zayne. Would Misha and I move into the compound? I was sure I'd see Zayne again, but things...things would be different.

I shoved those thoughts aside.

Tomorrow we would meet with Roth and the witches, and hopefully we'd find out something that would lead us to Misha.

Placing the phone on the bed, I glanced at the open door. Zayne had been gone when I woke up this morning, and him coming to me in the middle of the night felt like a dream.

I hoped it wasn't.

Rising from the bed, I walked to the window and opened the blinds just enough to see outside. The day was bright and the weather looked warm. Exhaling heavily, I rested my forehead against the wall. I closed my eyes as I folded my arms across my waist.

I missed Mom.

I missed Misha.

I missed Jada and Ty.

I missed Thierry and Matthew.

Mom was gone and I knew that everyone else was safe except for Misha, and I... God, I couldn't help but think about what Jada had said before. What kind of condition was Misha going to be in? Physically, I suspected a mess. The same emotionally and mentality, but I could help him get better.

With Jada and everyone, we could... We could make him better if he needed it. Misha was so strong, so I knew he was doing the best that he could. I knew he wasn't breaking. He was surviving—

"Trinity?"

Opening my eyes, I turned to the sound of Zayne's voice. He was in the doorway of the bedroom. "Hey," I said, waving awkwardly.

He stepped into the room. "You okay?"

I nodded. "Of course."

"Are you busy?" he asked. "Leaning against the wall?"

"Extremely busy. I try to do this at least once a day."

"Sorry to interrupt." He started to turn.

"What's up?" I pushed away from the wall and hurried toward him. Misjudging how far the bed jutted out, my calf smacked off the leg. "Ouch!"

"Damn, I heard that." He stepped toward me, his light blue eyes wide. "You okay?"

"Yeah," I muttered. "So, what's up?"

A look of doubt crossed his face. "Nicolai needs me to check in. Thought you might want to join me."

"Really?" My eyes widened.

"Sure," he said, and I was close enough to see the faint smile. "You'd asked if you'd get to meet Jasmine or Danika. Now's the perfect time. I can't guarantee both will be there, but I'm sure one of them will."

"I didn't…" I trailed off, realizing just then I hadn't believed him when he said I could meet them. I wasn't even sure why I had thought he wasn't being serious. "Okay. Am I dressed fine?" I glanced down at myself. Black leggings and tunic tank top may be too casual. "I can change."

"You look fine." Zayne chuckled. "We're only going to the compound, not the opera."

Picking up my phone, I narrowed my eyes on his back as he walked out the room. "I just want to make a good impression. I mean, I don't want them to look at me and think, Who's this messy-looking chick?"

Zayne chuckled as he went over to the island and grabbed his keys.

"It's not funny." I turned, finding Peanut draped over the punching bag. I shook my head. "What if they don't like me?"

Zayne looked over his shoulder at me, brows knitted. "I don't see how they wouldn't like you, but why would it matter if they didn't? They're not your clan, Trinity. They're barely even mine at this point."

The drive to the Warden compound was mostly quiet as I mulled over what Zayne had said. I wasn't all that bothered over him saying that these people weren't my clan. It was true, and who knew when I would see them again? What bothered me was what he'd said about himself. He didn't feel a part of his clan—his family? I didn't know what to say about that as I stared out the window. In a way, I knew how he felt, because I did know what it felt like to live with but not be part of a clan, but I also wasn't a Warden. For him to feel that way was a big deal.

I toyed with the hem of my shirt as we neared a bridge. In the distance, I saw something tall and white against the blue skies. I squinted. "Is that the...Washington Monument?"

"What? Yeah. That's it."

"Wow," I whispered, wishing I could see it more clearly.

"That's the first time you've noticed it?" he asked. "You should've been able to see it every night while we've been patrolling."

"I guess I wasn't paying attention," I lied, shoulders heavy. "One of these days when we have Misha back, I would love to see it up close and maybe visit the museums."

Zayne kept a hand on the steering wheel as he glanced

over at me. "I would tell you I think that would be fun, but I have a feeling Misha wouldn't want me around while you explore DC."

I grinned at that. "I think you'll grow on him."

"Really?"

"Yeah, you've grown on me." I looked over at him. "Despite the fact that you're sometimes a jerk."

Zayne shook his head. "I don't know. I think he'd still have a problem with me."

"Because of the soul thing?" I pointed out, and I wished he wasn't wearing his sunglasses so I could see his eyes. "Misha will get over that. I think you two would get along. You both like to try to boss me around."

"And you don't listen to either of us, so we do have that in common."

I rolled my eyes. "Whatever. So, what am I supposed to say if they ask me who I am?"

"Nicolai has already told them that you're here, from the regional seat, and that you're looking for a friend. That is all they need to know."

My brows lifted. "That explanation doesn't sound suspicious at all."

"Well, they can be as suspicious as they want, it doesn't matter." He hung a right, entering a heavily wooded area, and I finally felt like I could take a deep breath as the constant presence of demons eased off. "The clan members are good people, though. They could be trusted with knowledge of what you are."

Mom and I had thought Ryker was good people, but good people did bad things.

We neared a gate that opened as we approached. Up ahead, I saw the massive several-story brick building. It reminded me so much of Thierry's home that my chest ached.

I let out a rough exhale as Zayne followed the driveway and parked in front of wide steps. Nervousness filled me as I unhooked my seat belt and glanced over at Zayne.

He'd pulled his sunglasses off and placed them in the sun visor. "You look like you're about to puke."

"Do I really?"

One side of his lips kicked up. "Maybe not vomit, but you look extremely nervous."

"I am." I clasped my hands together. "I don't even really know why. I mean, you were right earlier. Everyone in there could hate me, but who cares?"

"They're not going to hate you," he said, and I saw him lift his hand. I stilled as he reached over, catching a few strands of my hair and smoothing the strands. "But you're wearing flip-flops. I probably should've told you not to do that."

Oh, no. "Why?"

"Because Izzy is going through this stage where she likes to nibble on toes."

"What?" I laughed, my toes curled. "For real."

"For real." He chuckled under his breath. "Come on, let's head in."

Deciding I was acting like a freak for no reason, I opened the door, stepped out and immediately tripped over the curb. Pitching forward, I caught myself with my hands before I ate cement. My sunglasses slipped down my nose.

"Oh my God, are you okay?" a female voice asked, ringing out from somewhere above me.

I cursed under my breath. Of course someone saw me. "I'm okay," I called out, feeling my cheeks heat.

Zayne was suddenly by my side, gripping my upper arms and lifting me up onto my feet. "You all right?" he asked, voice low.

"Peachy," I muttered, glancing down at my palms. The skin

was red, but not scraped open. I became aware of someone joining us at the bottom of the steps. I looked up, eyes widening behind my sunglasses as I stared up at a beautiful dark-haired female Warden who couldn't be more than a few years older than me. "You're really pretty," I blurted out.

She smiled as she glanced at Zayne, who was still behind me, still holding on to my arms as if he feared I'd fall again. "I like her, Zayne."

"I'm sure you do," he said wryly. "Danika, this is Trinity."

"Hi!" The girl thrust her hand forward. "I was wondering when I was going to get to meet you."

Zayne let go then as I went to take her hand, shaking it. "Usually I try to make a better first impression," I said.

Danika laughed as she waved her hand. "Don't worry about it." She squeezed my hand before letting go. "I'm really sorry to hear about your friend. I hope you find him."

"Thank you," I said, meaning it.

"How have you've been?" Zayne asked as he stepped around me, and I wasn't sure who went to whom first, but they were hugging, and it was a real one, full of affection. My heart squeezed again, because it was the kind of hug Jada and I gave each other—the kind of hug Misha and I shared.

"Good." Danika pulled back, clasping his arms. "You?"

"Perfect."

She tilted her head as if to suggest she knew better, but then she turned to me. "I hope you're keeping Zayne out of trouble."

"Uh, well, probably the other way around."

Danika's grin was sly as she slid Zayne a long look I couldn't decipher. We started up the steps. "Nicolai said you guys were coming over, and I got ridiculously excited."

"You're that bored?" Zayne asked as I carefully followed them up the steps, making sure I didn't fall again.

"Hell, yeah, I am." She laughed as she tossed glossy black hair over her shoulder. "Plus Izzy and Drake are teething, so I'm ready to throw myself out a window."

Baby gargoyles were a handful. Teething baby gargoyles were probably a nightmare.

Zayne stepped ahead and opened the door as Danika looked over her shoulder at me. "What do you think of the city so far?"

"It's nice, from what I've seen," I said, and then promptly ran out of anything else to say. Normally, I wasn't this awkward, but I was in rare form today. "I mean, I'd like to eventually see more, though."

"You should take her out, Zayne." Danika shoved him as she strolled past him. "Do you just have her locked up in your place?"

I lifted a brow as I took in the wide, circular foyer. There were a lot of doorways.

"All day and night," he replied.

"Sounds like a good time actually?" She giggled when he shook his head. "I think Dez and Nicolai are—"

A gray blur was suddenly coming straight for my face. Gasping. I stumbling back a step and lifted my arms out of reflex as someone shouted, "Izzy, no!"

Hands and wings smacked into me, and the next thing I knew, I was holding a squirming little gargoyle in my hands. She was a tiny thing but as heavy as a truck as she pounded her little fists on my arms. Her features took shape, and she was in her Warden form, her chubby face a slate gray and small horns parting a riot of red curls. She threw her arms around me and hugged me as tightly as a long lost friend would.

I was shocked into immobility as she murmured incomprehensible things and rocked in my arms, holding on to me for dear life. I stared over a small, flapping wing at Danika and Zayne. Both were gaping at us as I awkwardly patted the little girl on the back, between her wings.

"Hi there," I said, tightening my arms around the little girl as she kicked her head back and let out a wild giggle. I looked around her to Zayne and Danika. Both were staring open-mouthed at us. "I'm guessing this is Izzy?"

Zayne nodded.

"Yep," Danika said. "That would be her…and this would be my sister, Jasmine."

A moment later, a woman who bore a striking resemblance to Danika came rushing forward. "Oh my God, I'm so sorry. She was actually napping, and the next thing I knew, she took off and here she is." Jasmine reached for her daughter, grasping her by the waist, but Izzy held on. "Oh! I'm sorry. Izzy, let go."

Izzy did not let go, and she now had fistfuls of my hair. "I think she likes me."

"I think so, too," Jasmine agreed.

I glanced down and noticed that there was a small boy the same age as Izzy attached to the back of Jasmine's leg. He was peering out from behind his mother with big, blue eyes. "Hi."

He jerked back behind her. A second later, I saw one big blue eye appear behind her leg.

I grinned.

"Izzy, if you don't let go of this poor girl, you will not get any pudding for your afternoon snack."

The little girl immediately let go, wrapping her arms around her mother's neck.

"Wow, that worked remarkably fast."

Jasmine grinned. "This child will actually behave for pudding and that's about all. Again, I'm so sorry."

"It's okay." I smiled. "It was a nice greeting."

"Glad you think so." Jasmine turned toward where Danika

and Zayne stood. "Danika, can you do me a huge favor and grab Drake so I don't trip over him."

"Of course." She pulled away from Zayne and easily scooped up the boy, who promptly buried his face in her neck. "Drake is a little shy."

"And as you can see, Izzy is not." Jasmine grinned as she stepped back. "These two could not be any more different."

"Are they both shifting now?" I asked.

"Izzy can fully shift and hold it, but Drake can only partially shift so far," their mother answered as the girl twisted in her mother's arms toward me. "Izzy prefers to be in her Warden form."

"Drake just overthinks it, isn't that right?" Danika ruffled the little boy's hair and he lifted his head, sharing a tiny grin before shoving his face back down. "Izzy doesn't think twice about anything. She wants to do something, she just does it."

"My kind of girl," I said, playing with Izzy's hand as she reached for me again.

"Ours, too." Danika and her sister shared a look. "But she gives her daddy a heart attack about every five seconds."

Laughing, I glanced at Zayne and saw that he was leaning against the wall, ankles crossed and hands tucked into the pockets of his jeans. There was a faint smile on his face, a softness to the normally hard line of his jaw. I was struck by how much it reminded me of the day at Roth and Layla's place.

Zayne was here, but he wasn't a part of this.

My smile faltered as he tilted his head toward me.

The sound of male voices came from one of the closed rooms and then a door opened. A male Warden stepped out down the hall, and he was too far for me to see his face, but I recognized Dez's voice when he spoke. "Did Isabella attack someone again?"

"No." Jasmine laughed. "She was just overly happy to see Trinity."

"Is that so?" Dez swaggered down the hall and stopped to pluck his son out of Danika's arms. "Hey there," he said to me as he shifted Drake into the nook of one arm.

"Hi." I waved Izzy's hand at Dez, and Izzy cackled.

"How've things been?" He asked this of Zayne.

"Good. Nothing to share other than what I've already reported," Zayne replied, pushing off the wall. "How've things been here?"

"Normal, but we do have some news for you." Dez glanced at me. "This is something Trinity's going to want to hear, so I'm glad you brought her. Let's go visit Nicolai."

Zayne glanced at me, and I disentangled my fingers from Izzy's while Danika took Drake from his father. I walked over to join them.

"Remind Nicolai that he has thirty minutes," Danika said. "Or I'm leaving without him."

Dez shot his sister-in-law a look but she simply smiled back at him, and two things struck me as odd. One being the whole leaving without the clan leader part, which I hadn't even heard a male Warden threaten to do, and second, she was leaving? Like, the compound? By herself?

Danika's gaze met mine, and what I was thinking must've been written across my face. "Izzy takes after her aunt," she said, and Jasmine nodded. "I do what I want."

The corners of my lips tipped up. "I like you."

Danika winked.

"Come on." Dez motioned us. "Before you and Danika start chatting, because I feel like really bad things will come from that."

"Now I really want to talk to her," Danika called out.

"I'm not sure who would be the worse influence," Zayne commented, and I shot him an arched look. "You or Danika."

"Throw in Layla, and the entire house will be burning down around us," Dez commented.

"I heard that!" Danika shouted from the foyer.

I glanced at Zayne, but he showed no reaction to Layla's name or the fact that one of the clansmen had brought her up. I didn't know the details surrounding who had turned against her and who hadn't.

Dez opened the door, and I immediately smelled the faint scent of rich tobacco. I walked in, spying Nicolai behind a wide, large desk. He looked up from whatever papers he was flipping through as I inched into the room. Dez walked ahead, over a brightly woven throw rug.

"Danika wanted me to remind you that if you're not ready in thirty minutes, she's leaving without you."

Nicolai sighed, but when he spoke, his voice was laden with fondness. "Of course she will." He sat back. "Well, let's get the ball moving so I'm not chasing Danika through the streets of DC."

I opened my mouth to ask if she really was allowed to roam around the city, but I realized Zayne wasn't with us. I looked behind me and saw that he had stopped at the entry to the office. He seemed paler than normal as he slowly looked around the room, seeming to take everything in.

Then it struck me.

This had been his father's office.

My heart went out to him, and I started to turn toward him, but then he finally strode forward, those pale eyes focused on me. I waited until he was beside me and then I whispered, "Are you okay?"

"Always," he repeated, and then turned to Nicolai. "You have an update for us?"

If Nicolai or Dez had noticed his hesitation, they didn't acknowledge it, but then Nicolai dropped the bomb. "Bael was sighted last night."

"What?" I gasped as Zayne stepped forward. "When? Where?"

"Cal saw him on patrol around eight last night, near Franklin Square," Nicolai answered.

My heart started racing. This was huge news—news I hadn't been expecting.

"Cal is sure he saw Bael? Positive?" Zayne asked.

Dez nodded as he leaned back and picked something up off the desk. "Cal was able to snap a pic of him with his phone. We had the image printed out." He handed it to Zayne. "You think that's him?"

I darted to Zayne's side and peered down at the somewhat grainy image of a tall, dark-haired man standing outside a black town car. He was dressed in a gray suit and his black hair was slicked back. He was looking up, and even I could see the weird yellow light that had reflected off his eyes.

"That's him," I said, hope sparking alive. "That's Bael."

"It is." Zayne looked up as I all but snatched the photo from him. "Do we know who's in the car?"

I squinted. There was…someone in the backseat.

"Not sure yet, but we reached out to our contacts at the police department to get the tags run. The vehicle is registered to a local car service company. We're waiting to find out who the driver was and who they were transporting. As soon as we hear, we'll let you know."

Bael was in the city.

"This is good news," I said, looking up at Zayne. "Right? Once we find out who he's with, we can hopefully find him."

He nodded. "Not just that. Now we know where to start patrolling."

28

"Are you sure you're safe up here?" Zayne asked, offering me a hand as I reached the top of the fire escape of the building overlooking Franklin Square.

Staring up at him, I raised an eyebrow. He was in his Warden form, a beautiful, primal sight with his blond hair parted by his fierce horns. I placed my hand in his warm, hard one. "You sound like Misha."

"In other words, I sound like I'm asking reasonable questions?" He hauled me up with one arm, and I don't even know what happened.

Zayne either underestimated how strong he was or overestimated how much effort it took to lift me, but I ended up clearing the ledge and then some. My feet nowhere near the cement rooftop, I toppled forward, into Zayne. He dropped my hand and caught me with his arms around my waist.

"Whoa," he said, laughing as he sat me down on my feet. "And I'm supposed to not be worried about you up here?"

"That wasn't my fault." I tipped my head back. Silvery

moonlight sliced across his face. "You're like the Incredible Hulk."

"I don't know about that."

I expected Zayne to let me go and step back, keeping a respectable distance like he always did, but when he didn't, I wished I could see his eyes and I wished I knew what he was thinking. We weren't as close as we had been on the subway, but I could feel the warmth of his body.

I took a quick, shallow breath as I placed my hands on his arms. "You don't have to worry about me up here. For real, though."

"I can't help but worry about you, when we're over two hundred feet in the air." His arms loosened, and his hands slid to my lower back. "You're badass, Trinity, but I don't think you'll do well if you slip and fall."

"I'm not going to slip and fall," I told him. "And I can make some pretty awesome jumps." I pulled away, breaking his now-loose hold. "I can show you—"

"Yeah, no." He caught my hand, pulling me back toward him. "I don't need a demonstration. We're up here patrolling, not showing off."

"But I want to show off," I said, tugging on my hand, but his grip tightened. "I can clear the alley and go from roof to roof. Probably even over the street if I get a good running start."

"I really do not suggest that you attempt that."

"And what am I supposed to do if we see a demon or Bael down below? You'll just jump and I'm supposed to slowly make my way to the fire escape and climb down it?"

Zayne pulled me toward the center of the roof, his wings tucked back. "You can *quickly* make your way down the fire escape."

"That will make me very useful if you need help." I rolled my eyes.

"I'd rather have you alive than useful." Zayne let go of my hand then. "Besides, it's been quiet the last couple of nights."

Zayne was right about that.

But tonight felt different because we now knew Bael had been here.

As I moseyed away from the center of the building, Zayne was right behind me, like a shadow...like Misha. My heart squeezed as I reached up, rubbing at the center of my chest.

I missed Misha so badly it was a physical ache that I wondered how Zayne could be so distant from his clan. I spun toward him. "Can I ask you something?"

"You know, I would think something was wrong with you if you didn't have a question to ask me," he replied.

I snorted. "Well, you'll be able to tell if I ever get possessed."

"True." His wings spread out behind him, nearly blocking out the moon. "What is your question?"

"How often do you see your clan?"

There was a beat of silence. "Why?"

"Just curious."

"Weird thing to be curious about."

"So? Just answer the question."

"I check in with them often."

I inched closer to him. "Based on the way Danika and Jasmine acted, it seemed like it had been weeks, if not longer."

"Well, it has been a while since I saw them, and sometimes I check in with Nicolai or Dez over the phone or out here, in the city."

"So, how long has it been since you've been home?" I asked, and Zayne's wings snapped back, tucking close to him. I crossed my arms. "What? That is your home, Zayne."

"It doesn't feel like it. Not with my father gone and—" He

cut himself off and then he turned, stalking toward the ledge. "It's been a while since I've gone there."

"Don't you... Don't you miss them?" I asked. "I mean, I haven't been gone that long and I miss everyone so much it hurts."

"It's not the same." He hopped up on the ledge, perched there as he overlooked the city down below. "My clan is still here, in this city, and I can see them whenever I want."

"Yeah, you can," I said, hands curling into fists. "It must be nice to have that privilege."

His head turned to the side and a long moment passed. "You don't understand. Going back there...all I can think about is my father and how I wasn't able to save him and how I wasn't able to stop...stop Layla from being hurt. That place used to hold good memories. Great ones, but now...not so much."

I stared at the shape of him. "I know how that feels, Zayne, or have you forgot that?"

Zayne cursed. "No, I haven't. I'm sorry—"

"Don't apologize. Just...just listen to me," I said. "You told me that I wasn't responsible for my mother's death, and not to sound like an arrogant tool, but I am stronger than you. I could've ended Ryker's life in a heartbeat, but I didn't. You couldn't save your father—"

"It's not the same."

"How?"

Zayne rose fluidly and turned. "I was distracted with personal shit, Trinity. My head wasn't in the game. If it was, I could've stopped the attack."

I didn't know if that was true or not, but I had a feeling it wasn't that simple. "So, were you just moping around and doing nothing when he died?"

"No. I was fighting a wraith."

I threw my hands up. "Look, maybe you were distracted,

but it wasn't like you were doing nothing. His death wasn't your fault, and I have no idea what happened with Layla, but I'm sure that wasn't on you, either."

"Oh, that was entirely my fault." He came down to the roof. "I nearly got her killed, but it's not just that. It's more." He sighed, looking over his shoulder at the street. "I miss them. I do. I just need my space. That's why I moved out. It's why I didn't take over the clan."

"Because you feel like you failed your father?"

"Because I'm not sure if I...if I can do it." He was in front of me, wings outstretched. "I don't know whether I could lead the clan when I no longer believe that what they're doing is correct."

My eyes widened at the admission. "The whole killing de-mons indiscriminately thing?"

He nodded. "Just because we are told something is right doesn't mean it is."

I didn't know how to respond to that. The fact that Zayne was questioning the whole *all demons are bad* thing would be considered bad enough, but this was something I imagined the Alphas would be very, very unhappy to hear.

So would my father.

But after meeting Roth, Layla and, yeah, even Cayman, I thought Zayne had a point. They were helping me when my own clan had originally wanted me to just...move on.

"That's admirable," I said finally.

"What?"

"You," I said, nodding. "It's admirable that you're allowing yourself to see what probably less than one percent of War-dens see."

He cocked his head. "And what do Trueborns think?"

I lifted my shoulders. "I think... I think there's a lot for me to learn about, well, everything."

"Yeah."

"But—"

"I'm done with this conversation," he said, and I opened my mouth. "Seriously."

I snapped my mouth shut and then nodded. I was surprised he'd shared what he had. I felt like I'd scaled a fortress wall. As the warm breeze lifted the thin wisps of hair at the nape of my neck, I thought about the day Zayne and his clan had arrived.

"I used to climb the buildings back home when Misha would go atop one to rest. That's where I was when I saw you guys show up—on the roof of the Great Hall. I don't know if I told you that or not? Anyway, Misha hated it, always worried that someone would see me or I'd slip and fall," I said as I walked over to the ledge. "But I loved it—being this high and so close to the stars. I can't fly, so this is… This is the closest I can get to it."

Zayne cursed under his breath as I hopped up on the ledge, and he swiftly landed beside me, his large body angled to catch me just in case I lost my balance.

I grinned as I pivoted on the ledge and walked away from him. My peripheral was nothing but shadows and my night vision was basically utter crap, but my balance was on point. Up ahead, I could see where the building ended. When I'd been in the alley before, the gap between the buildings had appeared to be about twenty feet.

Zayne stayed right behind me. "What is up with your fascination with stars?"

Worrying my lower lip, I glanced back at him and then I lifted my gaze to the sky. "Can you see the stars? Right now?"

He didn't answer immediately, and I imagined it was because that wasn't a question he'd been expecting. "Yes. Why?"

"Because God has a messed-up sense of humor?" I exhaled heavily, about to talk about something that I talked about even less than I did my mother's death. I didn't want to, but I had gotten Zayne to open up just a little, so maybe it was... It was my turn. "My father is an angel—an *archangel*, Zayne. One so powerful and so...scary to most people that I don't even like to say his name. His blood pumps through me—his DNA—but so does my mother's and that of her family. Come to find out, they don't have the best genetics, and some of those flawed genetics made it through the mix."

"What do you mean?"

"I have what's called retinitis pigmentosa, and no, don't ask me to spell that. I'm probably not even pronouncing it correctly. It's a...degenerative eye disease that usually ends in partial or total blindness," I explained rather factually. "It's usually hereditary but sometimes people can just develop it. A great-grandmother of mine had it and it skipped a couple of generations, and I ended up the lucky winner of crappy eyesight. I have little side vision. Like if I look forward, I can't even see you. You're nothing but a blob of shadows. It's like having horse blinders on," I said, lifting my hands to the sides of my head. "And my depth perception is pretty terrible."

"Wait. Is that why I've seen you flinch if something gets close to your face?"

I nodded. "Yeah, if something comes at me from the side, I often can't see it until it's, like, right there, in my center vision. My eyes don't adapt well from light to dark, and extremely bright light is just as bad as extremely dark areas. There are... tiny black spots in my vision, kind of like floaters, and they're easy to ignore at this point, but I have cataracts already. It's a side effect of these steroid eyedrops I had to take when I was younger." I shrugged and started walking along the edge again. "Which is why the moon actually looks like two moons on top of one another until I close my right eye."

Stopping, I placed my hands on my hips and looked down at

the park against the street. The trees were just shapes of thicker darkness against lighter shadows even though the park was lit.

Zayne touched my arm, and when I looked at him, I saw that he'd shifted into his human form. "What does this mean exactly? Are you going blind?"

I lifted a shoulder again. "I don't know. Probably? The fact that I'm not completely human throws a wrench in the whole thing, and the disease requires a level of genetic mapping to see what the prognosis could be—I assume you know why that can never happen. But the disease isn't predictable even in humans. Some by my age are completely blind. Others don't develop symptoms until they're in their thirties. Maybe my vision loss will slow down because of the angelic blood in me, or it may stop entirely, but it has been getting worse, so I don't think my angelic side is doing that much good. I just don't know. No one can answer that. No one can even answer that for a lot of humans with the disease."

Zayne was quiet as he listened, so I continued. "When my mom noticed I started walking into things more often and having trouble navigating when it was really bright outside, she and Thierry took me to an eye doctor, and the man took one look at my eyes and referred me to a specialist. A lot of really annoying tests later, the disease was confirmed. It was a shock to say the least." I laughed. "I mean, come on. I'm a Trueborn. Fighting while having these huge gaps in my vision isn't exactly easy. So, how did this happen? But it is… what it is."

"I noticed some things, like the flinching and your steps seeming unsure at night, but I never would've guessed it," he said. "Never."

"Yeah, I don't think most people do. You know? Most people only think of the blind and the seeing, and they have no understanding or concept of everything in between. I don't hide that I have this disease." I looked over at him. "I've just learned to compensate for it, so much so that sometimes even I forget…but then I walk into a door or a wall, and then I'm quickly reminded."

"And the stars?"

A faint smile tugged at my lips as I recalled what the eye specialist in Morgantown had once asked me. "At my last appointment, about a year ago, my eye doctor asked if I could still see the stars at night. It was weird when he asked, because I had to think about it and I realized I couldn't answer the question," I admitted. "I hadn't looked up at the stars in, like, forever, and it sort of hit me, you know? That one day I would look up and I wouldn't see a star, and that would be it. I'd never be able to see something so…beautiful and simple again. Up until that moment, I'd taken that for granted. So, every night, I look up to see if I can see the stars."

Zayne didn't respond, but I felt his intense gaze on me. I started twisting my hair as I lifted a shoulder, unsure of what else to say. "So, yeah…"

A moment passed. "Can you see the stars now?"

I tipped my head back and lifted my gaze. It was a cloudless night and the sky was like a deep oil slick broken up by tiny dots. "I can see them. They're faint." Raising my hand, I pointed to two stars, one on top of the other. "Right there. Two of them." I closed my right eye and the two tiny blurs of white became one blur of white. "Oh, wait." I laughed. "There's only one star there."

"Yeah," he murmured, and when I glanced at him, he was staring up in the direction I'd pointed. "There's a star there." He looked over at me, and our gazes locked. "Do you see more?"

Feeling a little dizzy and silly, I looked away with great effort. I scanned the sky again. "I see a couple. Why? Are there a lot of stars?"

When he didn't answer, I peeked at him, and found that once again, he was staring at me, his head cocked slightly, causing a strand of blond hair to graze his cheek.

I kept twisting my hair as nervousness grew like a nest of birds waking up and taking flight. I looked away. "I'm guessing the sky is full of stars?"

"It is, but the only ones that matter are the ones you see."

My gaze flew to his.

He smiled at me. "You are… You are incredibly strong."

The comment caught me off guard. "What?"

"You're standing here talking about losing your vision like it's nothing. Like it's no big deal, and it's huge. You know that." Reaching over, he placed his hand on mine, startling me. Gently, he untangled my fingers from my hair. "But you're dealing with that. Living with that. If that's not the definition of strength, I don't know what is."

The nest of birds moved to my chest. "I don't think it's strength."

He pulled my hand away from my hair. "Trin…"

Flushing at the first use of my nickname and realizing I liked it when he called me that, I turned my gaze back to the two stars that were really one. "What I mean is, I don't think it's being strong. I can't change what's going to happen. Maybe one day there'll be a cure and it will work for me, but until then, I have to accept this and I can't dwell on it, because it *is* scary—it's scary as Hell to really think that all of this will be gone and I'll have to learn to live differently with the expectations of who I am and what I am, but I *have* to deal with it. And I do so by not letting it define me or consume every waking moment of my life. That's not strength. That doesn't make me special." I shrugged. "It just means I'm…doing the best I can."

Still holding my hand, he squeezed. "Like I said, the definition of strength."

As if I had no control, I found myself staring into his eyes again, thinking that it was going to suck one day when I couldn't see the stars, but it was going to be a damn shame when I could no longer see those pale blue wolf eyes.

"I can't believe you haven't told me until now."

"Don't take it personally. It's not something I talk a lot about, because I just… I don't know. I don't want people treating me different because of it." I turned to him. "I don't want you treating me different."

"I wouldn't." He stepped into me, careful of the fact we were still on the ledge. "Okay. That's not exactly true. I admire the Hell out of you, but I already admired you. So now it's more."

I tried to stop smiling, but I couldn't as I looked down at where he still held my hand. With the moonlight, I could see it.

"What are you going to do if it does get worse?" he asked.

"Maybe I'll get myself a seeing-eye gargoyle."

Zayne chuckled. "I can be that for you."

"Uh, yeah, I feel like you'd grow very bored of that."

"I don't think so." His fingers curled around my chin, bringing my gaze back to his. Air hitched in my throat. "I don't think…there's ever a boring second around you."

"You don't?" Needing a little space after discussing something so personal, I pulled free and backed up. "Good. I bet you can't catch me."

Pivoting around, I took off running on the ledge. I heard him shout my name, but it was lost in the wind as I picked up speed, the wind lifting my hair from my shoulders and sending it streaming behind me. I reached the edge of the ledge at a breakneck speed and there wasn't a moment of hesitation or fear. I jumped, surrounded by nothing but air, and in those brief seconds, right before I began to fall, I became weightless and I knew that was what flying felt like.

Hitting the ledge of the building across the alley, I tucked and rolled off the rest of the speed, popping back with a wild smile breaking out across my mouth.

Zayne landed a second behind me, fully shifted again, and his wings lifted out and spread wide. The roof was more lit here so I could see the stunned look etched into his features.

Tossing back my head, I laughed as Zayne stormed toward me, fully shifted once more. "You should see your face right now. Oh my God, you actually do look speechless." I spun away from him. "Didn't know that was an actual thing—"

Zayne was on me in a heartbeat.

I squeaked as he caught me, lifting me clear off my feet as he held me to his chest. He pivoted, pressing me back against the cool metal of a maintenance shed. Like the night in the subway, there was no space between us, and I don't know exactly when I'd curled my legs around his lean waist, but I had and I liked it.

A lot.

"You…" He glared down at me, the tips of his fangs exposed. "You…"

"What?" Clutching his shoulders, I was breathless and it had nothing to do with the jump and everything to do with how close we were.

"You're maddening," he said, pressing in, and a deep pulsing throb sent a shiver down my spine.

My eyes widened as I stared up at him. I wasn't even sure if he was aware of what he was doing. He was furious. That much was clear, but there was something heavier and thicker riding that anger.

"You're out of your mind." One hand slid from my waist, over my hip, down to my thigh. His hand clenched, the sharp claws snagging the thin fabric of the leggings.

Okay. He knew what he was doing.

"You're utterly reckless and completely impulsive," he continued, and I tipped my head back against the shed, finding it difficult to get air into my lungs. "If you do something like that again…"

"What?" I squeezed his shoulders as his wings lifted and came down, cocooning us. Before, the utter darkness had caused me to panic, but now, it made me bold, like I could do anything in the shelter he created. "What are you going to do?"

"Something." His words were hot against my neck, causing all my muscles to tense.

My fingers touched the edges of his hair. "You need to give me a little more detail on that," I told him. "Because I'm a hundred percent going to do that again."

"I'm going to need to get a leash for you." He shifted his body and my entire body seem to jerk against the unexpected hardness between his hips.

Oh God.

My heart was pounding as heat pooled. "If you got a leash for me, I'd choke you with it."

His husky chuckle burned my lips. "You would."

"*Yes,*" I told him, agreeing and giving permission for something he hadn't asked for but I wanted to give him. Something I think he wanted to give *me*.

He was so still and so quiet and then he said, "The second you kissed me in the training rooms, I knew you were going to be trouble."

"Is that why you ran from me?"

"I'm not running from you now," he said. "It seems I'm running *after* you now."

Then the barest brush of his lips against mine caused my entire body to arch. My lips parted, giving him access, and I felt the wicked tip of one fang against my lip. I shuddered against Zayne, and he made this deep, throaty groan that was nearly my undoing.

"We shouldn't..." He trailed off, dragging that sharp fang across my lower lip. "We shouldn't be doing this."

I couldn't think of any damn thing we should be doing right now other than this. "Why?"

"Why?" He laughed, low and soft against my lips. "Besides the fact this complicates things?"

"I like complications."

"Why doesn't that surprise me?" His forehead rested against mine. "You've been through a lot, Trin. You have a lot on your mind, and I'm not—"

A sudden screech ripped through the air, forcing us apart. Zayne lowered me to the roof and spun, tucking his wings so I wasn't smacked upside the head by one.

I didn't see them at first, not until the two creatures landed on the roof. They looked like bats—huge, walking bats. Moonlight streamed through their thin, nearly translucent wings.

"Imps," Zayne sighed.

I unhooked my blades and braced myself. Imps weren't known for their intelligence, but they made up for the lack of brains with their violent tendencies. "Don't they normally hang out in caves?"

"Normally. Guess they're out sightseeing."

"Do you think they're looking for me?"

"Well, we're about to find out."

One of them screeched and rushed Zayne. The other took flight and landed nimbly in front of me. It was too dark to risk throwing the blades so this fight was going to be hand to…bat wing?

I giggled.

"Do I really want to know why you're laughing over there?" Zayne asked, catching the imp around its neck.

Grinning, I darted back as the imp took a swing at me. I dipped under the demon's outstretched arms and sprang up behind it, then spun and slammed the iron blade deep into its back.

It let out a high-pitched shriek before bursting into flames. I turned in time to see the other demon do the same. I started toward him—

Jerked backward, I nearly lost my grip on my daggers as talons snatched me by my shirt. A stuttered heartbeat later, I was lifted off my feet. I shrieked as the imp started to take flight. The material of my shirt began to tear.

Zayne spun to where I dangled several feet off the roof. *"Christ."*

Lifting my daggers, I swept them back in wide, high arcs, catching the imp's hind legs. The wickedly sharp blades cut into the creature's skin and bone. Wet warmth sprayed into the air. It screamed, a sound that reminded me of an angry baby—if an angry baby was also part-hyena. The thing let go, and I was falling.

Into nothing.

A roar of wind and night air rose up to snatch me. I couldn't even scream as terror exploded into my gut as I fell.

Oh God. Oh God. Oh God, this was going to hurt. This was going to hurt bad—

Arms caught me around the waist, jerking me up and back

into a hard chest. The impact knocked the air out of my lungs, but I knew it was Zayne.

Zayne had caught me.

Air whipped around us as his wings spread out, slowing our fall, and then he landed in a crouch, the impact jarring me to the very core.

"Holy crap," I whispered as I blinked rapidly. My hair was plastered to my face. The handles of my daggers felt like they were embedded into my palms. "Holy crap, I didn't drop my daggers."

"Are you okay?" Zayne's voice was tighter than normal as let go of me, and I quickly spun toward him. "Trinity?"

"Yeah." Sheathing my daggers, I checked my shoulders. "It didn't claw me. I think it was trying to carry me off. Thank you." I looked up at him. "You probably just saved my life there."

"I think I totally saved your life there."

"Totally," I agreed, looking around and realizing we were in the alley near the fire escape. "Are you okay?"

"It got me in the chest." He looked down, cursing.

My stomach dropped as I reached for him as concern blossomed. "How bad?"

"Not that bad," Zayne said, stepping back from me. "But we should head back. I'm going to need to clean this up."

Worried, I quickly agreed and desperately tried to ignore the sudden, arctic blast rolling off Zayne.

29

The thin strip of light from the bathroom door pulled me from my sleep, alerting me to the fact that I had fallen asleep without Zayne.

After we got back to his place, he'd cleaned up in the bathroom and then had announced that he was making it an early night. The lights in the living room had turned off, a clear sign that he wanted his space, and I had stayed in the bedroom, thoroughly confused. Unlike all the nights before, he didn't come into my room and it had taken an eternity for me to finally fall asleep.

But either he or Peanut was in the bathroom.

Sitting up, I slipped my legs out from underneath the blanket. The cement floor was cool under my feet as I padded quietly toward the bathroom. I placed my hands on the door. "Zayne?"

"Sorry," came the gruff reply, several moments later. "I didn't mean to wake you. Go back to bed."

The corners of my lips turned down. He sounded...weird,

his voice terse and strained, more so than normal. "Are you okay?"

"Yes," he barked.

I bit down on my lip. Was he in pain? He'd been looking pale by the time we'd gotten back, but he'd insisted he was okay, and I'd asked that question about a half dozen times. Knowing I probably shouldn't, I went ahead and opened the bathroom door.

What I saw was a bloody mess. Zayne was in front of the mirror, shirtless, and he was... He was plucking something out of his chest with...with tweezers? Bloody towels were on the vanity and there was something milky in a mason jar.

"Good God," I exclaimed.

"Dammit, Trinity," Zayne growled as he turned away from me, reverting to my full name. "Do you ever listen?"

Not particularly. "I was worried."

"I'm fine."

"You do not look fine." He was a ghastly gray color, and his fingers, slippery with blood, trembled around the silver tweezers. "What happened?"

"It's nothing," he grunted, turning back to the mirror.

"It doesn't look like nothing." I inched closer to him, grateful that the sight of blood didn't freak me out, but what he was trying to do to his chest *did*. "Can I help you?"

"Yes. You can help by going back to bed." He did a double take. "And is that Elmo's face on your shorts?"

"Don't talk smack about my shorts." They were a gift from Jada—a gag gift, but they were the most comfortable shorts I'd ever owned. "Look, I really don't need you passing out or dying from trying to do surgery on yourself. So, stop acting like a stupid alpha male and let me help you."

His back tensed and then he looked over his shoulder at me. "Did you just call me a stupid alpha male?"

"Yes. I did."

One side of his mouth kicked up as he dipped his head, looking down at himself. Several strands of hair fell forward, shielding his face. "That damn imp got me in the chest."

"I know, but you should be healing…"

Reaching for the towel, he sopped up the blood leaking from his chest. "Yeah, well, one of its claws broke off in me. Got most of it out."

Ice trickled into my veins. "You…you have an imp claw stuck inside you?"

"Yeah, hence the tweezers."

I wasn't sure how much help I'd be with my eyesight, but I had to be better than him digging around in his own skin. "Give me the tweezers. You need to get it out. Now."

Zayne's head swung toward me sharply and he looked at me like I'd grown two heads.

"What? I can get the claw out. Me trying has got to be better than you digging around in your own skin."

"Are you sure you can do this?"

I narrowed my eyes. "I may be half-blind, but I will, without a doubt, do a better job than you're doing at this moment."

He stared at me for so long that I thought he was just going to tell me to go back to bed, and if he did, I might hit him, but then he grunted out, "Fine." Turning back to the sink, he turned the water on and dipped the tweezers under the flow. "The claw is only about an inch long. It's black."

Only an inch long? Jesus. I took the tweezers from him and then openly checked out his chest. The area he was digging at was above his right nipple, and I was eye level with that sucker.

I squinted, not seeing anything beyond torn-up flesh. "I'm going to need to—"

"I know what you need to do." His warm breath danced across my forehead. "Just do it."

Drawing in a shallow breath, I placed my fingers on either side of the deep cut and then pulled the sides apart. Zayne hissed in a breath, and my head jerked up. Those pupils were vertical again.

"Sorry," I whispered.

"It's okay."

Leaning in, I tried to ignore the minty scent that mingled with the metallic scent of blood as I looked for this inch-long claw. "How long did it take for you to realize a claw was stuck in you?"

"About when I got up and thought I was going to vomit. That's when I realized I wasn't healing. So, about an hour ago."

"You've been digging at this for an hour?"

"Yes."

"That's pretty terrible." When I peeked up at him, I saw that his jaw was tense. Sliding my hand along his skin, I pulled at the tear a little more. "Sorry."

"Stop apologizing."

"Kind of hard not to when I'm pulling apart your chest wall."

He coughed out a dry laugh. "You're not pulling apart my chest wall."

A second later I saw a small piece of blackness stuck in the middle of pink flesh. "So, um, are you still mad at me?"

"Mad at you for what?" he asked.

"For jumping off the building?" I got a good grip on the tweezers.

"I was trying to forget about that," he said dryly.

My gaze lifted to him. I wanted to ask him if he was trying to forget what happened afterward, too. The question burned the tip of my tongue, but I swallowed it back.

"I'm not mad at you, Trin."

Encouraged by the fact my nickname was back in usage, I

drew in a shallow breath. Concentrating on the claw, I lined up the tweezer and said a little prayer. "You didn't come in the room tonight to say good night...or anything."

He was quiet for a moment and then said, "That wasn't because I was mad at you." Zayne sucked in a sharp breath as I slid the tweezers in. "You have a really steady hand."

"I do." I bit down on my lip. "So, why didn't you?" I closed the pointy end of the tweezers around the edge of the broken-off claw.

"I'm not sure I want to talk about that when you're digging around in my chest."

Despite what that could mean, his words did make me grin as I tugged on the piece of claw. The tweezers slipped, and Zayne jerked. "Sorry."

He drew in a long, slow breath. "It's okay."

I tried again, getting the tweezers to latch on to the claw. "I'm kind of surprised an imp got an upper hand on you."

"Thanks for pointing that out."

"I'm just saying."

"I *was* kind of distracted."

"Not my fault." I tugged again and felt the claw start to give.

"I'm going to say that it was partially both our faults." Zayne tensed.

The damn claw wasn't budging. "Just how distracted were you?"

Zayne hesitated. "I think you could...feel just how distracted I was."

Hand stilling, I looked up at him. "Yeah, I could."

The centers of his cheeks flushed a faint pink. "Well, there's your answer."

A slow grin tugged at my lips. "You're blushing."

His eyes closed. "You know, most people wouldn't point that out."

"I'm not most people."

"I've noticed." A smirk appeared. "Haven't figured out if that's a good or bad thing yet."

"Wow," I murmured, and then I yanked hard. The claw slipped free as Zayne cursed under his breath. "Got it."

Stepping back, I held up the claw as I wrinkled my nose. "That's supergross."

"Thank you." He exhaled loudly and then reached for the towels, but I beat him to it.

Setting the tweezers aside, I picked up the towel and stopped the new flow of blood that was leaking out of him. The gnarly wound in his chest was already sealing up.

His hands fell back to his sides as I wiped up the blood. I healed quickly, but it was insane how quickly Wardens recovered. The color was already returning to his face.

"You look a lot better."

"I feel better." His gaze caught and held mine and then his gaze dropped, and I felt the intensity of his stare, all the way to the tips of my toes, before he dragged his gaze back to mine. He folded his hand around my wrist. "You have blood all over your hands."

I didn't say anything as he took the towel from me, and I didn't fight him when he set the towel aside and led me to the sink basin.

"I can wash my own hands," I told him.

"I know." He turned on the water and then opened a drawer and pulled out a tub of foaming hand soap. "Did you get any sleep?"

"A little." I looked up and saw us in the reflection. His head was bowed, brow lowered in concentration as he pumped soap onto my hands.

I got a little lost staring at our reflections, him so much taller and larger than me, blond and golden where I was darker. My gaze dropped to our hands as he slid his over mine. The water bubbled pink and red as it swirled down the drain. He washed my hands until there wasn't a speck of blood left, and then he retrieved a fresh towel from another drawer.

Drying my hands, he turned me away from the mirror. "You know what you asked me earlier?" His hands left my wrists and slid up my forearms. "About why I didn't come to you tonight?"

My heart rate sped up as I nodded.

"I couldn't, because I didn't think I could lie beside you after what happened on that rooftop." His voice was deeper, thicker, as his hands gripped my upper arms. He lifted me with ease, sitting me on the edge of the vanity. "And not touch you."

The heat from earlier returned, dancing over my skin. "What...what if I wanted you to touch me?"

His eyes flared an intense pale blue. "And see, that's the problem."

"Why?"

He lifted his hands, tangling his fingers in my hair as he dragged the strands back from my face. "Because we shouldn't, Trin. It will complicate things. Look at tonight—we weren't paying attention. The imp could've taken you. You could've been hurt."

"But I wasn't."

"I was, and that shouldn't have happened." His gaze searched mine. "I should know better, Trin. I know what happens when I don't have my head in the game. We make a good team—"

"We really do," I cut in, curling my fingers along the edge of the vanity. "We make a damn good team."

"Which is why this would be a bad idea."

"I think that makes it a damn good idea."

His laugh was strained. "Of course you would, but it's more than that."

"I'm not your father—"

"Jesus, I'd hope not."

My eyes narrowed. "And I'm not Layla," I said, and something raw flickered across his face, gone before I knew what it was. "You just need to learn how to multitask."

"That's all?" He laughed.

I nodded.

"Even if I learned to do that, you've been through a lot." One of his hands skated up my neck. Fingertips followed the line of my jaw. "I'm older than you."

"Oh, come on. You're *barely* older than me."

Thick lashes lowered as he traced my cheekbone, drawing a fine shiver from me. "You came here to find Misha, and you trust me to keep you safe while you're doing that. This feels—"

"Right," I suggested helpfully. "Because that's how it feels to me. Like I've been..." My cheeks flushed. "It feels right, Zayne. Are you saying it feels wrong?"

"No. I'm not saying that." Those lashes lifted, and there was intent in the way those pale eyes locked on to mine, to the shadows forming around his mouth. "You want to kiss me again, don't you?"

Every muscle in my body went tense. "Yes. I want—"

Zayne kissed me.

It was such a soft, beautiful kiss at first, his lips brushing across mine once, and then twice, and then the kiss deepened and there was nothing questioning or tentative about it. The kiss felt scorching, demanding and soul burning, a raw combination of pent-up need and explosive want.

He pulled me to the very edge of the vanity as he came forward, pressing with his body between my legs, and when he kissed me again, he left me breathless and exposed like a live wire. I curled my legs around his lower back as I slid a hand down his chest, mindful of the healing wound. His hand slid under my arm, down my back, and I thought I might be getting drunk on his kisses.

And then he was lifting me off the sink, backing up as I clutched at his shoulders and then the soft strands of his hair. He nipped at my lips as he bumped into the wall, and I laughed into his kiss, and he growled back at me. Somehow we made it into the bedroom and then he was laying me on the bed and he was coming over me, his body large and warm as he braced himself above me.

With the light of the bedroom to guide me, I reached out and touched his face. He turned into the touch, nuzzling my palm as he shuddered. When his eyes opened, I swore they glowed.

Neither of us moved or said anything for a long moment, and I swore to God, if Peanut decided to pop up right now, I would find a way to bring him back to life just to straight up murder him.

Peanut didn't appear but Zayne's stillness was starting to worry me. "Zayne?"

His throat worked on a swallow. "There's something I should tell you."

"What?" My gaze searched his face as I drew my fingers over the curve of his cheek.

He turned his chin, kissing my fingertips. "I've… I've never done this before."

My fingers stilled. My entire body stilled as his words sunk through. "You mean…you haven't done this?"

"Well, I've done *this*. I've done…stuff, but I haven't had sex." His gaze found mine and a small grin appeared. "Now *you* look struck speechless."

I blinked. "I'm sorry. I don't mean to, but I'm just shocked. I mean, you're—you're *you*. You're beautiful and you're intelligent. You're kind and you're funny and—"

"And annoying."

"Yeah, that, but—"

"And overbearing."

"And that, too, but—"

"But I still haven't done it," he said.

"Why?" I asked, and then immediately felt like an ass for doing so. "I'm sorry. I shouldn't have asked that."

"It's okay. I...I just haven't."

I was shocked, but I was also...relieved in a way. "I haven't, either."

A slow, heart-wrenching smile pulled at his lips. A real one, and it was the kind of smile that could break hearts and rebuild them.

"I don't know where this is leading," I said, tracing the curve of his shoulder. "I just know that I like you, Zayne. I really like you, and that has nothing to do with everything else that's going on. I want you, but we...we don't have to do *that*."

"No, we don't." He lowered his head and kissed the corner of my mouth, then he spoke again. "But there is other... *stuff* we can do."

And this time, when Zayne kissed me, he sipped from my lips, drank from my moans, as he ran his thumb over my cheek, tracing the bone. His touch was featherlight, but I stirred restlessly. Lust pricked my skin as he moved his fingertips down my throat, over my shoulder. A small sigh escaped me.

I hadn't been lying when I said I liked him—that I liked him a lot, and knowing that, *feeling* that, scared me a little. He was the first guy I'd ever been really attracted to, but it was so much more than that. It was his strength and his kindness, his beliefs, even the ones that had shocked me in the beginning, and his quick-wittedness. It was his inherent protectiveness, and even when he doubted himself, it somehow made him…human to me.

Something else lingered at the fringes of my thoughts, a sense of familiarity with him, of many moving pieces finally clicking into place.

It just felt right.

Zayne felt *right*.

Slowly, he moved his hand down the center of my chest. "You have no idea how long I've thought about this."

I placed my hand on his side, moving it toward his back, kneading the cords of bunched muscles. He dropped his hand to my hip and tugged me down, along the bed. Then he rose above me, using one arm to support his weight. Using one thigh, he parted mine and then lowered himself. Hard lines pressed against soft ones, and when he moved against me in a slow, undulating grind, I gasped and stiffened at the bolt of pleasure it sent through me.

"Is this okay?" he asked.

"Yeah. Yes. Totally."

He chuckled against my mouth as he rocked his hips again. Following his lead, I tipped my mine up as he shifted his head, moving his lips across the cheek he'd caressed moments before. "Have you thought about this? Us? Wondering what it would be like?"

"Yes," I whispered, spreading my legs, cradling his body. "I have."

His remaining hand slid up the flare of my hip, up my stomach. He stopped just below my breasts, his thumb brushing over the swell. My breath caught as his kisses reached the corner of my mouth again. I turned my head slightly. Our lips brushed.

"You don't have to worry about this going too far," he said.

My fingers curled against the skin. "I'm not. Are you?"

"Always," he murmured, and before I could question what he meant by that, he brought his head to the space between my neck and shoulder. Lowering his hands to my hips, he nuzzled my neck. He let his hand stray higher, nearly reaching the peak of my breast.

I didn't move, didn't say anything. Just waiting...waiting to see what he'd do.

"You tell me when to stop and I will."

"I know." My voice was thick, raw. "I...I trust you."

Zayne stilled and then he pulled away. For a moment, I worried that I'd somehow said the wrong thing, but then his hands reached for the hem of my shirt. "I would like to see you, touch you...taste you."

His words sent a dark shudder through me. *"Yes."*

He lifted up my shirt and I rose on shaky elbows as he pulled it off over my head and then my shorts went next. His sharp intake of breath was lost in the pounding of my heart. I lay back down, left only in thin undies, knowing that with his Warden eyes, he could see everything, and I fought the urge to cover my chest.

"You're beautiful, Trinity."

Then he lowered his head, flicking his tongue over a particularly sensitive part, causing me to moan and clutch his shoulders. He laughed against the skin of my breast, but it quickly turned to a groan as my hands ventured farther south, flattening over his lower stomach. He felt like satin stretched over rock, and I was enthralled by the way his muscles bunched under my touch.

I lifted my gaze as my fingers trailed over each hard ripple. *"You're* perfect."

"Mmm?" He pressed down, moving his hand and then his tongue to my other breast. "Do you want me to stop?"

"No. Not at all. Not even remotely."

"The best thing I've heard all year."

My laugh ended in a gasp as Zayne rolled me over him and sat up, my knees sliding on either side of his hips as he pulled me onto his lap. I gasped as the softest part of me pressed down on the hardest part of him. He still had his pajama bottoms on and I was still in my undies, but I could feel every inch of him.

His fingers sifted through my hair as his hand curved around the back of my head. He tugged my mouth to his and kissed me as I clenched his shoulders, allowing myself to settle into him. His answering groan sent shock waves through me.

"This seems very un-Warden-like," I whispered.

The hand at my hip tightened. "You'd be shocked by all the un-Warden-like things going through my head right now."

I shuddered, feeling dizzy and warm and alive. "Then show me."

And he did.

My head fell back as my breath came out in short gasps. His hands and mouth were greedy, and I *loved* it. My lower body started moving in tiny circles, and good God, I thought I could feel his pulse through the cotton of his pants.

I couldn't remember ever feeling like this, definitely not with Clay and not when I touched myself. This was… God, this was so much more; it felt like molten lava was running through my veins. Desire swirled inside me, leaving me feeling out of control and dazed.

My body arched into his, aching for him in such a way that it almost frightened me, but I did trust him. I trusted him with *everything*.

And when his mouth tugged on my breast and his tongue rasped over my skin, I stopped thinking. It was all about feeling and the raw, exquisite sensations shooting down to my core, warming and dampening me.

My hands slipped over abs that dipped and rippled. My hips rocked against him, and when he whispered in my ear, his voice was thick, smoky. I was panting against his mouth, my fingers trembling as they slipped over his skin and wrapped around the band of his bottoms. He was grabbing them, too, shoving the fabric down as he rose just enough to get the material to his thighs, and then there was nothing between us.

"God," he growled against my mouth.

His hand clasped my hip, urging me to move, to take what I wanted, but I didn't need urging. My body moved against his and he moved against me. The heat of his body, the friction and the dampness, and the way he nipped at my mouth—it was all too much and not enough. Tension between my legs built quickly, stealing my breath, shocking me. The coil tightened deep inside me, and our movements became almost frantic. His growl of approval seared my skin, igniting the fire, and I came in a blinding rush, muscles tightening and loosening all at once. Never, ever had I felt something so powerful, so deliciously obliterating.

Zayne's quickly followed, the hoarse, soul-deep shout smothering my cries as the release shook us, and then his mouth was on mine and he kissed me, and he kept kissing me as if he wished to not simply taste me, but devour my very being, and I...I wanted to be devoured.

I didn't know it was even possible to be kissed like that.

I don't know how, but we ended up on our sides, our faces inches apart, our legs tangled and his one arm under my ribs, curled around me, and the other around my waist. I didn't think I was ever going to breathe normally as we lay there, my heart still pounding.

"That was…" I cleared my throat. "I didn't know it could feel like *that* without even, you know, doing it."

Zayne's arms tightened and he pulled me to his chest, flesh against flesh. "I didn't, either."

I smiled, and when he kissed the corner of my lips again, my smile grew. He guided my head to the space below his chin, and I was surrounded by his warmth.

I had no idea how much time passed, but I could feel the lure of sleep tugging at me. "Are you… Are you going to stay with me tonight?"

His lips brushed my forehead. "Sleep, Trin. I'm not going anywhere."

30

"Any update?" Jada asked into the phone as I rooted through the clothes I'd packed, looking for something appropriate to wear to meet with witches. I felt like I needed something dark and badass.

"Bael was sighted the night before last." I pressed my phone to my shoulder. I hadn't told Jada that we were going to see witches tonight or that we were working with demons. I didn't think she'd understand when I barely understood myself. "We're waiting on some info that will tell us where to find him. I hope so at least, because I can't imagine…" I rocked back on my knees, closing my eyes.

"I know," Jada said quietly. "The good news is that you still feel the bond, right?"

"Right."

"So, he's still alive and that's all that matters right now."

I cleared my throat as I opened my eyes. "How is Ty? Thierry and Matthew?"

"Ty is amazing as always," she answered after a beat of silence. "Thierry and Matthew are okay, but they miss you."

"I miss them, too. Does Ty not miss me?"

Jada laughed. "Ty misses you, you dork."

"He better. Still no more attacks or anything like that?"

"It's been as quiet as a church mouse," she said, and I frowned as Peanut drifted through the wall and through my suitcase, stirring the clothes. "Boringly normal around here."

I couldn't stop my grin from forming. "That sucks...for you."

"And for you when you get back," she reminded me.

A weird twinge lit up my chest as I glanced at the opened bedroom door. "Sucks for me then."

"How's Zayne?"

I bit down on my lower lip, thinking about last night, about the way he touched me and made me feel, how he held me through the night. My face flushed at the heated memories, and I was at once grateful Jada and I weren't FaceTiming.

Zayne had stayed with me all night, and not only that, he'd kissed me this morning—kissed me so sweetly that just thinking about it now caused my chest to feel like there was a balloon inflated there.

And then he made me breakfast—waffles and bacon, and I sort of wanted to keep him forever.

"Trinity?"

"He's good," I said, keeping my voice low because he was in the bathroom, showering.

"I bet he is."

I giggled, wanting to tell her everything but knowing that right now was not the time. Plus, I knew she was going to have questions, ones I couldn't answer. Like did last night mean there'd be more last nights? Did it mean we were together? I didn't know. We really hadn't had that conversation. "Shut up—hold on." I lowered the phone as I saw Peanut making his way toward the bathroom. "Peanut! Don't you even think about it!"

The ghost threw up his hands and flailed all the way to the bed, throwing himself onto it. He sank through it, disappearing.

"What is he doing?" Jada asked.

"Being a freaking creep."

"I'm not a creep." Peanut's muffled voice came from somewhere in the bed. "I have to use the bathroom."

"Peanut, first off there are two bathrooms in here, but most importantly, you're freaking dead and you don't use the bathroom."

"Maybe I should let you go," Jada said, and I sighed. "Call me tomorrow, okay?"

"Okay. Talk to you soon." I dropped my phone on the bed as Peanut's head resurfaced. "Behave."

He grinned at me, though it was really just a grimace exposing all his teeth.

Shaking my head, I turned back to my clothes. I picked up a black tank top. It was one of those hi-lo styles, cut shorter in the front and longer in the back.

"What about this?" I asked Peanut.

He cocked his head to the side. "Why do you think I would know what to wear to go meet witches?"

"I don't know." I sighed, plopping onto my butt.

"I can't believe witches are real." Peanut's head was still the only thing visible. "I also can't believe I'm still surprised by anything."

"Same," I agreed.

"I also can't believe what you two were doing last night."

My eyes widened as I lowered my voice. "Were you creeping on us?"

"No. Come on. That would be gross." He paused. "But there was literally nowhere for me go in this place where I couldn't hear you two."

Oh my God.

The bathroom door opened, and I looked over my shoulder just in time to see a shirtless Zayne come out, running a towel over his wet hair. He was wearing jogging pants that were damp in...interesting places, making me think he hadn't taken the time to really dry off.

He glanced over at me. "What are you doing?"

"Looking for something to wear tonight." I lifted the tank top, struggling to behave like everything was totally normal. "Do you think this is appropriate?"

One side of his lips kicked up. "You can wear whatever you want to wear, Trinity."

"I like the way he says your name," Peanut commented.

So, I wasn't the only one who thought he said my name in such an interesting way. "Yeah, but I don't want to stand out."

"Don't think that's possible."

I lowered my shirt, grinning like a little idiot. When he turned to walk to his closet, I was watching him so avidly that Peanut giggled.

"Is your chest okay?" I asked.

"Yeah, I put some of that stuff on it this morning just in case, but it's fine." He pulled out a black shirt and put it on over his head. That was it. Dudes picking out clothes was so simple. "I figured we'd take it easy tonight, after you do the visit thing."

"Really?" What did *taking it easy* consist of? I glanced at the bed and felt my entire body flush.

I really needed to get control of myself.

He headed for the door, a pair of jeans in hand. "Yeah, we can grab something to eat."

Excitement thrummed through me. I was going to see witches and get to go out and eat dinner with Zayne like a normal person, like a—

I cut myself off before I let that thought finish. Ducking my gaze, I folded my shirt. "I would like that, but if the witches give us intel, we'll—"

"We'll act on that immediately," he agreed.

I dared to let myself smile. "Okay."

"Good." Zayne hesitated at the door. "You'll be ready soon?"

I nodded.

"I'll be waiting," he said, closing the door behind him.

The moment he was gone, I let myself topple, face-first, onto my suitcase.

"I think you like him," Peanut whispered.

I groaned.

"I think you really like him."

"Shut up," I said, closing my eyes.

"I think you like him a lot," Peanut sang, and I couldn't say anything, because obviously it was true.

I liked Zayne.

I liked him a lot.

The drive to Bethesda took longer than we anticipated, due to the traffic between the two cities. When we arrived, night had fallen and Roth was waiting for us in the parking garage, dressed all in black. He wasn't alone.

Layla was with him.

I'd decided to go with the leggings with skulls on them, which I had thought was superfitting to meeting with witches, and the black tank top, but seeing Layla in a pale blue dress, the kind that was flowing and flowery, made me wish I'd picked something...prettier.

I sighed. Too late now.

And besides, it wasn't like I could hid my blades in a dress like that.

"What in the Hell?" Zayne was muttering as he turned off the engine. He opened the door and stepped out as I did the same.

Roth and Layla approached us, their hands joined as Zayne came around the front of the Impala.

"Hi," I said, waving awkwardly at the demons.

Roth grinned at me while Layla sent me a brief, tense smile.

"I'm staying out here," Layla announced, smiling innocently up at Zayne. "To keep you company."

Uh-oh.

Zayne's jaw was working overtime, like he was going to crack some molars. "Just to give you guys a heads-up, Bael was seen two nights ago, over by Franklin Square. We patrolled over there but didn't see him."

"He was with someone, but we're not sure who yet," I added. "We're waiting to find out."

"That's a strange place for him," Layla commented, her pale brows knitted as she looked at Zayne. "I don't think I ever saw demons over there when I patrolled."

"You patrolled?"

She nodded. "I used to…tag demons so the Wardens could easily find them when they hunted."

I gaped at her. "I have so many questions."

"Layla's ability to see souls also means if she touches a demon, it lights them up for us Wardens to see. Gives them a glow," Zayne answered, arms crossed. "I wonder if you'd be able to see it."

"I don't know."

"It doesn't work on demons like Roth," Layla explained.

"But it did on a lot of the lower level ones. I'd tag them and Zayne would hunt them later."

"Ah, the good old days," Roth purred with a smile. "Right?"

Layla was staring at Zayne, who was staring at some place behind Roth.

"You used to hunt demons?" I asked, thoroughly confused, because, well, while she was half-Warden, she was also half-demon.

"I did. I used to tag every one I came across, no matter what they were doing," she explained. "I still patrol. Roth and I together, but I only tag demons that are actively bad."

"I don't really patrol, because I couldn't care less about what demons are doing." Roth grinned. "I'm just there to make sure Layla is good. Anyway, we should get this show on the road."

Still having no idea what was going on between Zayne and Layla but sensing he was not remotely happy about her being there, I reached out and touched Zayne's arm, drawing his attention. When I spoke, I kept my voice low. "You okay?"

He stared at me a moment and then nodded curtly. "Always."

Not sure I believed him, I glanced at Layla and Roth, discovering that they both were watching us closely. Roth appeared amused, but Layla looked...uncertain and like she wanted to...remove my hand from Zayne's arm.

"It's okay," Zayne said.

My gaze searched his and then I nodded. "Well, you two have fun, I guess."

Roth's brows lifted. "Probably best we get this over with as soon as possible." Angling his body toward Layla, he curled his fingers along her jaw and tilted her head back. He kissed her, and boy, did he kiss her. I felt my cheeks flush as I averted my gaze until Roth said, "You ready?"

I hesitated, because it felt like I should say something to Zayne before I left, but what? I had no idea, and it wasn't like I was going to kiss him or he was going to kiss me like that—though that would be nice—so I turned and started toward where Roth was waiting.

"Trin, wait a sec," Zayne called out.

My stupid heart did a little flip in my chest as I wheeled around and saw him striding toward me. "Yes?"

"You have your blades on you?" When I nodded, his gaze searched my face. "And what did I say before?"

"Use the *grace* if I have to," I whispered, fully aware that Layla and Roth could probably still hear me.

"Good." His chest rose as he glanced over at Roth and then back to me. "I wish I was going in there with you."

"Same," I murmured.

He opened his mouth like he wished to say more and then he gave me a lopsided smile before turning his attention to behind me. "Watch her back, Roth."

"I know," came the demon prince's reply.

"I should go now," I told him, a little disappointed I wasn't even getting a hug while also fully aware that we had an audience. "I'll be back soon."

Zayne let me get about a step away and then he caught my hand and pulled me back. My breath caught. Before I could guess what he was doing, he lowered his head and whispered, "Be safe."

Then I felt his lips on my temple, and my eyes briefly squeezed shut. It was a sweet, quick kiss, but it meant something to me. When I opened my eyes and pulled back, I saw the warmth in his pale eyes. I thought that maybe it might mean something to him, too.

Feeling ridiculously giddy, I nodded and then pivoted, hurrying to Roth.

The demon prince raised his brows at me and then whirled around elegantly. "Follow me, my holy roller."

I frowned at his back, but kept up with him as we walked outside the garage. The streets were lit by bright lamps.

"So, we're going to a club?" I asked, realizing we were walking across the street, toward a hotel.

"More like a restaurant. It's a private one." He reached the door before me, holding it open. "Probably not what you're going to expect."

Already it wasn't.

Stepping into the hotel lobby, I looked up at the silver ceiling lamps that cast a glow across the black marble floors that reminded me of moonlight. Roth led us over to an elevator, and it opened before we reached it. I looked over at him.

"Spooky," he said with a grin.

My eyes narrowed, and he chuckled as we stepped into the elevator and as soon as he hit the button to the thirteen floor, which caused me to blink.

I turned to him. "I thought hotels didn't have a thirteenth floor?"

"This one does."

Okay. That was spooky, but as the doors closed, I glanced over to where Roth had retreated in the corner. "Can I ask you something?"

"Sure."

"What's up between Zayne and Layla?"

He lifted his brows. "What makes you think there's anything up between them?"

"Besides the obviously awkward as Hell meeting at your place and what just happened out there? Zayne looked like he would rather mate with a porcupine than wait with her."

Roth blinked. "Nice imagery." Shaking his head, he crossed his arms, and it was then that I noticed a tattoo on his biceps.

I squinted. It looked like a...*kitten* curled up in a little ball? That couldn't be right. Demons with kitten tattoos? My eyes were getting way worse. "What do you know about them?" he asked.

A great sense of unease blossomed in my stomach. "I know they grew up together and that he...he feels bad about never accepting her demon side."

"He told you that?"

I nodded. "And he told me what happened to her—what her clan did and that it was his fault."

A muscle flexed in his jaw. "Did he tell you what happened that caused that?"

I shook his head. "Only that he feels responsible."

"Of course not," he muttered, and the elevator slid to a halt and the doors opened. "We should finish this conversation afterward."

"But—"

"Afterward," he repeated, stepping out in the hall. "Come on, Trinity. We need to focus, and if we have this conversation, your head is not going to be in the right space."

I wanted to push, but he was right, so I dropped it for now. The hall we walked was long and narrow, and when it curved to the right, I saw what appeared to be a restaurant packed with human-shaped forms.

Roth spared me a quick grin. "Told you it's not what you expected."

"You were definitely right," I murmured, turning my attention to a young woman who stood at the hostess desk.

She barely looked at me as she focused on Roth, her already thin lips becoming nonexistent. "You again."

"Rowena, did you miss me?" Roth smiled as he rested his forearms on the hostess stand. "I missed you."

"No," she said, taking a step back from him. "I did not miss you. Are you here to see Faye?"

Roth nodded as he straightened.

The woman sighed so loudly there was a chance she cracked a rib in the process. "Follow me."

Rowena led us through the maze of tables, past people who looked like, well, normal people. They all stared at Roth like they knew exactly what he was and none of them seemed overly thrilled about it as they scooted their chairs in, giving him wide berth.

I didn't know what I was expecting exactly. Okay. I was expecting women in a long black dresses and men in robes, chanting mystical words and fires—lots of fires. I was not expecting people in jeans and summer dresses eating fried calamari.

I was kind of disappointed.

We came to a round booth that was occupied by a pretty young woman with short dark hair. She looked up as Rowena deposited us there, surprise splashing across her face, quickly followed by wariness.

"Hello, Faye," Roth said.

"Roth." The woman started to stand up. "This is a surprise— Oh!"

Something happened.

Something *really weird*.

A...shadow drifted off her body, breaking apart into a million tiny black dots. They dropped to the floor and spun together, swirling and rising back up, together forming a—

"Holy crap." I jumped back, pressing my hand to my chest as my *grace* sparked alive inside me and a huge snake, at least ten feet long and as wide as me, appeared no more than a foot away.

The snake threw itself at Roth, its thick body weaving and

wiggling as it rested its diamond-shaped head on Roth's shoulder, its red tongue darting in and out, wiggling.

It wasn't trying to kill me.

It wasn't trying to kill Roth.

My mouth dropped open. It reminded me of a happy dog—if a happy dog was a giant freaking snake, but it was squirming around, its tail thumping on the floor. Wait. Did snakes have tails? I had no idea, but I felt like I needed to sit down.

"Hey, girl, miss me?" Roth scratched the giant snake's head. "I know. It's been too long."

I blinked slowly. "That's...that's a giant snake."

"It is." Roth kissed its nose. "This is Bambi."

"The snake's name is *Bambi*?" I squeaked.

"I have a thing for Disney," he answered, and I found that even more disturbing. "She's one of my familiars, but she's currently on loan to this witch—"

"That wasn't the deal," Faye said, and then shut it when Roth sent her a look I couldn't see.

A familiar? Holy Moses, I'd read about them, but of course had never seen one. They looked like tattoos when resting, but came off the skin and were alive upon summoning. Only the most powerful of Upper Level demons had them.

My gaze shot to his arm. The kitten tattoo was still there. Was that also a familiar? A *kitten*?

"Bambi, this is Trinity. She's a *friend*," he continued as the snake weaved and then twisted its long, thick body toward me.

My eyes widened.

"And what do we do to friends?" Roth said. "We don't eat them, Bambi."

"She...she eats people?" I asked.

"She eats all manner of things. Sometimes demons, sometimes people. She hasn't eaten an angel. Yet. Thumper, on the other hand, has fried an Alpha," Roth answered.

"Thumper?"

Grinning, Roth pulled up the side of his shirt and all along his taunt waist was a vibrant blue and gold...

"Oh my God, is that a *dragon*?" I whispered.

He winked. "That it is." He let go of his shirt. "Have a seat, Trinity."

Giving Bambi wide berth, I scooted into the booth opposite Faye, and Roth sat down next to me. A second later, Bambi flopped across Roth's lap, and I scooted as far as I could go as the snake stared up at me with unholy red eyes.

"What can I help you with, Roth?" Faye asked, glancing at me curiously.

"We're in need of information," he answered as he idly rubbed the top of Bambi's head.

"That much I figured." She tucked a short strand of hair back from her ear. "I'm sorry. I don't mean to sound rude, but who are you?"

"A friend of Roth's," I said, thinking that was a sentence I'd never thought I'd say before, and based on the way the demon was smirking, he thoroughly enjoyed that statement. "I'm looking for a friend. A Warden who was taken by a demon."

"A demon who's suddenly become very active in the city," Roth added. "His name is Bael."

"You know that we rarely...consort with demons." She reached for her glass of red wine, her hand trembling slightly.

Faye was nervous.

"I know you consort with demons and all kinds of things when it benefits the coven," he replied smoothly. "So, let's cut the political blessed-be bullshit about how you guys are good witches who worship trees and hold hands, singing 'Kumbaya.'"

My brows rose.

"You and I both know differently," he said, the teasing grin gone from his lips. "A large posse of humans attacked a War-den settlement. They were working with Bael, and there is no way he possessed all of them."

"Which begs the question of how one demon could amass a small army of humans willing to die for him," I chimed in. "I think I know the answer."

Faye stiffened.

"As do I." Roth tipped forward. "Has your coven, perhaps, aided a certain demon with an enchantment spell? Possibly one that allows you to control humans? And let's not pretend that such a spell does not exist."

Her lips pursed. "There is such an…enchantment—a spell. One not often used and typically forbidden."

I was momentarily distracted by the sound of a little en-gine running next to me. I glanced down at Bambi. Was that snake…purring?

Bambi looked at me, showing its forked tongue.

Alrighty, then.

"But you guys like to do what's forbidden," Roth coun-tered. "Did you help Bael with such a spell?"

Taking a drink of her wine, she then shook her head as she swallowed hard. "You're not a Warden," she said to me.

"No, I'm not."

"So why would you care about an attack on a Warden set-tlement?" she asked Roth.

"Did I say I care?"

I shot him a withering look.

"Did your coven help Bael with this enchantment?" he asked.

"If we did, and that's a big if, we're not responsible for what he did with the spell," she said.

My brows snapped together. "Not responsible? That's like setting fire to a bush and walking away from it and then that fire spreads to an apartment building and takes out the whole thing. You didn't intend for it to happen, but you're still responsible. What did you think he was going to do with such an enchantment? Use it to convince a group of humans to do charity work?"

Roth snorted.

The witch's grip tightened on the wineglass.

"I'm growing bored with this conversation, Faye." Roth leaned back. "Did your coven have contact with Bael?"

She was quiet for a long moment. "You do realize how much this could blow back on us if it gets out we were divulging...others' activities?"

Roth continued petting Bambi's head as he looked over to me and smiled. "And you do realize I don't give a flying crap about what blows back on you? You should be more worried about getting on my bad side."

"Well, of course, but—"

"But what you don't realize is that you really do not want to get on *her* bad side," he continued, and I lifted a hand, wiggling my fingers. "Answer the damn question."

Faye eyed me for a long moment and then she shuddered. "Just so you know, I advised the coven against aiding anyone with such a spell, but I was outvoted. It wasn't a demon who came to us two months ago."

Hope had sparked and then died in my chest. "It wasn't a demon?"

She shook her head. "It was a human who came and asked for that spell."

I looked at Roth, wondering if she was telling the truth or not.

"Who was the human?"

Faye pressed her lips together as she gave a little shake of her head. "It was... His name is Josh Fisher."

That name meant nothing to me.

"Josh Fisher?" Roth repeated. "Do you happen to mean Senator Josh Fisher, the Senate Majority Leader? *That* Josh Fisher?"

I felt my heart skip a beat as Faye nodded. "That would be him."

"Why in the world would a senator want that kind of enchantment?" I asked, dumbfounded. "And not use it to, I don't know, sway votes or something?"

"I don't know why he needed it—"

"Do you get people looking for that enchantment a lot?" Roth demanded.

Faye stiffened. "Well, no. This was the first—"

"So we can safely assume that this enchantment was used to virtually turn humans into cannon fodder."

"Bael was seen with someone two nights ago. We don't know who it was or if the person was human or not," I told Roth. "But the senator would have to know demons to know that witches could do something like this, right?"

"Right." Roth eyed Faye. "Unless he was a witch, but I'm going to go out on a limb here and say he wasn't a witch, right?"

"Right," Faye muttered.

I tipped forward, resting my arms on the table. "Do you know why he wanted the spell?"

"We didn't ask." She finished off her wine. "Some things are better not known. He offered a rather large sum of money."

"How convenient," Roth murmured. "You cannot tell me that not one of you was a wee bit concerned about what a goddamn senator would do with such a spell? Was money that desperately needed?"

"Money isn't the only thing he offered," she said, crossing

her arms. "He offered something else that's highly coveted—something none of us have."

"And that is?"

"A nephilim," she whispered.

I stilled as I stared back at the witch. "And why would you want a nephilim?" I asked even though there was a part of me that already knew.

"There are many spells that need…parts of a nephilim," she answered. "Bones. Tissues. Hairs."

Anger flared as I glared at the woman who was talking about *my* parts like they were seasonings for a pie.

"And why do you think a senator would have access to a creature that was wiped out a millennium ago?" Roth asked.

That creature was currently getting nudged in the thigh by a giant freaking snake. I glanced down and Bambi stared at me with big, hopeful red eyes.

Faye looked around before saying, "Because he said he knew one was alive and that he knew how to get it."

"How?" I asked.

"He said he had the nephilim's *Protector*."

My skin pricked with the need to reach across the table and punch the witch in the face. "Did he happen to tell you where he had this…*Protector*?"

She shook her head. "Only thing that he told us is that he expected to have this nephilim by the end of the solstice."

"The solstice is in a few days," I said as Bambi nudged me again.

"It is," she said with a shrug. "So we'll find out shortly if he's able to hold up his end of the bargain."

"He won't be able to." I reached down, barely touching the top of Bambi's head. The scales were rough and cool to the touch. "That you can count on, so I hope that money was worth those innocent human lives."

A muscle flexed in her jaw.

"You've only interacted with this senator?" he asked. "Not Bael?"

She shook her head. "Correct."

"You can find out where they have this Protector, can't you?" I asked. "Can't witches do…scrying spells?"

"Not on Wardens or demons," she answered. "It only works on humans."

"We don't need that to find the senator," Roth advised.

Bambi pressed up against my palm, obviously not pleased with my lack of effort. I grimaced as I put a little pressure on the snake's head. She hummed in response.

"Is there anything else you can tell us?" Roth asked.

Faye sat her empty glass on the table. "I know he wasn't working alone. When he came to us, he was on the phone constantly with someone who appeared to be giving him the orders," she explained. "That's all I know."

That was news and not great news. One Upper Level demon to deal with was bad enough, and if there was a possibility of more?

I sank back against the booth.

"Thank you for being so helpful," Roth said with a hint of sarcasm. "I think it's time that we leave." Tapping the snake, he leaned back as he lifted her head from my leg and withdrew from the booth, allowing both of us to stand.

"I'll see you soon." Roth patted Bambi's head and then gestured at Faye with his chin. "Go back to her."

The familiar wiggled and then let out a very human-sounding sigh before breaking apart into the dots that formed a thick shadow. The mass drifted back to Faye, inking itself on the witch's arm.

"Roth," Faye called out as we stepped away from the booth. "We'll be leaving soon. You should be doing the same."

A chill swept down my spine as the prince turned back to her.

"The whole coven is leaving," she continued.

Tiny hairs on the back of my neck stood up. "Why?"

"*Something* is here and we want no part of it." Her dark gaze slid to me. "But I have a feeling you'll find out what that something is sooner rather than later."

"Well, that's creepy and not remotely helpful, but thanks," I said, shaking my head as I turned away. Roth followed me into the hall. "You think she was talking about this demon that's killing Wardens and other demons?"

Roth lifted a shoulder. "I don't think it's a demon."

"Then what could it be?"

He looked at me curiously.

"I just don't get it." I stopped in the center of the hall. "Why is a senator involved with this? What does he think he can gain? It can't be money. And if this senator has already bartered away most of me, then what does Bael plan to do with me? Just kill me?"

"Well, he is a demon. Demons like to kill stuff, especially..." He leaned in and whispered, "Angelic stuff."

I rolled my eyes. "That can't be it. It cannot be that simple and stupid."

"Some demons are that simple and stupid. So are a lot of humans," he went on. "Sometimes the most obvious answer is the stupidest one."

I stared at him a moment. That was about as helpful as the witch. "This is good news, though. We find out where the senator is, we should be able to find out where Bael is, right?"

"Should," Roth answered. "If Bael has let the senator know where he is. The senator could always be possessed."

"Don't rain on my parade," I told him.

"I'm just thinking of all the possible avenues," he replied.

"There could be a lot of dead ends, Trinity. If Bael is using this senator to do his dirty work, there's a good chance that Bael was smart enough to cover his bases. This may not be as simple as going to this senator's house and getting all your answers."

"I know."

He inclined his head. "Do you?"

I did, but I was hoping it was that easy. I turned and started for the elevator, mulling over what the witch had told us and the creepy warning that I had a feeling had to do with whatever was killing both Wardens and demons. This meeting might not have given me all the answers I wanted, but it wasn't a complete loss. We had another avenue, and it might be a dead end like Roth suggested, but I was going to find out. I reached for the call button on the elevator.

Roth spoke then, three little, earthshaking words. "Zayne loves Layla."

31

Every muscle in my body locked up. "What?"

"He's been in love with her since they were kids," he said. "And Layla loves him. She's loved him since she was a child. They were even together for a while."

Slowly, I turned to face the demon prince. We were close enough that I could make out his expression. There was no smirk or laugh to his lips, no animosity to his amber eyes, no malicious intent.

"Layla just loves me more," he continued. "And I know, if Layla and I had never met, she and Zayne would be together. Hell, sometimes I'm surprised that she didn't choose him over me." He sighed. "He's a far better man than I could ever hope to become."

So thrown by what he was saying, I was at a loss for words. All I could say once I got my mouth to move was, "He loves her?"

Roth leaned against the wall. "Yeah. I mean, as of six months ago, he did. I can't imagine that kind of love—you know, loving someone for years and years and years—has faded *that* quickly."

A tiny fissure opened in my chest, proving to me just how much I'd come to like Zayne—how much I liked him without even realizing it.

Why should that be so surprising?

That was why I'd trusted him so much last night. That was why I couldn't tear my eyes off him when I was around him. That was why I'd confided in him about my vision and talked to him about my mom.

Maybe it wasn't love, but it was definitely something that was potent and powerful and could be hurt, because whatever it was, it was hurting right now.

Tipping his head back against the wall, Roth let out a sigh. "You like him, don't you?"

My jaw clenched from how hard I was clamping my mouth shut.

"He probably likes you, too. He liked Stacey."

I blinked. "Who is Stacey?"

"Layla's best friend." He tilted his head toward me. "She and Zayne were pretty close after, well, everything that had happened between him and Layla. They weren't together. Well, I mean, I try not to get up in their personal business, but I think they were just…distracting one another."

"From what?"

"From their grief," he answered. "There's a lot you don't know, Trinity. Like you don't know that the reason Layla's clan attacked and nearly killed her was because Zayne kissed her and she took a piece of his soul."

I sucked in a shaky breath.

"And you don't know that he punishes himself every day because of that," Roth continued. "Why else did he move out on his own? Why else did he refuse to take his father's seat of power?"

"He told me it was because he needed space and that he didn't agree with what his clan was doing," I reasoned.

"And I'm sure he was telling you the truth. He just wasn't telling you all of it." Roth's face softened. "I'm surprised his clan didn't speak up when you became involved and went to stay with him."

"Why would they? I doubt they talk about his...his past relationships with random strangers."

"Yes, but you're a Trueborn and must be protected at all costs, right?" There was no mocking in his tone. "And he would step right over you and lay down his life for her this very second."

I sucked in air around the sting those words delivered. Looking away from Roth, my chest rose and fell heavily as I tried to shake off what he was saying—trying to tell myself that Roth was a demon and he was just messing with me, but...why would he do that?

And I'd seen the way Zayne acted around Layla, heard the way he talked about her and how he avoided speaking about her at all costs.

Roth wasn't lying.

I closed my eyes.

"Yeah, you like him. Did you guys hook up?"

My head jerked in his direction. "Excuse me?"

"I'm only asking, because I know he didn't do that with Stacey. They fooled around, but they didn't, you know, go next level."

"How in the world do you know that?"

"Unfortunately, I've heard one too many conversations between her and Layla," he replied dryly. "They share everything. So, did he? You know, go next level? Because if he did, then I'm over here talking out of my ass and I'm about to have a party, because trust me, no one wants to see Zayne move on more than me."

Pressing my lips together, I shook my head. "No party."

"Damn," Roth sighed. "Look, like I just said, no one wants to see him with someone more than I do—see him really *with* someone, moving on, and living his best fucking life, but you're barking up the wrong tree there." He pushed off the wall and came to where I stood. Leaning around me, he hit the elevator button. "So, that's what's going on with Zayne and Layla. Ten years of loving what you can never have and then losing it once you realized it had always been within your grasp."

The elevator dinged, signaling its arrival.

Roth and I were quiet as we rode the elevator down and walked out into the humid night air. I was in a daze from what Roth had said, but a part of me realized I shouldn't be so surprised. The signs had been there, but I just didn't know Zayne well enough to read them.

A sharp slice of pain lit up my chest at that realization. I'd thought I'd gotten to know him well, especially after all the nights we'd talked about everything and anything, but in reality, it had been mostly superficial stuff he'd shared.

Neither of us spoke as we entered the parking garage, and my heart was thumping heavily as we rounded a pillar, and I saw Zayne and Layla, standing in front of his car. There was a couple of feet separating them, and their heads were bowed together like there were discussing something very important. My stomach started flipping around as they both looked up.

"Well, Trinity, this should be a fun evening for the both of us." He cut off toward Layla—toward the girl Zayne was in love with. "Hey, Shortie."

My steps slowed, and as I drew closer, I could read Zayne's

expression as he stared at the ground. He didn't look mad or as irritated as he had when I left him. He just looked…sad.

Pressure clamped down on my chest, and I didn't know if it was for me or for him or for this whole situation.

He lifted his chin and whatever he was feeling was closeted away as his gaze met mine. I saw it then. A veil slipping over his face, cloaking everything he was feeling. No emotion, nothing deeper than the surface.

"What did you guys find out?" Layla asked, her voice sounding hoarser than I remember, as if she needed to clear her throat.

"We found out that it was a senator who came to the witches to get the enchantment," Roth explained while I just stood there, trying to get my thoughts back on track. "Josh Fisher, the Senate Majority Leader of all people. He offered up a Trueborn, in pieces basically, to the coven for the enchantment, claiming he had the Trueborn's Protector."

"What in the Hell?" Zayne demanded, turning to me.

"Basically." Roth draped an arm around Layla's shoulders. "So, we do know that Bael is working with the senator."

"Find Senator Fisher and perhaps we find Bael." Zayne was still staring at me. "This is good news."

I nodded slowly, finally finding my voice.

"I'll make some calls. Gideon, one of our clan members— damn near a tech genius—will be able to ferret out the senator's address," Zayne said, and that was good news. He was already reaching into his pocket, and he made a quick call. "We should have something in a couple of hours."

"You guys are going to his house once you get the information?" Layla asked.

"Yes," I said, ignoring the sudden sharpness in Zayne's face. "We should—"

"Give it until tomorrow night," Roth suggested. "Layla and

I have some things to take care of tonight, but we'll be your backup if you get his info and decide to go in."

I opened my mouth, but Zayne spoke before I did. "Don't think that will be necessary."

"Don't think I care," Roth replied.

Layla pulled away and smacked the demon in the chest and then she focused on us—on Zayne. "You have no idea what you're going up against. It could be just the senator. Or there could be human security, and if that's the case, you need us—"

"Because I will take care of the humans and not feel remotely bad about it," Roth explained. "You know, if the humans pose a problem to us."

I snapped my mouth shut.

"Not just because of that." Layla shot her boyfriend a look, and he simply grinned. "But I'm under the impression that the clan isn't really helping with this, not actively, and you should have backup just in case things go south."

"She's right. They're right," I said, crossing my arms. "It would be foolish for us to do this without help."

Zayne exhaled and then nodded. "Once I hear back from Gideon, I'll text you guys the address and we'll be up tomorrow. Eight sound good?"

"Sounds good." Roth took Layla's hand. "We'll see you guys then." He started to turn and then stopped, looking at me. "Sorry you didn't get all the answers you were looking for."

Sucking in a sharp breath, I knew he wasn't just talking about Bael or Misha. He was talking about Zayne. I nodded and then turned, making my way to the passenger side of the Impala.

Zayne followed, opening the door for me.

So polite.

Always the gentleman.

"Gideon will be able to get us the information we need," he said, and there was a hint of remoteness to his tone.

"I know."

Leaning against the passenger door, Zayne shoved a hand through his hair. "We've got some direction, but with Bael being involved with a senator, that could also mean bad news in the long term."

"It does." I sighed, beyond frustrated and emotionally and mentally stretched too thin as I looked up at Zayne. "We're closer to finding Misha, though. At least there's that."

Zayne was quiet as he turned his head, staring in the direction Layla and Roth had disappeared to. "I feel like...we're missing something. That it's right in our faces and we're not seeing it."

"Yeah, well, Roth thinks it's because Bael just wants me dead. Like he found out I existed and was, like, let's take all these elaborate measures to kill her."

Zayne's brows lifted.

"But that doesn't make sense, because why keep Misha alive? With the bond, I'm stronger. He's stronger. And if they know enough about Misha and what he is, then why haven't they killed him?"

"I don't know." Zayne stepped back. "But we're not going to find the answers here."

No, we wouldn't.

I buckled myself in as Zayne closed the door and jogged around the front before climbing in behind the wheel. While I knew I should be focusing on what the witch had said, all I could think about as he coasted out of the parking garage was what Roth had told me.

My heart started pounding all over again as I glanced at Zayne, his features cast in shadows. I looked out the window, trying to think of a way to bring it up, because we needed to talk about this. Maybe if last night hadn't happened, we wouldn't need to, because it wouldn't have been my business, but now it was my business.

"You okay?" I asked, my hands surprisingly damp as I rubbed them along my knees.

"Yeah." He looked over at me. "Why?"

Why? I blinked slowly. "You're really quiet."

"I am?"

"You are," I confirmed, wondering if the distance in his tone was really there or if it was my imagination. "How... how did things go with Layla?"

"Good."

I arched a brow. "Good?"

"Yeah, it was good."

"Doesn't seem like it."

He shot me another quick look, but he didn't respond.

Frustration grew, but so did the sudden sick feeling that tasted like bitterness and dread in the back of my throat. I lifted my hands. I didn't plan on blurting it out, but it just happened. "Roth told me."

Zayne didn't immediately respond, so I twisted in the seat toward him. He was focused on the road, his jaw a hard line. "Told you what, Trinity?"

"About...about you and Layla."

No response. None. Not even a brief glance or flicker of emotion that I could see.

"He told me that you're in love with her."

That got a reaction, not the one I was expecting, but something. His lips twisted in a wry grin as he slowly shook his head. "He told you that?"

"Yeah," I whispered, and waited for him to say something, anything, but there was nothing. "Are you?" I asked. "Are you in love with her?"

He exhaled as he kept one hand on the steering wheel. A moment passed, one that was so long that I already had my answer.

The same answer I'd had before I even asked the question.

Tensing, I focused on the blur of darkness outside the window. I opened my mouth and then closed it, because there were so many things I wanted to say I didn't even know where to start.

"I will always…care about her," Zayne said, his voice quiet. "Always."

I flinched as the breath caught in my throat. "You don't have to answer my question. I already know. I don't even know why I asked."

"What did he tell you?" Zayne asked.

"Enough to… I don't know. Get my head on straight, I guess," I muttered. "What was last night?"

Oh God.

The moment that question left my mouth, I wanted to catch it and shove it back down my throat, but it was too late.

"What did he say to you, Trinity?" he repeated.

"He told me that…that you're in love with Layla, and that you've been in love with her for years. He told me that you guys were together and that she took a part of your soul." Once I started going, I really couldn't stop it. "He even told me about some girl named Stacey and that—" I cut myself off before I said anymore. "He told me enough."

"Jesus," Zayne muttered. "Why even ask me what I feel or think when he seems to have laid all my business out for you?"

"Oh, yeah, like you've been entirely forthcoming with information any time I asked you about Layla," I snapped, anger replacing the sting of hurt. I latched on to it. Anger was better, easier to deal with it. "You failed to mention last night, when you were listing all the reasons why we shouldn't do what we did, that the most important one was that you were still in love with someone you can't have."

"I didn't realize you and I were going that deep," he shot back, and my head swiveled in his direction.

My lips parted on a sharp inhale that went nowhere as that burning sting returned, sharper than before. The knot in my throat was back, and suddenly I was so uncomfortable in this seat, in my skin, that I wanted to be far away from here. Anywhere. On the street. By the river. In a den of hungry demons. *Anywhere*. My shoulders tensed as I slowly pulled my gaze from him.

"Shit," he hissed. "Trin, I didn't mean for it to sound like that. I didn't—"

"Can we just not talk right now?" I cut him off.

"No, we need to talk. I'm in a… I'm in a weird space right now. I wasn't expecting her to be here tonight and…and all that shit that comes with her. I wasn't expecting Roth to gossip like a damn old lady. I wasn't expecting last night—"

"Yeah, well, neither was I, Zayne. I wasn't expecting to like someone who is in love with someone else." My fingers dug into my knees. "And I *really* don't want to talk about this anymore."

"You don't understand."

"You're right," I said, blinking back stupid tears—tears I refused to let fall. I wasn't weak like that. I was a damn trained fighter. I wouldn't cry. "I've never been in love with someone. So yeah, I don't understand."

"Trin—"

"*I don't want to talk about this.* What part of that do you not understand? I just don't. Okay? I'm tired and I want to go home— I mean, back to your place."

A beat of silence. "Thought you were excited about grabbing something to eat."

Not anymore. "I'm not hungry. I just want to go back."

"Right. We can do that."

And we did that, in perfect freaking silence—silence that followed us into the elevator and ended when I walked into his place, stalking toward his bedroom door.

"There's food in the fridge if you change your mind," he said.

Slowly, I turned back to him. "Are you going somewhere?"

"Yeah. Out."

I took a step toward him, realizing I didn't want him to leave…and I didn't want him to stay. I wanted him to force the conversation and I also didn't want to talk about it, and I was thoroughly confused by these conflicting violate emotions.

"Where?" I blurted.

"I don't know."

He started for the elevator and then stopped and faced me. For a moment, that wall was down and I could see it all. Sadness. Anger. Disappointment. Most of all, a feeling I'd recognized anywhere—*yearning*. Then he turned from me. "I'm sorry, Trinity. I just need… I'm sorry."

And then he left.

I knew why he left and I knew why he'd been so quiet on the ride back here. And I now knew why he'd never had sex before and why he hadn't pushed for it with me.

It was because he'd been in love with Layla since he was a boy and he was still so obviously in love with her now.

I took a breath and it got stuck in a sudden knot in my throat. I looked down at my hands, watching them close into limp fists. My chest…it ached like I'd been punched center mass, and I didn't know why I felt stupid and silly, but I did as I stared at those doors, because all I could think was that he'd done those things with me last night, he'd touched me like that, he'd held me like that, all the while he'd still been in love with Layla—in love with a half Warden, half demon who was in love with the Crown Prince of Hell.

Did he even see me last night? Feel me? Or had he been seeing Layla instead, pretending that I was…

A strangled sounding laugh parted my lips. "God."

I had no idea how long I stood in the center of his apartment, staring at the closed elevator doors. Could've been minutes or hours before I walked over to the couch and sat down, numb to the very core.

Peanut drifted over to me, from where I had no clue. "Trinnie?"

I shook my head, not trusting myself to speak.

"Are you okay?" he asked. "Where's Zayne?"

I opened my mouth, but what could I say? I had no idea where he was. "Everything is—"

The elevator door dinged and Zayne's voice suddenly filled the silent apartment. "You know what, Trin. Screw this. We need to talk about this."

"Well, there he is," Peanut announced.

Eyes widening, I shot to my feet and turned around, and yeah, there he was, striding across the living room. He tossed his keys onto the island. "Roth had no business telling you what he did," he said, coming around the couch. "That was not his place. He may think he knows everything about me, but he doesn't know jack shit—"

"We have company," I blurted out.

Zayne snapped his mouth shut as he looked around while Peanut waved at him, unseen. "The ghost?"

"The ghost has a name," I reminded him. "Peanut."

"Peanut. Okay." Zayne thrust a hand through his hair and those strands immediately slipped back against his cheek. "Peanut, can you give us some space?"

Peanut lowered his hands as he looked over at me. "He's… he's talking to me."

"Yes. He's talking to you."

"For real?" An awed expression filled Peanut's face. "No one talks to me except for you, even when they know I'm here."

"Well, he's talking to you now, Peanut." I glanced at Zayne. "Isn't that right?"

Zayne nodded. "Yeah, Peanut, I'm talking to you. Can you give us some time alone?"

I turned to Peanut.

"Normally I would love to be here for what I am sure is going to be a superawkward conversation, but since he's asking, I'm going to give you space," Peanut said, and I thought it was kind of messed up that he was doing it because Zayne asked and yet never did it for me. "I'll give you some space and check out what Gena is doing."

"Okay. He's leaving— Wait. Who is Gena?" I asked.

"She's this supercool girl on the fourth floor who can see me. She's been marathoning *Stranger Things* with me," he said, and I blinked. "See you later, alligator!"

"Wait!" I reached for him, but Peanut blinked out of existence. I turned to the door. "Oh God, he's been hanging with some kid on the fourth floor that can see him. I don't know if that's a good thing or not, but that sure does explain why he hasn't been around all that much."

"Maybe it's a distant relative of yours," Zayne commented wryly.

I shot him a dark look as I shoved my hair back from my face. "I'll have to figure out what to do with that later." I inhaled deeply as I lifted my gaze to his and those pale blue eyes snagged mine. Suddenly bone weary, I let out a ragged breath. "What did you want to say to me?"

His eyes searched mine. "Roth should've kept his mouth shut."

"Why? So that we would continue whatever it is we're doing and I'd have no idea you wanted someone else?" I heard his words from earlier. *I didn't realize you and I were going that deep.* A sharp slice of unease cut across my chest as I took a step back and then sat on the edge of the couch. "That's messed up."

"No, that's not why. He shouldn't have involved himself, because it's none of his business—"

"I asked him. He didn't bring it up. I asked him what was up between you two. He answered."

"Still wasn't his place."

I stared up at him, and yeah, maybe Zayne was right. Maybe it wasn't Roth's place, but it didn't change what was said or the fact I knew the truth. Swallowing hard, I looked away.

"He shouldn't have told you, because I didn't want this to happen. With everything going on, the last thing I wanted was for you to get hurt."

God.

Why did those words make me feel worse?

"I'm not hurt." That was a lie. It felt like there was an imp claw stuck in my chest. "I...I don't know what I was thinking last night," I said, curling my hands around my knees as my gaze fell to the blank TV. "It's not like I thought you were madly in love with me or something. I mean, I figure I annoy you too much for that, anyway, but I didn't know there was someone else."

"There isn't someone else."

"There isn't? You may not be with Layla, but you're in love with her, and that means there's someone else you'd rather be with and that means I'm...I'm second best. I'm—"

"You are *not* second best, Trin." Zayne sighed, and my heart squeezed. "I know this is hurting you. Shit. Hearing you say this is killing me."

"Really?" I tilted my head. "How exactly is it killing you, Zayne?"

"Because I do care about you. Because last night was—"

"A mistake?"

"No. It wasn't a mistake to me. Was it to you?"

A huge part of me wanted to say that it was, to lash out, but all I could do was shake my head as I stared down at my hands, wondering how I got here. "Did you...?"

"What?"

I shook my head again, heart pounding and my throat boarding as I looked up at him. "Did you want to do that with me last night or were you thinking of her?"

His eyes widened. "Jesus, is that a serious question?"

"The first time I kissed you, you launched yourself off me like a rocket, and any other time we've gotten close, you've pulled away. It wasn't like you jumped my bones last night. I had to... I had to convince you," I whispered, stomach twisting as I realized that was true and I couldn't look at him. "You listed all these reasons and I—"

"You didn't have to convince me. What I feel for Layla— what I've felt for her had nothing to do with last night. At all. What we shared was damn near perfect," he continued, and I felt the couch shift when he sat next to me. I jerked when I felt his fingers under my chin. "Sorry," he murmured, tilting my gaze back to his. "There isn't a fucking moment of last night that I regret."

I blinked.

He held my gaze for a moment longer and then looked away. "I've known Layla for what feels like half my life. Longer, really. She was... She was just this little girl at first, following me around and being...well, a nuisance. I imagine it was a lot like you and Misha."

Squeezing my eyes shut, I took a ragged breath. I wanted him to shut up. I wanted him to keep talking. I wanted...

I didn't know what I wanted.

But Zayne kept talking. "As she grew older and so did I, I knew she had a crush on me, and it was easy to ignore at first, because she was younger, but then she wasn't and she was going to public school, something she'd begged and pleaded for my father to allow, and I looked forward to her coming home each day and telling me about her day. I knew she liked me, but it wasn't something either of us acted on."

"Because she wasn't a full-blooded Warden?" I opened my eyes.

He was still staring down at his hands when he let out a rough laugh. "No. Because her mother's abilities manifested differently in her. You know about some of them, but she can't kiss anything with a soul. She'll feed that way."

My eyes widened.

"That would make pursuing a relationship...difficult, but I trusted her. I never feared that she'd harm me. She just didn't trust herself," he said, tipping his head back. His throat worked on a swallow. "I don't know exactly when I realized that how I felt for her wasn't anything...brotherly. It was before Roth came into the picture. That I do know, and I dated, but I just wasn't into anyone because of her. I would flirt with her, but she never thought I saw her like that. No matter how many times I flirted with her or dropped hints that I was...I was into her, feeling the same way, she just didn't see it. Then Roth came along."

"I... Roth said you two were together at some point?"

He lowered his chin and nodded. "We were. We tried. It's a long story, but Roth pushed her away because my father threatened him to get him to stay away from her. Roth obeyed out of fear for her, and it was my chance—it was our chance to try to make it work. We both saw that and we took it, but it didn't last."

"Because you tried to kiss her?" I asked, thinking that not being able to kiss would suck, but there were all kinds of things you could do that didn't involve mouth on mouth.

"We were actually able to kiss. We'd thought it was because she was able to control her abilities, but she had Roth's familiar on her at the time, and it altered her abilities—"

"Bambi?" I asked. "Or another one?"

"Bambi." He looked at me. "How did you know?"

"I met her tonight. She was on that witch."

"That damn snake kind of grew on me." A faint smile appeared and then faded. "When Layla got hurt by my clan, she was dying. The witches had a cure and Roth bartered for it. They wanted Bambi, and he gave her to them. I hear losing a familiar is like losing a part of yourself, but that's how much he loves Layla."

"Oh," I murmured.

"Anyway, the last time I kissed her, Bambi wasn't on her, and she accidentally fed on me," he said. "Took just a small piece of my soul, but that wasn't what ended us. She chose Roth, and the whole time she was with me, she really just wanted him. She loved me. She still loves me, but she…she just loves Roth more."

I winced. That was the same thing Roth had said.

"Afterward, I was pissed. I felt like I'd been used and then discarded." A muscle flexed along his jaw. "I was angry at her for a long time."

"You seem like you're still angry at her."

Zayne looked over at me. "I'm not."

"Really?"

"No. If anything, I'm angry at the situation, because I didn't just lose a relationship with her, I lost someone who was basically my closest friend. Things changed. They changed for her. They changed for me," he said. "And I know I've seemed angry with her, and I have been, but not because she broke up with me. It's because she still tries to treat me like nothing has changed. Like she can demand to know what's going on in my life and who I'm with. I was hanging out with a girl, and Layla got in the middle of that."

"Stacey?"

"God, what didn't Roth tell you?"

"Sorry," I muttered. "He made it sound like Stacey had lost someone?"

"She did. Her boyfriend. He was also Layla's friend." He dragged a hand through his hair. "Stacey and I are friends. We...made out a few times. Things were kind of awkward afterward, because of us both being close to Layla. I haven't seen her in a while." He lifted a shoulder. "Anyway, Layla thinks I owe her... I don't know what. Acceptance? I've already accepted that she's with Roth. Forgiveness? It took me a while to get there, but I have gotten there. To go back to the way things were before, like none of this happened? I'm not sure if that's ever going to be possible, and it's kind of messed up that she expects that of me."

"Kind of?" I repeated. "I kind of think it's super-messed-up, to be honest. I mean, this wasn't that long ago, right?"

"December," he said. "Not forever ago, but not yesterday."

"No." I studied his profile, unsure how I felt after hearing all of this. That was seven months ago, not six, and I didn't know how long it took to get over a broken heart. "I don't know what to say right now."

That was true, because knowing this helped me understand, but it didn't ease the ache in my chest. Or the simmer of jealousy in my gut, because I wanted…what Zayne felt for Layla, for him to feel that for me.

How could Layla not have chosen Zayne?

He was loyal and kind. He was smart and funny. He was strong and protective. He was the good guy with a very wicked side, if last night was any indication.

Zayne wasn't perfect, but damn, he was close.

"Roth should've kept his damn mouth shut, because how in the Hell is he supposed to know how I feel or know what I want when I don't even know?"

I clutched my knees. "What do you mean?"

Zayne shook his head. "I thought… I thought I did. Hell. For the last seven months, I thought I would only ever really want one person. Like really want to be with her, and that was how I felt until you laid my ass out in the training room. I wanted *you* then. Right there, on the damn mats. You have no idea how much restraint I had to use to not…" His hand curled in his lap, his knuckles bleaching white. "I don't even think I ever wanted *her* like that. It was like a damn punch to the gut."

My lips parted.

"It shocked me. That's why I jumped off you. I've never felt such a…raw reaction to someone. I…I don't know what I'm doing when it comes to you. When I'm with you, I don't think about her, and I sure as Hell don't see her. I see only you. I just don't know what that means. All I do know is that I never meant to hurt you."

I believed him.

Tears crowded the back of my throat as I nodded. I did believe him, and somehow that made me want to let go and cry. I looked away, having no idea where that left me—left us.

No, that was a lie.

I did know.

"I like you, Trin, and I care about you. I do, and I know it means something," he said, and when I didn't look at him, I felt his fingers curl around my jaw, tilting my head back until I met his gaze. "And I do want you. Hell, I'm coming out of my skin from wanting you, and I feel like I'm… Like I'm drawn to you. It's the craziest thing. Like I know where you are in the room without looking. When I told you back in the Potomac compound that I felt like I knew you, I wasn't full of shit then. I do feel like that, and I…I can't explain that."

But.

There was a *but* lingering between us.

Zayne liked me. He cared for me. He wanted me. But he'd been burned. Badly. There was a fortress around him that didn't just have to do with Layla, but also with his father and his own reckoning with his clan's responsibilities. He didn't know what he really needed.

I might not know what it was like to be in love or to love someone like he had, but I thought… I thought you knew if you really liked someone, that if there was a potential for that, even if you didn't know a person for weeks, months or years, you just *knew*. And if you knew you really liked someone, you'd reach out and seize it. You'd chase after it.

And I knew that I really liked him, and I knew that even as messed up as things were right now, if he felt the same way, I'd reach out and seize it. I'd chase after it.

But I was pretty sure that, even with everything he'd said, he wasn't going to go down that road with me. He wasn't seizing or chasing anything. He wasn't ready.

"It's okay," I said, and I forced a smile even though this didn't feel okay.

It felt horrible.

Zayne's fingers splayed across my cheek, and my eyes drifted shut. "Trin…"

My smile started to wobble, and I knew it was time for me to get some space. Everything had to be okay. I needed his help. He was going to need mine, and me crying wasn't going to make things okay or any less awkward.

His thumb slid over my chin, just below my lip, causing me to suck in a shallow breath. I felt that gentle sweep all the way to the tips of my toes. "Are things really okay?"

I nodded, opening my eyes. "Yeah, I understand."

Doubt clouded those beautiful eyes of his, but he smiled as he dipped his chin, pressing his lips to the center of my forehead. The kiss was like the one earlier in the garage, sweet and gentle, and completely devastating.

Pulling back, I slipped free and rose on unsteady legs. "I think... I'm tired. I mean, I am tired. I'm just going to head to bed." It wasn't even eleven o'clock yet. "Thank you for talking to me."

He opened his mouth, but seemed at a loss for what to say. Finally, he managed with a dry rasp, "Please don't thank me right now."

My chest spasmed as I nodded. I turned before I could do something...impulsive and reckless, like say screw the real, painful heartbreak that was sure to come down the road and climb into his arms, because I thought he'd let me do just that.

That he'd welcome it.

I couldn't do that...because I was already starting to fall for him, and I couldn't let that happen.

I had to be smarter than that.

I *would* be smarter than that.

Because I'd finally found someone I wanted, I *yearned* for, and I wasn't going to play second fiddle to a past he was still working through.

Hurrying around the couch, I went straight for the bedroom, stopping at the opening. "Good night, Zayne."

He remained on the couch, and as I started to close the door, he said, "Good night."

I closed the door.

And I locked it.

32

I didn't cry.

I wanted to, but the tears built and built and went nowhere as I lay on my back, wishing I was looking at stars.

I couldn't remember the last time I'd let myself cry. When Mom died? No. Holy crap, even then, I'd held it in. Sure, I'd felt the burn of tears in my throat and in my eyes, but I'd never let them out.

I couldn't let them out now.

I didn't get much sleep. Every time I did fall asleep, I jerked awake what felt like minutes later, pulling myself out of nightmares surrounding a bleeding, dying Misha or dreams where I was following Zayne but could never reach him no matter how fast I ran or how many times I called his name. That happened all night, so when I finally awoke in the early morning and could see the faint light of dawn seeping under the heavy blinds, I gave up on sleep.

I rolled onto my other side and reached for the worn book on the nightstand. Curling my fingers around the frail binding, I pulled it close to my chest and held it there as I closed my eyes.

I needed to get my life right.

That's what I realized in those early-morning hours as I lay in Zayne's bed, holding my mother's book to my chest. I thought about what had happened last night between Zayne and me. I thought about what the witch had told Roth and me, and I thought about what could be happening to Misha at this very moment.

I didn't for one second think that Bael just wanted to capture, kill and then sell me in pieces to the coven. There had to be more behind this, and that was what I needed to focus on. Not whatever had happened between Zayne and me.

I was going to find Misha, and then I'd help Zayne and his clan find this thing that was killing them, and then Misha and I would go home. Zayne... He would just be a memory. Hopefully, when I had some distance, it would be a good memory, but even if it was still a sad one, it wouldn't matter, because I would have Misha and Jada. I would have my duty—Misha and I would have our duty.

But what if tonight led us nowhere?

The demon took Misha to get to me. He'd already sent Hellions and imps after me. What if the only way I was going to find Misha was to give Bael what he wanted?

Me.

I squeezed the book to my chest as my stomach dipped and twisted. That sounded...insane and reckless, but I would be willing to do it. If we didn't get answers tonight...

I must've dozed off again, because I woke to find Peanut sitting on the edge of the bed and my mother's paperback stuck under my chest.

"Morning," Peanut said, swinging transparent legs. "Well,

it's almost afternoon. You should get up and, I don't know, do something productive."

I frowned at him.

"And you may want to get up soon, because I think Mr. Brooding Hot Gargoyle Man-Boy is making bacon."

Bacon?

I'd get up and face Zayne completely naked for some bacon.

I shifted onto my back, pulling the book out and placing it on the nightstand. "What time is it?"

"Time for you to get right with your life."

I rolled my eyes.

"It's almost noon," he replied. "Is everything okay with you and Zayne? When I came back, you two weren't all snuggled up like little cuddle bugs."

I didn't want to even think about the fact that he'd seen us together, and I also didn't want to acknowledge the way my chest spasmed. "Things are fine," I said finally.

"Sure didn't seem like that last night."

"Speaking of last night..." I sat up and pushed my hair out of my face. "Who is this girl you've been talking to?"

"Gena? Oh, she's awesome. She saw me a couple of days ago when I was checking out the lobby. She's introduced me to *Stranger Things* and I've introduced her to *Star Wars*. You know, the original three, which are the only ones that count."

I didn't know how I felt about someone else being able to see Peanut. "How old is she?"

"Fourteen? I think? She's cool. You'd like her. I should introduce you two."

My stomach pitched. "You haven't said anything about me—about what I am?"

He rolled his eyes. "Duh. No. I'm not dumb. But if she can see me, doesn't that mean she's like you?"

"Not exactly." I rose. "She's probably got an angelic ancestor somewhere down the family line, but it's not the same. I'm—"

"A special snowflake?"

I shot him a narrowed glare. "No. I'm first generation. I'd like to meet her at some point, but right now I'm going to shower and start getting my life right."

"About time."

Ignoring that, I went into the bathroom and took a quick shower, letting the hot water wash away what felt like a layer of funk. When I was done, I combed out the knots in my hair and changed into a pair of leggings and a lightweight, comfy shirt with a happy face in the center of the chest.

Peanut was gone from the bedroom. I stopped at the door and took a deep, calming breath.

I can do this.

I could walk out there, see Zayne and act…act right. I could do it. I had to do it.

So I did it.

As I opened the door, my stomach grumbled at the scent of bacon. Zayne was at the kitchen island, plucking the crispy strips out of the pan. My steps slowed as he lifted his head and looked at me. Even though I couldn't see his eyes from where I was, I could feel the intensity in his stare.

A wave of awareness shimmied over my skin as I forced myself to keep walking towards. "Morning," I murmured. "Or afternoon."

Zayne placed a couple of strips of bacon on a plate, and as I drew closer, I saw the faint smile on his lips as he tucked a strand of hair back behind his ear. "I was just about to see if you were awake."

"I am," I said, and then realized how stupid that sounded. I went to the fridge and pulled out the bottle of juice. "Did you sleep well last night?"

"Yeah." He turned, placed the tongs in the pan and dropped his hands on the island. "Actually, that's a lie. I slept terrible last night."

My gaze flicked to his, and I sucked in an unsteady breath. "I didn't sleep all that well, either."

"Sorry," he murmured, lowering his gaze. "Hopefully the bacon and the news I have for you will make up for it."

"Bacon pretty much fixes everything." I sat on the stool, tucking my bare feet on the rail. "What news do you have?"

"Gideon called this morning," he said, speaking of the Warden from his clan. "He got us the address of this senator. His primary address is in Tennessee, but he's got a house just across the river, near the restaurant where we met Roth."

"That's good. So, we're going to check it out tonight?" I could feel Zayne's gaze on me as I munched on my bacon.

"Yeah, but I also got some more news." He waited until I glanced up at him. "Gideon was able to track down the car that Bael was seen in. It linked back to a car service that deals only in government officials and diplomats. He reached out to the driver and, through some convincing, was able to get a list of who was being driven that day. It was only one person."

"Let me guess. Senator Josh Fisher?"

"Yep." Picking up a strip of bacon, he pointed it at me. "So, we had our suspicions before, but we definitely know now that Senator Fisher and Bael are connected."

Hope sparked. "God. I know I shouldn't be happy to hear this, but it's—"

"It's a clear lead. A connection."

I nodded, letting out a shaky breath. "Tonight could be—" I cut myself off before I let hope carry me away.

Zayne caught on, though. "You could find Misha tonight. Or maybe we find information on where Misha is." He pushed off the island. "It's okay to have hope."

"Is it really?" I wiped my hands off on the paper towel that had magically ended up in front of me. "Because what if we find nothing?"

"We might." He came around the island, and I tensed as he stopped beside me, angling his body in between the other stool and me. He was so close that I could feel the warmth rolling off him. "But it doesn't hurt to have hope that it will work out in the end."

I thought that maybe too much hoping led to nothing but hurting, but I kept that to myself as I lowered my gaze. I ended up staring at his chest. He was wearing a gray cotton shirt that didn't have a single splatter of grease on it. I had to think that took serious bacon-frying skills.

I drew in a deep, slow breath and caught the faint scent of winter mint. I swallowed. "Thank you for breakfast. I...I would say that one of the days I'd return the favor, but I don't think you'd like that."

"Why?"

"I can't even boil eggs."

He chuckled. "I'm sure it's not that bad."

"Oh, no, it is. Once I tried to make a grilled cheese sandwich and got the bread and cheese stuck to the pan," I told him, toying with the napkin. "And then I almost burned down Thierry's house, because I was convinced that I could make fried chicken. I'm a disaster in the kitchen."

"I can teach you how to make grilled cheese," he said, and my gaze flicked to his. There was a warmth in his eyes that I wanted to fall into. "How about we try that tomorrow for lunch?"

My stupid, stupid heart skipped a happy little beat, and if my heart was right in front of me, I would've punched it. I stared down at my hands. "I don't know."

Zayne picked up a piece of my hair and tugged gently. "Learning how to make grilled cheese will change your life."

Against my will and better judgment, my gaze lifted to his.

"Just say yes, Trin."

I should say no, but because I was a grade-A glutton for punishment, I nodded.

Zayne smiled then, and it felt like a reward, which made me want to punch him now. That smile faded, though, as he drew his fingers down the length of my damp hair. "You locked the door last night."

I stilled.

Zayne let go of my hair. "I...I wish you hadn't."

Air lodged in my throat.

"But it was probably a smart idea."

Zayne had tried to come to me last night. Either because he couldn't sleep or because maybe he'd heard me waking up over and over.

But he still had tried to come to me after everything, and I didn't know what to think about that other than Zayne was most likely right.

It was probably a good thing I had locked that door.

Exhaling slowly, I pulled my gaze from the heavy thicket of elms. Dusk had fallen and we were on our way to Senator Fisher's house, just outside of Bethesda.

We'd already passed several homes so large that even I could see them, but for the last mile or so, all I'd seen was trees.

Zayne's phone rang, and he reached for it from where it sat on his thigh. "It's Roth," he told me, and then answered. "What's up?"

I watched him and saw that a muscle flickered along his jaw, probably in response to something Roth said.

"Sure thing. See you in a few minutes." Disconnecting the

call, he placed the phone into the slot along the door. "We're going to pull over here and walk the rest. Roth and Layla are almost here."

I nodded. "Sounds like a plan."

Zayne parked just off the old gravel road. The trees hid the car from anyone on the road, and when I climbed out, I was immediately grateful that my shirt was loose as humidity smacked me in the face.

Zayne came around the front of the Impala, joining me. "We head west, through the woods, Gideon told me, and we should come to a gate. Roth and Layla will meet us there."

I nodded, feeling the weight of the daggers attached to my hips as I stepped off the gravel and skidded down the little embankment. I scanned the trees. With dusk quickly turning into night, this wasn't going to be exactly fun.

"Are you good?" Zayne asked, a few steps ahead of me.

I started to say yes, because I didn't want to be a hindrance, but I couldn't see crap in front of me and the terrain was completely unfamiliar. "I...I don't— I can't see a lot."

Up ahead, Zayne stopped and turned to me. A second later, he was right beside me. Without saying a word, he took my hand, and I flushed. "It's, like, rocky—the ground. Plus, there's a lot of fallen trees and branches."

"Okay," I whispered, a little embarrassed and a little grateful. "Normally it's not this hard. Back home, I can run the woods like nothing, because I'm familiar with the landscape. I'm sorry—"

"Don't apologize." He squeezed my hand. "It's no big deal."

"You don't have to hold my hand," I pointed out as he led me around something large on the ground—a rock or branch.

"I don't have to. I want to." He caught a low hanging branch, holding it out of the way as we dipped under it. "And remember, I told you I would be your seeing-eye gargoyle whenever you needed me."

Shaking my head, I laughed. "Well, you're doing a really good job at it now."

"Oh, I plan on excelling at it."

I pressed my lips together, unsure how to take his light, teasing tone. I decided I could stress about it later, because Zayne's steps slowed.

We were at the fence.

Slipping my hand free, I stared up at the lit cement pillars and the closed gate. I took a deep breath, tasting the fresh air that mingled with the crisp winter mint of Zayne, and—

"It's weird," I said.

"What?" Zayne angled his body toward mine.

"I don't feel any demons. The only time I haven't felt demons was when we were at your clan's compound…and here." I looked up at the gate. "I guess I was expecting to feel them here."

"That's got to be a lot to deal with in a city like DC, constantly feeling them."

"I'm getting used to the varying degrees." Lifting a hand, I dragged my palm over my forehead. "But if the senator is hooked up with Bael, wouldn't there be demons here?"

"That doesn't mean anything, really," he replied, and I glanced over at him. A long moment passed as everything around us slipped farther into shadows. "Trin, I—"

I felt them then.

So did Zayne.

A hot breath along the back of my neck, and sudden heaviness in the air around us. We both turned to the gate just as a form appeared out of the shadows, on the other side of the gate.

"Roth," Zayne said, stepping forward.

The demon prince stopped, and I squinted, seeing someone else behind him. I was guessing that was Layla. "We scoped out the house first. Appears no one is home."

"Crap," I muttered.

"Not bad news," Layla spoke up. "We can get in and look around, see if we find anything."

She had a point.

"And the senator will probably be home at some point to-night," Zayne said, and I nodded. "Well, let's get to some breaking and entering." Placing his hands on the center of the gate, he twisted. Metal grinded and then gave way. The gate parted, swinging open. He stepped aside. "After you."

"Show-off," I murmured.

He chuckled. "What? You can't do that?"

"I'm strong." I nodded in Roth and Layla's general direc-tion. "But not that strong."

"There was an alarm on the house, but we disarmed it be-fore we came out here," Layla said, and I wondered how that was accomplished without alerting the alarm company. I fig-ured that was due to Roth. "We haven't gone in yet."

"Okay," I said as we walked up the thankfully flat surface of the driveway.

Zayne fell in step beside me as Layla said, "Did you guys look into this senator? We did today, and he's probably the last person you'd think would be involved in anything demonic."

"Or the first person, if you ask me," Roth chimed in. "The illustrious senator is involved in a lot of charities that benefit at-risk youth. Goes to church every Sunday. Comes from a long line of Baptist pastors. Married once, to his high school sweetheart, who passed away from breast cancer two years ago. Since then, he's also been involved in health care reform and women's services."

The corners of my lips turned down. "Why would you think he would be the first person?"

"Because it's always the last ones you suspect, in my experience. The ones who hide their dark souls rather than show the world what a shit ball they are," he replied, and I shook my head. "And the fact that even though he's involved in all these good works, he voted down every reform or bill that would have actually helped people in need."

"Oh." Well, that last part sort of sealed the deal.

"If we don't get to meet the senator tonight, Layla's going to try to find him so we can get a look at his soul, but I have a feeling we know how that's going to turn out."

Our pace picked up as the sprawling, one-level ranch house came into view. Floodlights kicked on, and I winced at the sudden harsh glare. Roth and Layla headed around the house, toward the back.

My heart was pounding as we walked under a breezeway and Roth stepped up to the back door. He turned the knob, snapping the lock in two.

"Now who's the show-off?" Layla said.

"Me," Roth quipped. "Always me."

Glancing at Zayne, I took a deep breath. Nervousness filled me as I followed Roth and Layla inside the dimly lit house.

Zayne was behind me. "I haven't seen any cameras yet, but keep an eye out for them."

"Sure thing, boss," Roth replied.

We started opening door after door, revealing empty bedroom after empty bedroom, and with each vacant, normal-looking room, more disappointment surged through me. By the time we checked out all the bedrooms, the living room, a kitchen and a den, I knew Misha wasn't here.

I didn't think Misha had ever been here, and if I had been honest with myself from the moment we learned about the senator, I'd known deep down that he wouldn't be here. It would've been too easy.

"Here's an office," Layla called from the other wing of the house as I stood in the middle of a large, sunken living room.

There were photos framed on the walls, and as I walked over to them, I could see that they were of a family. Their faces were nothing but blurs, but I imagine the senator's living room was no different from millions of others. I reached up, touching the black, matte frame of one photo. Dust covered the tip of my finger.

"Trin?" Zayne called from behind me.

I turned, arms at my sides as I opened my mouth, closed it and then tried again to find words. "He's not here. Not Misha. Not the senator. Nothing. I don't think anyone has been here in a while."

"Trin." Zayne's voice was soft as he stepped toward me. "I'm—"

"Don't say it." I held up my hand. "Please don't apologize right now. This is just another dead end, and Misha is out there, somewhere, most likely being tortured to death, and what are we doing?"

"We're trying to find him."

"What if we never find him? What if we don't find him in time?" My heart was pumping too fast as I turned away. I didn't make it very far.

Zayne snagged an arm around my waist, pulling me toward him. I protested, but he folded his arms around me, one hand folding along the nape of my neck. I shuddered at the contact, and when I felt his breath along my forehead, I squeezed my eyes shut.

"We're going to find him," he said. "We will."

Resting my cheek against his chest, I didn't give voice to

what I was realizing. That the only way I could get to Misha was by using myself as bait.

"Hey." Roth's voice intruded. "Layla has found something I think you guys are going to want to see."

Zayne was slow to pull back, but he didn't let go. His hand was still curled around the nape of my neck. "We will, Trin."

Swallowing hard, I nodded.

"What did you find?" Zayne asked, sliding his hand off me.

"Follow me."

I got my feet moving, ignoring the curious look Roth sent my way. We followed him back to an office lit by a desk lamp. There were walls of books. A freestanding globe. More pictures of what I was guessing was the senator's family. Layla was behind the desk, her hair nearly white in the glow of the lamp. She was staring down at what appeared to be large papers that covered nearly the length of the desk. Roth walked over to the globe and started spinning it as Zayne joined Layla.

There was a weird twinge in my chest, seeing them together, and I ignored it, because that twinge was so, so wrong. Crossing my arms, I walked to the desk.

"What is it?" I asked, since I couldn't make out any of it.

"It looks like..." Zayne turned over a paper. "It looks like plans for a school?"

Layla peered around him. "Yes." She pointed out several marks. "These are classes...and over there are dorms. What is...?"

Zayne leaned in. "Nursery?"

The globe stopped spinning. "What kind of school has a nursery?" Roth asked.

Unease slithered down my skin. "That's a good question."

Zayne shook his head as he lifted a thin sheet. "There's a company name here. Cimmerian Industries. Have you heard of them?"

"No. But the word *Cimmerian*—" Roth's head jerked to the side, and I felt it.

Pressure settled between my shoulder blades, and my head jerked up as Roth lifted his chin, his nostrils flaring.

"Demons?" I asked, reaching for my daggers.

"You can feel them?" he asked while Zayne and Layla stopped riffling through the papers. "And know it's not us you're sensing?"

I nodded. "I feel you two, but this is more...intense."

Roth inclined his head toward me, and I'd swear he pouted. "I don't feel intense?"

"Wow, Roth. Sensitive, aren't you?" Zayne planted a hand on the desk and vaulted over, landing in a crouch. As he rose, he shifted.

The gray shirt split up the center and down the back as his skin turned from golden to deep gray and wings unfolded behind him.

It was a rather impressive sight to behold.

I dragged my gaze from him to Roth. "What I mean is that I can feel you and Layla, but I can feel the presence of...*more*."

Roth appeared appeased by that answer.

"Layla, do you have your phone on you?" Zayne asked, striding toward where I stood.

"Yeah," she answered.

"Can you take pictures of all that real quick?" he asked. "And text it to me?"

Layla whipped her phone out of her pocket. "On it."

My fingers curled around the handles of my daggers as I strode toward the windows. I could see nothing beyond them. I unhooked the weapons. "Do you think the senator and possibly Bael are returning?" I asked, even though that didn't make much sense to me. There were no headlights out there. No car coming up the driveway. "Or something else."

"If it's Bael, he's about to get the surprise of his life," Zayne growled. "Look at this. Can you see it?" he asked, turning to me.

I squinted as I saw what looked like...like fog rolling over the driveway and the front yard, so thick it was like a wave of storm clouds on the ground. "I can see it."

"This can't be good." Zayne's wings tucked back.

"I got the pictures." Layla came around the desk, slipping her phone into her pocket. "I don't see a car coming up the driveway and I haven't seen a single camera anywhere."

"Well, what's coming our way is a crap ton of demons," Roth said, his voice low. "And I don't believe in coincidences."

"The witch told you about the senator," Zayne said. "Is there a chance that she would've given the senator or Bael a heads-up? Thrown us under the demon bus?"

"If she did, she's not only a stupid witch, she'll be a dead witch," Roth snarled, and I saw him shift. His skin thinned as an oily darkness seeped out, turning his complexion from olive to obsidian. His wings were nearly as wide as Zayne's, but he had no horns.

"Holy crap," Layla whispered. "How many are there?"

My heart skipped a beat as I strained to see anything in the fog outside. "I don't see anything..." I trailed off as several shapes began to take form in the thick mist. "Oh, Hell."

There were...*dozens*, some tall and some small. Some walked. Others crawled. There were even some in the air. I'd never seen so many demons in one place.

I turned to Zayne. "I thought you said there weren't a lot of demons around?"

"Yeah," he drawled the word out. "There weren't."

"I think they're all here now," Roth said as he glanced at Layla. "If things go south, I want you out of here. Go home to Cayman—"

"Are you high?" Layla demanded. "If things go south, I'm going to kick some butt."

"Layla—"

She held up a hand. "Do not forget, I'm a badass."

"There's about forty-plus demons out there."

Forty-plus? God.

Zayne towered over me as he spoke. "If you need to use your *grace*, do it. You got it? If you tire out afterward, I'll make sure nothing gets between you and me."

Heart thumping, I nodded. "Got it."

"If you're staying, you should get ready, Layla," Zayne advised as the things in the fog stilled ten or so feet from the house.

Layla shifted then, drawing my attention, and I didn't understand what I saw. She looked like she normally did, except she had wings—black, feathered wings.

"Feathers. You have feathered wings," I said dumbly.

"I do." Layla's left wing twitched as she grinned at me. "It's a long story, but the gist of it is that I almost died and, well, this is what happens now when I shift."

I stared at her. "You look like an…an angel. If an angel had black wings."

"I'm no angel." She lifted a shoulder. "I'm just…unique."

"That you are, babe," Roth replied, extending his hand to her. She took it, and they stood side by side in front of the window. He leaned down and whispered, "I know you're a badass. Won't *ever* forget that."

I looked away from them just in time to see one of the tall forms come toward the window. It stopped too far out for me to make out details.

"It's an Upper Level demon," Zayne explained, knowing the features were nothing but a blur to me. "It's not Bael. I've never seen this one. What about you, Roth?"

"Like I said before, I'm not friends with all demons."

Zayne snorted.

"Hello?" the demon outside the house called out, sounding like he was there to sell Girl Scout cookies or something. "We know you guys are in there." He lifted an arm and waved. "Hiya! What do we have? A...half-breed daughter of Lilith. A demon prince who's been very, very bad. A Warden who keeps strange company, and an actual, living and breathing... Trueborn?"

"Well," I said, brows lifting. "Is there a breed of demons that have X-ray vision?"

"Not that I'm aware of," Roth muttered.

"Are you wondering how we know?" the demon called out, and I rolled my eyes. "I'd be happy to tell you guys, and I hope we can make this a pleasant experience for everyone involved. Let's start by me introducing myself. I'm Aym, but some know me as Haborym. I'm a handsome little devil, but don't let my pretty face and charming disposition fool you. I'm a Grand Duke of Hell, ruling over twenty-six legions of demons, and half of them are here with me tonight," he purred. "I've burned castles and entire cities to the ground, leaving nothing but ash and death in my wake when I don't get what I want. Just, you know, a heads-up."

Roth yawned.

"Oh, and you could consider me...Bael's personal assistant," Aym continued. "So, now that we know who I am, do you have any questions?"

"Yeah," Zayne called out. "Why did we have to get stuck with such a damn talkative demon? This makes killing you so much more time-consuming."

"For once, Stony, you and I actually agree on something." Roth laughed.

There was a deep, rumbling laugh that rattled the windows, causing my eyes to widen. "The Warden speaks first. Interesting. You don't want to chat? Fine. We're here for the Trueborn."

"No shit," Roth muttered.

"Give her to us and we'll let you all go about your merry little ways." Aym paused. "Pinkie swear."

"Not going to happen," Zayne replied. "You might as well move on to option B."

"Well, option B is you all die. Starting with you, Warden. I'm going to burn you alive."

My stomach twisted sharply while Zayne seemed not at all affected. I stepped forward and called out, "What do you want from me? To cut me up and give to the witches?"

"Ew," Layla murmured.

"Not at all, my dear little nephilim," cooed Aym, and I stiffened. "We just want to love you and hold you and become the very best friends ever."

"Wow," I said, hands tightening on the dagger as Layla and Roth exchanged a look. "Where is Misha?"

"Your Protector?" he asked. "Why, he's right here, waiting for you."

My heart might've stopped in my chest. It felt like an eternity that I was frozen, and then I reacted without thought or hesitation.

33

It all happened so fast.

Zayne spun and I heard him shout as he launched himself at me. Roth and Layla both turned, but none of them were as quick as me. Not when I didn't want to be stopped.

I was at the door that led outside before any of them could reach me. There was no sense of reservation as I gripped the doorknob and turned, snapping the lock into pieces as I tore the door open.

Humid night air washed over me as I flew outside, scanning the line of demons. I didn't see Misha, but then again, I wouldn't have been able to see him in the first place in fog even the full moon couldn't penetrate.

"Where is he?" I screamed, spinning toward Aym.

The demon was suddenly in front of me, and he was handsome. Tall and blond, impeccably groomed. "He said you were impulsive," the demon said, and my breath caught. "Gloriously so."

He reached for me just as something large slammed into him, knocking him back into the fog.

Zayne.

A tremendous shift to the air took place as the mist scattered. The liege of demons charged, so many so fast that for a moment I was stunned.

Nightcrawlers.

Hellions.

Imps.

Ravers.

It was a damn demon party.

Roth shot passed me, catching what appeared to be a Hellion. He flew into the air with the creature, tossing it back into the side of the house. Layla sprang up beside a Raver, catching it by the shoulders as she brought her knee up to the creature's chin, snapping the neck back, breaking it. A Nightcrawler charged Layla. She spun, but he was fast.

But I was faster.

I let the dagger go and it struck the Nightcrawler in the face, knocking it backward. It was nothing but ash when it hit the ground.

Layla spun toward me. "Holy crap, thank you."

Darting forward, I couldn't see the dagger in the grass. It was too dark, and there was no time to search it. "Misha!" I shouted, darting across the lawn, straight toward a Hellion. It grabbed for me, but I dipped under its arm and spun around, slamming the dagger into its back. A hot spray of blood hit me as I whirled around.

Thick tendrils of mist scattered as Zayne flew backward, hitting the ground with enough impact that I stumbled. I turned to him as he flipped to his feet.

He sent me a quick look. "This demon is as annoying as I thought. Find Misha and get out of here."

"Not without you."

Zayne gripped my shoulder, pulling me toward him as he lowered his head so I was at eye level with fierce, pale blue eyes. "You find Misha and get the Hell out of here. I'll find you. Wherever you go, I will find you."

I let out a ragged breath as our gazes connected. Too many unspoken words surfaced. Too much I needed to say to him, and there was no time.

His claws caught on my shirt and then he let go, shoving me back as he flew forward, hitting a fully transformed Aym with a closed fist in the stomach, doubling the demon over.

The demon... The demon had two heads.

Spinning around, I caught a Raver in the knee. It swung toward me, mouth open and teeth snapping as I jumped back. I feinted to the right and then whirled around, thrusting the dagger into its hairless chest.

Jerking the dagger free, I whipped around as a Nightcrawler headed for Roth. Another cut in front of me, rushing the demon prince. A Nightcrawler leaped over me, rushing toward Layla. She rose, her wings lifting her high—

The Nightcrawler's claws caught her in the midsection. He spun, throwing her sideways. She screamed as she fell backward, landing on a wing with a crack that sickened me.

No.

A roar of anger shook the ground as Roth launched into the air. I turned as Zayne spun. I saw the moment he realized Layla was down. His jaw hardened and then he turned back to Aym as Roth landed behind the Nightcrawler. Roth was like a cobra striking. His hand shot out, cutting through the demon's back. He jerked his arm back, and the Nightcrawler folded into itself, crumpling like a ball of paper.

Imps screeched as they dived low, aiming for Zayne. I

shouted his name, and he spun, tossing Aym over his shoulder as he shot into the air, catching an imp by the neck.

On the ground, Ravers rushed past me, their claws digging into the soil, kicking it into the air as they went for Roth and Layla. Imps circled like buzzards.

There were too many.

They surrounded Roth and Layla, swarmed them as Roth struggled to get Layla to her feet. One of the imps snagged Roth's wing. He shook them off, but they kept coming. Two had ahold of his wings again and they start to pull. The demon prince howled as Layla tried to gain her footing.

I had to do something.

Layla and Roth were demons, but I couldn't let this happen. I couldn't. If the imps tore Roth's wings, he would be down for the count, and Layla, God, she was already done. Her arms were streaked with inky darkness, and her wings were gone. She'd shifted back into her human form, and now she was as vulnerable as a newborn kitten.

Stepping back, I lifted my left hand and took my dagger, dragging it down the center of my palm. I hissed through my teeth as my skin split open. Blood welled. I squeezed my hand closed as my heart pounded fiercely.

I knew the moment they scented my blood in the air.

The imps stilled. The Hellions skidded to a halt and slowly turned. The Nightcrawlers tossed their heads back and sniffed at the air. My blood did what I needed it to. The demons were now focused on me, and not Roth and Layla.

I smiled. "Dinnertime."

Aym whipped around, shifting back into his human form, his mouth gaping open and elongating, stretching wide and distorted as he let out a wail that raised all the tiny hairs over my body.

"No!" he shouted. Or maybe it was Zayne. I wasn't sure,

but it was definitely the demon that yelled, "She must be taken alive!"

Lowering my bloody hand, I knew the lower level demons were beyond hearing Aym's order. The imps let go of Roth's wings and flew at me. I was prepared, clenching the dagger as I ran toward the first, leaping up and spinning, slamming the dagger deep into the chest of the imp. It screamed, and we both went down in a tangle of arms, and demon wings.

I rolled, tossing the demon off me, and then sprang to my feet. "Get Layla out of here, Roth!" I yelled at him as I dipped and narrowly avoided an imp's clawed feet. "Get her out of here now!"

Roth didn't hesitate.

Scooping Layla up, he crouched and then took off like a missile, disappearing into the sky as I whirled to face what sounded like a herd.

All the demons were coming for me now.

Sheathing my dagger, I gave in to the adrenaline pumping through my veins as the *grace* stretched me to the seams, demanding I let it out…and I let it take over.

Light filled me, buzzing through my veins as the corners of my vision burned white. Muscles tensed as pure golden-white light erupted down my arm, forming the sword. The moment the handle formed against my palm, I screamed and swept the sword high, catching the nearest Hellion in the waist, cleaving it in two. I spun, shoving the sword through the chest of another demon. Yanking the sword back, I pivoted and caught a Nightcrawler along the thighs, cutting *it* in two.

A cyclone of violence and blood surrounded me as the world constricted to each blow I delivered, each blow I took as the demons tried to get to me. Bodies piled around me, dying on top of one another before they could burst into nothing but ash and fire. I felt nothing but righteous rage as I cut down demon after demon, blood mixing with sweat—

Pain exploded along my side and I stumbled forward, the sword flickering and fading as I lost my hold on the *grace*. I spun toward the demon responsible for the burning pain along my side.

The demon was dressed in head-to-toe red pleather. Her long blond hair was pulled into a high ponytail. When our eyes locked, the demon's mouth dropped open and stretched grotesquely. The eerie whine sent a shiver down my spine. But more than anything, the sight of a female demon threw me through a loop. She was an Upper Level demon, obviously drawn by my blood.

She struck out, her hand catching me in the stomach with a shocking quickness, knocking the wind out of my lungs.

All right, then. If she wanted a bitch fight, she was going to get one. "You really don't want to do this, honey."

She cocked her head to the side as she circled me. "I'll eat you alive, bitch."

"As charming as that sounds, you're not my type." I shot forward, dipping under the demon's outstretched arm, and coldcocked her in the jaw.

Stumbling back a few feet, the demon spit out a mouthful of dark blood. "That wasn't very nice."

The demon moved fast, hitting me in the chest and knocking me to the ground. My back throbbed, but it was a speck of pain in the big scheme of things. Pushing up, I spun around and planted my foot in the demon's stomach. We exchanged and dodged blows. The female was fierce, scrappy and so not above hair pulling.

She got a good grip on my hair and tossed me to the ground. Really ticked off now, I sprang to my feet and returned the favor as blood trickled out of my nose. Grabbing ahold of the blond ponytail, I yanked her head forward as I brought my knee up. The resulting sickening crunch of the demon's nose breaking filled me with unmeasurable glee.

"Like I told you," I said, slamming the chick's face into my knee again. "You don't want any of this."

"Screw you," she spat.

Done playing around, I released her and whipped out my dagger, delivering the final blow with a deep thrust to the chest. I pulled the dagger out, breathing heavily as she caved in on herself.

"Trinity!" Zayne shouted, and a moment later he was beside me, circling an arm around my waist and hauling me back as a wall of flames went up no more than a few feet in front of me.

Gasping, I clutched his arm with one hand as he spun me around, taking me to the ground as flames roared over our heads. His wings slammed down on either side of me, stabbing the ground.

"It's Aym," he growled. "He's killing the other demons."

While that was surprisingly helpful, it wasn't out of benevolence. Aym needed me alive, and he was willing to kill his own kind to ensure it.

As soon as the flames retracted, Zayne rose, lifting me onto my feet. The scent of burned earth and ozone assaulted my senses as my vision focused on the blond demon.

"You two have no idea what is about to go down," Aym taunted, flames rippling from his fingers as he stalked forward. Sparks hit the trees. They went up like nothing more than dry twigs. "But you're going to find out."

Zayne reacted, and since he was standing to my side, I didn't see him until it was too late. His arm swung back, catching me around the waist and shoving me as the demon charged us.

I skidded backward over the yard and caught myself on the

wall of the house while Zayne took flight, crashing into the demon as flames burst from him.

"Dammit," I shouted, pushing off the wall. I grabbed my dagger, but as the two twisted and turned, there was no way I could get a clear shot at Aym without wounding Zayne.

They were like two Titans battling it out, going toe to toe, punch for punch. The demon had also shifted, his skin now a deep maroon, and with each punch he landed, flames erupted, and the scent of charred flesh hit the air.

The fire... The fire was burning Zayne.

"No," I whispered, heart dropping. I shot forward but braked as a wall of flames shot up in front of me, burning intensely and forcing me back before burning out, leaving the ground charred.

They were a blur of twisting, angry bodies, and then suddenly Zayne was flying backward and slamming into the house. I spun then, launching the dagger at the demon. It caught him in the shoulder and he staggered back as Zayne lifted himself up. I spared him a quick glance. One of his wings was completely blackened, and half of his body—

Oh God, no. *No.*

I had to get him out of here. I had to—

Aym launched into the air, coming straight for me. The *grace* stirred alive inside me once more as I stood there, more than ready to end this stupid, mother—

Zayne caught the demon and they fell behind me, sliding across the ground and into the wall. I whirled around, and it was then when I saw the shocked look etched across the demon's face and Zayne yanking his head back, his horns and claws dripping with gore.

"Damn," gasped Aym, and a second later Zayne tore into his neck. The head went in one direction, the body in the other. Both erupted into flames before hitting the ground.

And that was… That was impressive.

Gross.

But impressive.

Zayne was on one knee, and I realized he was trying to stand. His wings folded into his back, disappearing into the slits above the shoulder blades and closing over skin that was suddenly pink in some areas and…and reddish black in others. Oh God.

Lurching forward, I didn't reach Zayne in time. He fell to the side, against the wall, completely in his human form.

"Zayne!" I shouted, dropping to his side. Horror seized me as I stared down at him. I picked up his hand. "Zayne!"

"I think… I think I'm a little sunburned."

I choked on a wet-sounding laugh. "A little. Oh God, what were you thinking? I could've—"

"His fire…would've scarred you…would've killed you."

It would've. His Warden skin protected him, but only to a certain degree, because the splotches of white among the charred skin told me he had third-degree burns. Horror exploded into my gut. "Zayne…"

"It's…okay." He shuddered, eyes screwed tight. "It'll be… okay."

There was no way this would be okay. No way. None. It was horrific and panic clawed at me as exhaustion flooded my every pore. He was badly injured. "I'm going to get you out of here. I'll call Nicolai or Dez, and I'll get—"

"Misha," Zayne moaned.

I shook my head, heart pounding. "We'll find him later, but you're the priority now. You—"

"No," he said, eyes closing and opening, his gaze focusing beyond me. *"Misha."*

"It smells like a barbecue in here—a Warden barbecue."

I stopped.

My heart stopped.

Everything stopped.

Almost like I was moving in a dream, I turned toward the sound of the familiar voice, a voice that didn't make sense. I scanned the yard and who I saw couldn't be there. There was no way.

Because I saw Misha standing in the moonlight.

"I knew we could always count on your impulsiveness."

34

It *was* Misha—his curly reddish-brown hair dark in the moonlight, his face handsome as ever and his stance familiar, wide legged and shoulders thrown back as if he could challenge someone with just the way he stood.

Misha.

For what felt like an eternity, I was locked up, unable to move as I watched Misha take a step forward, and then elation powered through me so fiercely that I cried out as I started to scramble to my feet—

Zayne's hand tightened on mine. "Don't," he groaned, voice raspy and low. "Something...something isn't right..."

I swiveled back toward him, confused. "It's Misha," I said. "It's—"

"You should probably listen to him, Trin," Misha said. "Especially since it doesn't look like he has much time left."

Cold air traveled down my spine as I twisted back toward Misha. "What?"

"You look so surprised." Stopping a few feet from me,

Misha ducked his chin. The burning trees cast a reddish glow across his face. He was... He was grinning. "I wish you could see your face right now."

"I...I don't understand." I stayed kneeling beside Zayne as I lifted my other hand, pressing my palm to my chest, fighting the urge to run to Misha—to throw myself at him and to touch him, to hold him, because I...I didn't understand this. "How did you escape—"

"Escape?" He toed Aym's ashes with his boot, smirking. "And that's what he said you'd think."

"Who? Aym?" Glancing down at Zayne, I saw this his eyes were open. He was silent, his grip looser on my hand, but I knew he was aware of what was happening. I squeezed his hand and then let go, rising on shaky legs.

Misha laughed. "Not that idiot. God, whoever told us that demons were intelligent and conniving obviously hadn't met half of them."

Unease spread as I pulled my hand free of Zayne's. "What's going on, Misha? Did you escape?" But if that was the case, why hadn't he helped me or Zayne? "What—?"

"What am I doing here?" he asked, spreading his hands. "I have a better question to ask. Did you really think you were the only special one?"

"What?"

"*What?*" he mocked, tilting his head. "You did, didn't you? This whole time, you always believed you were this chosen one—the Trueborn who would someday be called upon, and I was the Protector, your faithful fucking *shadow*, trailing behind you."

Stunned, I started toward him but stopped when I grew close enough to see the hatred twisting his features.

I shrank back, my stomach churning. "What are you talking about? What has he done to you?"

"He chose me," Misha said. "That is what he did. He chose *me*."

"Who? Bael? Who are—?"

"God, you should be smarter than this," he said. "I know you are."

I stared at him, heart thumping heavily. "Okay. I don't know what in the Hell is up with you, but we can figure this out. Together. Obviously, the demon did something to you—"

Misha shot forward and his hand snaked out, landing across my face with a stinging blow that knocked me back a step. "He did nothing to me! Bael is just a tool to get to this moment. All I needed was for him to create a distraction. Get in, get me and you, but he messed that up. Just like Aym messed up tonight."

Tasting blood in my mouth, I slowly turned my head back to him. "Did you seriously just smack me?"

"I will do so much worse."

I drew in a *very* deep breath as I met his glare. Something… something terrible had happened to him. Was he possessed? His eyes were normal, a vibrant blue. He looked like the Misha I knew, the Misha I loved, but he sounded nothing like that.

"Did you know that a Protector bond can be broken without the Trueborn's death?" Misha asked, laughing when he saw the widening of my eyes. "You didn't, did you? No one taught us that. Then again, your father never really taught us anything."

Instinct took over, and I backed up, keeping enough space between us so he wasn't in my blind spots.

"All it takes to break the bond is a Protector killing an innocent," Misha said. "I'm not going to kill you, Trinity. Not now. But eventually, I'm going to have to break this bond, because you *are* going to die."

Ice drenched my veins as horror filled me. "Misha, this isn't you. You don't talk about killing innocent people—killing anyone like it's nothing. *This isn't you.*"

"I don't think it's nothing," he admitted, a muscle clenching. "But I have to do it. He showed me the way. He taught me everything when he chose me. He showed me how to keep it hidden, and it worked. I've been planning this for years."

Years?

I shook my head, stunned by what he was saying and terrified that it was the truth, and this was him, and that he was right—I'd never seen it. Because if that was the case, I couldn't fix this—fix him.

"Who do you think was behind Ryker? He never came to the training rooms before, but he did the one time you decided to show your *grace*?" He chuckled upon seeing the horror dawning on my face. "Who do you think goaded him into his fear and his anger? Who do think pulled those strings?"

Heart stuttering, I shook my head. "No."

"*Yes.*"

"No," I whispered. "*No.* You couldn't have. He killed my mom. He *killed* her—"

"She had to go," he spat, and I stiffened at the loathing that dripped from every word he spoke. "She was figuring out that Thierry had made a mistake. You never saw it, but then again, I'm not surprised. It has always been about you—about what life you didn't have, about how you were bored or how you were lonely and how you'd never find anyone if you stayed in the community. It was always about making sure you were safe and you were protected. It was always about how important you were and what you wanted and needed, and it was *never about me!*" he roared, shaking the ground.

I flinched at the truthfulness of his words, because that was me. Oh God, that was so me.

"It was never about me until *he* chose me and showed me

the way. And he knows I will succeed because you…you won't kill me. You can't." His chest rose with a deep breath. "So, for once in your life, you're going to listen to me, and you're going to come with me. If you don't, I'll make you, and you're not going to like it when I do."

A strangled sound closed off my throat. "And Clay?"

"Oh, I had nothing to do with that. He was just a jerk who obviously had a bone to pick with you," he said. "I don't think he intended to kill you. I think he just wanted to scare you. The mask was a nice touch. I copied that."

My stomach twisted even further. "Misha, please… You can't be behind this. Someone has turned you. Someone has—"

"Showed me how important I am for once!" he yelled, and I jerked.

I shuddered. "Who is 'he'?"

"The Harbinger," Misha said, and he smiled. "He's already been here. He's what they are hunting and will never find. He showed me what's coming, Trinity." Misha shook his head. "You're going to be a part of it."

"How?" I demanded, dragging in deep breaths. "How am I going to be a part of it, and then what? You break the bond and then kill me? What happens to you, Misha? You're going to live with yourself after all of this? I trusted you. I love you, and you can do this? To me? To us?"

"I can and I will," Misha said, lifting his chin. "And, Trin, there's never been an 'us.' It's only ever been you."

That was worse than a slap in a face. It was a knife to the heart.

"It's time for a new era."

"A new era?" I shook my head. "Have you lost your mind?"

Misha sprang at me, giving me no room to doubt that he fully intended to do what he'd claimed. And maybe it was the shock of it. Maybe it was the fact I couldn't believe what was right in front of me, but either way, I just didn't move.

The first blow knocked me on my ass, stunning me. The second blow, a kick to the back, woke me the Hell up. I sprang to my feet, and the third blow never landed as I jumped out of his reach, panting.

"You're exhausted. You used your *grace*. You should've stayed down," he said.

"And you should know better than that."

Misha's lips pulled back in a sneer. "So be it."

Then he shifted, shirt ripping and skin hardening to stone. He came at me hard and fast, stunning me with his brutality.

Fighting Misha was like fighting myself—if I was a Warden falling down an out-of-control rage spiral. He deflected nearly every blow I sent his way, and Misha's fists connected with parts of me more times than I could count. It was savage and raw, and I felt all the hatred Misha had inside him and had kept buried until now with every fist and kick, the last one bringing me to my knees.

Blood poured from my nose and mouth. My lip felt wrong. Split. I spit out a mouthful of blood, arms shaking as I pushed up onto my feet. I refused to look at Zayne's crumpled body, knowing I couldn't afford the distraction, and squared off with Misha once more.

He took an angry swipe at me, nearly digging his claws into my stomach. He was fast in his attack, cutting and jabbing at me until he backed me up against the wall of the house.

Through it all, his own words kept coming back to me, words he'd spoken to me over and over during the years of training.

Fighting is *simply anticipating the next attack*. Find the muscle tremor. Watch where Misha looks...where he positions his body... *He will tell you where he strikes next without words.*

But it wasn't enough.

Misha had my strength, and he knew all my moves, all my weaknesses. I knew he could defeat me.

Misha's spin kick caught me in the jaw, snapping my head back and taking me to the ground once more. I rolled onto my side, moaning as I blinked blurry eyes. I tried to sit up, but pain brought me back down to the scorched grass. Gasping, I wheezed as I tried to get my lungs to expand. Pain lanced across my chest. Something...something felt broken. A rib? Multiple ones? I wasn't sure. My eyes drifted shut.

"Stay down." Misha stepped over my legs. "I'm going to put this one out of his misery."

No.

"Not going to happen," Zayne growled, and I opened my eyes to see him pitch forward as he struggled to rise. I rose onto my elbow, panting. "I'm going to rip your throat out."

"Really?" Misha chuckled as he knelt beside Zayne. "It was supposed to be you."

I had no idea what Misha was talking about, but it didn't matter. I needed to get to my feet. I needed to... I needed to stop Misha, because he would kill Zayne.

And I could not, *would* not, let that happen.

I pushed to my feet, swaying as my *grace* came to life inside me once more, burning through my veins and muscles, bone and tissue, lighting up every cell. Fire snapped through me as I summoned the sword and felt it respond, hot and heavy in my grasp.

I was nothing more than storm and fury as I stepped forward and Misha looked up at me. He rose.

"I love you," I said, and Misha's eyes widened. There was a flicker of surprise, almost as if he couldn't believe I was going to do it, and for a brief second, I didn't know what he wanted from me, what he expected. Didn't he know me at all? Didn't he know there was no way I'd let him kill Zayne?

That I'd let him take me?

Why didn't he realize that?

Misha reached for me.

But I lifted the sword high as it spit white fire.

Screaming filled my ears, drowning out everything around me and in me, and a distant part of me realized that it was me making those sounds, it was me wailing as I swung the sword down on Misha.

The white flames burned bright, and I thought there was a moment our gazes locked, a moment when I saw the boy I grew up with staring back at me through familiar beautiful blue eyes, but then the flames swallowed Misha, and within a stuttered heartbeat, he was gone. There was nothing left of him but ashes—

A sudden icy feeling poured into my chest, knocking the air out of my lungs. I took a step, but my legs collapsed and I landed on my knees, not evening feeling the pain.

Oh God.

A shudder racked me from bones to muscles, and when it receded, taking the iciness with it, I couldn't...

I couldn't feel *it*.

I lifted a trembling hand and pressed it to the center of my chest, just below my breasts. I couldn't feel *it*—the bond.

It was gone—broken, and that meant, Misha was... He was truly gone.

35

The *grace* recoiled deep inside me, pulling back. The sword collapsed into itself and the corners of my vision darkened as I stared at the spot where Misha had stood. I opened my mouth, but I could make no sound, as if my throat had sealed itself off. There was a vast emptiness inside me, a hole…

Misha was gone.

Bending at the waist, I drew in a shallow breath that hurt. The breath went nowhere, stuck in my burning throat. My hands shook. My entire body trembled as raw, unbearable pain swallowed me and questions pounded through me. How could this have happened? How could Misha do this? How could he become this lost, and I never saw it? I lifted my hands and stared down at them. My fingers trembled. So did my legs. My entire body rattled.

I'd killed Misha. I'd had to, but I killed him and I—

Zayne.

Pulling myself back from the brink, I scrambled to my feet and staggered toward him. Every part of my being focused on him. Zayne was here. He'd been hurt. Bad. I had to help him. He was the priority. Not Misha. Not me. Zayne. I dropped to my knees beside him. I reached for him but stopped, unsure of where I could touch him.

"Oh, Zayne," I whispered. For a heart-stopping moment, I didn't know what to do. His eyes were closed, and a horrible fear surfaced. It was so bad that wild panic dug deep and it eased only a little when I saw his chest finally move.

He wasn't in his Warden form, seeming to have lost the strength to shift back. Half his body was…charred, ruddy and black. There was a terrible gash across his chest, deep enough to expose the muscles beneath the skin. Whatever injuries I had, which seemed like a lot, were nothing in comparison to what had been done to Zayne.

What he had done to himself to protect me.

"I need to get us help," I said, touching his left cheek, where he wasn't burned. The breath I took was shaky. "Do you think—?"

"I'm sorry." His voice was hoarse when he spoke. "I'm so sorry."

I shook my head, wanting to touch him more but afraid of hurting him. "What are you sorry for? You—"

"Misha," he groaned, his eyes opening into thin slits. "I'm so sorry."

If I thought my heart was incapable of shattering even more, I was wrong. It cracked wide open as I blinked back my tears. "Don't," I whispered, gently brushing the hair back from his face. "Don't apologize for him."

"I know…" His breath shuddered out of him as his face tensed. "I know how much he…means to you and you…you shouldn't have had to do that."

His face blurred as I fought back tears. "Thank you…" My voice broke.

"He…he hurt you." Zayne shuddered.

"I'll be okay…" I would, but Zayne… "Do you think you can get up? Or do you think you can at least shift?"

"I…I don't think so," he said, and that was bad. If he could shift, it would kick in his healing abilities, and if he stayed in his human form, he'd keep getting worse until he—

I cut that thought off. "I'm not going to let you die, Zayne. You annoy me too much for me to let you die."

A huffing, pained laugh came from him. "That doesn't… make any sense."

"It makes complete sense," I told him. "You need to shift."

"You…you need to go before more…demons show up," he said, his chest rising and then sinking. "You're bleeding all over. I smell it. Ice cream."

"I'm not leaving you, Zayne. I need you to concentrate and shift. If not, you—you're going to die a virgin, Zayne. Do you want to die a virgin?"

He laughed and it ended on a choking sound that sent my heart plummeting. "I cannot believe you just said that."

"Me, neither, but come on, Zayne. Please. God. Please, don't do this. I…" *I really like you.* It might even be deeper than that. I might even be falling…falling in love with him, and I couldn't lose him. Not now. Not ever. "I really like you, Zayne."

"I think…that was pretty evident a few nights ago."

Despite everything that had happened and everything that could still happen, I flushed as I picked up his hand and felt that jolt that always came with skin-to-skin contact with him. "I need you, Zayne. So, I'm not going to let you die. You're going to shift and then we're going to get out—"

I felt it then, the hot breath along the back of my neck. Every muscle in my body tensed as I twisted at the waist, prepared to lay waste to anyone or anything—

A form came out of the smoke and fire, taking shape. It wasn't until he was a few feet from me that I realized it was Roth.

I relaxed.

A little.

"Hell," Roth muttered, going straight to Zayne. He dropped to his knees beside the Warden, reached for him but stopped, hands curling around empty air. "I came back as soon as I could. I…"

"He's hurt. Bad. We need to get him out of here and get him help," I said.

Roth glanced at me then, his amber eyes luminous, and the look he gave me robbed the air from my lungs. Everything he didn't dare speak was in his…his pained expression. Everything I feared resided there.

Too late.

That was the look Roth gave me.

It was too late.

"No," I whispered, trembling.

Roth's lips parted. "I—"

Something happened right then.

It started with a shimmer of light that looked like fireflies had invaded the yard. The tiny hairs rose all over my body as Zayne lifted his head off the wall. I looked around, seeing thousands of twinkling lights, as if the stars had descended from the skies. The fires around us flickered and then went out.

Fear exploded in my gut. Not for me. Not for Zayne. But for the demon prince who was so very much unlike a demon, who loved Layla and cared enough for Zayne that he came back.

My head whipped toward where Roth crouched beside

Zayne, whose eyes were closed again. "You need to go," I told him. "Now."

Roth was staring at the lights now, his eyes wide. "Is that...?"

"Yes." My mouth dried. "If you stay, he will kill you. You know that, right? You can't take him. No one can. You need to go. We'll be okay." I hoped at least. "But you won't be."

For a moment I thought Roth would argue and say something arrogant, but common sense prevailed. He seemed to know this wasn't an Alpha that his familiar could swallow up whole. What was coming was death for him. He looked at me, nodded and then turned to Zayne. "Don't die," he growled. "It would upset Layla."

And then Roth was gone, moving too fast for me to see him. Letting out a shaky breath, I focused on the twinkling lights.

"Am I... Am I seeing this?" Zayne asked, and I wasn't even sure he was aware that Roth had been here.

"Yeah." I swallowed.

My grip on his hand tightened as blinding white light poured into the yard, dripping from the burned trees and running down the walls of the house. It was so bright that my eyes stung and I had to look away.

I knew who it was.

I knew who was coming.

Zayne struggled to sit forward, throwing an arm back against me as he shifted his large body so that I was partially blocked. Even horrifically injured, he was trying to protect me, and I tried to tell Zayne it was okay, but then the trumpets sounded, rattling the walls and our eardrums. I winced, placing my hands over my ears as the horns blared once more. When they stopped and the light receded, Zayne was staring into the center of the yard, his spine stiff.

"Holy…" He trailed off.

Lifting my head, I lowered my hands and looked to where Zayne was staring.

He stood in the center of the driveway, his long, wide-spread legs encased in leather and his torso and chest shielded by golden battle armor. His arms were bare and his skin put off a luminous glow that made it difficult to tell exactly what his skin tone was. His hair was fair, brushing his shoulders, and from what I could make out of his features, he looked no older than Nicolai, though I knew he was ageless.

The air stirred as his wings lifted behind him, white and feathered, stretching at least ten feet on either side of him.

Michael, my father, sure liked to make an entrance.

"What a waste," the archangel said as he stared at what remained of Misha.

I flinched at his words.

He walked toward us, the grounds trembling under his weight, and I realized at once why he was here.

Horror punched through my gut as I dipped under Zayne's arm, planting myself between him and my father. "Don't," I said, staring up at my father. "Please don't force this on him."

My father halted.

I swallowed at the look on his face, one that said he was shocked that I dared to question him or stop him. "You saw what happened when you forced this bond. Please don't do it to Zayne." My voice shook. "Please don't force him to take this bond."

"What?" Zayne was leaning on his side.

"He's going to force you to become my Protector, like he did to Misha," I said, crouching in front of Zayne. "I will not allow it. I will not allow you—"

"You will allow nothing." My father cut me off, his all-white eyes pulsing. "And you assume too much."

I lifted my chin. "I don't assume—"

"You assume too much just by speaking." He cut me off again, focusing on Zayne. My father's upper lip curled. "You do not impress me."

"Good to know." Zayne groaned as he forced himself into a sitting position. I scrambled backward, supporting his weight as he met my father's glare.

My father continued to sneer. "Your faith in demons disturbs me greatly."

"I…I imagine it would," Zayne replied. "All things considered…"

The sneer faded. "But here we are, as we should have already been. The mistake was made ten years ago. It will not be made again."

"Mistake?" At once, I remembered what Thierry and Matthew had said, what Peanut had overheard. Them speaking about a mistake. The same thing Misha had said my mother had been close to figuring out. "What mistake?"

I didn't think my father would answer, but then he said, "Protectors are predestined at birth, linked to their charges before they even meet. They thought it was Misha based on how quickly you took to him when you first met. They were wrong."

"They?"

"Those who have taken care of you. Thierry. Matthew." His all white-eyes shifted to Zayne. "Your father."

"*My* father?" Zayne repeated.

"Your father was supposed to retrieve *her*," he said, inclining his chin toward me. "Not the half demon."

My mouth dropped open.

Zayne shook his head, groaning at the movement. "I don't… I don't understand."

"Me, neither. I mean, I get it. You're saying I was never supposed to be bonded to Misha, then why did you bond me to him?" My thoughts raced. "Why didn't you step in? Why—? You should've—"

"It was not my job to step in, nor is it your place to question what I should have or should not have done," he said, eyes sparking white light. "I did not realize the mistake was made until after you were bonded. I decided to see what would happen."

I was thunderstruck. "You...you decided to see what would happen?"

"After all, it must have been a part of the grand plan," he replied, and then he shrugged, as if it was no big deal, and all I could do was stare as a shudder worked its way through me.

He didn't even care.

He didn't care that Misha was never supposed to be bonded to me, or that Misha was now dead. He simply just did not care.

And why was I surprised? Angels didn't have emotions. They didn't even have a soul, not like humans did.

My father's shoulders straightened. "Do you, Warden, accept this bond, forsaking all others and all duties, to become her Protector until death breaks this bond?"

My breath caught.

"Yes," Zayne groaned. "Yes, I will become her Protector."

Panic blossomed. This was happening too fast. "Zayne—"

"Then it shall be done." My father placed a hand on the side of Zayne's ruined face, causing him to gasp in pain. He placed his other hand on mine, and then I felt it.

Heat rushed through his palm, in and out of me, flowing through the archangel and into Zayne. His body bowed and the *grace* filled him, irrevocably connecting him to me. Zayne was awash in heavenly light, completely indistinguishable. I could scarcely breathe as I felt the warmth pouring into my chest, replacing the bond once held with Misha, erasing the hollow emptiness left behind.

The pain—oh God, the pain of Misha's betrayal was still there, but...but Zayne was *there*. I felt him deep inside me, taking root, his essence becoming a part of mine.

Then I felt more.

Two heartbeats instead of one. Mine. His. Together. And that...that was something I'd never felt with Misha.

When the light receded, Zayne was slumped over, his hands planted against the ground, his burned and torn skin and chest healed.

Seeing that, knowing that he was going to be okay, was almost too much to take. I started to shake.

My father leaned in, whispering in Zayne's ear. I couldn't hear what was said, but whatever it was caused Zayne's eyes to widen and his gaze to swing toward me. A look of dawning understanding filled his expression. I didn't get a chance to question what was said to him.

"Rise up." Michael removed his hands from us. "For what has begun a millennium ago is now at the door. The Harbinger has arrived." His voice deepened, booming like thunder, and the words he spoke sent a cold chill straight to my core. "The end is upon us. Stop it, or all mankind is lost."

36

"Trin."

The soft brush of fingertips against my cheek stirred me awake. I blinked open my eyes and found myself staring into Zayne's pale blue ones fringed in thick, brown lashes. His golden skin was unmarred—not even the faintest hint of pink remained from where he'd been burned. It was almost like he'd never been hurt. Almost like last night hadn't happened. That we didn't go to that senator's house and end up surrounded by demons. Almost like Misha hadn't showed, and I...I hadn't had to kill him. All of it felt like a nightmare, a really bad one that haunted you throughout the day, slipping in and out of your consciousness when you least expected it.

But there was a warmth in my chest, a ball of light beside my heart that beat in step with Zayne's.

Last night *had* happened, and Zayne was now... He was my Protector.

Out of the ten years I'd been bonded to Misha, I'd never

felt what I felt now. With Misha, it had been a connection, but with Zayne, it was as if a piece of him existed inside me.

And it was weird.

Drawing in a shallow breath, I sat up and pulled my legs out from under a rainbow-colored quilt I hadn't fallen asleep with. Hair fell across my face as I pulled my gaze from Zayne's and looked around the unfamiliar room. It was small, oval room and there were playpens across from the couch that I'd been dozing on. I was in the DC compound. We'd come here last night after...everything, and while Zayne met with Nicolai and the rest of his clan, I'd left to call Thierry, and Jada, and somehow I'd roamed into this small room while Zayne told his clan what had happened last night—what Misha had done, what he'd hinted at and what my father had warned.

I hadn't wanted to be there for the blow-by-blow of what I'd already lived through, and there had been more pressing matters. I'd needed to call home.

Telling Jada and Thierry and Matthew had been one of the hardest things I'd ever done. There'd been tears from Jada and Matthew, and stony silence from Thierry—silence I knew came from a place of great shock and guilt, because, like me, he couldn't believe it and he couldn't understand how he hadn't seen it. The call had ended with Matthew leaving to come here, and I'd promised to come home to see Jada as soon as possible.

I had no idea how I'd dozed off, but after using the *grace* twice, I shouldn't be surprised even though my injuries had been healed when my father had restored Zayne.

"You doing okay?" Zayne asked as he made a show of lifting his hand. His fingertips grazed my cheek as he tucked my hair back, out of my face. "You've been sleeping for several hours. I checked on you a couple times."

That explained the quilt that had been draped over me. I

placed my hands on the cushions beside me. I nodded, even though I wasn't sure what I felt.

"Have you heard from Roth or Layla?" I asked.

He nodded. "Both are fine. Roth said you made sure that he got out before your...your father showed."

"Yeah."

A beat of silence and then, "Layla's okay. Resting. Because of you. You probably saved her life."

"I don't know about all that."

His head tilted to the side. "Trin, she's says if you hadn't—"

"I'm just glad she's okay," I said, cutting him off, and then I felt it. A burst of frustration that tasted like pepper in the back of my throat. It wasn't me. It was Zayne. "You're frustrated."

"Well, yeah. I'm a lot of things right now. Frustrated is one of them—"

"I can feel it. I can feel that you're frustrated," I told him. "Do you feel me? Feel anything I'm feeling?"

Zayne sat beside me, and when I looked at him, his blond hair was a mess of tumbled waves. His gaze dropped, and then wordlessly he picked up my hand that was closest to him. He brought it to his chest, to his heart. Air hitched in my throat. He knew what I was asking.

"I feel it," he said, keeping my hand to his chest. "I feel *you*, but I've felt something since the first time I met you. Like I've always known you. We talked about that, but I thought... I'd thought it was just something weird. Maybe both our imaginations working overtime, but there was also this...jolt that I'd feel whenever we touched."

"I felt it, too." I leaned toward him. "With Misha, it wasn't like that. I mean, I could feel him. Like, I knew we were connected, but it was more of a mental thing. Not physical. Not like this."

Zayne lowered our joined hands to the space between us. "Maybe it's because...this was meant to be."

I closed my eyes. Meant to be. Him. Me. Protector. True-born.

"God." He coughed out a short laugh. "If what your father said is true, and since he's *the* freaking Michael I'm assuming it is, then it *was* supposed to be you. My father was supposed to bring you here and not..."

And not Layla.

Swallowing, I gave a little shake of my head as I opened my eyes. "I just don't understand. I don't understand how any of this could've happened or why."

"Well, maybe we'll have some answers soon," he said. "I came to wake you. Matthew's here. He's with Nicolai. You ready to see him?"

Not really, but I nodded, and when Zayne rose, he brought me with him.

The moment I saw Matthew, it was like I was ten all over again, and the only thing that was going to make me feel better was one of his hugs.

I let go of Zayne's hand, and I didn't care who was in the room. I raced toward him as if he was holding a plate of cupcakes. I threw myself at him, and he caught me, wrapping his arms around me, and when I took a deep breath, he smelled like... He smelled like *home*.

"Girl," he said, lifting me off my feet for a brief second. "I am so very sorry."

I dug my fingers into the back of his shirt, holding on for dear life, because Matthew...he represented *before* to me. Before I came here with Zayne. Before Misha...did what he did. I didn't want to let go, so I didn't, for what felt like an eternity.

Matthew had to untangle my arms from him like I was an

octopus. When he led me to a chair, I saw that Nicolai was in his office, behind his desk, and Zayne...he was right beside me, standing there like a sentry.

Like he'd always been there.

Matthew sat in the chair across from me, and I looked at him, really looked at him. There were shadows under his puffy eyes and taut lines at the corners of his mouth. He started to speak.

"It was a mistake," I said, placing my hands on my knees. "That's what my father said. That I was supposed to be bonded to Zayne all along?"

"We didn't know, Trin. We thought we were doing the right thing." He glanced at Nicolai and then Zayne. A long moment passed. "Your mother was supposed to bring you to Abbot. That is what she told us, and to this day, Thierry and I have no idea why she didn't do that. Maybe she just felt safe with Thierry—with me—and you took so well to..." He sat back, drawing in a ragged breath. "You took so well to Misha. We thought it was him. We started training you two together, and you were bonded. We didn't think anything of it until...he arrived."

I glanced up at Zayne, and while his face was impressively stoic, I could feel his confusion mingling with mine.

"You two seemed to find each other immediately," Matthew went on. "Like you were there to see him arrive, and he...he knew you were in the Great Hall when none of us knew you were there. He found you that night you were hurt. He knew, and Misha didn't."

"It's true," Nicolai said, drawing our gazes. He was focused on Zayne. "We were all sitting around, and suddenly you got antsy. Said you needed fresh air. We were outside for no more than a couple of minutes before we ran into her."

Zayne nodded slowly and then he looked at me. "I didn't know she was hurt. I just had to get out and keep walking."

"Protectors are chosen at birth. That is what we're told, and it seems to be true. That even though you two were never bonded, you could sense her." A faint smile came and went as Matthew dragged his hand over his face. "That's when we realized it was you. We just didn't know what to do, and your father…"

"He didn't clear anything up. He just let all of this happen." I sucked in a sharp breath. "Misha wasn't a bad person. I know he wasn't. You have to know that, Matthew. He was good and normal and—"

"And he was never supposed to be your Protector. We made a mistake, Trinity, and mistakes…" He shook his head. "I still don't know how he got to this point. I think…maybe the bond twisted him, made him susceptible to Bael's influence, made him feel and think the way he did." Matthew bowed his head. "It's the only thing that makes sense."

Maybe it did.

Maybe Matthew was right that this bond, forced upon the wrong Warden, had slowly poisoned him, but I wasn't so sure. The things he'd said—he'd said the Harbinger was here, the same thing my father had said.

Matthew knew that. As did Nicolai. I'd told Matthew and Thierry on the phone. Zayne had repeated everything to his clan. It was easier to think that it was the bond that had done it. I wanted to think that was the case, because if it had been Misha—if it had been him all along—I wasn't sure how I was supposed to process that.

How I was supposed to move on from that?

I walked through the unfamiliar woods at dusk, following the well-worn path along the ground. I had no idea where it was going, but I figured Zayne would find me when his session was done inside the compound.

Matthew was still there, and they were talking about what was found at the senator's home—a home we'd just learned had been razed to the ground this morning. It was all over the news, and people were saying how lucky it was that the senator was in his home state of Tennessee during what they believed to be a freak electrical fire.

Obviously, the senator was a bad dude and we needed to find out exactly how he was connected to Bael and what he planned to do with that school.

I should be in there with them, but I just couldn't sit still any longer. I needed space, because I...

I hadn't cried yet.

Not a tear.

I didn't know why. I felt like there was something wrong with me, because it wasn't like I was trying not to process what had happened. I was. I was dwelling on it. I was stressing over it, replaying nearly every day of the lives Misha and I had shared, realizing there had been signs of his unhappiness—but this? His discontent had opened him to influence, because he *had* to have been manipulated.

Misha had meant the world to me, and I hadn't even known him. Not really, and that was as tough to swallow as his betrayal. But I still hadn't cried and I didn't understand that—

I tripped over a fallen log, catching myself before I fell.

Sighing, I straightened and kept walking as the woods got thicker and more fireflies appeared, flickering in and out of existence. Misha had called them lightning bugs. When we were younger, we'd catch them in our hands and chase one another with them.

My chest ached as I rounded a thick tree and came upon... a tree house?

Yep. That's what it was.

A tree house with what looked like a huge observation deck. I looked over my shoulder in the direction of the main house. I was still on their property, so I was betting this had been for Zayne once. For Zayne and Layla.

Now my chest hurt even more, because I really did like Zayne, and if things had been complicated before, they were sure as Hell a mess now, because Protectors and Trueborns…

That was a big No.

And I felt it then, a burning in the back of my throat and behind my eyes. I smacked my hands over my face and took several deep breaths, but those breaths seemed to fuel the ugly, raw mess of emotions expanding in my chest and building and building until I couldn't hold back. I couldn't swallow them down or shove them away. I couldn't push them to the back of my thoughts. They were tearing and ripping and clawing free.

The tips of my fingers dampened, my cheeks became wet and when I opened my mouth the scream that tore loose was full of anger and sorrow and rage. It sent the birds in the trees around me flying and it ended only when my voice gave out and my throat become raw. I took a step, and I just couldn't take another. I plopped down in the plush grass under the deck, my hands still over my face. I rocked onto my back and I curled onto my side, pulling up my legs as far as they would go.

I wanted my mom—I wanted one of her hugs, right then, more than I'd ever wanted anything in my life, and I wanted Misha. God, I wanted Misha—the Misha I knew and loved, and not the one who hated me. Not the Misha I'd had to *put down*.

Not that one.

I wanted to go back and prove to him over and over that he was special and that he mattered, and I…I hated that. Fucking hated that, because I didn't do this to him. I didn't make him become this way. I didn't turn him into what he became. It wasn't my fault.

But it felt like it was, and I screamed again, but it made no sound as it still tore at my throat, because I wasn't just crying for Misha.

I was finally crying for my mother—giving in to the grief that had been building for over a year, the pain and anger of her loss compounded that it had been Misha who had caused it. It had always been him, and I wanted to hate him. I did, but I wanted to hate him more, because maybe if I did, it wouldn't hurt so bad.

I didn't feel the bond in my chest warming. I was so caught up in the maelstrom of emotions, I didn't feel Zayne's approach. I felt him only when he crouched beside me, picked me up and shifted me into his lap, his strong arms wrapped around my shoulders.

The grief and the pain poured out of me in big, ugly sobs, and it hurt—all of it hurt, and I didn't think it would ever stop. But through it all, Zayne held me tight, so close that even if there wasn't this strange new bond feeding him what I was feeling, he would've known.

He just held me, one arm folded over me and the other moving up and down the length of my back, slow and soothing, and finally, *finally* the tremors eased off, and the tears dried up.

I didn't know how much time had passed, but when it was all over, the back of my head ached and my throat felt raw.

And I had not only torn the front of Zayne's shirt by pulling on it, I had drenched it.

*Awk*ward.

Easing my fingers from the material, I pulled back. Zayne didn't let me get too far, though. "I'm sorry." Wincing, I cleared my throat.

"Don't apologize," he said, and I was grateful it was too dark now for me to see his face, but I felt his hand on my neck. He moved slowly as he raised his hand to my cheek and caught the tangled mess of hair there, gathering it and pulling the strands back from my face. "Do you feel better?" he asked, his voice soft.

"No," I muttered. "Yes."

"Which one is it?"

"I don't know." I took a couple of breaths. "I feel better. That's the right answer."

"I don't care about the right answer, Trin. I just want the truth."

I spread my hands against his chest. "I...I feel like I've been suffocating, and...I don't feel like that anymore."

"Then that's a start." He brushed back the hair on the other side of my face.

A few minutes passed as Zayne continued to hold me, his hand curved around the side of my head, his thumb sliding up and down the line of my cheekbone. "I was selfish. He was right about so many things. It was always about me. I was always thinking about me and—"

"You weren't selfish. He was. Selfish and possibly delusional," Zayne said. "What he did was on him—on him and no one else."

"I want to hate him, Zayne. A part of me does, but I..."

"I know. I get it. I do." There was a moment, and then I felt his warm lips against my forehead, and that went a long way, longer than it should've. "You're going to be okay."

I was.

I knew that.

I would be okay.

This was going to hurt, and this was going to haunt me like a ghost, but I would be... I would be okay.

And I needed to put some space between Zayne and me before I did something impulsive and that was sure to have consequences.

Balancing myself, I shifted off his lap and onto the grass beside him. Our thighs touched, as did our arms. I didn't move farther away. It was like I...I had to be close enough to be touching, and I had no idea if that was the bond, or if that was me.

Zayne cleared his throat. "I left when I..."

My shoulders slumped. "When you felt me?"

"Yes."

"This bond thing is going to be really...inconvenient."

"Not at this moment," he replied. "You needed me, and I needed to be here."

His words stole their way into my heart even though I knew better—because those words came from the bond and not from his heart. I knew this, and yet they were inking themselves into my muscle and onto my skin.

"What did they say?" I asked, focusing on the important things. Entire conversations I'd bailed on. "About the Harbinger?"

Zayne leaned back against the tree trunk. "They're worried. Whatever this thing is, it's been working at this for a while, and if Misha was involved with it, it wanted you, and it's still out there."

I shivered as I rested against the trunk. "I don't think it's a demon."

"Neither do I," he said, and I felt his head turn toward mine. "Nicolai doesn't, either."

And that left the big question. What could it be?

"You know," I said, feeling weary as I let my eyes drift shut. "My father could've filled us in. Given us some direction. Maybe a spoiler. Something."

Zayne was quiet for a moment, and I remembered seeing my father whisper in his ear. I turned my head toward his, and realized our mouths were inches apart.

"Did he tell you anything?"

"Nothing about the Harbinger." His breath coasted over my lips as he spoke. "We got this, Trin. We only have to stop the end of the world with little to no direction."

"No big deal."

He chuckled, and my lips curved up at the sound and the feel. "None at all."

We both fell quiet, even though there was a lot left unsaid between us, but I felt what wasn't spoken through the bond. What was flaring alive deep in me was doing the same in him. It was *there*. Desire, need and...yearning.

There was yearning for something more. It was there even if I wasn't sure what that meant, even though his heart might still belong to another, and it was there even though he was now my Protector.

It was still there.

"Trin?"

"Yeah?"

"I know we have an apocalypse and all to stop, but I've been thinking about something you said."

"God only knows what that is."

He chuckled again, and I smiled, knowing he probably could see it. "You said you liked being on the roofs of buildings, because it was close to the stars and the closest you could get to flying. You also said flying was the one thing you were jealous of."

"I did say that."

"Do you want to fly?"

Pulling away from the tree, I twisted toward him even

though I couldn't see him. My hands landed on his knees. "Are you suggesting what I think you're suggesting?"

"You want to see the stars?" Zayne asked, and I nodded emphatically, knowing what he meant, and when he took my hand, I folded my fingers over his like I had the day I'd left the community. I felt him begin to shift, his skin hardening under mine. "Then hold on tight, Trin. I'm going to get us as close as we can go."

★ ★ ★ ★ ★

Acknowledgments

Writing *Storm and Fury* was uniquely difficult for me. It wasn't because it was a spin-off of a series I hadn't visited in a while, even though that is never easier. It wasn't because I was expanding the world, rewriting it in a way. It was because Trinity shared the same progressive eye disease as me. Retinitis pigmentosa is a group of rather rare genetic disorders that involve the breakdown and eventual death of retina cells. Less than 200,000 people suffer from it. It's a progressive disease, typically resulting in significant constriction of vision (tunnel vision) or blindness. There's no cure or treatment at this time. If you're diagnosed with RP, you're going to get that talk. The what-to-expect-in-the-future talk. You're told that your vision will continue to shrink until there's nothing but a thin pinprick of vision left or nothing at all. You won't know when it will happen. How long it will take or when you will go blind, but you know it's coming. It's scary. No lie. When I was diagnosed in my early thirties, I almost didn't believe it. I ignored it at first. Well, I ignored it for years until my doctor at the Wilmer Eye Institute asked me, "Can you still see the stars at night?" And you know what? I couldn't answer the question. I couldn't remember the last time I even stopped to look up at the stars, and that was a wake-up call for me. Because one night when I looked up at the night sky, all I would see would be darkness, and I wouldn't even know the last time I saw the stars. I didn't want that to happen. Denial is just as bad as wallowing in it. I had to face that I was going blind, that it was happening, and I needed to make adjustments, and I wanted people to learn about RP.

Like Trinity, RP doesn't define who I am. It's just a part of me, and through her, I wanted to hopefully educate people on diseases like RP. Ones that are silent and not always visible. When people look at me and interact with me, they often cannot tell that I can barely see them. When I ask for help from strangers, I'm usually dismissed, because nothing looks "wrong" about me. I hope that after learning about RP, it will make people more empathetic to everything in between the blind and the seeing. And maybe, hopefully, one day there will be a cure.

I want to thank my agent, Kevan Lyon, my subrights agent, Taryn Fagerness, Tashya Wilson and the entire team at Inkyard Press, my publicist, Kristin Dwyer, Margo Lipschultz, my assistant and friend, Stephanie Brown, Stacey Morgan (who told me the first version of this book sucked and it did), Andrea Joan, Vilma Gonzalez, Jen Fisher, Lesa and Andrew Leighty. The following people are always an inspiration on many different fronts: Sarah J. Maas, Jay Crownover, Cora Carmack, KA Tucker, Kristen Ashley, JR Ward and so many more.

Thank you, Liz Berry and Jillian Stein for always making sure I will see the stars.

Special thanks to all my JLAnders and reviewers, and to you, the reader. This book wouldn't be possible without you. I owe you everything.

Thank you for reading Storm and Fury!

Trinity and Zayne survived the battle,
but the war is just beginning.
Turn the page to read an excerpt from

Rage and Ruin

book 2 of The Harbinger trilogy!

Only from Jennifer L. Armentrout and Inkyard Press.

1

I blinked open achy, swollen eyes and stared straight at the pale, translucent face of a ghost.

Gasping, I jerked upright. Strands of dark hair fell across my face. "Peanut!" I pressed the heel of one palm against my chest, where my poor heart pounded like a steel drum. "What in the Hell, dude?"

The ghost, who'd been sort of a roommate of mine for the past decade, grinned at me from where he floated midair, several inches above the bed. He was stretched out on his side, cheek resting on his palm. "Just making sure you're still alive."

"Oh my God." Exhaling raggedly, I lowered my hand to the soft dove-gray comforter. "I've told you a million times to stop doing that."

"I'm kind of surprised you still think I listen to you half the time."

Peanut had a point.

He had an aversion to following my rules, which were only, like, two rules.

Knock before entering the room.

Don't watch me while I sleep.

I thought they were quite reasonable rules.

Peanut looked like he had the night he died, way back in the '80s. His Whitesnake concert T-shirt was legit, as were his dark jeans and red Chuck Taylors. On his seventeenth birthday, for some idiotic reason, he'd climbed one of those massive speaker towers and subsequently fallen to his death, proving natural selection was a thing.

Peanut hadn't crossed over into that shiny bright white light, and a few years ago, I stopped trying to convince him when he said to me, quite clearly, it was not his time. It was far past his time, but whatever. I liked having him around... except when he did creepy crap like this.

Pushing the hair out of my face, I looked around my bedroom—no, not my bedroom. This wasn't even my bed. All of this belonged to Zayne. My gaze flicked from the heavy sunlight-blocking curtains to the bedroom door—the closed bedroom door that I'd left unlocked the night before, just in case...

I shook my head.

"What time is it?" I leaned back against the headboard, keeping the blanket close to my chin. Since Wardens' body temps ran higher than humans' and it was July, so it was most likely hot and sticky as a circle of Hell outside, Zayne's apartment was like an icebox.

"It's almost three in the afternoon," Peanut answered. "And that's why I thought you were dead."

Damn, I thought, scrubbing my hand across my face. "We got back pretty late last night."

"I know. I was here. You didn't see me, but I saw you. Both of you. I was watching."

I frowned. *That* didn't sound creepy at all.

"You looked like you'd been through a wind tunnel." Peanut's gaze flickered over my head. "You still do."

I'd felt like I'd been in a wind tunnel. A mental, emotional and physical wind tunnel. Last night, after I'd had a complete and utter breakdown by the old treehouse at the Warden compound, Zayne had taken me *flying*.

It had been magical, up there with the cool night wind, where the stars that always looked so faint to me became bright. I hadn't wanted it to end, even when my face went numb and my lungs began to strain with the effort to breathe. I'd wanted to stay up there, because nothing could touch me in the wind and the night sky, but Zayne had brought me back down to Earth and to reality.

That was only a handful of hours ago, but it felt like a lifetime. I barely remembered coming back to Zayne's apartment. We hadn't talked about what had happened with… Misha, or about what had happened to Zayne. We hadn't talked at all, really, other than Zayne asking if I needed anything and me mumbling no. I'd gotten undressed and climbed into bed, and Zayne had stayed in the living room, sleeping on the couch.

"You know," Peanut said, drawing me from my thoughts, "I might be dead and all, but you look way worse than me."

"I do?" I murmured, even though I wasn't surprised to hear that. Based on the way my face felt, I probably looked like I'd face-planted a brick wall.

He nodded. "You've been crying."

I had been.

"A lot," he added.

That was true.

"And when you didn't come back yesterday, I was worried." Peanut floated upright and sat on the edge of the bed. His legs and hips disappeared a few inches into the mattress. "I thought something happened to you. I was panicking. I couldn't even finish watching *Stranger Things* I was so worried. Who's going to take care of me if you die?"

"You're dead, Peanut. No one needs to take care of you."

"I still need to be loved and cherished and thought of. I'm like Santa Claus. If no one alive is here to want and believe in me, then I'll cease to exist."

Ghosts and spirits didn't work that way. At all, but he was so wonderfully overdramatic. A grin tugged at the corners of my lips until I remembered I wasn't the only one who could see Peanut. A girl who lived in this apartment complex could also see him. She must have watered-down angelic blood kicking around in her veins, like all humans who were able to see ghosts or displayed other psychic abilities. Enough to make her…different from everyone else. There weren't many humans in existence with traces of angelic blood, so it was a shock to learn that there was one so close to where I was staying.

"Thought you made a new friend?" I reminded him.

"Gena? She's cool, but it wouldn't be the same if you ended up as dead as a doornail, and her parents aren't choice, you know?" Before I could confirm that *choice* meant *good* in '80s speak, he asked, "Where were you last night?"

My gaze shifted to that closed, *unlocked* door. "I was at the compound with Zayne."

Peanut inched closer and lifted a wispy hand. He patted my knee, but I felt nothing through the blanket, not even the cold air that usually accompanied Peanut's touch. "What happened, Trinnie?"

Trinnie.

Only Peanut called me that, while everyone else called me Trin or Trinity.

I closed my sore eyes as realization sank in. Peanut didn't know, and I wasn't sure how to tell him when the wounds left by Misha's actions hadn't scabbed over yet. If anything, I'd just slapped a weak-as-Hell bandage over them.

I was holding it together. Barely. So, the last thing I wanted to do was talk about it with *anyone*, but Peanut deserved to know. He knew Misha. He liked him, even though Misha could never see or communicate with Peanut, and he'd come to DC with me to find Misha instead of staying behind in the Potomac Highlands Warden community.

Granted, I was the only one who could see and communicate with Peanut, but he'd felt comfortable in the community. It was a big deal for him to travel with me.

Keeping my eyes closed, I drew in a long shuddering breath. "So, yeah, we…we found Misha, and it wasn't…it wasn't good, Peanut. He's gone."

"No," he whispered. And then louder, he repeated, *"No."*

I nodded.

"God. I'm sorry, Trinnie. I'm so damn sorry."

Swallowing around the hard lump in my throat, I met his gaze.

"The demons—"

"It wasn't the demons," I interrupted. "I mean, they didn't kill him. They didn't want him dead. He was actually working with them."

"What?" The shock in his voice, the way the one word pitched to near glass-breaking levels, would've been funny in any other situation. "He was your *Protector*."

"He set it up—his abduction and everything." I pulled my knees up under the blanket, pressing them to my chest. "Even made it so Ryker saw me that day using my *grace*."

"But Ryker killed…"

My mom. I shut my eyes again and felt them burn, as if there could possibly be more tears left inside me. "I don't know what was wrong with Misha. If he's always…hated me, or if it was the Protector bond. I found out that he was never supposed to be bonded to me. It was always supposed to be Zayne, but there was a mistake."

A mistake that my father had known about, and not only had he done nothing to fix it, he hadn't seemed to care about it at all. When I'd asked why he hadn't done anything, he'd said he wanted to see what would happen.

How freaking messed up was that?

"The bond could've twisted him. Made him turn…bad," I continued, voice thick. "I don't know. I won't ever know, but the *why* doesn't change the fact that he was working with Bael and this other demon. He even said that the Harbinger had chosen him." I flinched as Misha's face formed in my thoughts. "That the Harbinger told him he was special, too."

"Isn't that who's been killing Wardens and demons?"

"Yeah." I opened my eyes once I was sure I wasn't going to cry. "I had to…"

"Oh, no." Peanut seemed to know without me even saying it.

But I had to say it, because it was the reality. It was the truth I would live with for the rest of my days.

"I had to kill him." Each word felt like a kick to the chest. I kept seeing Misha. Not the Misha in the clearing outside the senator's house, but the one who'd waited for me while I talked to ghosts. Who'd napped in his Warden form while I sat beside him. The Misha who had been my best friend. "I did it. I killed him."

Peanut shook his head, his dark brown hair fading in and out as he became more corporal for a moment and then lost his hold. "I don't know what to say. I really don't."

"There's nothing to be said. It is what it is." Exhaling, I stretched out my legs. "Zayne is now my Protector, and I'm going to be staying here. We need to find the Harbinger."

"Well, that part is good, right?" Peanut rose from the bed, still in a sitting position. "Zayne being your Protector?"

It was.

And it wasn't.

Becoming my Protector had saved Zayne's life, so that was a good thing—a *great* thing. Zayne hadn't hesitated to take the bond, and that was before he'd found out it was always supposed to have been him. But it also meant Zayne and I... Well, we could never be more than what we were now, and it didn't matter how badly I wanted to be more or how much I liked him. It didn't matter that he was the first guy I was ever seriously into.

I tipped my head back instead of suffocating myself with the pillow. Peanut became a blur as he drifted toward the curtain, though that had nothing to do with his ghostly form. "Is Zayne up?"

"He is, but he's not here. He left you a note in the kitchen. I read it while he wrote it." Peanut sounded rather proud. "It says he went to see someone named Nic. I think that was one of the guys who came with him to the community? Anyway, he left maybe a half hour ago."

Nic was short for Nicolai, the Washington, DC, clan leader. Zayne probably had unfinished business with him since he'd left whatever meeting they'd been having last night to come find me.

Zayne had *felt* my emotions through the bond. That strange new connection had led him right to the treehouse. I wasn't sure if I was amazed by that, annoyed or really weirded out. Probably a mixture of all three.

"Wonder why he didn't wake me." Pushing the cover aside, I scooted to the edge of the bed.

"He actually came in here and checked on you."

I froze, praying I hadn't been drooling on myself or doing anything weird. "He did?"

"Yep. I thought he was going to wake you. Looked like he was debating it, but all he did was pull the blanket over your shoulders. I thought it was totally bodacious of him."

I wasn't sure what *bodacious* meant, but I thought it was... God, it was sweet of him.

It was so like Zayne.

I might have known him for only a few weeks, but I knew enough to be able to picture him carefully pulling the comforter over me, and doing it so gently that he didn't wake me.

My chest squeezed as if my heart had fallen into a meat grinder. "I need to shower." I stood on legs I expected to be shaky but that were surprisingly strong and stable.

"Yeah, you do."

Ignoring the comment, I checked my phone. I'd missed a call from Jada. My stomach tumbled. I placed the phone down and padded on bare feet to the bathroom, flipped on the light and winced at the sudden brightness. My eyes did not care for bright light of any kind. Or dark or shadowy areas, either. Actually, my eyes pretty much just sucked 95.7 percent of the time.

"Trinnie?"

Fingers lingering on the light switch, I looked over my shoulder at Peanut, who'd moved closer to the bathroom. "Yeah?"

He cocked his head, and when he looked at me, I felt stripped bare. "I know how much Misha meant to you. I know it has to hurt something bad."

Ending Misha's life hadn't hurt me. It quite possibly had *killed* a part of me, replacing it with a seemingly bottomless pit of sour bitterness and raw anger.

But Peanut didn't need to know that. No one did.

"Thank you," I whispered, turning away and closing the door as the burn hit the back of my throat.

I will not cry. I will not cry.

In the shower, with its multiple jets and stall large enough to fit two fully grown Wardens, I used the minutes under the hot, stinging spray to get my head straight.

Or, in other words, compartmentalize.

I'd had my much-needed breakdown last night. I had given myself time to cry it all out, and now was the time to put it away, because I had a job to do. After years of waiting, it had finally happened.

My father had called on me to fulfill my duty.

Find the Harbinger and stop it.

So, there was a lot to sift through and file away in my mental cabinet so that I could do what I was born for. I started with the most critical. Misha. I shoved what he'd done and what I'd had to do all the way to the bottom of the cabinet, tucked under my mother's death and my failure to stop that. That drawer was labeled EPIC FAIL. The next drawer was where I sent the cause of the blackish-blue bruises covering my left hip and the length of my thigh. Another bruise colored the right side of my ribs, where Misha had delivered a nasty kick. He'd kicked my butt and then some, but I'd still beaten him.

The usual feeling of smugness or pride over having bested someone who was well trained didn't surge through me.

There was nothing good to feel about any of that.

The bruises, the aches and all the pain went into the drawer I called BUCKET FULL OF NIGHTMARES, because the reason Misha had managed to land so many brutal hits was because he knew I had limited peripheral vision. He'd used it against me. That was my one weakness when fighting, something I needed to improve on, like, yesterday, because if this

Harbinger discovered just how poor my vision was, it would exploit it.

Just like I would if the shoes were on other feet.

And yeah, that would be a nightmare, because not only would I die, so would Zayne. A tremor coursed through me as I slowly turned under the spray of water. I couldn't cave to that fear—couldn't dwell on it for one second. Fear made you do reckless, stupid things, and I already did enough of that for no good reason.

The top drawer had been empty and unlabeled until now, but I knew what I was filing there. That was where I was putting everything that had happened with Zayne. The kiss I'd stolen when we'd been back in the Potomac Highlands, the growing attraction and all the *want*, and that night, before we were bonded, when Zayne had kissed me and it had been everything I'd read about in the romance novels my mom had loved. When Zayne kissed me, when we'd gone as far as we could go without going all the way, the world had truly ceased to exist outside us.

I took all of that, along with the raw need for his touch, his attention and his heart—which most likely still belonged to someone else—and closed the file.

Relationships between Protectors and Trueborns were strictly forbidden. Why? I had no idea, and I guessed the reason the explanation was unknown was that I was the only Trueborn left.

I closed that drawer, which I simply labeled ZAYNE, and stepped out of the shower into the steam-filled bathroom. After wrapping a towel around myself, I leaned forward and wiped a palm over the mist-covered mirror.

My reflection came into view. As close as I was, my features were only a little fuzzy. My normally olive skin, courtesy of my mom's Sicilian roots, was paler than usual, which made my brown eyes seem darker and larger. The skin around them was puffy and shadowed. My nose still tilted to the side, and my mouth still seemed almost too large for my face.

I looked exactly as I had the evening Zayne and I left this apartment to go to Senator Fisher's house in hopes we'd find Misha or evidence of where he was being held.

I didn't feel the same.

How could there not be a more noticeable physical manifestation of everything that had changed?

My reflection didn't have an answer, but as I turned away from it, I said the only thing that mattered.

"I got this," I whispered, and then repeated louder. "I got this."